Praise for Deb Caletti's Books

A Heart in a Body in the World

★ "Caletti rips apart the contradictions of a society that commands women to be compliant and pleasing and then blames them for male responses to their attractiveness, however violent they might be. **This timely, well-written novel is crucial reading** in the days of #metoo."

—*Booklist*, starred review

"**This novel is full of sorrow and rage, but also beauty and hope and so, so much wisdom.** Annabelle's story will resonate deeply with so many women that it's tempting to call it a novel of the time. But really, **this is one for the ages.**"

—Gayle Forman, author of the #1 *New York Times* bestseller *If I Stay*

"Caletti's novel **dazzlingly maps the mind-blowing ferocity and endurance of an athlete** who uses her physical body to stake claim to the respect of the nation."

—E. Lockhart, *New York Times* bestselling author of *We Were Liars*

Girl, Unframed

★ "**Caletti delivers the near impossible:** a page-turner grounded in thoughtful feminism."

—*Booklist*, starred review

★ "Caletti offers a **riveting, meticulously plotted mystery** with plenty of drama alongside an exploration of objectification and the male gaze."

—*Publishers Weekly*, starred review

One Great Lie

★ "A **potent story** of how one young woman finds the power to write her own story."

—*Kirkus Reviews*, starred review

★ "The introspective and quiet narrative is **beautifully written, with rich sensory details and nuanced explorations** of sexuality, artistic motivation, loneliness, and jealousy."

—*School Library Journal*, starred review

THE
EPIC
STORY
OF
EVERY
LIVING
THING

THE
EPIC
STORY
OF
EVERY
LIVING
THING

DEB CALETTI

LABYRINTH ROAD
NEW YORK

Text copyright © 2022 by Deb Caletti
Jacket art copyright © 2022 by Seema Surana

All rights reserved. Published in the United States by Labyrinth Road, an imprint of Random House Children's Books, a division of Penguin Random House LLC, New York.

Labyrinth Road and the colophon are trademarks of Penguin Random House LLC.

Visit us on the Web! GetUnderlined.com

Educators and librarians, for a variety of teaching tools, visit us at RHTeachersLibrarians.com

Library of Congress Cataloging-in-Publication Data
Names: Caletti, Deb, author.
Title: The epic story of every living thing / Deb Caletti.
Description: First edition. | New York: Labyrinth Road, [2022] |
Audience: Ages 14 and up. | Audience: Grades 10–12. | Summary: When Harper Proulx and her newfound sibling travel to Hawaii to track down their sperm donor father, Harper finds a deep-sea diver obsessed with solving the mystery of a shipwreck, and the experience forces her to face even bigger questions.
Identifiers: LCCN 2022011306 (print) | LCCN 2022011307 (ebook) |
ISBN 978-0-593-48550-7 (trade) | ISBN 978-0-593-48551-4 (lib. bdg.) |
ISBN 978-0-593-48553-8 (ebook)
Subjects: CYAC: Identity—Fiction. | Fathers and daughters—Fiction. | Family life—Fiction. | Sperm donors—Fiction. | Deep diving—Fiction. | LCGFT: Novels.
Classification: LCC PZ7.C127437 Ep 2022 (print) | LCC PZ7.C127437 (ebook) |
DDC [Fic]—dc23

The text of this book is set in 11-point Maxime Pro.
Interior design by Cathy Bobak

Printed in the United States of America
1st Printing
First Edition

For Theo

CHAPTER ONE

MARRIAGES: In this city, April 1, Captain Joshua A. Patten, 26, master mariner, of Rockland, Maine, to Mary Ann Brown, 15, daughter of Mr. George Brown, seamaster, and Mrs. Elizabeth Brown, both of East Boston.

Boston Post, April 1, 1853

HARPER SCOOCHES HER FOOT THIS WAY, AND THEN scooches her foot back. It's always so hard to know what to do with your hands. Why are you so suddenly aware of your hands when you're trying to take a good photo, when they usually just do their own thing? Right behind Harper, the sheer rock face of Rattlesnake Ridge sits like a headstone against the murky green of Rattlesnake Lake. When she posts those names, it's all going to sound hazardous and thrilling, even if Harper has never seen any kind of snake there, just cagey squirrels darting around, and regular old crows staring menacingly. That murky green—it can be fixed in a second with a saturation edit. Ezra crouches down and then stands back up, snapping away. He's great at getting a variety of angles. Right now, all of this is incredibly important to Harper. Crucial, even.

Later, much later, when Harper looks at those images, she'll see a girl who lives at the surface, who doesn't have a clue about what's beneath it, including a bomb, an actual bomb, lying dormant, but not for long. She'll see a girl who has no idea that she's about to have a fateful meeting with another girl, and with a creature, too—a strange, glowing creature, the most beautiful underwater alien you can imagine, something with a soul, for sure. A creature that moves like a secret, mysterious heartbeat, in, out, rising from that old wreck as if to tell important truths about resilience, about what matters and what lasts. That wreck with a hidden story, as Harper has a hidden story.

But even more, when she looks at those images, she'll see someone just standing there at Rattlesnake Ridge, worrying about her hair, completely unaware of what's going to happen to her in a matter of hours.

"Is this good?" Harper shouts to Ezra.

"The mountain's coming right out of your head," he shouts back, and so Harper scoots to the left.

"Head tilt or no?" she shouts to Ezra.

"Sure," he says.

Harper smiles, but it's the kind of smile that doesn't make it to your eyes. Even she can tell that, so she tries again. She tries to beam. She's pretty sure a person doesn't naturally beam, that beaming takes effort. Ezra *click-click*s a bunch more.

"Let me see."

Ez hands Harper her phone. He's done this enough times to know it might be a while. He takes out his own phone to keep busy, thumbs flying as he texts, head bent down. He has the best hair. Dark curls, a mess of them. And he's the best boyfriend, too.

Sweet. The chunky-sweater, *hey, do you want to try this* kind, offering you a bite. Always letting Harper know that he's thinking about her when they aren't together. Always saying how lucky he is, and loving her body just as it is, and even being nice to Harper's mom, who doesn't think he's good enough for her and sometimes shows it. Melinda Proulx, who teaches economics at their local community college, wants Ezra to be a go-getter, to have *goals,* to have the résumé of an up-and-coming CEO, even though he's only seventeen. To be in student government, or an intern at Amazon. To be athletic, at least.

Ezra—with that mix of traits from his Cuban mother and his Jewish father, and his sometimes retro-rumpled clothing choices (a long scarf, his dad's old overcoat)—he looks artistic or something, which Harper loves. Pretty much, Ezra actually just likes to read, and be with his family, and he has to work hard to pass his classes, but he has that undefinable vibe of being *interesting.* When she posts photos of both of them, they look interesting *together.* It's a bonus.

Harper makes sure not to have too much lovey couple stuff on her page, though. It's a delicate balance. When you look at someone's posts, you want to feel slightly, pleasantly, voyeuristically envious, but not hostile, I-hate-you envious. She's known for a hiking-outdoor-adventure vibe, lots of mountains and waterfalls and lakes and meaningful nature images, featuring Harper doing adventuresome things. But people like it when you break things up occasionally—shots of you with your interesting boyfriend, a sprinkling of adorable animals, some just-regular-life moments, and a few romantic yet unchallenging objects, like a rumpled bed or a latte or a croissant.

Harper's pretty sure she could work at an advertising agency with all the stuff she's figured out. Or maybe a false advertising agency, because the truth is, the idea of *actual* adventures is pretty terrifying. People fall off cliffs and drown in lakes and get buried under mountain avalanches. Do you know how many mosquito bites you'd get if you actually went hiking in a bikini? And what about all the deadly diseases that mosquitoes carry? Seriously, if she were truly going on mountain treks as often as it seems, how would she ever get her homework done? Or go to school at all? Or even have time to *post* all these photos of herself on forest trails with the sunlight coming through the trees? Take Rattlesnake Ridge, right there. In addition to its lack of rattlesnakes, that dramatic rock rising above the arc of green water makes it look like they hiked for miles into a hidden corner of paradise, when they're really just a few steps from the parking lot, and a short drive from Seattle. Luckily, Washington State is full of places like this, and close to home, too.

Last year, during the first months of the pandemic, Rattlesnake Ridge sure wasn't a hidden corner of paradise; it was *packed*. To cure the wall-scratching claustrophobia and sheer boredom of quarantine while still avoiding other human beings, everyone headed to the mountains and the beaches, which meant that everyone was now at the mountains and the beaches. They eventually closed all those places, which was kind of like closing down nature. Harper and her mom, under the same roof for weeks, drove out here, but the Ridge was so crowded, they turned right around and went home. Harper's mom made her use hand sanitizer *and* wipes, even though they didn't get out of the car.

Harper scrolls through the photos Ez just took. In some, her arms look big, she thinks, the way they're squished against her sundress. In others, you can only see the bad side of her hair. It's all she can see. Fat arms, bad hair. Fat arms, bad hair. Ugh.

"Hey, Harp. Ready?" Ezra zips his phone into his bag. "I've got to get back. I told my mom I'd watch Binx." Binx is Ezra's little brother, who's three. These are more things to love about Ez—his sweet family, his mom and dad, the way he's so cute and patient with that tiny terror, always making sure he has a couple of Band-Aids in his pocket, because Binx loves Band-Aids. The little guy is always sticking out a perfectly intact arm or knee and saying, *OWEE,* and after you carefully attend to the invisible wound, he'll run off happily. Man, if only it were that easy with every wound you can't see.

Harper wants to ask Ezra to take a few more photos so she can hold out her arms and smile with her lips closed, but he has to get home, and she doesn't want to be one of those girls who treat their boyfriends like an assistant, with no lunch breaks or vacation days. She isn't going to make him trek everywhere carrying tripods and lights, asking him to lift her up in his arms as her dress cascades down, in one of those *no one would ever wear that outfit in a desert* type shots. Well, she isn't going to make him do that *again,* not after he gave her the silent treatment for a whole weekend that time.

"Ready. And hey, thanks," Harper says. When Ezra looks up, his eyes are so green. Of course, she knows they're green, and sometimes she makes them greener in his photos, but, wow. She has one of those moments where you actually *see* someone you normally go around forgetting to see. "Come here." She tugs his

T-shirt and kisses him. She sticks her hand in his back pocket like it's her back pocket.

"The monster will be in bed by seven-thirty, if you want to swing by." Ezra loops his arms around her.

"Calculus test. Ez, I'm failing . . . ," Harper moans.

"Yeah, can I fail like that?" He makes a face. He struggles with Algebra II. In truth, Harper's grade has only dropped to an A minus.

On the drive home, Ezra has Armor Class Zero playing, and he pounds the steering wheel in rhythm, and spring is painting yellow light over the mountains on either side of I-5, and the clouds are as fluffy as beaten egg whites. The trees rise grandly, doing their important job of making oxygen and keeping the ground solid and sheltering deer and birds and the occasional black bear. It's all the best version of April, so different from the last one, when they were panicked and scared, locked in the house since virus intruders were everywhere, scrolling death tolls while struggling with the boredom of online school and the dull irritation of captivity. This spring is hope plus future plus promise, at least mostly. It's the world offering itself, reminding you it's still here. But Harper barely notices. She's trying hard not to reach into her purse for her phone. She wants to fix those photos so bad. That phone is practically shouting at her in there. She wishes Ezra would just hurry up and get them home. He's going sixty-five, but it feels like he's dawdling by enjoying the music like that.

Harper picks at the crack in the plastic of Ezra's seat, because anxiety is jetting under her skin. She feels this big ticking clock of expectation. Everything seems crazy and urgent every single second. She tries this trick that Ada's dad told her, where you inhale up the imaginary side of a triangle for five seconds, exhale down the other side for five seconds, and pause along the bottom for another five. But triangles morph into geometry, which slides into calculus, her enemy, and tests and failure and that semitruck on their ass.

"I love this song," Ezra says, in spite of climate change, fat arms, pandemics, and grades.

It's times like these that make Harper wonder: If she had the kind of family that Ez does, would she be optimistic and easy-going, too? If she had more than a mother and a mystery, would she feel *safe*?

One thing Harper knows without a doubt: all that stuff you hear about body positivity and self-acceptance, the ending of body-shaming, et cetera, et cetera—it's a shining vision for the future maybe, but it sure isn't true yet. If it were, we wouldn't have treatments to make your hair glossier, heels to make your legs longer, Spanx to make you slimmer, sticks of makeup to contour your face, things that, if you imagined a guy doing them, you'd laugh. There wouldn't be so many apps to help you edit your lips and nose and body, either, Harper thinks as she sits on her bed in her room, using one of those apps to edit her lips and nose and body. Hopefully, no one will be able to tell. The only thing worse than *having* the faults is people knowing you *fixed* the faults.

Do guys go to this much trouble with their photos? It sure doesn't seem like it. Every now and then, one of those strange, creepy dudes who follow you out of nowhere will appear, the kind who have only a handful of photos on their profile. Wearing aviator sunglasses in one, shirt off in another, thinking he's hot shit in a suit, drinking a beer on a Jet Ski. And clearly, they think they look *amazing,* even when they seem gross and they're old and she's not, so just *stop,* for God's sake. One bad selfie in the mirror, and they're like, *Hello, you stud.* Harper can't imagine having confidence like that.

On her bed, with the travel posters of places she's never been on the walls around her, her ignored calculus book splayed open, sipping a half-drunk can of Mountain Dew she'll ditch before her mom sees (more than forty grams of sugar per can, and uniquely dangerous to the pancreas), Harper deletes all the imperfect images. She pushes the little trash can, and, poof, the mistakes are gone. Goofy expressions, closed eyes, or looking off in the wrong direction, zap. She's reached the *fuck it* stage, so she chooses the one where she's standing, fake beaming, Rattlesnake Ridge in the back, green water, teeth now white, arms now slim, contrast up, brightness up, shadows down, saturation raised a few notches, filter—dramatic. It looks pretty good. It looks casual.

Captions. Her fingers fly, tap, tap, tap. *Nature all around.* No. *Beauty all around.* Nature or beauty? Maybe just *Nature* with a heart emoji. Or *Nature* with a heart emoji and a tree emoji. You're supposed to ask a question because that always gets more "engagement." *Afternoon escape. What's YOUR favorite time of day?* But does she really and honestly care what anyone's favorite time of day is? Not just kind of but *really* care? She herself can tell when someone asks a question just to hook people into answering. There'll be a sudden landslide of comments, too, and she'll have to respond. *I like it just after the sun rises!* Or *Sunset, because ROMANTIC.* It'll be another expectation on the tipping pile of expectations. She settles on *Next up: vegan tacos.* It sounds carefree and spontaneous.

Next, hashtags. #allaboutadventures #hiking #tourtheplanet #awesomeearth #roamtheplanet #beautifuldestinations #explore #optoutside #earthpix #paradise #rattlesnakeridge #beautyallaround. When she was little, there weren't even hashtags yet. When she first heard the word, she kept thinking *hash browns.* Now they're such a regular part of life, her mind almost *thinks* in them. #morninglight #whatsforbreakfast #icandrivemyselfcrazy-withhashtags.

She presses the magic word: *post.*

The image joins all the others—Harper at Mount Rainier, Harper pondering a lake, Harper next to an ironic billboard, open road stretching ahead. Her and Ezra at a beach bonfire. Her and Ezra at a trailhead. Her tussling with Ezra's dog, Nudo, in golden light. Her with Soraya (#bestfriends), her with Soraya and Ada (#pals #lucky). Her on a wintry trail, wearing mittens and a woolly hat; her in a flouncy dress and boots, kicking fall forest leaves; her on a hike with a red backpack; her with a steaming mug; her on a rock with a retro map. Lots of leaping and leaning and perching on the edges of things, docks, cliffs, shorelines. Never too high, though. Never honestly on a ledge.

In all those photos, she looks confident, happy, sure of herself, at ease. She looks ready to meet any challenge. She looks *brave.* But she's none of those things. Fear follows her around like Binx follows Ezra, whining and asking nonstop questions. *Why, why, why? How, when?* And the biggest: *What if?* Harper's mind is a constant spinning washing machine full of white laundry, with one red T-shirt in there, threatening to ruin everything.

The world, and Harper in the world: this is the problem. The world is too big—it spits tornadoes and unleashes hurricanes, and it holds viruses that, in a matter of days, can wreck life as you know it. That's hard to forget. And Harper is too small. How can she stand up against stuff like that? She can't even drive yet! She doesn't *want* to drive yet. That semitruck on Ez's ass was going a million miles an hour! Next year, after she graduates, she's supposed to go to college and choose a major, and she doesn't even know what she *likes,* let alone what she wants to *be.* When she asks herself those questions, she only feels an emptiness inside, like something critical is missing. Or some*one.* Which, of course, is true.

On Harper's best social media account, though—Instagram, the one with all the followers—she's not empty. Whatever she's supposed to be is *right there.* It's her perfect body, and it's her own world. *She* isn't a go-getter. *She* doesn't have *goals. She* isn't athletic or in student government or an intern at Amazon. But she has her face and her body in those squares. The way she looks on that page, the way people respond to her—it's who she *is.*

Harper hears the garage door hum and rattle. A moment later, her mother shouts down the hall. "Hey-ey!"

"You're early," Harper shouts back.

"Hello to you, too."

Harper hears her mother's heels drop on the floor and her purse clunk on the counter. Her mom heads to the kitchen sink so she can wash her hands for thirty seconds with antibacterial soap, something they still do, something they might do forever, right up to their elbows, like a pair of surgeons. Next, Melinda Proulx will aim for her bathroom, where she'll wipe off her mascara with those little cleansing cloths piling up and up in our landfills. She'll change into a tidy tracksuit, pour a glass of wine, and demand the details of Harper's day. The level of wine in those glasses has gotten higher and higher, Harper's noticed, one *glug* turning to a *glug, glug, glug*.

While she waits for dinner, Harper just scrolls through her feed, bored. She's offered to cook a million times, but her mom always sighs and says, "That's okay, *I'll* do it," with an almost admirable determination to make Harper feel guilty. Soraya's dog has a cone, which Harper already knew, but Ada has a new makeup vlog she didn't even mention. Soraya and Ada are still her best friends, even if the relationships feel weirdly new and awkward since they returned to school a month ago. Ada's been spending more time with Olivia, that girl in band, since their parents let them hang out in person last year, while Soraya's parents, like Harper's mom, made her stay home. It was frustrating to see posts about Ada and Olivia doing stuff together, or Ada and her family on vacation, when Harper couldn't go anywhere. She didn't know who to be mad at—her mom, or Ada's parents, or their governor. And she doesn't want to feel this little crack of divide, either, but even now it's hard to forget Ada all free and normal-looking at that hotel pool last summer.

Harper spies on Olivia, who just posted an enchilada in green sauce, and then she spies on Ezra's ex-girlfriend Brie, who *really* has the perfect life. Shooting hoops with her dad while looking gorgeous, so, yeah. You can almost hear the air escaping, *sssss*, from Harper's self-esteem as that little dart makes a direct hit, haha. She's totally aware of it, but it doesn't mean she can stop it.

Swapping over to breaking news, Harper scrolls past a shooting in a mall and a child dying in a fire, two-second tragedies as she swallows the last of her Mountain Dew. Next, "The One Kind of Bread That's Wrecking Your Body," and "Ten Things That Happen When You Eat Tahini," and "If You See This Terrifying Insect, Call the Authorities Immediately." On another social media platform, she sees a cat in a jail cell. A *Hello, April* in script against a field of flowers. A drawing of a bird. A real bird. A bagel, a muffin. A broken toe, gross. She watches Ada line her lips. Soraya interrupts with a text about this girl, Lola, who said something mean about the way Soraya talks, too high-pitched. *Am I high-pitched?* Harper knows that Soraya is seeing the little bubbles of thought as Harper types. They are definitely bubbling too long, as Harper measures how to respond. *Of course not,* she lies. *Ignore her.* The bubbles stop and go flat.

Harper looks at some other stuff that's recommended for her—really great nature shots that are pretty much like every other really great nature shot. Beautiful, well-lit girls in bold or pensive poses. Unique photoshopped art that's like all the other unique photoshopped art. After millions of people do unique things, there aren't a lot of unique things left. A mug next to a book. A highway, stretching into the distance. A selfie in a mirror, a selfie in a mirror, a selfie in a mirror. Sisters, an airplane wing. The moon. A shoe.

But then something happens.

The something.

Something shocking.

She opens her own page again, to check out the likes and the comments. She's thumbing through them mindlessly, like, like, like, when she sees it. A comment from @summerknights4666.

Wow. You look exactly like my friend Dario. EXACTLY.

Oh wow. Wow.

Her heart starts thumping so hard, it's like a wild animal inside her. The comment radiates. It's almost hard to look at. She blinks, paralyzed.

She also feels a quiet dread.

Not again.

In panic, hardly breathing, she searches through @summer knights4666's friends. The name is easy to spot: @DarioD.

Oh God, okay. She clicks.

The account isn't private, but it's rarely used, with only a few photos. The boy, Dario, is about Harper's age, maybe a little younger. There he is in a museum, standing next to various vintage airplanes. Next, a fuzzy image of a stage with a cello player on it. A gaming high score. A Christmas tree. In every other photo, same as a checkerboard, there's also a photo of a small white dog. With his beard and his somber expression and his gentlemanly demeanor, he resembles a Civil War soldier in those sepia portraits. #*Walter.*

And Harper doesn't even need to enlarge those photos of Dario D. next to the airplanes to see it.

They could be twins.

If you shortened Harper's hair, you'd barely be able to tell them apart. And it isn't just the slope of their foreheads, or that ridge in their noses, or their supposedly rare combination of auburn hair and blue eyes. It's the way his shoulders go up a bit in that museum shot, the way Harper's do when she's excited. That recognition—it's *felt*. It's old. It goes back so far that it doesn't have a name.

And it's undeniable.

That thing she has, her face, her image—he has. That thing she is, he is, too.

CHAPTER TWO

> Joshua is still waiting for the *Cordelia Lawrence* to be ready for sea. Quite impatiently, since he is eager to add to his reputation as a young and rising seaman. Father would be pleased, since we have heard that *St. Andrew* and the other vessels under his command have apparently made some of the swiftest passages on record.
>
> Mary Ann Patten to her mother,
> Elizabeth Brown
> New York, December 4, 1853

"HARPER! COME ON!"

Dinner. She didn't even smell it, or hear the pans. She drops the phone on her bed like it's burning. That rectangular technical marvel seems dangerous. In the kitchen of their small house, her mother is wearing the blue tracksuit with the slimming white stripes down the legs and arms. Harper can see that the corners of her eyes are still red from her new Retinol Resist Anti-Aging Wrinkle Cream. "Set the table, please," her mom says.

All she can see in the silverware drawer is Dario D. And when they sit down to eat—kale with mushrooms, walnuts, and brown rice—Dario D., Dario D. Harper's mother moves a hill of nuts to the side of her plate. Healthy omega-3 fatty acids, but high in calories. Recently, Harper has spotted her pinching a chunk of imaginary flab at her sides, the way those mean mothers in the grocery store grab the arm of a misbehaving kid. And brown rice . . . They are still working through the multiple huge bags of it, along with the cans of vegetable broth and boxes of rubber gloves Melinda Proulx madly gathered as everything was shutting down. Back then, those were some of the things you believed might save your life. "I hope you were studying up there," her mom says. "If you didn't always wait until the last minute, your retention would be better."

"I haven't been waiting until the last minute. How was your day?" Oh, if her mother knew what Harper's day had just brought, she'd lose it for sure.

"It was fine. Same old, same old. *Honey.* Slow down. This took me forty-five minutes to make, and you're eating it in two seconds."

Harper mimes eating super slow, like her batteries are dying.

Her mother makes a face. "Also, FYI, and I'm only bringing this up for your own benefit. I popped on to your GradeShare and saw you're still at a ninety-four percent in calculus."

Everyone knows this is called helicopter parenting, but honestly, it's one of those huge military-transport types, with two propellers, loud enough to cause permanent deafness, and capable of chopping your head off if you get too close.

"Maybe I'll just stay at ninety-four percent."

"Harper." Melinda uses that weary-plus-exasperated tone that says, *We've been over this a hundred times.*

"Okay, okay!"

"You've only got two more tests before the final. Do you really want a ninety-four to mess up your GPA? If you had more extracurriculars, I wouldn't be so worried about your grades. You can't try a sport, at least, in the fall?"

"*No one's* going to have a bunch of extracurriculars when we didn't have any for a whole year. And I don't want to be on the basketball team." Harper has trouble walking and bouncing a ball at the same time.

"There are a hundred other options, Harper, please. What about Girlz2Power? Quinnie is in that." Quinnie is the dream daughter of Melinda Proulx's best friend, Denise. Denise also has a dream son, Garret, who took Harper to a few dances before she met Ezra, but he was self-centered and awful. "That group is doing all kinds of things! Raising money for menstruation education in Africa, lobbying big business and the entertainment industry about their depiction of women . . . It's inspiring."

"I don't feel like being inspiring. Wait. I sort of *am* inspiring, on Instagram. I'm up to almost ten thousand followers."

"Yeah, I don't think admissions officers are going to care about Instagram. How are you going to get into a great school, let alone get a scholarship? With only one season of track and band, your grades *have* to be strong."

For a second, Harper understands it, kids who act out because they can't tell someone to SHUT UP. Her mother has more sides than this, though—she does. Sometimes she searches for overwater Tahitian bungalows they could stay in someday, even though they could never afford that, or she suddenly sings into a wooden spoon while cooking. Occasionally she'll meet a new man and get all giddy, before it gets disappointing and she ends things. And then there were all those days they spent together during lockdown, just the two of them, like soldiers sharing a trench, hating each other every now and then, definitely hating the war, but bonding during it, too.

"Honey." Her mom's voice softens. She puts her hand over Harper's. "I'm sorry. I'm only saying this because I want the best for you. Because I love you."

Her mom looks tired and stressed, with that red at the corners of her eyes. And her gray roots are starting to show through her dark hair again, a quarter inch of truth, meaning she's overdue for her date with the L'Oréal box, when Harper has to make sure the back is fully squirted with dye before Melinda puts on the plastic cap and sets the timer. On the kitchen TV, the wearying world plays out on the news. Her mom works hard to pay for everything by herself, and she juggles a lot—her job, their house, Harper herself. She's trying to be a good mother, and a good daughter (to her long-dead but much-admired father, economist Raymond Proulx, and her own exacting mother, Patricia Proulx), and a good friend, and a good teacher, while cooking nutritious meals, and keeping a watch on current events, and downward-dogging, and lowering her cholesterol, and guarding them against new variants, and getting her yearly breast panini, aka mammogram.

Honestly, if she knew about Dario D., she might reach the tipping point.

"I love you, too," Harper says.

And she does. Even if the way her mother says "menstruation" makes Harper want to strangle her.

After dinner Harper calls Ezra, and Binx insists on talking, too. *Wo?* he says, and then waits. Harper asks him questions, but there's only the sound of Binx breathing, like those movies of an astronaut adrift in space. They hang up, and Harper yells good night to her mom, who's watching a documentary about tsunamis. A wave is rising. Harper brushes her teeth. In the mirror, she sees Dario D.'s cheekbones.

She wants to stay up all hours searching for him, but this seems dangerous. Melinda, with her bouts of insomnia, might see the glow from her screen, and Harper would have to slam the laptop closed and patiently endure a lecture about the need for adequate rest. She'd better wait until she's alone. The secret is electrical, a live wire. Something that's hers and only hers, which is the great part about it. It's hard to explain, but she doesn't even want to tell Ezra, because, wow, who knew, but *a secret* can fill that empty space in you. At least, for the first time in a while, Harper is honestly excited. She can't wait for the next day.

In the morning, when her mother leaves for work, Harper fakes sleep. For the millionth time, she thinks about how hard it would be to act dead on TV. Melinda kisses Harper's head. An hour from now, she'll text to make sure Harper hasn't overslept. Of course Harper hasn't overslept. She's never overslept in her whole life. It would be so awesome to be the wayward delinquent her mother worries she is.

When Ezra drives them to school, Harper watches the familiar scenery through Dario's eyes, and during that stupid calculus test, Dario sits on her shoulder like a cheat, and during lunch, she sits distractedly with Dario at the table, ignoring her friends. God, she wants to know everything about him! Ada's face is contoured beyond recognition, shiny with bronzer, but Harper/Dario tells her she looks pretty. Maybe he wouldn't even do that. Maybe he's not even very nice. He seems nice, though. He has kind eyes. *Are you okay?* Ezra asks. *Are you okay?* Soraya asks. *Are you okay?* Harper's favorite teacher, Ms. Mahmoudi, art, asks.

What are they seeing on her face? *Their* face. No idea. She lies and tells them she has a stomachache. Somewhere in Edmonds, Washington (according to his profile), maybe Dario's stomach hurts, too.

After Ezra drives her back home, Harper kisses him like *I'd better go,* and not like *please don't go.* Ez moved here last summer from California, and she and Ez met when school was still online in September, in American government class. The first time she saw him in his Zoom square, she got that feeling, the one where you know someone will be an important part of your life. They started joking around in class, to the point that other kids started teasing them, and then they FaceTimed for a while. After a bunch of huge, horrible fights with her mom, plus negotiations, phone calls, and online surveillance stalking, confirming that Ez and his family truly *didn't* ever go anywhere or see anyone, Melinda finally allowed Ez and his family to be part of their "pod" so Harper and Ez could see each other. Now they've been a couple long enough to know what various kisses are saying. *I'd better go* means homework or stomachaches or babysitting Binx. *Please don't go* means kissing all delicious in the car until Rainey, the neighbor boy, sets down some awful cap gun or whatever dangerous toy he's playing with right then and starts to stare, or until they see the rustle of Mrs. Wong's blinds. Since her mom returned to work, they sometimes go inside to get skin on skin under Harper's sheets. Ezra is Harper's first real boyfriend, but Ez knows his way around a condom thanks to his ex-girlfriend, the unnervingly beautiful Brie.

"Talk tonight?" Harper asks.

"Talk tonight," he says. "Feel better."

She and Dario need to be alone.

Harper meets Dario on Google. She shuts her bedroom door and actually sits at her desk with her laptop, because this is serious. She's Harper Proulx, Private Eye. Harper always thought she was a pretty skilled investigator, until she figured out that *everyone* is a pretty skilled investigator lately. Anthropologists of the future will probably see that the human brain expanded at this point in history, and the reason will be that we acquired the ability to hunt down photos of an ex-girlfriend, Google Earth a particular backyard in California, and examine fine details of changes of clothing to determine locations and timelines of events.

It helps that Dario D. has an unusual first name. Sucks if you're searching for a Jason Smith. Edmonds is small, too, only one high school. *Dario* and *Edmonds High* nets her Dario Damaskenos, and his second place in dramatic interpretation in the Edmonds Debate Team's win over Roosevelt. Hmm, notable. Especially after Harper's own high verbal PSAT scores, and the fact that her mother regularly says, *Don't be so dramatic.*

A thrill of glee rises with *Damaskenos*. No Jason Smith here—it's a jackpot. *Damaskenos* offers up Dario's address, and the news that Dario has two moms, Dana Damaskenos and Reba Shelton, while Harper has her single mom. Dana: a systems analyst at Google, but seeking new opportunities for advancement. And Reba: owner of a small bakery in Edmonds, playfully called Buns. Harper likes her already. She finds an aunt wishing Dario a happy birthday (in June, a year after hers), and there's a cute photo of him as a toddler running through a sprinkler, exactly like the one of Harper as a toddler running through a sprinkler. His house is a nice, not-fancy Northwest Contemporary on a suburban street. Down the road, the Google Maps camera has caught two dogs and a garbage truck with a guy smoking inside.

Weirdly, she can't find much more about Dario than his profile with those few photos. He likes history, for sure. He's standing proudly by those war airplanes, and Reba also tagged him on a few articles she posted: a review of a new biography of Winston Churchill (yawn), a German World War II ship found in the Baltic Sea that was sunk with 1,083 people aboard (eek), and super-ancient World War II veterans taking a trip in a B-25 bomber ("I'll remember it for the rest of my life," said a ninety-six-year-old army vet). There's no intel on the importance of Walter.

Dario seems quiet and studious, like Harper herself. They both also have a streak of high-achiever competitiveness, she can tell. Maybe he's anxious, too—when she zoomed into the debate team photo, he's doing that same thing she does, pinching his fingers together. But, wow, how eerie, it's just occurred to her—the most important way that they're the same is something she'll never see, because it's an empty space. They share the exact same absence, and this realization is so strange that the need to know Dario becomes a *craving*.

Man, she wishes her mom had a bakery.

Oh, ow, her neck aches. She's missed a bunch of texts from Soraya, back on the subject of her too-high voice, and Harper's mom will be home any minute. She hasn't posted anything yet, either, and if you don't stay on top of it, engagement goes down. When Harper first started on Instagram in middle school, it was just bad photos and silly stuff, inside jokes, and pursed lips with sexy poses, even though no one had even kissed anyone yet. But then, freshman year, she made her feed public and took more time with her photos. It all made her kind of uncomfortable, but everyone was doing that then.

One day, though, they were all on Ada's dad's boat, and Ada's brother had given her this huge blue plastic cup of beer. She'd never even had it before. Boom, a little alcohol confidence and a push of a button, and, oh God, there she was in a bikini on Instagram, a beautiful lake behind her. And, hey, maybe her body *wasn't* an essay test she'd failed completely, with a big fat minus at the top, because suddenly there were all these likes. When she and her friends tried to hike up Mount Si (seriously, it was her first hike, and they barely went a mile), she posted another cute shot, and bling, bling, bling, it was like confetti coming down.

She wanted to make it happen again, the confetti. And again. Harper plus nature seemed to be the equation, so she kept doing it. It was kind of amazing, because here she was, a girl who always hoped there wouldn't be a group project, or a skit, or a relay race, or an oral report, yet new followers kept arriving, like an audience, the number ticking up, up the more she posted.

And then it was hard to stop, because it was like caffeine, the way it gave her a buzz, but also because it seemed like she owed those people something, *followers*. It made her think of the time when Mark, this man her mom briefly dated, taught her how to ride a bike. *Pedal, pedal, pedal!* he called, because if you stopped, you'd crash.

Still, what a great discovery. If you don't want anyone to see you, let everyone see you. This carefully crafted version of you. It's the safest hiding place ever.

Now Harper finds a shot from when she and Ezra went kayaking on Lake Union. She's standing by the water, the boat at her feet, and she looks carefree, but right then, an airplane flew by so low, Harper worried they were under terrorist attack. She uses a quick filter, Halo's Dancer, which sounds like a racehorse but gives her a heavenlike glow. Her legs look kind of pocked in her shorts, so she smooths them and makes a mental note to check for an invasion of cellulite the next time she passes a mirror. #springday #seattlelife #liveyourlife #joy #fountainfun.

Hashtag who cares, because there are way more important things to think about.

Dario D., Harper says to herself, and when she does, there's a flutter in her stomach, like a deck of cards shuffling.

The question, the real question, that Harper asks herself now: *How many more of us are out there?*

CHAPTER THREE

> The waiting is unbearable, at least for Joshua. I am happy he is still here. I know you do not approve of the modern practice of a shipmaster taking his wife to sea, but I have inherited a love for blue water from Father and the boys, and being alone in the city for months at a time is a dark prospect.
>
> Mary Ann Patten to her mother,
> Elizabeth Brown
> New York, July 15, 1854

HARPER HEARS THE GARAGE DOOR GO UP. HER MOM IS home, so she'd better hurry. It's dangerous, but she's got to see this. It's urgent.

She takes a screenshot of Dario and slides it to the left of her desktop. And then she clicks open a folder and removes a photo of someone else. This girl's hair is longer and lusher than Harper's, and her eyes are bluer and brighter, but maybe she just has better editing apps. Her mother, M. Haviv, is a French translator. Her father, Roen Van Den Berg, owns an art gallery. Her mom has dark skin, and both parents have dark hair and dark eyes, but their daughter doesn't. Simone has Harper's and Dario D.'s rare—the rarest—combination of auburn hair and blue eyes, and she's a freshman at Berkeley, art major.

Simone's last name, Van Den Berg, is Dutch, and it means some kind of hill or mountain, and Roen means "secret." After checking in on Simone multiple times daily, Harper knows this and a hundred other things, too. Simone is charming, and everyone is in love with her, guys, girls, maybe Harper, too, though her feelings sometimes edge over into the ugly territory of envy. Simone has a cat—first name: Merci, last name: Beaucoup. Her dorm room, and her room at home, are extravagantly decorated, with draperies and white lights and art film posters, which all shout *whimsical yet intelligent*. She has a creative, enchanting profile, with way more followers than Harper, featuring photos of her as a maiden and a mermaid and a sorceress, surrounded by lightning bolts, lying on a bed of moss, walking through a forest with a leaf tiara, gazing into the eyes of an adoring unicorn. She's Harper's older, more beautiful replica. She looks perfect, and dramatic, and imaginative. And she seems to have the thing Harper doesn't, an ability to handle stuff, to be in the world without fear. He, the mysterious He, will probably like Simone better, even if she always misspells "definitely."

Harper has known about her since December, when she got the message. *You look JUST like my friend Simone.*

Now Harper slides Simone's image next to Dario's. Finally, she slides her own image next to theirs.

They look like suspects in a crime. It isn't a crime, but when you see faces that are exactly like yours, it *can* feel like something's been stolen. And, oh, those faces are exactly like hers, or at least so similar that Harper's heart begins to thud so hard that she puts her hand to her chest.

She stares at the three of them with awe, and thrill, and utter anxiety. And wonder, too, at how it happened. The World Wide Web is so vast that it's something you can hide in. But the World Wide Web is so vast, you'll surely be found.

"I've been slammed back-to-back, so I couldn't look. *Well?* Tell me," Harper's mom says. She wants to know about the calculus test. Multiply this by basically every school night, and try not to run around screaming while battling the urge to fail on purpose. Melinda jabs a forkful of turmeric cauliflower with chard, low in calories and an excellent source of fiber.

Also on the plate: a side of brown rice. Harper hates seeing those big bags of it in their garage. The rice, the bottled water, the Clorox, it makes the trauma of the pandemic swirl. When and how does that distress stop? *Will* it ever stop? Harper always worried about stuff anyway, *before*—Ebola, and biological warfare, and ticks and Lyme disease, and serial killers, and weird headaches, and men in vans, and the biggest butcher knife, and the dentist maybe hitting a nerve, and dolls, and clowns, and characters in costumes, et cetera. But now, even after their vaccines, when she's no longer crossing off each day they endure on her pandemic calendar, there is so much more to fear—deadly handrails and lethal doorknobs, the fatal aerosol droplets from a friend's sneeze, ventilators and overrun hospitals.

And she and her mom and Grandma—they've been *lucky*. Her mom didn't lose her job, and they had a small house to quarantine in, not a tiny apartment, or the streets. They've stayed healthy, unlike poor Mr. Wong, who one day was out in his front yard with his trowel and little garden fork, and a few days later, not. Boom. Gone. If *she* feels like a bad guy is perpetually stalking her with his hands about to grab, how do those people, people like Mrs. Wong, hundreds and thousands of them, suffering and grieving, *cope*? How do they go on? And she's still supposed to care about *calculus*.

"I did *fine*. Ninety-eight. Two little points."

"Do you know what my father used to say? 'Never let it rest, till your good is better and your better is best.'"

A rational jury would say a murder right now would be self-defense, but Harper is carrying around a hidden generosity. She lets it pass.

"Can you put down your phone at dinner? We've discussed this a million times. What are you looking at that's so important?"

"Dog befriends miniature horse." Harper shows her.

Melinda can't help herself. She fights a smile, but a small one sneaks out. "Cute."

"Look at them sleeping all cuddled up."

"I never see your eyes anymore."

Well, yeah, *exactly*. A phone can be the drawbridge you raise, so no one comes into your personal castle. It's funny, Harper always thinks, all the talk about lack of privacy and phones, when sometimes it's the thing that *gives* you privacy. She doesn't want her mom to see her eyes. She might see Dario D., Simone, and Harper's betrayal, especially.

Maybe it isn't generosity she feels. Maybe it's pity. Those things probably go together a lot.

It's the bomb before the bomb: Melinda Proulx has absolutely no idea that there are more of them.

After Harper and Ez say good night and hang up, Harper shoves her arm between her mattress and the box spring and yanks out the notebook like a pickle in a giant sandwich. Her mother has one, too. They're supposed to be twin gratitude journals, and Melinda writes in hers every day *(Sunset. Good health. Mom's enduring charisma.)* as if gratitude is an assignment. Something you can get an A in if you're diligent.

Harper's journal isn't full of gratitude, though. She opens the pink leather cover. She's never particularly liked pink, and now pink seems little-girlish. Her mom gives her a lot of pink stuff, though, including a Swiss Army knife, should she ever need to convey her femininity while fighting for survival in the wilderness. In her baby pictures, Harper is *always* in pink attire—dresses with ruffles, T-shirts with unicorns and hearts and glitter. Unicorns and hearts and glitter, pink-handled razors, and deodorant that smells like lilacs or baby powder just don't send the message that she's capable of managing difficult times. They send the message that she's capable of handling Valentine's Day, maybe, which, okay, does have its moments of stress. If she had kid clothes with dump trucks and dinosaurs on them, and deodorant with the words "Arctic" or "Blast" in the name, or razors with five blades that can mow down a hair like a saw through a tree trunk, according to the ads, she'd perhaps feel more equipped to deal with the rigors of life, or at least a complicated remote control, but who knows.

Inside the pink journal are the tiny letters *MF* written in the corner. This is what she named the mysterious blank space in her life. She was going to fill it full of facts as she found them, but she still only has three.

Student.

University of Washington.

Lakeview Reproductive Medicine.

Instead, it's jammed with questions. *Where does he live? What does he look like? What does he do? What's his family like? Do they know? Am I like them? Does he have any other (real) children? Does he have any special talents? Does he have any terrible illnesses? Is he interesting or boring, like, does he have some exotic background (royalty or family history or unusual occupation)? Does he know I exist? Would he like me if he knew me? What was he like when he was my age? Was he bad at math? Was he in student government or an intern at Amazon with a 4.0, or not? Would we get along? Does he ever think about me? Why did he do it, exactly? Was there some reason other than the money? If he met me on the street, would he recognize me?*

Some of these are the same questions, over and over, said in different ways. Honestly, they are all probably the same two questions.

Was I wanted? Would he love me?

Which are maybe both a single question. The one that knocks around in the vast, echoey space inside her.

Do I, whoever that is, matter?

Harper's mother, Melinda Proulx, can't answer these questions about *MF*. And she refuses to answer the ones she *can*. For example, what was the whole experience even like? Did she get to pick him out of some big binder or something, the way you hear? Did she get to choose certain qualities, like auburn hair or blue eyes or a musical talent? This is all Harper knows: Her mom was thirty-two, had just gone back to school to get her doctorate at UW, and was a new hire at Seattle Central College, where she still works today. She hadn't yet found a guy who met her standards, and everyone (her own mom, mostly) kept talking about the clock ticking, and she wanted a child. So, after much careful consideration and research, she went to the Lakeview clinic and used an anonymous donor to make it happen. This is pure Melinda Proulx—goal oriented, efficient, unromantic. Anything beyond those few details, Melinda will not discuss. The message is clear. Sperm is not a father. Sperm is not DNA, or the other half of you. Sperm does not belong to an actual human man; it belongs to science. Sperm was a means to an end, an insignificant, irritating, inconsequential detail.

But it's more than that to Harper. Sperm is mystery. Alchemy. Molecular mojo. Squirming carriers of eons of DNA. Definitely deserving of a more regal, respectful name, instead of one that belongs on the Top Five Worst Words list, along with "phlegm," "moist," "pustule," and "ointment," all things that leave only a slime trail before they vanish.

Sure, sperm is science. But science is the most magical thing there is.

MF—My Father. Harper has no idea if the actual man himself belongs in a gratitude journal, but his role in her creation does.

Still, being thankful that you exist is pretty basic, no-frills stuff, like those off-brand sodas on the bottom shelf of the store, labeled only COLA.

Maybe she should have labeled the journal *MA. My Absence*. Because absence can have a very loud presence, that's for sure. *Absence* is an entity, with all of an entity's annoying habits, possible joys, and devastating effects.

She almost jumps when her phone buzzes. A text from Ezra.

Forgot to even ask! How's your stomach? Weeping emoji.

For a minute she has absolutely no idea what he's talking about.

And for another minute she feels terrible for being the kind of person who lies and wants to keep a secret from him. Seriously, how long can this go on anyway? The secret is another bomb, ticktock.

Nothing a hot dog won't fix, Harper texts, and adds a dancing spear of broccoli.

A little bling of a heart appears, and she sends a little bling of a heart back, and then her phone is quiet again. In the notebook, Harper turns to the very back.

Simone's name is there already, along with her most essential facts, which Harper has gathered like a conscientious squirrel collecting nuts for a possible hard winter: Simone's address, her phone number, her account handles. Harper tried to make the writing look like calligraphy, which of course ensures that it doesn't look at all like calligraphy. But that night, for the second time, she gets one of her nicest pens and swirls it first so as not to mess up the letters.

The point is, she wants to make it as beautiful as it deserves.

Dario Damaskenos, Harper writes. And next to that his address, his phone number, his account handle.

She makes sure to leave room for whatever else, *whoever* else, she might find. Because if sperm is mystery and alchemy, it is also definitely and seriously *abundant*. How abundant? She forgets. This is one problem with Google—it's super easy to look stuff up, so it's super easy to forget whatever you look up, too. She taps the question in again. Oh wow, wow—that's right. Up to *two hundred million* sperm per *milliliter* of semen.

Her imagination goes wild. Wild enough to envision herself as one tiny, meaningless speck in a great sea of other specks. Seeing herself in those like-like-liked Instagram squares, she can feel pretty special, but, God, what a joke.

CHAPTER FOUR

When Joshua is at last assigned a ship, I will accompany him, it has been decided. There has been an increase in acceptance of the practice of wives on board, and Joshua does not want to leave a young lady of seventeen alone in the city. There are notices of cholera on every street corner as well, with word of imminent quarantine. We are taking care to avoid all ardent spirits, drafts of air, and cold water, as advised, and we are keeping a regularity in the hours of meals and rest, but even a tumultuous sea beckons in comparison to the dire warnings.

> Mary Ann Patten to her mother,
> Elizabeth Brown
> New York, October 10, 1854

IN EZRA'S BACKYARD, EZRA AND HARPER, ALONG WITH Ezra's mom, Yanet, each take turns blowing into the little plastic tube of an inflatable baby pool until they get dizzy and pass it to the next person. This casual sharing of spit would have been unthinkable a short while ago, a perilous act. It's strangely warm for April, since the rampant use of fossil fuels has increased concentrations of greenhouse gases. Anytime Harper hears the words "fossil fuels," she thinks of dinosaurs, and what happened to them. All it took was one asteroid. Weird, Harper thinks, how they got wiped out by something so big, and how we almost got wiped out by something so small.

Now all the dolphins and whales and seahorses around the sides of the pool are plump, and the garden hose is trickling water in, and Binx is running around in his Spider-Man underwear, slippery with sun lotion. Nudo, their German shepherd, drinks out of the pool with his big pink tongue. When Binx first started to talk, he called everything he liked *Nudo*—noodle. This included the dog that Adam, Ezra's dad, found wandering the parking lot of Red Apple Market with no ID and no one stepping up to claim him, no matter how many ads they placed. Nudo's origins are even more mysterious than Harper's.

And then, suddenly, the tiny, coconut-scented superhero is gone. "Where'd he go?" Ezra asks.

"No idea." Harper wasn't looking. She was trying to get a good shot of the glass of pineapple soda next to her as she lounges in a sundress decorated with lemons, her mind whirling with fruit hashtags. It's not hiking and mountains, but people love a good sundress, even if she got it on clearance at Ross.

"Ma?" Ezra shouts.

"He's in here!"

They do this all the time, Ezra and his parents, like a sports team jointly keeping an eye on the ball. This is Ezra's family— a dad who saved a dog from a parking lot, a mom who delivers a cold drink, a wading pool with dolphins. It feels so different from one mom and a sperm donor.

"I look silly." Harper shows Ezra the image.

"Nah." Something's bothering him.

"What?"

"Nothing."

"Don't say nothing when it's something," Harper says, reasonably.

"Don't tell me don't," he says, less reasonably. The thing is, he never takes that tone with her. *That tone,* definitely a Melinda Proulx expression. At home Harper's tone is monitored like everything else that might escalate into the territory of imminent disaster: rising waters, air pollution, viral load, weight. Her impoliteness is a danger, evidence that circumstances might get out of control. Right that second Harper sees what her mom means, but it's all fine. When she shoots Ezra a hurt expression, he even apologizes. "Hey, sorry. Just tired." They're so good together.

Binx races back out. He flings a naked Barbie, a rubber triangle of pizza, and a tiny astronaut into the water. Harper can see the headline: HOLLYWOOD ACTRESS FOUND DEAD IN POOL AFTER OVERDOSE.

"A tragic end to a fairy-tale story," she says.

Ezra laughs. Binx shoves a pair of flat water wings at him.

"Bwow," Binx commands.

"Please," Harper says. "Please bwow."

Binx glares at her, his hair shiny in the sun. Ezra puffs into more little tubes. He scoots and yanks until the wings are on, and Binx's arms are lifted from his body like a muscly wrestler. He plops into the four inches of water.

"Want to go to Edmonds tomorrow?" Harper asks.

"What's in Edmonds, besides the ferry and lots of retirees?"

"The beach?"

"A photo thing?" He watches Barbie ride a pizza raft.

"They have a good bakery. I thought we could get your dad those chocolate croissants he likes." Harper didn't think that. It came to her just now. She really wants to spy on Dario D.'s mother, maybe even see Dario D. himself.

"Ma's got her knitting class. I said I'd babysit the beast."

"NOT A BABY," Binx protests from the pool. The astronaut dives, heading the wrong direction in the hydrosphere.

"Shoot," Harper says.

"But I'm looking forward to Soraya's thing tonight," Ezra says. "I'm glad the weather's going to be good."

Soraya's Third Annual Avengers Party, celebrating Soraya's all-time favorite film, which apparently premiered in April back when they were kids. Mostly, it's an excuse to wear costumes midway to Halloween and eat Soraya's mom's shawarma, pretty much the only food in the movie. She couldn't do it last spring, but now it's been transformed to an outdoor event, same as almost everything else.

"I told you, I can't go," Harper says.

"Um, *no*."

"I had to have. I know I did. Maybe I told Soraya twice."

"Harp," he exhales. "God, I spent all day yesterday making a Captain America shield out of a garbage can lid." Now that he mentions it, Harper can see a little red and blue paint under his fingernails. His long legs are crossed at the ankles, and he's wearing some bohemian-looking sandals and a really cool geometric sunrise-over-mountains tee and a woven bracelet. Harper's heart fills with tenderness, and she hopes he isn't really mad, because he looks so adorable right now, the perfect, tousled, outdoor-adventure-y, artist-type guy.

"I'm so sorry! I *hate* to miss it! But it's my mother's turn to host the EW meeting, and she's going ahead with it, you know, for the people who are vaccinated. Twice a year, every year. Well, *almost* every year."

"Ew?"

"Empowering Women. Leaders in business in the community, blah blah blah. I'm expected to circulate so she can show me off as evidence of her success."

That's when Harper sees it. The briefest lift of his eyebrows. You can't always tell what Ezra's thinking, but it's clear right then. *Yeah, I know how you feel.*

Wait, really? Does he think that *she* does that, shows him off as evidence of her success? And, oh God, does that mean she's like her mother? Well, sure, she *does* do that a little, but who wouldn't? She and Ezra have been a couple for almost a year. Seven months, but close enough. They say *I love you.* They have sex, a few times on the leather couch in the basement of this very house. She went on a weekend trip with his family to Orcas Island, when everyone was escaping to Airbnbs, and she regularly goes with them to get takeout from Las Margaritas. The point is, it's a real relationship. Everyone sees them as Ezra and Harper, Harper and Ezra. Yanet encourages her to eat whenever she gazes into their fridge full of stuff that isn't brown rice and tofu and Broccolini. She squeezes Harper's shoulders with affection, and Adam hands Harper a burger on a paper plate like she's a part of the family. She loves *all* of them, even Binx, who can be a real butt, and Nudo, who sometimes sniffs with inappropriate enthusiasm as he tries to get the intel. Harper has photos of her and Ezra from homecoming and the holidays, and there are, of course, lots and lots of photos of him on her page #sohot #boyfriend #lucky #whatacutie with so many comments: *You guys are ADORABLE together! OHMYGOD, GIRL!* Flame emoji. *I want one!* Weeping emoji. *Cutest couple evah. The way he looks at you, sigh!* There's *a lot* to show off!

Still, sometimes, like right now, like after those eyebrows, if she's being truly honest, she wonders if she really knows him. Or knows what love is. Or if Ezra really knows *her*, either. Half of her is a blank, so how can he? And she hasn't even told him about Simone or Dario D. She explained her absent father the way she usually does, that she was an in vitro baby and that he was anonymous. People usually leave it alone after that. If she *does* tell him about the others, how will he feel about her? That's the real question. Because when *she* looks at their three photos together, it's like she's a copy and paste. A doughnut on a conveyor belt, with a doughnut in front and a doughnut in back, going on times infinity.

"Is he peeing in the pool?" Ezra asks. Binx has gone completely still, his eyes glazed in concentration, as the pizza hits a wave and Barbie takes a spill.

"He's definitely peeing in the pool."

"Binx!" he calls, but it's clearly too late.

"What do you love about me, Ez?" Harper asks. There are so many ways she can be a better person, starting with not asking stuff like that, ugh.

Ezra makes a face.

"Name three."

"I can name twelve thousand," he says.

That night at Harper's mom's thing, Harper's the one who brings the trays around, offering tiny napkins and the healthy appetizers her mom gets from Trader Joe's, like creamed greens on crackers and corn-filled cones. Sometimes a girl just starts craving a block of cheese and a cupcake, that's for sure.

They haven't had these parties for a year and a half, and it's weird to have so many people gathered in their house, even though her mom required everyone to be vaccinated and has every door and window open as if they've just had a burnt-toast, blaring-smoke-alarm emergency. Her mom debated whether to have the party at all, as if she were the leader of a country weighing the opening of its borders. A few people have their coats on because it's freezing in there, and her mom flinches every time someone goes into the bathroom, and she occasionally passes Harper and furtively whispers, "Wash your hands," as if they're in a sordid, underground sex den of iniquity, instead of their own living room with canvas art reading LIVE, LOVE, LAUGH.

On these nights (*important for networking and visibility,* her mother says) you can count on a few things: one woman will drink too much; one will laugh in a super loud or unusual way, like a honking goose, for example; and her mother will introduce Harper around like she's a visiting celebrity who also happens to be a waitress. In the morning her mother's Spanx will be slumped over the side of the bathtub, lying collapsed and dripping after a tough night at work, hand-washed in cold water, exactly like the tag recommends.

"Will you study economics?" a young woman asks her after snagging a creamed green. "Like your mom?"

"Not sure yet," Harper says, and smiles. They always ask her this, too.

Jazz plays. Harper doesn't think her mother even likes jazz. Clusters of laughter explode; heads bend toward other heads in conversation. "Let me introduce . . ." Her mother grabs her elbow and introduces her to each Realtor–accountant–program manager. Melinda holds her back straight, which might be the Spanx, but she's also in her element, discussing productivity, things you can measure, things excelling and exceeding and surpassing other things.

Harper smiles and shifts around in the black skirt and white blouse and heels she wears for these events. She circulates. She's Barbie on a pizza raft, at the mercy of other forces.

It won't be long until she can flee. Her mother folds into a group, and Harper can hear her mention the name of her long-dead father, the famous economist Raymond Proulx, whom no one has ever heard of. She swirls her wine and says economic principle–type things, like Rational People Think at the Margin, and Future Consequences Count, and All Choices Invoke Cost.

It's safe. On her way through the kitchen, Harper takes a swig from a bottle of wine and shoves an eggplant round with cashew butter into her mouth. In her room she opens a box of Little Debbie Swiss Rolls, hidden for this occasion, sets one on a cocktail napkin, and FaceTimes Soraya. Soraya is dressed in all black, an

Avenger assassin. She looks cute with her dark hair pulled back in a little ponytail. It's loud over there, even in her backyard, with maybe, like, six people. That number isn't just pandemic precaution; it's Soraya's usual idea of a party. She and Soraya are introverts, and Ada's an extrovert, someone who's energized by social activities, at least according to that quiz they took. Ada pops her head into the screen and makes a face, proving the point.

"Hey, Harp! Can't talk," Soraya says. "We're just about to start the movie. My dad set up this whole outdoor theater. And your boyfriend has been telling my mom all about this great Lebanese restaurant in Havana, and now she's following him around like she's in love."

"Ezra's been to Havana?"

"Wait. Ben's screaming for paper towels. Someone spilled something. Hey, I gotta go."

"Okay, see you guys."

Soraya disappears into her world—Harper's world, she thinks. And Harper's mother has disappeared into *her* world, maybe Harper's world, too. But what if none of these people are really her people, and none of these worlds are her world? Perhaps she belongs to a stranger's world, and that's why she always feels so alone.

If she sometimes acts like her mother, in what ways does she act like her father? He's a mystery to her, so she's a mystery to her.

Right at this moment, he's *somewhere* doing *something*. He could be living on the other side of the Earth, or down the street. He could be sleeping in a tent in Yosemite, or battling dengue fever, or reading a book. He could be passed out drunk, or clipping his toenails, or drinking milk straight out of the carton. Or else, he isn't somewhere doing something, and he's dead, and she's missed the chance to ever know him. She thinks she would sense it if he were dead, but what she senses is that he's *out there.*

How should you view a man who anonymously fathered children? And maybe, just maybe, *many* children? It seems sinister, preposterous, wildly generous. Or else it was simply meaningless to him, in a way it can never be meaningless to Harper.

Meaningless. The word knocks around inside her. If it was meaningless to him, how much does she matter, really? Identity is a calculus problem.

She takes her gratitude journal out from underneath her mattress. She sets her finger on his name: Dario D. Harper has never tried to reach out to Simone. She's way too intimidating.

It's too late to call, isn't it? But it's only nine, and a Saturday night, and Dario D. isn't some senior citizen who's gone to bed already. His phone number is a mixed message: go, stop, yield. She's light-headed.

In Harper's life of shouting posts and attention-getting shots, and blingy comments, and the casino-like flashing of lights and words and images, this is one of the quietest things she's ever done.

It's a compromise: a text, not a call.

Oh God. This could go very, very wrong.

Hi Dario. My name is Harper Proulx. You don't know me, but I think we have someone in common.

Pushing *send* is like leaping from the side of a boat when you don't even fully realize you decided to jump. Suddenly you're in midair, and then swallowed by a blast of water so cold that you know without a doubt that you're alive. In it, anyway. Finally in.

She could throw up. Her palms are sweating. She paces a few circles in her room. Her phone sits silent, and they are both unchanged.

Wait.

Wait, wait, wait.

She sees the bubbles that mean he's typing. Oh God! *He,* an actual human being! The first moment of connection.

I think we have each other in common, he says.

CHAPTER FIVE

Joshua has just been offered command of a ship, *Neptune's Car,* of Foster & Nickerson of this city. The ship is ready to sail this day, prepared for the circumnavigation of the Earth, but for Captain Forbes, who has unexpectedly sickened. It is the largest clipper ship ever built in the Commonwealth, two hundred sixteen feet long, forty feet wide, with three masts reaching nearly twenty-four feet, and has been on only two record-setting voyages since its launch just shy of our wedding day. Joshua has declined, however. He told the owners that he cannot leave me, his new bride, alone for so long a time.

Mary Ann Patten to her mother,

Elizabeth Brown

New York, January 12, 1855

THERE ARE SEVERAL THOUSAND TV SHOWS ON AT ANY minute, and probably five thousand movies, and 1.45 million books in the Seattle Public Library, and countless stories and words and more words online, and yet it only takes a few words to tell the story that sits between Harper and Dario.

You already know who I am? she texts.

Same as you know me, he texts back.

Lakeview clinic?

Yup, he answers. *Want to talk?*

Now? Right now? No way. That's like jumping over the side, all right. Smack into waters jammed with stinging jellyfish.

Tomorrow? Like, late morning? Maybe eleven?

Tomorrow, he agrees. *Eleven.*

He sends a smiling emoji, and she sends one back, and then the bubbles go flat.

What is she thinking? Tomorrow?! Why did she suggest *that*? She could have at least given herself some time to think about actually *talking*. But then again, tomorrow! Wow. She gets to speak to him in a matter of hours, a guy who's technically her brother. It's all so strange. You'd have thought we'd hit the peak of strange when the entire world was strange, Harper thinks, but this is like those nesting dolls, when you find another one inside the larger one. Harper is alone in her room, but not. Dario seems to fill actual space. Dario D. stretches to every dust-clumped corner, and he practically busts through the window. Harper paces the small space of her room, mouthing *OhmyGodohmyGodohmyGod.* Her body is made of electricity, jumpy, jumpy, jumpy. She nervous-eats another Little Debbie. Her mind is a bag of snakes, floppy, wiggly, uncontrollable, dangerous.

She posts an image of her face in the mirror hanging behind her door. She's in her room, not outside in nature somewhere, and she looks slightly deranged. But she still has her makeup on from the party, and her hair looks good, and she needs them now, her followers. The hearts and likes rush in, and so does the calm reassurance. It's like a blankie and pacifier, or, better yet, a soothing cocktail of self-esteem.

Down the hall, jazz plays and glasses clink and Harper's mother laughs.

Harper's a horrible person, she's sure. She's her mother's one and only, her special project, the *best thing she ever did.* Her mom took care of Harper's sore throats and made her nutritious meals. She rubbed her back that day Harper was overwhelmed and sobbed because there was the pandemic *and* riots *and* wildfire smoke. She made Harper that eclipse viewer thing out of the All-Bran box so they could share the moment together, the moon passing between the sun and Earth, when the light got weird and the birds went silent. It all means that Harper owes her. Harper feels so guilty at her disloyalty. But then again, Harper's mom made them have twin haircuts in the sixth grade, and played the left hand of the piano while Harper played the right during her eighth-grade piano recital, and is adamant that Harper's entire future depends on getting into a high-profile university. And sometimes she texts Harper's own friends (a recipe Soraya might like, an article about the basics of investing for Ben). Is this what happens when a person tries too hard to make you into herself, only improved? If you're lucky, you kick your way to freedom, into the bright light of your own imperfect self.

This is all probably the Little Debbie talking, because the only thing Harper is brave enough to do right now is keep a secret, and hang up her black skirt and white blouse for the next gathering, and wipe off her makeup with her mother's little white cloths so her pores don't clog. Clogged pores can lead to catastrophe, if the soap commercials are to be believed, though there's never a guy in those commercials, talking about his complexion or uneven skin tones, now looking dewy and transformed.

The not-driving thing is a problem when you want to rebel, Harper realizes. Luckily, she doesn't generally want to rebel. Rebelling sounds as frightening and risky as skydiving, and there's always someone to take her wherever she wants to go anyway. Harper's mom, who will press her to the point of torture about her grades, and colleges, and extracurriculars, and friends, and, and, and, never presses her about driving. *I don't want to force you,* says the woman who forces everything else. The few times Melinda took her out to practice, Melinda was a nervous wreck, and Harper did terribly, they both agreed, as if driving were something you're innately good at or not. She'd likely worry every second Harper was behind the wheel of a car, too. Besides, her mom always likes the time with Harper in the car, she says. It's when Harper *opens up* and they can have *real conversations,* and maybe Harper *is* more relaxed with her mom literally in the driver's seat.

But it's a problem when you want to go somewhere in secret. It's a problem when you want something to be *yours.*

So, Harper walks that day when she's about to speak to Dario D. She tells her mom she's meeting Ezra to get coffee at Butter, the bakery a few blocks away in Green Lake. It's strategy: offering a fictional wrongdoing to hide a worse, real one, because . . . white flour, hidden calories, a muffin is a cake, who's kidding who. The butter in a croissant, gasp, and a scone is a total loss. But luckily, Melinda's a little too hungover from the party last night to care too much.

Harper does pass Butter on her way to Green Lake before the appointed hour. The great smells crook their nasty, evil little fingers at her, urging her not to be empty. She wants to go somewhere quiet, but where's that? Even at ten-thirty on a Saturday morning, the parking lot of Green Lake is jammed, and bikes are whizzing around in a cyclone of Lycra. People are marching their way to ten thousand steps, cardio-ing their hearts out, as their dogs trot along beside them, at the mercy of their owners' fitness goals.

Harper hurries as if she's late, but she's never late. Ugh, she's early, same as always, and so she fills the time by worrying if she's in a spot where her phone won't work, worrying if she has the time right, worrying that she should have brought a charger in case her battery dies, basically worrying about all the little things that keep you busy so you don't worry about the big things.

And then, finally, there he is. Right on time. His number appears on the screen, but so does his face. Oh shit! They didn't agree on *that,* a video call, and she starts to panic. She didn't plan on him *seeing* her.

"Oh my God, I look bad," she says.

"Don't be ridiculous," Dario says, as if he's known her forever, almost like a, uh, *brother.* "Let me see. Take me out of your . . . coat, I guess? Something blue."

"T-shirt," Harper says, and turns the phone to reveal herself.

"Blue like your eyes," he says. Dario's hair is longer than in the photos. More moppish, and his face is narrower, and he's—

hard to tell—shorter? Thinner. It makes him look young, or maybe he just seems vulnerable, his face there on the screen, his voice sounding like a middle schooler's. They stare at each other. Behind him, there are travel posters on his bedroom wall. "OH MY GOD," he says then, snorting and laughing with nerves. He can barely get the words out. It's the sort of hilarity that's nerves gone wild. "Blue like OUR eyes."

Harper starts laughing, too, because it's all so weird. He's laughing hard enough that the phone bops around and Harper gets a glance of his room. "*I* have travel posters," she says.

"What?" Dario looks at her, blinking.

"Your travel posters. I have them, too."

"Weird. So *weird*," he says, but it's the most inconsequential thing, the posters. Ada has them as well, and she isn't Harper's sister. She *hopes*, haha.

They stare some more. His face is an archaeological site. Everything is. She spots a potato chip bag and a bottle of Mountain Dew. It's like finding out that early man used the same tools you do. There's too much to say, so it's hard to talk. "How did you know who I was? I mean, that we—" she asks.

"My friend Summer."

"Oh right." She'd totally forgotten about @summerknights 4666.

"I should tell you. I've already met another one of us."

"What?"

Her face flushes as a sickening feeling fills her. *Another* one of us. Like they're one whole entity. Different bees, but just bees, emanating from one hive, and, God, how many are there? Once you hit the hive with a stick, they just keep coming and coming.

"A guy."

"Wow." Harper's stomach feels gross, but she's also curious, and jealous. Dario's already ahead of her with information. She doesn't know if she should tell him about Simone. She has no real evidence. Nothing for sure.

"He's kind of an asshole."

"Really?" This seems impossible. She isn't an asshole, most of the time anyway, a usual, generic amount, and Dario doesn't seem to be one, and suddenly there are all these possible calculations of similar and different, instead of just similar. And another strange thing, with that summation, she feels an instant bonding with Dario. The two of them together, the asshole not belonging.

"Mercer Island. Plays *football.*" He makes his eyes large and shocked and shakes his head like, whoa, huh? Harper does the same back.

"His mother must play football," Harper says, and Dario cracks up. Oh man, it's awesome making him laugh. She wants him to like her, but he's also one of those people you realize you can be funny with.

"He didn't know about . . ." Dario searches for words. He seems embarrassed. Maybe even a little immature for his age. "How he was *conceived,* until last year. They weren't going to tell him at all, but some aunt let it slip."

"Oh God."

"Did you always know? I've always known. My mothers had these books . . . this, uh, sperm, wearing a top hat, tap-dancing toward the egg."

"I was maybe five?" Harper's mother had made her sit down. She spoke with the same somber tone as when their gerbil, Muriel, died. Harper understood similar things as with Muriel, too: It was what it was, and nothing could be done about it. A mystery involving larger life forces that one had to accept. Also, same as Muriel, Harper's mother treated her carefully for a few days after the news. She got ice cream and a unicorn floor puzzle. The questions—those came later, when other people, kids, teachers, whoever, started asking them. Does your dad cook, too? Where is your dad? Could your dad help? She saw them, dads, zipping coats and bringing in the treats and standing next to partner moms or dads. For a while, it was mostly something other kids had that you didn't and never would, like a bouncy castle on your birthday. But then it seemed more than that. Definitely more. That emptiness inside her felt like a longing, like his absence had created a space that was destined to be permanent.

"He was pissed, finding out that way. So no wonder he has a chip on his shoulder." Dario takes a chip from the bag and sets it on his shoulder. That Dario D.—he's an odd one.

Out of nowhere a small white-and-brown dog leaps up into the frame and snatches the chip. He crunches in victory. Harper recognizes Walter. It looks like a trick they've done before. Or maybe Walter just looks like a circus dog in person.

"Hey, is that . . . ?" If she uses his name, Dario will know the extent of her spying, so she stops there.

"This is Walter." Dario rotates the dog to look at the camera, and then he kisses Walter's cheek.

"Hey, Walt," Harper says.

"He's not a nickname kind of guy. I forgot when I named him that Walt was my horrible shop teacher who always smelled like cigarettes and stared at us like a creep."

"Oh my God. Walter, then."

"He's a stray."

"Ah." It makes Harper think of Nudo. And all the dog-members of families who have mysterious origins. They know very little of their own stories, and they seem to manage. It's one of their great strengths, dogs, Harper thinks, the lack of existential crises. "The football player from Mercer Island . . ."

"Wyatt. Groveland. Like Groveland Park?"

"No idea." She shrugs.

Dario giggles. Seriously, he's kind of a goofy kid, but Harper feels like she's known him forever. She doesn't know anything about him, not really, but tell her DNA that. It *recognizes* him. It was the way she felt about Ez when she first saw him in that Zoom box, where she just knew they were going to have a future together, but also, as she paces around on that grass at Green Lake, a past together, too. "Me neither. That's just what he said. 'Wyatt Groveland, like Groveland Park?'"

"We'll have to look it up."

"I did. Boring. A park. A million Grovelands, nothing specific."

"You get right on it, the research."

"Who doesn't? But I like history." She remembers him by those airplanes. "Do you?"

"Eh." She wobbles her hand to say *sort of.* And then she writes his name down in her mind: *Wyatt Groveland.* When she goes home, she'll write in her notebook with her good pen. "Do you know any more about him?" She doesn't mean Wyatt Groveland; she means MF, but Dario understands.

"Probably same as you. Student at University of Washington.

Height, hair color, weight, ethnicity, medical stuff . . . They said not to be concerned about that lactose intolerance thing. Are you concerned? Hey, we just met. Maybe it's too early to ask you about dairy." Dario D. snickers.

"Wait, what? Medical stuff? Weight? I don't know any of this."

"You don't?" He seems more than surprised. He seems shocked.

"How did you find out?"

"Um . . . I'm not even . . ." Dario looks kind of panicked, like there's nowhere to run now.

No. No!

A gross dread flows into Harper's whole body. An awful awareness of being kept in the dark *on purpose.*

"Just tell me."

"Oh man. My mothers had all the information," he confesses.

"Mine said he was anonymous. That it was closed." Her cheeks flush. Harper looked it up—the rules varied in different states and countries, but the default in Washington was open information, unless the donor specifically wanted it otherwise. "She said he requested it."

Dario looks sad. He shakes his head. In pity. For her. Now she feels furious at her mother, but jealous, too. One of Dario's moms owns a bakery, and they let him know everything this whole time, and they were *honest,* and it seems like a bounty.

"She *lied.*" Wow, Harper has been both guilty and smug about her own betrayal, but her mother betrayed her first. Open! Her whole life, open! Fury threatens to take over everything else— this reunion, hope for more information. She watches a woman stretch one leg to her head and hold a pose. Two others with bare midriffs run without sweating. A couple walks past, with two children in waterproof suits, utterly protected from the possibility of raindrops or mud puddles. This is all Harper's fault for being curious. It's too much. Too much information, too much feeling, too much world. This is what you get when you step out into it. Feelings, annihilating feelings, more than you can handle.

"Hey, hey. Maybe you *do* have an anonymous one. Someone else. Maybe it's not even the same guy," Dario says.

"Look at us."

"It's the same guy."

"How could she *do* this?"

"Anonymous doesn't exist anymore, regardless," Dario says. He's the type of boy to use words like "regardless." "You'd spit in a tube sooner or later and find a bunch of relatives either way."

"Tell me about him."

"Are you sure?"

"I'm sure. I promise you, I'm sure!"

"Six foot one. Auburn hair, blue eyes, duh. You know that's rare, right? Like, one of the rarest combinations, red hair, blue eyes."

"I know."

"Greek and Irish on his father's side, Scottish and Dutch on his mother's. High cholesterol. No increased risk for significant medical conditions. The lactose thing."

"Greek, like you, right?"

"Right. Sometimes people choose ethnicities to match one of the parents, you know? My moms picked him with numerology, though. The Greek was icing on the cake, the cake being me. I can find out more after I'm eighteen. Wyatt turns eighteen this year. He's going to look and tell me what he finds."

A real him exists. MF—with his own mother and father, his own arteries and organs. Harper knows this logically, but the telescope suddenly focuses. For the millionth time, right there at Green Lake, she plays the game Maybe That's Him. She waits for an auburn-haired man about the right age to pass. There's one—incredibly overweight, but he's doing his best to jog, his feet skating slowly along the ground. Maybe that's him. Another one—Harper's terrible at heights, but he seems about six feet tall, and he's carrying a fishing pole to the edge of the lake as a boy walks beside him, holding a tackle box to his chest. Maybe *that's* him. Or another guy, sitting on a bench, hunched over, disheveled, smoking, a Starbucks cup beside him. He looks horribly depressed. The story might have a bad ending. It might be better not to know.

It might be better to stop right there, with the sudden find of Dario D. and Walter. They seem like a bonus. Like a happy enough ending. Like an ending she can manage. It makes her think of that bracelet Soraya's mom gave Soraya. It was supposed to be inspirational, and Soraya loves it, but it makes Harper uncomfortable. *Beautiful girl, you can do hard things.* Couldn't it just be *You can do hard things*? Do you have to be beautiful *and* resilient? Does any guy's dad ever give him a bracelet that says, *Good-looking boy, you can do hard things*? But the point is, she doubts she can do hard things, all by herself, even with a bracelet urging her on.

"Hey, Dario? I've got to go. This is all pretty overwhelming."

"You're not going to disappear, are you?" Dario looks panicked again. "This isn't the last time we'll talk, is it?" Walter hears the anxiety in his voice and jumps around on Dario's lap, filling the screen. "Walter, ow. Get off."

"No, of course not," Harper says, but she isn't sure. Then again, it's funny, but she almost misses him already, before they've even hung up. There's so much more she wants to know.

"There's so much more I want to know," he says, speaking her very own thoughts. "You seem like such an interesting person. Your boyfriend, too. He looks awesome, like an artist or something."

"He's not an artist, but he *is* awesome." She thinks of Simone, an actual artist, and then, why not, she tells him. "I think there might be another one of us, besides your Wyatt. I haven't talked to her or anything, so I have no real proof, but she looks exactly like us."

"Oh yeah?" He seems really unimpressed.

"Simone Van Den Berg. She's a student at Berkeley. You said Dutch—her dad is Dutch."

It's strange, how he doesn't seem shocked, or even all that interested.

"So that makes four of us," Harper says.

Dario makes a face.

"What? What's going on?"

"I don't know if this is the right time. I mean, you said you were overwhelmed."

"Oh my God, what?"

"Sometimes a person isn't ready. You shouldn't force it."

"Dario. *Tell me.*"

He sighs. "I said Wyatt was someone I *met.* In person. But I didn't mean he's the *only one.*"

Harper's body is suddenly aching, and a coldness ripples through her, as if she's coming down with a flu. Or maybe even *that* virus, something awful. Dire. Her cheeks flush again. "Dario. What are you saying?" She can barely speak.

"Well, I should just . . . Are you sure?"

"I'm sure, I'm sure!"

"Maybe I should just show you."

He stands. He moves to a different wall. There's a poster there, one Harper doesn't have. A big white sheet, with circles and lines. It's the kind of thing you see on TV, when a detective is trying to nail down a murder suspect. There are photos, too. Small photos, of people with her auburn hair and her blue eyes and her nose. And names. *Sullivan Cleary. Lara Brooks. J. C. Mandelli. Liam O'Patrick. Jasmine Bauman. Finn Lange. Eamon, Sophia, Mia, Oliver, Jack . . .*

"Oh my God," she breathes.

"Are you okay, Harper? Are you okay?"

"Oh my God."

This is when Harper learns the truth about herself.

She is the child of her mother, Melinda Proulx, who has one daughter, and her father, an unknown man, who has forty-two daughters and sons, so far.

CHAPTER SIX

A sudden turn of events! Joshua has gotten permission for me to accompany him aboard *Neptune's Car.* In twelve hours, we will set off on a voyage around the world. Joshua is calling it my bridal tour—a honeymoon voyage around Cape Horn to San Francisco, and then outward-bound again to China, then London. We will flee this cholera epidemic by heading into the great and terrible ocean, but there is nothing to fear as long as Joshua is at the helm.

> Mary Ann Patten to her mother,
> Elizabeth Brown
> New York, January 12, 1855

ONCE AGAIN, THE BEAUTIFUL THING ABOUT HARPER'S phone right now, right when she learns about all the others, is that it's a world. The whole world is in her palm. She can visit a museum in Paris; she can see what's happening in Bosnia, or Soraya's backyard. She can look inside restaurants she'll never go to, or view trailers of films she'll never see, or watch gamers playing a game she doesn't play, or a guy freaking out at a haunted house she'll never visit. People dance as she sits still. She can watch a cartoon bear with a hockey stick, a cat climbing a drape, the rating of a variety of chicken nuggets, a guy opening a box with a personal-sized fan inside. Or a music video, music video, music video.

But she can shut it, too. Just like that—in her own palm, *gone.* Who can shut down a whole world when it's too much? She can, when it's in her hand. The real one, out there—that one is wild and uncontrollable, but this one isn't.

She ends the call with Dario. Boom, finished. His face disappears, his voice vanishes, and she can suddenly understand the whole ghosting thing. How you can just pretend that someone doesn't exist anymore, and make all the regrets and bad feelings go away. Mostly. Mostly, you can move on, tell yourself it never happened. That would be way easier than dealing with the fallout and feelings of what did.

Pretend she never called Dario. Pretend she was never curious. Pretend she kept the door shut.

She walks home. She's so upset, no, *furious,* that she's not even in her own body. Is she ever in her own body? What does that even mean? She doesn't remember the walk home. She's under that tree at Green Lake, and then, poof, she's in the kitchen of their small house.

Thank God, Melinda Proulx, the traitor, isn't home. There's a note on the counter. Why did she leave a note? Why not just text? Why have those moments where she's *too* tech savvy, appearing on Harper's feed with her suffocating comments and heart emojis, befriending Harper's friends, knowing all the newest channels everyone likes before Harper does, texting her every five minutes when she's out, and then *a note*? Too tech savvy and then utter helplessness, some screaming fit because there's a paper jam in the printer or a weird, freak-the-hell-out error message on her laptop, or she's sure something important has disappeared, when of course it hasn't. You know who wants to disappear? Harper.

Visiting Grandma. Made some hummus, in the fridge.

Fuck hummus!

Grandma is Grandma Patricia, who lives across Lake Washington, in Bellevue. It's either twenty-five minutes away with no traffic, or twenty-jillion hours away with, but they don't see her that often. Melinda calls her every few days, and afterward, she sighs, complaining that she's part of the sandwich generation, which means she has to take care of Grandma Patricia and Harper, and that no one takes care of her. Honestly, Grandma Patricia doesn't seem to need much taking care of. She has her friends and her yoga class and her 401(k) and her IRA and her SEP, whatever those are. Her face is always made up with the circles of rouge on her cheeks, and colorful scarves hide her saggy neck, and in the bathroom are those little perfect towels that you aren't supposed to use, embroidered with *P.P.* Whenever Harper sees them in the bathroom, she *wishes* she had a sibling. They would laugh, P.P. in the bathroom, haha! They would wipe their hands on the backs of them and whisper stuff and smirk secretly.

Her mother, that liar, will likely be gone for hours. Good. Harper is so pissed that she imagines terrible things happening to her, and her not returning, and Harper living alone like Pippi Longstocking without the horse. Pippi always looked so satisfied. Pippi never seemed confused and full of longing for what she didn't have.

Harper starts to cry. But then, no! *No!* It's unbelievable, her mom hiding MF from her like this. A lie, her whole life! Which actually means *millions* of lies. God! She's furious. Harper wants to ruin and wreck. She wants to fling those LIVE, LOVE, LAUGH canvas prints to the ground and stomp on them. Fuck LIVE, LOVE, LAUGH! She wants to kick over the Target mid-century modern accent tables, and the air purifier that removes pollutants, allergens, and toxins. She wants to fling her mother's modest collection of crossbody bags from the window, rip their mildew-resistant, antimicrobial shower curtain from its rod, tear apart the memory-foam pillows, and cut those resistance bands in rainbow colors into rainbow shreds. She wants to throw every squirting bottle of gelatinous hand sanitizer out the freaking window.

How could she do it? How could she not tell Harper, or let Harper know about half of her? How could she try to own her like that?

She goes to her room. Slams the door hard enough that stuff on her dresser rattles. If a door slams and no one is there to hear it, does it really slam? She sees that she's missed a call from Ezra. She doesn't want to hear about a party she didn't go to because she was dutifully passing gross appetizers.

Tears keep fighting their way forward. Honestly, she could break right down, but that's too terrifying. It's too large. Her chest is squeezing. She can barely breathe. Is this a heart attack? Can you get a heart attack at her age? There's supposed to be a shooting pain down her arm, she thinks, and maybe she *does* have a shooting pain, or maybe just a sore muscle from hauling that tray of wineglasses around last night.

She hunts around on her phone. Symptoms of a heart attack.

Uncomfortable pressure in chest, pain in arm, nausea, light-headedness, cold sweat, check, check, check. Risk factors. Diabetes, smoking, high blood pressure, menopause. Okay, no. High cholesterol! MF has that! MF—this can also stand for Mystery Figure. Or Many Fucking children.

Other reasons for chest pain: injured rib, peptic ulcers, collapsed lung, costochondritis, whatever that is. There are so many things that can go wrong, you don't even know what they all are.

Anxiety attack.

Harper tries to do the triangle breathing thing. She breathes Forty-Two Children up, and Forty-Two Children down. What if there are *more*?

Harper opens her page. Her last post, the hurried one of herself in the mirror, has gotten three hundred forty-five likes and a bunch of comments. She scrolls, hitting *like* to all their likes. Sometimes you almost need their like of your like to their like. She scans her feed. A dog dressed like a shark, a hair removal kit, Neuschwanstein Castle, a tattoo of a pine cone, something with gravy. A girl in a white bikini doing a headstand poolside.

Harper can't do a headstand to save her life, but she finds the photo of herself in her white bikini, the one they took at Discovery Park, where she's lying inside a heart that Ezra helped her draw in the sand. His hearts are always so perfect. Sunrays and salt water! #beachbabe #bikinigirl #swimwear #beachlife #girlswhowander #girltraveler #beachphotoshoot #summervibes #getoutdoors #liveyourbestlife. Post. In come the little flame emojis, the faces with heart eyes, the comments. *Wow! Love your swimsuit! Absolute babe! You're killin it! 100%! Hottie!*

She flips back to the other girl in the other white bikini. She zooms in on her face, tries to see if there's something in her eyes, something more than the smile on her face. Is she really that happy and confident? Is everything truly going that well? Harper clicks on her profile. She's got a jillion followers, and yeah, of course. She looks perfect. Always, always happy. Happy on cliffs, happy on a wakeboard, sultry on a pool floaty, sexy sipping a drink through a straw. Is she on a *yacht*? Everything appears rich and abundant. Shiny, golden. Capable, fearless, confident— beautiful girl, she can definitely do hard things, even without a bracelet. Is it possible she's just learned that someone has cancer, or did she just get a DUI, or is her boyfriend about to leave her? Is she fighting with a friend, or battling depression? Is she scared of doorknobs and handrails? Does she lie awake at night, thinking about earthquakes?

Did she just find out that her father has forty-one other children?

It sure doesn't seem like it. Look at her! There's even one of those *here's me without makeup* shots where she looks perfect. God, Harper hates those. Her abdomen seems hard enough to knock on, and you can bet she's wearing some lavender deodorant, and she probably shaved those thin, ropy calves with a pink-handled razor, which means she's solved all of it, the mystery of being unafraid in the frightening world, how to be full of actual self-esteem on a diet of glitter and hearts. Harper slides into outright jealousy. The emptiness inside merges with something hard to identify. Fury plus sadness plus a permanent anxiety plus aloneness plus what's-the-point-ness. Harper just can't *do* all of this.

The white bathing suit is so white, and the smile is so bright, and the pool gleams, and the sun sparkles. Outside, the sky, her sky, the one there, in the real world, has turned to a muddy gray. Dim and monochromatic.

And now Harper herself is another bomb, along with the bomb of Melinda Proulx, and the bomb of MF and all his offspring, and the real bomb, the most dangerous one, right under the surface of the ocean. A bomb she doesn't even know about yet, one that will be detonated in a mere eighteen weeks, destroying everything around it for miles and miles. She has no idea that certain things had better happen, and fast.

A dump truck with a plastic giraffe and a tiny plastic chef in the back rides across Harper's ankle and smashes into a superhero in a spaceship.

"POWEE," Binx says as the chef tumbles out onto the grass.

Ezra hops the little chef back and forth and talks in a tiny man voice. "Mon dieu! How am I going to cook ze boeuf flambé if I have ze broken leg?" Apparently, he's a French chef.

"I will help you," the superhero says as Binx wiggles him out of his ship and flies him over, making tending gestures.

"Ah, oui oui. Zis is much better, ze gentle person who doesn't smash and bash into me," Ezra says.

"Wee-wee!" Binx cackles with the thrill of a potty joke.

"Somebody send ze ambulance," Ezra says. Harper zooms a circus train car to the rescue as her phone buzzes.

Dario. Dario for the millionth time this week. *Call me.*

"Who keeps texting?" Ezra asks.

"Soraya," she lies. Ezra's eyebrows go down. Harper's a terrible liar. She wouldn't have believed her, either. "She got in a fight with her mom." Once again she adds a nugget of truth, so at least part of her believes it.

"That creepy guy online again?" Ez asks, concerned. A twenty-five-year-old has been DMing Soraya, and she had to block him after he sent a dick pic that, on first glance, Soraya thought was a purple corn dog. Every single person Soraya tells that story to says, *When have you ever seen a purple corn dog?!* And she shrugs and turns red. Sometimes you can have the world in your hand, and gross stuff will pop into it, too.

"No, um. It's *private,*" Harper says, with the kind of inflection that means personal stuff.

"YOU BE THE NURSE," Binx says, and shoves a plastic tiger into Harper's hand.

"She can be a doctor," Ezra says.

"There might be only three thousand nine hundred left of me in the world before we go extinct, but I am an extraordinary doctor," the tiger says, hopping around on its back legs near the chef.

Ezra makes a *Harper, stop* face.

"Ah, merci, merci, Dr. Tigresse," Ezra says. "You are ze miracle worker. Now I will make for you a fluffy crepe."

Binx's eyes go wide. Potty jokes are one thing, but a shocking swear word like "crap" is next level.

Nudo races around and then wiggles on his back on the lawn, giving himself a grass scratch, showing off his belly and balls without the slightest embarrassment.

"Do you think Nudo ever wonders about his old family? Like, where they went? Or if he misses them?"

"Harp, look at him. Does it seem like it? He's just living his life." Somewhere MF is doing the same. Not scratching his back on the grass, but the living part.

Of course, this is the time to spill the whole story. Well, long ago would have been better, but now here's a chance again. The problem is, the whole situation with MF is only getting weirder and more complicated and harder to reveal. She makes a promise: when the perfect moment comes, she'll tell him everything.

At Ezra's house they finish dinner, some delicious kind of fried beef with onions and rice. Ezra's mom and dad always make good, meaty stuff. Filling stuff. There's always warm, soft bread, butter. Dessert. Cookies, or rice pudding, or ice cream. Yanet seems to think food is a fun, great, satisfying thing, not an imminent hazard. It's like visiting a sunny, abundant planet when you come from a vast, icy one. Yanet calls her stretch pants her friendly pants.

All during dinner Harper can hear her phone buzzing in her purse on their kitchen counter. Yanet hates phones at the table, so Harper has tucked it away, but it's vibrating with need and demand, and everyone's pretending not to notice. When they're finished and she sneaks a look, Dario has texted six times. It's the same stuff he's been saying for days.

Hey, I'm REALLY sorry. That was too much too soon.

I'm so SO sorry.

Please don't disappear.

Photo of Walter, plus *Can we try again?*

This is so weird. Call me?

Okay, I'm done texting. See ya.

Dario's a stranger, Harper reminds herself, even if he doesn't feel like one.

"Hey, before you go, I've got something to show you," Ezra says.

"What?"

"Surprise. Just a sec."

She sits on the floral couch in Ezra's basement, where they mess around when his parents aren't home. Yanet and Adam are in the family room above, watching some TV show. Harper can hear the *mrphh mrphh* of television voices, and the thump of Ezra's feet as he runs up the stairs. A few moments later, after she's flipped through the Zabar's catalog on the end table, mentally choosing the chocolate babka over the bagels, and the New York Breakfast Basket over the Salami & Cheese Crate, she also hears the appreciative whoops and laughter of Ezra's mom and dad. Then Ezra's feet come pounding down again.

"Hide your eyes," he says.

"You're making me nervous."

"Surprises can be good things, Harp."

"They can?"

"Ready?"

"Ready," she says.

And now there's Ezra, standing in front of her, wearing a retro navy-blue paisley tuxedo jacket, slim black trousers that hit above the ankles, a white shirt with a pointed wing-tip collar, and a bolo tie, circa the 1990s. It's dweeby and fabulous, and, man, does he look *interesting*. The kind of interesting you just need a calm confidence to pull off. It doesn't look like a costume on him. It looks like style.

"Dad's tux from prom. There's even a ticket in the pocket that says 'Keep This Ticket,'" he says, and shows her.

"It's fantastic." Slightly embarrassing, you know, but fantastic. Harper plays a fast and furious film of him and her at the dance together with him dressed like that. Even in her imagination, she watches what other people are thinking before she can relax, but Ez is relaxed from the moment they join their friends under the covered football field, where they're having the dance this year. Too many parents are still nervous about a packed gym.

"Yeah? It's okay?" Ezra's eyes are shy. God, she wants to put her hands all over him.

"*Yeah*. Geez. My dress is so boring." She's going to wear the same one she wore when she was her mom's date at a fundraising dinner for the community college before the pandemic, when people still regularly did things like that. The dress is *elegant*, according to her mom, who picked it out. *Elegant* means being understated, quiet, sticking to the rules, *not sexy*. Sexy always makes her mom very, very nervous. Sexy is maybe dangerous, but sexy also means growing up and leaving her. With Melinda, it's like Ezra's always on a job interview. The message to Harper is, *This is not forever.*

"You'll be your kind, funny, beautiful self no matter what you wear," he says, and brings her in close. He really believes those things about her, but Harper doesn't. She thinks she has to be those things 100 percent of the time in order to be them at all. And sometimes she's selfish, dull, and downright ugly, and that's the truth.

"Oh my God, wait. Just a sec." She pushes her hand against his chest to get free, reaches for her phone. "Go over by the door." If she stands back, she can get the top of his head without getting the popcorn ceiling in the frame. The door isn't bad, actually. The grain of it is kind of artsy with the paisley. Again, this is totally off brand, but people are going to go wild when they see him. "Maybe, like, lean with your chin in your hand or something."

Dazzling Ezra stops. "Harper . . ."

"What?" Shit, shit! He has that look again. Like a landslide of disappointment just slid down his face. "What, Ez?"

"Just *your* eyes," he says. "Only you."

There's no need for him to be embarrassed! Her followers love him as much as she does.

CHAPTER SEVEN

I climbed the ship by a rope ladder like any man, and we are now ready to depart. The thousands of bags of cargo have been lifted from the hull (animal hides, linseed, castor oil, gunnysacks, and thread), and now the hull has been filled again with lard and flour and meats and sugars, leather goods and hardwares, coal and spices, coffees and teas and whiskey. What a sight, the transfer of all those bags of goods. But more importantly, the ship herself! Oh, if only you and Father could see her, all sixteen hundred tons of her, three masts reaching twenty-four feet, carrying twenty-five sails that will spread as wide as seventy! She is made of white oak, with red pine decking and ceilings and copper fixtures. Our private saloon is finished in maple and rosewood and mahogany, with gilt mold-ings and columns, mirrors and floral carvings. On each side of the galley, there are the most beautiful staterooms I have ever seen, each with its own private bathroom and washstands and mahogany writing desk, and even the crew quarters are spacious, with a roomy galley, and an extra deck above the forecastle at the bow. What luxury, what comfort and ease! And leading us at the prow is the majestic figurehead of King Neptune, with his tumbling hair and forked trident.

Mary Ann Patten journal entry

January 13, 1855

DARIO MEANT WHAT HE SAID. AFTER HIS LAST MESSAGE goes unanswered, he's silent. No more texts. No calls. He's given up. And she just can't do it. She can't do one Dario, let alone forty more siblings. All those tiny photos keep swimming in her mind. People with glasses, people without, smiling, shy, long hair, short, all with different lives but with the similar auburn hair, and with the same father. But how are they related? Really related? DNA doesn't mean you should spend Thanksgiving together. Then again, should those people be insignificant? Because MF has a history, a story, a legacy that's also hers and theirs. MF's great-grandfather's grandfather did something, who knows what, came over on some ship or fought in some war, probably, and he met the great-grandmother's grandmother, et cetera, et cetera. That hidden story is also Harper's story.

Still. Forty other siblings plus Dario, plus Walter, including some guy named Wyatt, who's an asshole, and Simone, who's intimidating beyond belief, and even that's too much information. It's like an overstuffed closet, so full that if you open the door, a hockey stick and a handbag and a barbell are sure to tumble forward and knock you out.

And what's she supposed to do with her mother and the lies between them? It's not more stuff in the closet—it's a *whole other closet*! In that awful pandemic, it was the two of them against the world. No, it has *always* been the two of them against the world. Harper may have the biggest family she's ever heard of, but in reality, she relies on one main person for her general safety and well-being. Until she's out on her own, she's as dependent as Nudo, reliant on his people for everything, only she's reliant on her one and only adult. Nudo can't get pissed and walk away. Nudo can't bring some immense, bomblike topic to the table, even if he could talk. Harper feels it in the deepest parts of her—this stuff has the potential to blow them apart.

For the next two weeks, instead of pulling the pin on the grenade, Harper chooses a different plan, a favorite among passive and powerless people: sullen irritation. It's not an awesome plan. Still, it's better than nothing, so Harper shoots angry, exasperated glances and exhales and eye rolls at her mother at every opportunity. Because, God! How dare Melinda say *I trust you* (which anyone knows means *I don't entirely trust you*) when they talk about the after-dance party Trace is throwing in his backyard? How dare she nag about calculus when she's been so calculating? Let alone the generally annoying stuff, which has now risen to the level of criminal: Her mother's fork scraping her plate. The hum of her electric toothbrush for a full two minutes (gum disease equals heart disease). The way she silently counts when Harper washes her hands. Or the way she scowls if Harper puts sugar on her oatmeal, and then lists the dangers of sugar, period: diabetes, inflammation, fatty liver disease (ew), how it's *an addiction,* as if Harper is headed for a stint in rehab.

"These are the teen years they warn you about," Melinda Proulx says to the clerk at Michaels when Harper gives a huge, irritated sigh at the stack of coupons Melinda hands over. They're purchasing the art supplies for Harper's AP Lit project, and the line is long behind them. The clerk is barely older than Harper herself and only *beep-beep*s each coupon across the scanner.

And then one night Ada comes by. Harper's mom loves Ada because Ada is Harper's smart *and* popular friend, compared to the quiet and studious Soraya. Melinda just stays and stays in Harper's room with them, talking and talking until Harper starts slamming stuff down. "*Hormones,* right?" her mom says to Ada, as if they're on the same team, dealing with an impossible Harper. As if hormones, too, are an invading terrorist group, destabilizing the government in charge. After that books arrive at their house: *Hope for Parents of Defiant Teens, How to Parent Your Troubled Teen While Keeping Your Sanity.* They sit on her mother's nightstand with certain page corners folded down, as Harper maintains her 3.9 overall grade point average, is polite to teachers, and feels like a felon when she and Ez park down the street to make out if her mom is home.

She wants to confide in Ezra. Badly. Ez, though . . . He loves her kindness and her humor, he always says, and there is nothing kind or humorous about how she's feeling. Some truths about her are dark, and she has dark thoughts. Sometimes she hates her mother. Who ever says that? No kind person. The person Ez thinks she is never would. He never would. Hiding is better, even if she knows ugly, mean stuff is eking out between the cracks of her. Sarcasm, unhappiness, lies, secrets. Quick, better post some-thing. A shot of herself on Tiger Mountain, where there are no tigers, her hair windy-tousled as she stands serenely in a field full of wildflowers. But her secret self wanders a barren, lonely planet, a girl in a desert with only cactus and cracked earth around her, like the only person remaining after the plague.

Harper and Soraya are smushed up together in the closet of their physics class. Like, their faces are practically touching. A few minutes before, Mrs. Shannon in the main office got on the intercom, saying *This is a drill,* and then the drama teachers, Mr. Tecante and Ms. Sharpton, and the band teacher, Mr. Burr, came running down the halls dressed in black, holding up cardboard machine guns as the students all piled up the chairs and tables over the windows. Now she's in the closet with Soraya on one side and that quiet boy, Drake Osmond, on the other, with a few other kids around them. Of course it crosses her mind how close they all are in that small space, how any one of those kids' breaths could've killed her. *Could* kill her? Are they really fine now, since they've been vaccinated? Should they even be doing drills like this? Do you forget school shootings now that there's been a virus? Do you go back to the shootings now that there've been vaccinations?

God! When you have to prioritize potential tragedies, there are too many of them. And when will they ever be able to truly relax about the virus? When are they safe, finally? When will she ever be able to stop thinking about it? Someone's on her foot.

They're supposed to be silent, but some kid always cracks a joke or something so it won't get too real, and someone always farts, God. The first time they did the active-shooter drill, they used kids with fake blood on them, and a few students ended up crying in the counseling office, so they stopped with the bodies anyway.

"You okay?" Soraya whispers. They've known each other since elementary school but only became best friends in the ninth grade when they were lab partners and had to dissect a fetal pig. During the worst of the pandemic, Harper's mom and Soraya's parents let them see each other a few times in their yards from, like, thirteen feet away, because they were all the same type of ultracareful people. Still, she and Soraya aren't the kind of friends you see in teen movies, sharing every secret. She and Soraya don't talk about sex with their boyfriends (if Soraya is even having sex with Jax, probably not) and don't stay up late and paint each other's nails or bond by dancing to some song that was popular in the 1970s. Harper does know lots of stuff about Soraya, though—that Jax's new haircut bothers her, and that she feels like they're a boring old couple already, always watching TV when he comes over. That her mom is strict, and that Soraya thinks her dad likes her sister, Yasmin, better, since she's the super–high achiever who got an internship at NASA and went on to Stanford, when Soraya mostly just likes to read her old *Lord of the Rings* books. Soraya's mom is a page at the Seattle Public Library, and Soraya's both proud and embarrassed about this. She calls her mom her "best friend," but she is Harper's.

"Well, Mr. Burr is about to gun us down," Harper whispers back.

"No, really. I mean, *lately*. Are you mad at me?"

"Mad at you? No, of course not."

"You seem upset. Like, all the time."

And this is when Harper does it. Speaks the truth.

"I'm sorry I'm so awful lately. I just found out that my biological father had forty-one other kids," Harper says. Maybe she just wants to hear it out loud. Or sort of out loud in that closet, where they are practicing tragedy. She wants to see how it sounds. Well, it sounds completely outrageous.

Soraya actually snorts and starts laughing. Harper kind of laughs, too. It might be nervous laughter partly, because they can hear the pretend-screams in the hall. But then Dani Dre shushes them, and they're shamed into silence. Finally Mr. McNulty, the principal, walks around the halls in his orange "police" vest, freeing them.

"You're hilarious," Soraya says.

Dario gets further away. That day at Green Lake takes on a dreamlike quality. It's almost as if it never happened. Harper quits looking at Simone's feed. *Feed*—food. It isn't. Harper still feels almost hollow and hungry.

The week before the spring dance, Harper's mom starts texting her articles. The "spring dance" used to be called junior prom, but it's been scaled back to a covered area on the football field and has now been demoted to a less-exciting name. Seniors keep telling them how lucky they are to have it at all, having missed theirs, plus plays, and choral concerts, and tryouts, and games, and their siblings' graduations, and, and, and. Her mom has some retro idea of proms and lost "virginity," probably from movies. "The Lasting Regrets of Sex Too Soon" is one of the articles. "Top Five Sexually Transmitted Diseases in Teens (Number Two Will Surprise You!)" is another. Then the tone changes. "One in Five Teens Are Victims of Date Rape." Screaming-face emoji. "Date Rape Drugs, Your Invisible Enemy." Emoji of a martini glass. "Eighteen Percent of Teen Girls Will Be Assaulted by Age Seventeen!" Well, there's no appropriate emoji for that one.

For God's sake, Mom, STOP, Harper texts. She basically had to leap on Ezra to get him to kiss her the first time.

You need to be informed. You need to be prepared. You need to have the facts.

Maybe we have too many facts. You didn't have facts when you guys didn't wear seat belts or bike helmets or whatever in the old days.

We wore seat belts! We wore bike helmets.

You know what I mean. You didn't have the internet.

Ignorance is NOT bliss.

What about the other percentages? Of all the things that don't happen? Harper asks, but then her mother goes silent.

Fine. Fine! Passive aggressiveness is another favorite weapon of the powerless.

Harper texts: *FYI "virginity" isn't even a real thing. It's just a gross old concept that says we all better be women-hating heterosexuals or else. I'll worry about my purity when guys worry about theirs.*

That'll freak her out, Harper's sure. Even with a silent opponent, having the last word makes you feel like you won.

The night of the dance, Soraya and Jax and Ada and Maya and Trace and Fiona and Harper and Ezra have dinner in Soraya's backyard. Then they go to the football field that still looks like a football field even if it has balloons and a cover. It's hard to hear the music because it echoes and disappears into the empty bleachers. It's still May, and it gets cold after dark, and everyone has sleeveless dresses. So they leave early for Trace's house. Maybe next year things will be completely normal, whatever that means. Probably, there's no going back. Not when you realize every person in the entire world can suddenly be in danger in, like, *days.* Handshakes and stuff like that are probably gone forever, too. People will read about them like some quaint custom in Victorian times. Maybe they'll even seem creepy, like curing disease with leeches.

At Trace's the guys take off their ties, and Ez loosens his bolo, and the girls remove their sparkly shoes because they hurt. Since it's supposedly okay for small groups of vaccinated people to be inside, they hang out in Trace's rec room and play video games. They drink a slightly spiked punch Trace's permissive parents made, and they snack on a variety of those frozen appetizers from Costco. They aren't the kind of entitled, troubled kids who get arrested or suspended, or caught doing something they shouldn't be, like Kara Wainright, caught with weed at school, or Wilson Bellis, who got drunk and stole his own dad's BMW. They're nice and responsible and sometimes wish they *were* entitled or troubled, because worrying about your SAT scores all the time gets so exhausting. Ez brings the paper plates to the kitchen trash. Maya wraps the cords neatly around the controllers. Soraya tries to clean a ketchup stain from the couch using spit and a napkin. No hotel rooms are smashed and no drugs ingested.

But yeah. Later Harper and Ez do have sex. In his car. It's great for the first few minutes, but then really uncomfortable and then fast. She can't concentrate because her head is on the door handle at an awkward angle. She pretends she's having an amazing time and tosses in a few moans, even if Ez would be horrified if he knew her neck was jammed. Afterward he whispers *I love you,* and Harper whispers it back, and they readjust, and Harper has her head on his chest, sort of, with the steamy windows around them. It's an embarrassing thing to admit, but she doesn't feel very strong or ready to face the perils of the world like high cholesterol or school shooters or virus-laden bat droppings. Here are Ezra's ribs, though, and his skinny ankles wound with hers, and there's the vulnerable wing-flapping of his heart, and she feels safe. He's capable, so at least one of them is.

When she gets home, she can feel the strained silence of her mother hovering but pretending not to hover. In bed, finally, she hears the toilet flush in the bathroom, meaning her mom is definitely still awake. She's literally creeping down the hall now (Harper herself knows those particular creaks in the hall floor), and then there's the soft click of her mother's door.

It's late, but the internet is like a 7-Eleven, open twenty-four hours. You can't get great healthy food there, but you can get hot dogs that have been spinning around for hours, and pepperoni sticks, and gigantic Cokes. Propped against her pillows in the dark, Harper posts a series of photos, #prom. It's not hashtag #outdoorlife, but, watch, they'll get even more likes, because *prom* is an Instagram staple, equivalent to the pasta on every restaurant menu. Now her followers can see Ez's wing tips with her sandals, the rows of string lights overhead (cropping out the football field scoreboard), her and Ez together under a tree (in the parking lot, you can't tell), a group shot.

Next she does something she hasn't done in weeks. Maybe because it's three a.m. and fatigue has stolen her barriers. She looks at Simone Van Den Berg's page.

Why, why, why does she do it? Right when all of it is almost tucked away? *Why?*

Because, oh God! There she is, sitting under a tree in a forest, wearing a gauzy white dress like a nymph. But that's not the shocking part. What's shocking is who *else* is in that photo with her.

Walter the dog, sitting on her lap like he's found a new friend.

CHAPTER EIGHT

I am doing what I can to make a comfortable home here, while Joshua is focused on his boast to beat the *Westward Ho* to San Francisco, constantly poring over the current charts and the *Maury's Guide*. I've arranged all our books and movable articles so they will not dislodge with the motion of the ship, after losing forevermore items that have rolled under the washbasin and beneath the bunks. Joshua says it's quite strange to him to have me on board, and it looks rather odd to him to see ladies' clothing hanging in the stateroom! He is proud that I have only once been seasick, even though the pitch and roll can be so bad that one can hardly keep in bed. If the sailors feel the expected aversion at a woman aboard a ship, they are mostly silent about it, busy on watch and calling their peculiar sea phrases, some familiar and not— "Mainsail haul! Tacks and sheets! Hard-a-lee!" We have breakfast at half past seven, dinner at half past twelve, tea at six, a walk on the deck in the moonlight with Joshua, and I am generally in bed at eight. Sleep is difficult with the sway of the ship and the constant noise of ropes and rudder and the ringing of the bells indicating a change of watch, and the tramping of the men overhead every morning, swabbing the deck.

The largest problem for me is that there is very little to do, save for keeping Joshua company. This he considers my most important job, though he is often too occupied to look up. I walk with him on the deck in pleasant weather, play cards with him, muse of the past, present, and future. I try to oversee the steward's work in the pantry, but it is not needed. I have tried to entertain myself by singing, but failed. Mrs. Lanfear, in *Letters to Young Ladies on Their Entrance into the World,* writes that young ladies, "in the early periods of life, resemble the flowers in our gardens in the spring of the year," but I am not succeeding at blooming. One gets so wretchedly lonely at sea that I have almost forgotten how to laugh.

Mary Ann Patten journal entry

January 28, 1855

"WHAT HAVE YOU DONE, DARIO?"

"I don't know why you're so upset."

"I saw Walter. In that photo with Simone Van Den Berg."

Harper's head is pounding, she's so tired. She slept maybe an hour last night, tossing and turning and finally giving up as soon as the sun rose. Her mother is still asleep. The whole neighborhood looks asleep. Outside now, where her mom can't overhear, the morning light is tangerine with a side of lemon, and birds twitter and tweet, and Mr. Wong's daffodils are a stubborn row of optimism, outlasting even him, though Harper doesn't really see any of it. Hopefully, no one sees *her*. She looks unhinged, barefoot and pacing, wearing her pink FUTURE LEADER nightshirt that Grandma Patricia gave her for Christmas last year.

"So? I can't believe you're calling me this early on a Sunday." Dario's sitting on his bed, those same posters behind him. Only now Harper knows what's on the other wall, too: all of them, her probably-siblings. Dario's sleepy face looks especially young. He's wearing a grandpa tank top. This is their first fight, Harper supposes. They skipped the tussling over Legos and who hit who first and who got to sit in the front seat and went straight to this.

"What do you mean, 'SO'?" she semi-shouts. Mrs. Wong's curtains rustle. She's barely been outside since Mr. Wong died, only shuffling to the mailbox in her housecoat and slippers, or trotting through her high grass to catch one of her escaped chickens. "I gave you her name. I didn't say you could contact her. Let alone meet up! She lives in Berkeley. I mean, that's a special trip."

"Not for some people. For some people it's just a weekend. And it's not like you uncovered some great mystery. Her name was on my list. I just hadn't gotten to her yet. Hey, in case you forgot, she's my sister, too."

Heat rises in Harper's face. "How can you use that word?"

"How can you not?"

"Half. *If.*"

"No *if.* It's for sure. And half is enough to count."

Mrs. Wong is definitely peeking, keeping an eye out for possible danger, who can blame her. Harper tries to calm herself. She sits on the curb. "Dario . . ." It's a plea, but she has no idea what she's pleading for. All at once she realizes why she's so angry.

She feels left out.

"How do you know who all those people are anyway? I mean, like that Wyatt guy, and everyone on your wall?" Harper asks. She kicks at a leaf with her toe. The neighbor's garage door slides up, and out comes Rainey with his skateboard. No kneepads, no helmet, nothing. Great.

"There's a registry. Since our father is open ID. You can't try to reach out to him until you're eighteen, but there are these donor sibling registries. And the Lakeview clinic has this whole private forum. You can connect with the other families there. My moms have been emailing and chatting with a few of the other moms for *years.* Wyatt's mom and dad connected when he found out. They needed some support, since Wyatt was so pissed."

"*They* needed support?"

Dario ignores her. "And I found a few on MyHeritage.com, too. It's pretty wild when some aunt pops up. My moms opened an account for me when I was thirteen. They thought I'd be more well adjusted if I knew my origin story from an early age."

"Are you more well adjusted?"

"Than who? Wyatt? You? Sometimes I might as well be a cow in a herd, but other times it's kinda nice. You're, like, my people."

Oh man, the words melt something in her. Or maybe *fill* something in her. Or maybe just open a teensy window. But the word "herd"—that one is terrifying. "So, you've talked to all these . . . ?" She doesn't say it. She can't use a word people legitimately search for on pillows and greeting cards, *Sisters Are Forever*, all that. Hey, *Happy birthday, Sister, from all of us* would fit now. Gasp.

"Of course not. I don't go blasting my way into people's lives. *You* contacted *me*, remember?"

Harper's silent. But then: "What about Simone? Did *she* call you?"

"I had reason to think she'd be open to talking."

Harper scowls. "You sound like a CIA operative."

"She has information," he says, using a CIA operative voice.

"Real funny."

"Harper, she does."

Her stomach sinks. Dread weight.

"I saw a blog post she wrote," Dario says.

"You mean you stalked her." Harper's one to talk.

"You're one to talk," Dario says. "Maybe we should meet in person. This isn't stuff you just say on the phone, and I gotta go. Someone's staring at me because now, thanks to you, he's up early and has to pee." Dario swings his phone around, and now Harper's face to face with Walter's somber, insistent stare.

She pulls her T-shirt way down over her knees. "Okay. Fine. We'll meet."

"My mom has a bakery in Edmonds, if you like almond croissants."

"Is there a single soul on this earth who doesn't?"

"Maybe at, like, eleven?"

"Today?"

"No, in sixteen *more* years. *Yeah,* today."

"Oh wow. All right. Hey, no problem. I'll do it. What's the name of the bakery?"

Dario cracks up. Seriously, he's in utter hysterics. "You totally know already."

"Oh my God!" Harper says in exasperation.

"You do. *Stalker?* Takes one to know one." He thinks he's hilarious. But Harper doesn't feel like laughing. She feels like Mrs. Wong, peeking out to see what awful thing might happen next.

"What kind of information?" she dares to ask.

"You sure you want to know?"

"I'm sure." She's mostly sure.

"You won't freak out and disappear?"

"Tell me."

"She knows who he is," Dario says.

When Harper steps through their front door, her mom is standing in the foyer, wearing her chenille robe, her hands on her hips. There's a splotch of something on the collar of the robe. Red wine or ketchup or chocolate, something that speaks to the depths she wallowed in last night as she waited up. Now her eyes blaze, and her hair's wild.

"Oh super. This is just fantastic. Look who's home. Perfect. So, where have you *really* been all night?"

"Here. I've been here! What are you talking about? You heard me come in."

"Uh-huh. But I didn't hear you *sneak back out.*"

"I was home! I was home the whole time!"

"Which explains why you're walking through the front door at seven-thirty in the morning wearing *this*." She plucks at Harper's FUTURE LEADER nightshirt as if it were some sexy corset from Victoria's Secret.

"I went *outside*. After coming *inside* last night!"

"Uh-huh. You know what really gets me? If you could just be honest with me, if you could have said you wanted to stay out all night, we could've talked about this. We could've been open and sharing about your virginity, about sexual exper—"

Harper interrupts. And, yeah, she's shouting. "There is no such thing as 'virginity'! Do you hear my quote marks around that word? It's a patriarchal concept that has no business even being in the twenty-first cen—"

Now her mom interrupts, and *she* is shouting. "You basically *told* me you were going to do this. You dangled it right in front of my face! We could have *talked*. You didn't have to resort to such *games*. I could have made sure you had protection!"

"If there *were* such a thing as 'virginity,' it would be *my* business! Okay? *My business.* My protection! I wouldn't *want* to talk about it. I can fumble around and figure it out, same as every human being has since forever!"

Her mother leans toward her, nose twitching like a rabbit's.

"Are you sniffing me? For what, *weed* or something? I've never done drugs in my life! I *came home*. Right at three a.m. The curfew we agreed on, just for this one dance."

"*No one* gets up at seven-thirty in the morning after staying out until three. I know what goes on at prom. I'm not stupid."

"Yeah, from silly prom movies, where everyone's losing their non-virginity!"

"Not just. I was young once, Harper."

This is one of the saddest things she's ever heard her mom say. She's not even *that* old. Then again, her mom is honestly a whole book of lived experiences that Harper has no idea about. "I can't believe this. I seriously can't believe this!" Harper shoves past Melinda. She stomps to her room in a rage. She slams the door, and the mirror on the back shudders. She can see her reflection shuddering, too.

"*You* can't believe it? *You* can't?" her mother yells through the door.

Ticktock, because yes, a bomb is ticking under their roof, all right. Like that other bomb Harper doesn't know about yet. That one is ancient, a bomb from an old war, sunk down into the sand in the deep waters of one of the most beautiful places on Earth. It's not as ancient as all the precious stuff around it, though. The destruction that bomb will cause is unimaginable.

Harper fumes, tossing clothes from her drawer because she wants to look good for Dario D., a brother she's never met. She chooses a sundress. Her hair's still semifancy and stiff with hair spray from the night before, good. But, ugh! Now she has to figure out how to get there, since Edmonds is about a twenty-minute drive away. What was she thinking? She'll have to pay for an Uber out of her babysitting money, and then drive there masked, riding with all the windows down. It feels as dangerous as committing an armed robbery. An Uber plus a bakery means she'll likely do the Covid mind games afterward, too. For at least five days, she'll be sure she has a fever or a heaviness in her chest. She'll take her temperature a hundred times and go around sniffing things (coffee, toothpaste, mustard) to make sure she hasn't lost her sense of smell.

But these are the prices you have to pay to (oh God!) actually and finally *meet* your medical-miracle blood relatives.

She scrolls through her phone, just wasting time until she can head out to the bakery. She looks at all the likes and comments for her last post, those dance photos. Her mom has liked and commented on every single one, something she does even though Harper has asked her not to a million times. She also always sends Harper DMs, even though they live in the same house. Can you block your own mom if she's your stalker? Harper posts a quick shot of her non-prom dress in a suggestive puddle on the floor. In fifteen more weeks that bomb's going to blow, but now she watches a skateboard crash and the unboxing of a neon-pink stuffed sloth. She looks at pancakes in the shape of a teddy bear, a hedgehog with a crown, a panda eating a melon, midriff, midriff, midriff.

CHAPTER NINE

I read and reread every *Godey's Lady Book* I brought, until I can read no more. "The Home Shall Be Made a Paradise," "Unselfishness in the Wife," advertisements for Ayers Pills for nerves and liver, Modene for unsightly hair removal, Fashions and Fancies, new corset patterns. Joshua found me reading the logbooks of the *Car*'s first two voyages, kept by Captain Forbes, and warned me against it. The first voyage brought hurricane gales through the Strait of Le Maire, and on her next, a hellish and perilous journey across the Pacific to Singapore, and onward to Calcutta. On that trip her highly armed sailors fought through the pirate-filled waters of the Malacca Strait, and then battled monsoons and stifling heat. Then the mutiny of twenty-three of her sailors, who refused all orders from the apparently boorish Forbes, who confined them belowdecks. He locked them in chains, deprived them of food and water, and threatened to shoot them. On the return trip, the ship was battered by another hurricane, and a man was washed overboard, and for two days she clashed and fought the waves until they finally reached New York. Thankfully, we will not face this degree of drama and misfortune with Joshua as our captain! Much of the time I am only fighting back boredom. On this great sea of the world, it creates a feeling of extreme confinement and indifference to everything. I am darning a pair of Joshua's pants, and am once again thumbing through *Practical Instructions in Stay-Making,* and advertisements for hats, caps, and furs.

Mary Ann Patten journal entry
February 7, 1855

IT'S WARM OUTSIDE ON THIS LATE-SPRING MORNING, AND even warmer in that snug bakery, where the smell of butter wraps its arms around Harper and hugs. The little town of Edmonds is bustling, and so is the store. They're probably happy about that. When she—okay, okay!—*stalked* the bakery's social media page, she saw that Buns had to close during the pandemic, then quickly adapted to curbside, and was open again, with thanks to loyal customers and a GoFundMe set up by a devotee of their almond croissants. Now there's the whoosh of the espresso maker, and the *tink*s of forks on plates and cups on saucers, though the tables are still spread out at a distance, a few out on the sidewalk. There's the happy chatter that comes when people are eating uplifting things, because, thank goodness, bread has gone on being bread.

Some people are wearing masks and some aren't. They've

been told that vaccinated people don't need to, but it's hard to know what to do. It's unnerving to Harper, having her face showing again. She hasn't been back in a restaurant-type place without a mask yet, and this, they've heard again and again, is especially perilous, so she puts it back on, the do-I, don't-I mask tango.

When she spots him at a corner table, though, Dario, plain-faced, open, offering, brave, Harper takes her mask off again and stuffs it in her purse. His whole face, her whole face, it feels crucial. As she approaches, he stands, and the commotion around her vanishes.

"Hey," he says, and smiles. They stare at each other. She just looks at Dario and tries to keep it together, because her throat is tightening, and her eyes are filling, and when she tries to speak, no sound comes out. He even has a crooked bottom tooth, same as she does. This boy in his jeans and T-shirt (sporting an image of George Washington flexing his muscles, with the words HISTORY BUFF underneath), shoving his moppish hair from his forehead in nerves, seems to step right into some hollow space inside her. It's strange, but she's also hit with a wave of loss. So many days have already gone by without him. Harper can see Dario's mom Reba, in her cotton skirt and flowy T-shirt and wavy hair, behind the counter. She's trying not to look at them but is definitely looking at them, making sure Dario is okay.

Dario steps forward and hugs Harper. He has thin arms, and he's shorter than she is, but part of her is sure she's met this stranger before. He's familiar. It's déjà vu, but in no way nagging or unsettling, just . . . *certain.* When her mind offers her the words "home" and "shelter," everything tumbles out of the closet she's been afraid to open. Her chest heaves, and she starts to cry. Dario pats her back as if she were a baby, and then she feels the tiny scratch of paws on her legs. Looking down, she sees Walter, looking worried, apparently quite sensitive to large emotions.

"Walter," she says, wiping her nose. She leans down and pats his head. "You're a good boy."

"Hey, what about me? I am, too," Dario jokes. You can tell he's an only child. Maybe that's unfair to only children, but hey, she's one, too. "Wow. You're tall." It's funny hearing Dario's voice in person and not on the phone. He's *right here*.

"My mom is tall," she says.

"Mine is . . ." He gestures toward the counter. "Kinda not." It's true. Reba is shorter and square compared to Dario. She notices them looking and gives a little wave. Now Harper sees two almond croissants already on the table next to Dario, plus two white cups with the fancy sort of lattes everyone takes pictures of, a feather design in milk. The guy behind the machine looks familiar, and then Harper realizes it's Nate, ex-boyfriend of Soraya's sister, Yasmin. His lattes are pretty perfect.

They sit, and Dario pushes the croissant plate toward her. "Here. It's good to see you." It's something you'd say if you haven't seen someone in a while, and that's what it feels like. Like she hasn't seen him in a while. Like she already knows him from long ago. It's a reunion with someone she's never met.

"It's good to see you, too," she croaks, because she's about to cry again. That he exists at all, it squeezes her heart and her vocal cords. *I've missed you* feels more accurate. But she could never get those words out without weeping, because, God, she's realizing that maybe she's also been lonely, like, really lonely, for a long time. And maybe not just pandemic-lonely, but no-one-has-ever-really-known-me lonely. The deepest kind.

The croissant is an offering, and maybe a test, so she takes a bite. Also, it looks amazing. It *is* amazing. "Ohm mygd isho good," she says with her mouth full. No wonder someone started a GoFundMe page.

"Right?" he says. He takes a bite of his, too, and they sit there beaming at each other, powdered sugar dotting their bulging cheeks. They've missed a lot of years looking at each other.

"I like your shirt," Harper says. Dario flexes his muscles, same as George. Dario's muscle is a little apricot pit. You can tell they don't prioritize macho shit at his house.

"I wonder if he likes history." He—they both know who Dario means. The all-important, gigantic-in-their-minds, missing, mysterious He. Maybe they should always capitalize it, like you're supposed to for God. "My moms only like it okay. Not the way I do."

Harper doesn't have one particular thing she really loves, so she doesn't know what to say next. Did He, giant God *H*, have some particular trait of hers? And then she notices it, on the floor by Dario's chair. "Your laptop?"

"It's just easier to navigate on that when there's a lot of information."

Her heart thuds. "A lot?"

"Well, not a lot. I just wanted to show you what led to what." He's already unzipping the bag, setting the laptop on the table. He lifts the top.

She flicks her finger toward the camera. "You should put a Post-it over that."

"The camera, really? Do you think someone's watching?" He waves his arms and does a little dance. He takes a sip of his latte, tipping the cup to make a foam mustache. "Far better is it to dare mighty things, than live in a gray twilight!" He gestures with one pointed finger. "Or something."

"No idea," she says.

"Teddy Roosevelt." He licks his upper lip.

Dario. He's a little dweeby, for sure.

"Don't be surprised if they *are* watching you," Harper says.

"Who's 'they'?"

"I don't know." Honestly, she has no idea. Some hidden force of evil, trying to steal nude shots and credit card information. Or convince you to buy stuff you never thought to buy before, like an at-home electrolysis kit. "Haven't you ever just talked about something, and then, boom, an ad for it appears on one of your feeds? My boyfriend—"

"Ezra."

"Yeah, Ezra, stalker! Once, he was telling me how his dog, Nudo, attacked their Roomba, and two seconds later I had an ad for a Roomba. I swear to God, once, I was just *thinking* about shrimp, and I opened my phone, and there was a Red Lobster ad for all-you-can-eat scampi. It's creepy. There are cameras everywhere, too, you know. On traffic lights and buildings? Have you ever notic—" She's talking too much out of nerves.

"Here," Dario says, ignoring her. He's pulled up a blog post on a site called *Simonerelda Isle*. "Simone, she used the same name on a few accounts. It led me to her blog."

"I didn't see *that*."

Dario smiles smugly. "Superior stalking skills, hey, sis?"

"Oh my G—"

"Harper, I'm just messing with you! You should see your face."

"You butthead," she says.

"Anyway. I read all the posts going back a few years. And there were a couple that jumped out. One talking about sending a contact request to her biological father. And then another one about not getting an answer. And then *another* one, about how she tried again after she'd won some art award at college, hoping maybe he might like her better if he knew she'd been a success at something. Like, maybe he'd answer then."

"That is so sad." How awful. He didn't even reply? Maybe he's an asshole, a trait he shares with that guy, Wyatt. She'd never have imagined in a million years that Simone could be insecure. And Harper already knows about that award she got, so there. Simone mentioned it in a post, accompanied by a photo in which she'd painted her face to look like a palette, with splotches of color all around. It seemed so bold and confident.

"But then I read one where she called herself a mutt, in a proud way. She said her mom was Israeli and French and both her dads were Greek and Dutch and Irish, though her actual dad had some Persian, too. When I read that, I knew you were right. I knew she was one of us. She wasn't on the sibling registry, but I was sure she must have reached out to him through Lakeview. And so, I called her." Dario drops a piece of croissant down to Walter, who gulps without chewing.

"And?"

"We talked for hours. She told me her origin story." This is the phrase, Harper understands. Origin story. It sounds like Darwin and something from the Bible, both. "Her mom and her actual dad decided to use donor sperm because the dad has a family history with pretty severe mental health issues. She knew about the whole thing from a young age. When she turned eighteen, just a couple of years ago, she contacted Lakeview and got the information. Her parents were nervous about it. Worried for her, you know, what she might find, if she'd be disappointed, but nervous for themselves, too. Some parents feel . . . dismissed, or threatened, or whatever. My moms are cool about it. They're my real parents, and we both know it, and they aren't freaked out by it." Harper looks over at Reba and smiles. Reba gives a little wave again. She's the kind of warm, friendly person you just want to hug.

"My mother would for sure freak," Harper says.

"Simone handled it by . . . Well, she told her parents she wanted to know his medical history. Simone has some issues with depression. After, you know, they were trying so hard to avoid that."

"She does?" This seems impossible.

"I guess. But who doesn't right now, right? My little cousin does, and she's ten. Anyway, Simone sent him a couple of messages through Lakeview but didn't get a reply, like I said. She still hasn't heard anything."

"But she got his name."

"His name, and a photo. An old one. Are these things you want to see?"

She's so nervous, she just sits there and paces in her mind. Sometimes she can feel climate change, floods, tidal waves, and wildfires right inside her own body. She feels that asteroid, aiming right for her.

"A photo."

"Yeah."

"His name."

"Yup. Would you rather have someone here with you?"

"Well, you're with me," she says. "And Walter." Reba, too. Even though Harper isn't related to Reba by blood, she's related by story.

"You can hold him," Dario says.

Walter looks up, offering his services. She gives his head a scratch. "I'm okay. Let's do it."

Dario taps the keys of his laptop.

Harper waits.

And then, there it is. A photo of him, her father, the actual, real man. Not a man, a boy. A guy. He doesn't look very old. He stands against a brick wall, wearing baggy tan pants with pleats (pleats!) and a T-shirt with a half-zipped neon windbreaker over the top. Harper tries to summon some sort of feeling as she looks at him. She definitely sees their eyes. The color, but also the tilt of them, and something in the shape of their faces, too. His hair, their hair, is that particular shade of auburn, cut in a spiky fashion, and— "Oh my God, the tips are *bleached.* He looks so . . ."

"Boy band, circa 1999." Dario smirks. "Like the guy on my mom's old NSYNC T-shirt."

"He's wearing a *necklace.*" It's a little jarring. She expected to see a man who looked like a *dad.* This is a kid who might think Doritos are a breakfast food. Still, Harper could almost throw up, and her throat gets tight with tears again.

"If you zoom in . . ." Dario does. "It's a Celtic thing."

Harper squints. "He looks so *young.*" He's someone she could tutor in calculus, someone who might drive a Mustang with furry seat covers.

"This was twenty-plus years ago. The oldest sibling is twenty-one. Hey, he was *cool.*"

Maybe to Dario. "That brick wall . . . I know it from somewhere." In a plaza, near a large white building.

"Red Square." Dario opens another tab—a photo of the main plaza of the University of Washington campus, made of red brick.

"Man, you're thorough."

" 'You don't let go—you just press forward!' " Dario says, finger up again.

"Teddy Roosevelt?"

"Alicia Keys. Reba loves her." He gives a fist pump to his mom behind the counter, and she gives one back. Maybe Harper's newly found father is a little disappointing, but Dario and Reba sure aren't.

"Wait, though," Harper says. There's something Dario hasn't told her yet.

"Did you think I forgot?"

"I'm ready."

"His name—his name is Beau Zane."

CHAPTER TEN

After two days of seas too rough to write, we have now hit a calm approaching the doldrums just after we crossed the equator. Fifty-six days out, there is no wind at all, even if Cape Horn is right there in sight. Joshua hopes we are not more than two hundred miles behind the *Westward Ho* and is pressing every slight breeze and zephyr. The boredom of the voyage is endless, and on the ship I am a Nobody, not even on the crew list. Beauty, health, and temper are the personal qualifications universally considered to be of greatest importance to the female sex, but out here they leave a bitter hollow. I cannot bear another glimpse of a knitted women's headdress pattern, or an article on female cleanliness, or an ad for vanishing cream, vanishing cream, vanishing cream! Thankfully, hidden in the depths of the ship's library, I have discovered two volumes by ladies of the sea who were infected by the literary microbe: Mrs. Captain Wallis's *Life in Feejee,* and Mrs. Lucy Cleveland's *The Voyage of the Zephyr.* Inspired by the strength and example of those wives who came before me, I have begun to read the few medical texts on board, in case it should fall to my lot, as it did Lucy's, to take charge of some duties.

Mary Ann Patten journal entry

March 9, 1855

BEAU ZANE, BEAU ZANE. IT'S THE NAME OF A MOVIE STAR, or a cowboy, or a dropout. After Harper leaves Dario at the bakery, feeling dazed and holding a white bag full of treats, Beau's name and his image make up for lost time in her brain. *My father, Beau,* she practices saying aloud, as if she's introducing him. *My mother, Melinda, and my father, Beau.* She pictures the guy with the bleached hair tips pushing her in a swing. She pictures him wiping peaches off her baby chin with a kitchen towel. She pictures him in the auditorium during her first-grade play when she was a shy cloud. She pictures crying on his shoulder, and him just *getting it.* She pictures everything being different if he'd been in her life.

But then all those beautiful wishes are gone, and she pictures him rejecting her after she reaches out. She tries *not* to picture him handing over his vial of sperm and leaving. What did he do after that? After fathering forty-two children in one go? Head to Burgermaster? Turn some tunes on in the Mustang? Brag to his boy band friends? Or maybe it wasn't in one go. He could have returned again and again, like regular visits to Starbucks, his name on a cup, ugh.

By the time she gets home, Dario has emailed her everything he and Simone and Wyatt now have—a folder labeled *BZ*, real initials where her MF has always been. The BZ and the MF seem like two different people, honestly. She says an abrupt goodbye to the MF of her imagination. It's sad to see him go, compared to this new stranger. Now the mystery of Simone and Wyatt, the need to see and know them, two more people who look exactly like her, hums inside as well. She was right about that closet. Everything is tumbling out, and she can't stop it. Mostly, she doesn't want to stop it. All of this is part of her, and she can't forget the feeling of Dario stepping into some lonely space.

She pumps herself up for *let's do this*. Reckless and rebellious, Harper eats two cookies from the white bag as she reads what Dario sent. It's kind of disappointing and thin, information-wise. Student at UW, health records, same stuff she already knows, plus an old address in the University District, a phone number that now connects to a nail salon. They have his name, but no idea who he is. Or rather, no idea which Beau Zane is theirs. Beau Zanes live all around the country. Dario and Simone have narrowed the possibilities by age and appearance. There's a Beau Zane who lives in Salt Lake City but used to live in Bellingham, Washington (reddish hair). A Beau who has so many addresses, he seems on the run from the law: Carmel, California; Key West, Florida; Port Huron, Michigan; Bonne Terre, Missouri; Sitka, Alaska; Freeport, Texas (no photo). A Beau who actually *has* run from the law—he committed an armed robbery in Portland, Oregon, too close for comfort to Seattle, and was caught in Beaverton after a chase ensued (does he have their nose?). Another Beau is the owner/operator of a Jiffy Lube in Nevada City, California. A Beau Zane sells Nissans in North Carolina, and another manages a casino in Reno, and another is a teacher at a Christian school. All of them have the same auburn hair and maybe, years ago, could have been that guy in the photo, but it's hard to tell.

There's also the sculptor in the UK. Next to his name in the document are the words *DO NOT CONTACT* in bold. The minute Harper sees it, she calls Dario.

"You miss me already?" he answers.

You know what? *Yeah.* She misses him and Walter, and even Reba, who grasped Harper's hands in her warm ones and handed over the bag of baked goods before saying goodbye. "No," she says. "It's been, like, *an hour.* What's with the sculptor?"

"Nothing, nada. Simone was sure it was him. She *wanted* it to be him. He had the right hair color, but that was it. He was an artist, you know, so Simone was like, THAT'S THE GUY! She found his gallery, and then his agent, and then his home number, and talked to *his wife,* big mistake. I mean, imagine, you're living your life and some stranger calls you and asks if your husband was a sperm donor in college, because he might have forty-two kids."

"Heart attack possibilities."

"Right. Plus threats and tears, and a call back from the UK Beau Zane, saying he's never even been to the US."

"Oh."

"We—me and Simone and Wyatt—have now agreed not to just call random people until we're sure."

"Okay. That seems smart."

"Harper?" There's a rapping at her door, and then Harper's mom opens it and peeks in. The whole idea about knocking is that you're supposed to wait for an answer before proceeding, but Melinda always skips the middle part. Her voice is soft, ready to make peace after their post-dance-non-virginity argument. Harper *wants* peace. It's only been her and her mom her whole life, except for Grandma Patricia, who straightens every knick-knack Harper touches, and smooths every bedspread she rumples. "Can we talk?"

"Hey, I gotta go."

"If you want to get togeth—"

She doesn't even let poor Dario finish. She slams the laptop shut. The intel on all the Beau Zanes is right in plain sight.

"Who was that?" Melinda's soft tone slides away, like a lovely blop of Jell-O into a garbage disposal. "And what was on your laptop?"

"A *friend*. And nothing. God! School report."

"You don't have a school report."

She's right, of course. "Why are you so paranoid?"

"I can tell when someone's keeping a secret, okay?"

Harper folds her arms and stares out the window. Her mom sighs and looks up at the ceiling as if God might give her answers, but only Freddie Mercury looks back. Ez gave her that poster and a Queen's Greatest Hits playlist after he blasted "I Want to Break Free" and she didn't know who was singing it. It's her favorite song now.

"Harper, maybe we need a reset," Melinda finally says after a long standoff silence. "I owe you an apology about last night. I spoke with Yanet. She told me Ezra was home sometime after three. His brother woke him up at five-thirty a.m. by jumping on him and singing 'Baby Beluga.'"

"You called Yanet?"

"You can't blame me for being worried!"

"Worried? Why is *worry* always a parental excuse for bad behavior?"

"How would I *not* be worried, Harper? You haven't been acting like yourself lately, *at all*. The front door has been slammed so many times, I practically need a repairman. This is a very high-risk time for people your age. And you won't let me *in*. What's happened to us? We used to sleep in the same bed at night until you were in kindergarten. I brought you into this world. You're my miracle child. We're a *team*. I need *transparency*, not this . . . coldness. I'm not your enemy."

"*Transparency?* You've got to be kidding me." Harper glares at her. She drills the guilt of Melinda's own lies right into her, and her mom feels it. Harper sees her flinch, and her eyebrows form a V of puzzlement that Harper knows, *knows,* is fake. She can see the performance of it, bad acting, as bad as Ryan Avery playing Jean Valjean, the tormented former prisoner, in their school play.

"What? What are you saying?"

Beau Zane. The name sits right there on Harper's tongue, waiting to spring out. But the private knowledge of him also feels so deliciously powerful. Too powerful to just give away in a moment of anger.

Harper shakes her head. Examines her fingernails in a way that tells her mom the conversation is over.

"What's in *there*?" Melinda nods toward Harper's desk. The white bakery bag.

Harper reaches in, pulls out a cookie. "Heroin?"

"Harper! You know that white sugar . . ." Melinda trails off. Takes a big, cleansing breath. "Let's sit down together for a nice dinner tonight, and you can tell me all about prom. I didn't even get to hear everything! I want all the details! Look, I apologize if

I misjudged you. To be clear, I think you're an amazing human being. Incredible. You—you are so beautiful and talented, and I believe in you, I do! I could see that you were gifted when you were only two years old. I gave you this shape sorter—"

"And you used to time me."

"Oh my God! You were so fast! And I don't say it enough, but I always admire your creativity, too. I don't think art is a solid career choice, but you have an *eye*. Your Instagram account. It's always so professional and unique! You're incredible, and you're going to do great things."

Harper shakes her head and exhales slowly. She hates all that praise. It's not true, and even more, she doesn't want to be incredible. She *can't* be incredible, not like the girl in the white bathing suit by the pool. She wants to be just okay. That's an achievable goal. That's a goal that's not so *intense* all the time. After a year of being afraid of unwashed fruit, and taking her temperature ten thousand times when her throat was maybe scratchy, plus all of the *all*—A Million Terrible Things That Might Kill You Today— she just wants a little calm.

"Oh, you *are* incredible, though!" Melinda says. "Don't shake your head! And the thing is, we're bound to have these conflicts right now. We're so close, and next year you'll be going to *college*." Melinda's voice wobbles, and Harper feels awful for being such a shit. "I don't know what I'm going to do without you. The thought of you leaving . . . It wrecks me." Melinda presses her palms to her eyes and stops herself from crying before looking up again. "All of this . . . *strife*, it's not unexpected. It's just a normal part of the *separation process*."

Maybe she's right. Maybe Harper's stress and upset isn't just about Beau Zane and her mom hiding the details about him.

Because when Melinda says that right then, about going to college and moving out, a whoosh of terror shoots through Harper, like a horrible gust through a fairy-tale forest where a child wanders, lost. Harper sees college students all the time when she visits her mom's campus, and they all look like . . . adults. Some have *beards*! They stride from one class to another with a sense of purpose. Or else they stroll and look at their phones with a casualness that suggests that the world is no big deal. Some college classes have three hundred people in them!

Right now, as Harper's mom stands in the doorway of her room, the line between Harper and that real, enormous, and unpredictable world seems very thin. And it's filled with a complicated maze of tasks, too. What are taxes, really? How does the stock market work? Insurance, rent, oh God, *jobs*—how do you go about any of it, let alone all of it? Not the babysitting-the-twins-down-the-street job, or the summer parks-and-rec job, but a job-job, a résumé job. How much does a cell phone even cost? Who will kill the big spiders? And there are mysterious filters in things, like the coffeepot and the refrigerator water thingy. Oh God! She bites her lip with anxiety, gets a taste of her lip gloss, a pale peach named Spring Fling. What if she gets sick? What's the difference between a decongestant and an expectorant? Tylenol and the brown ones? What if she gets *really* sick? Ventilator, hospital sick? She still can't shake it, that siren coming down their street and stopping in front of the Wong house. Mr. Wong, the long, unmoving lump of him, buckled into that stretcher. Mrs. Wong's arms reaching up to him as he disappeared through the ambulance doors. Harper wants to sob with grief just remembering that.

Who will take care of her if no one is taking care of her?

Maybe Ezra can. He knows a lot about those things. He can put chains on his car when it snows, and he was brave enough to pick up Nudo's rainbow vomit after he chewed up that pack of crayons.

It's all too big, and she's much too young.

Life seems impossible to navigate. Terrifying, too.

Beautiful girl, you can do hard things.

No.

She's pretty sure she can't. Which earrings with which skirt, yeah. Art shots of her feet dangling off a dock, no problem. Not real things, though. Not world things.

CHAPTER ELEVEN

The astonishing feats of the prior ladies of the sea have taken root within me. Their bravery and acts of fortitude described in the hidden tomes have propelled me to seek my own acts of fortitude. I have acquainted myself with the pills, medicines, herbs, plasters, and oils in the medicine chest, and after consulting Hollis's *A Companion to the Medicine Chest, with Plain Rules for Taking the Medicines, in the Cure of Diseases,* I have treated a man for fever with a powerful dose of Calomel of Julep. As well, I have removed a cinder in the eye of another by putting in a hair and some flaxseed, cured a blister on the chest of a third with liniment, and the foot of a fourth man by applying a poultice. It is a relief and a pleasure and a great freedom to be of use! One's abilities can be a mystery to one's own self!

Mary Ann Patten journal entry
March 20, 1855

"HARP, CAN WE STOP?" EZRA PANTS. HIS FACE IS RED AND sweaty. One of his knees is banged up and sporting a crosshatch of red scrapes from falling on ice-slushy rocks and landing on his tripod. He's getting farther and farther behind her.

"We're almost there!" Harper shouts over her shoulder.

"You've been saying that for hours," he whines. It's been a longer trip than they (all right, *she*) thought. First the drive to Mount Rainier, which was a good three hours with traffic, and now this hike on the Plummer Peak/Pinnacle Saddle trail. It's only four and a half miles round trip, but it seems like forty, with its steep, rocky inclines and patches of snow still left from winter, melting rapidly on this unseasonably hot first Saturday of June. Harper, in part, wants to prove to herself that in terms of hard things, she can at least do this, actually and really hike a trail that was marked as family-friendly in the guide. The rest of her just wants to get some great shots for her page.

"They said it was one of the best views of the mountain, with fewer people! We should see it any minute."

"Fewer people because no one wants to go through this hell," Ezra shouts. It's not like him to be so dramatic, but he'd rather be home reading. At least, that's what he's grumpily muttered five million times so far.

"They said there might be mountain goats!" *They*, the all-knowing internet they. You can't even always tell who *they* are, but they certainly have more knowledge than you do, firmer opinions, too, about weather, and current events, and films, and books, and even the most random items, like nail clippers and Halloween masks. *They* are also always stepping into dangerous, uncharted waters and reporting back: *I stopped eating bread for seven days, and this is what happened! I did yoga for seven days, and this is what happened!* And *they* have the inside information on "the best" coffee, restaurants, woolly socks, workout gear, appointing or withholding stars like stingy, egomaniacal generals. You can forget that "the best" is only an opinion. You can forget that stars and likes aren't truth.

"You only wanted to be here because you saw @hikinggirlls's post of a panorama from the top of here with all those likes."

"Someone said their nine-year-old did it easily! A quick scramble to the top!"

"How do you know if that person even really has a nine-year-old? How do you know if they've even left their house in the last ten years? What do you know about that fucking nine-year-old? Maybe he had enough sunblock and water to make the whole trip. Maybe he didn't get dehydrated and almost fall off a cliff in order to get a shot of you posing in front of a distant glacier that no one will be able to see anyway!"

Harper stops. Ezra's never sworn at her in anger before. When she turns to look at him, it's awful. He's shaking his empty water bottle at her. His hair is plastered to his skull, and a pair of gnats have died on his forehead. And it's true—his nose does look like it's getting sunburned.

"Have mine." Harper hands him her water bottle, which only has a thick half inch of warm spit backwash left.

"I NEED TO PEE," he snarls. He sets down the tripod and the backpack Harper borrowed from her mom. It was a gift from Bruce, one of Melinda's ex-boyfriends. Those boyfriends—they never last very long. Melinda enjoys when they take her to dinner and stuff, but when they want to move in or get serious, they get on her nerves. Bruce was "just okay." That guy Mark, who taught Harper how to ride a bike, he was "just okay" too. No one ever climbed to the peak and made it all the way to the top.

"Fine, pee, then," Harper sort of snaps back, but in truth, guilt is rapidly filling her. She can hear him rustling in the brush. Still, why just stand around and wait? She takes her phone out of her pocket. No bars. A little closer to the edge of the trail, not close enough to be dangerous, of course, she windmills an arm around, trying to get service. There. She checks her page. Her last post is an image she took this morning, her water bottle and boots and a fruit bar on a rock. *Challenge accepted! Goal stressss. What are your favorite ways to motivate yourself?* #hardhikeahead #motivation #almost summer #justdoit, et cetera, is getting a flood of comments. *Bribe yourself with a treat after! Doing it with a buddy always helps me! You got this! Hear you, girl. Breathe, Queen!* Next she takes a quick look at her feed. Nail art, grass beach hut, couple kissing, ferret in a clothes hamper, airplane wing, airplane wing, airplane wing. Ezra returns, zipping up his shorts.

"We're going back," he says.

"It's got to be, like, twenty more steps," she says. She feels bad, but they're almost there.

"WE HAVE ENOUGH PICTURES, HARPER," Ezra says.

Harper goes silent. She never wanted to be one of those girlfriends who treat their boyfriend like an assistant, but she *is* one. "Ez, I'm sorry. I shouldn't have been so focused on my stupid photos."

"Harp, *I'm* sorry. I'm tired. It was a long drive. We have, like, a hundred pictures. You look great in all of them. I don't know what you're looking for. And it's roasting. How much hotter is it going to get out here?"

"Do you want me to check?"

He puts his head in his hands. Harper thinks he might cry. "Evfy questin nntt hv answr."

"What?"

"I *said*, 'Every question doesn't have to have an answer.' Sometimes it's just better if they don't. Sometimes it's better just to *wonder*. We can't even wonder anymore! We lost wonder."

His voice has gotten all reedy and distressed. She's never heard him like this. "Let's just go."

Ezra only looks at her with those pleading eyes and shakes his head as if she'll never understand. She picks up his (Just-Okay Bruce's) pack and swings it over one shoulder and starts back down. It's a bad place to have a fight. If you're going to fight, you want to be close to home, or any exit point, not almost two hard miles to your car and another three hours of a silent ride home. Harper hears every crunch of their shoes, every bird tweet, every unnerving slither in the grass. She can practically hear the sweat roll down Ezra's face.

And, well, she hears something else, too. Just as they're finally off that mountain, with Ezra's car in their sight line, a whoosh of a text comes in. And then another whoosh. The arrival of a text during a loaded silence always feels like one more rude wrongdoing. Your phone should be silent during tense times, and when it isn't, it's like the phone itself is mocking and shouting and sticking its tongue out at the mad person.

Whoosh.

Ezra exhales, unlocks the car, *beep beep, kachunk.*

Harper sits in the passenger's seat, in a pool of her own regret. She silences her phone without even glancing at it, feeling like a naughty child. She *is* a naughty child, she's sure. At least, a selfish and unthinking one.

"Go ahead and look," Ezra says. Her phone, that wrongdoer, sits in her lap.

"Just in case it's an emergency," she says. A lie used by all badly timed text checkers.

And then . . . holy shit. It's from Dario.

We found him, it says.

It's been two months since Harper discovered Dario, two months of keeping this secret from Ezra and her friends and her mom. A secret this large is a calculus problem, because sometimes it seems like *only two months,* and sometimes like *a whole two months.* Her wrongdoing of not sharing this news grows exponentially and very nearly loops back into itself, because she really can't say anything now. More and more this seems like the only option, staying silent, especially right this minute, watching Ezra's profile as he drives, her phone with that text sitting in her lap.

It briefly crosses her mind that maybe this is how her mother feels, only in years, not months. Sometimes, ugh, seeing another person's point of view is exceptionally inconvenient.

But wait. *Her* secret-keeping should be totally understandable, right? And any anger that might come her way is just mean, because this is *huge.* How are you supposed to deal with something this big? Forty-two children! And a Beau Zane, mystery man–father. The question of him, it's been filling 95 percent of her brain. As she studies for her calculus final, it's Harper and Beau Zane, Nissan salesman. And as she finishes up her end-of-year project for Lit—that papier-mâché mask of Viola in Shakespeare's *Twelfth Night*—she's the daughter of Beau Zane, armed robber. As she tutors Ezra for his Algebra II exam, it's her and Beau Zane at the Jiffy Lube in Nevada City. Every day after she posts some photo of herself at Green Lake in a cute summer outfit, or some mountain shot from a few years back, she lingers on the Facebook profiles of the Beaus and gazes at fishing trips and family gatherings, mothers in hospitals, a Thanksgiving turkey, an alarming political post or two. She searches their eyes in the tiny photos she can find online, sure that she'll know him when she sees him, but she doesn't.

She hasn't yet reached out to Simone or Wyatt or any of the thirty-nine others, either. After all, Wyatt is *kind of an asshole*, and Simone is fabulous. Simone is a slice of chocolate cake on a plate in a French bakery, desirable, layered, perfect, and Harper is more of a Cronut in a Safeway, she's sure, with a cheap, uncertain identity. Made of similar ingredients, but worlds apart. Dario, though—he's only a year younger, but he's a funny little semibrother kid who's really growing on her. He's even texted her meaningful stuff, like his newborn photos, showing his moms standing on their front porch with a bundled him in Reba's arms, and a report he wrote in the ninth grade about his "origins," describing how a beautiful combination of love and nature and science and mysterious human connection allowed it to happen. Harper almost cries when she reads it.

But Dario has never sent anything like this.
We found him.
Harper stares at the words, her heart thumping. It's Saturday,

and there are only three and a half days left of school before summer vacation, so it's that time when hope and possibilities are already right there waiting. But this is HOPE in capital letters. Excited, anxious, stressed hope, but HOPE. Ezra eyes her from the driver's seat. She turns her phone upside down in her lap, fingers circling the rounded corners.

"You can answer," Ezra says.

"I know I can. You don't have to give me permission," Harper says. He doesn't have to act like he's in the driver's seat while sitting in the driver's seat! Still, no way is she going to answer that text. Even if Ezra knew all the details, it's too personal. She doesn't want to find out if her father is the Nissan salesman or the prisoner as an angry Ezra sits less than a foot away.

Well, of course Ezra feels the secret. He knows that text isn't from Harper's mom or Soraya or any of her other friends. "Who is it?" he asks. He sounds jealous. Ezra never sounds jealous. He's usually calm, secure, and cozy, a guy version of your favorite quilt.

Harper's caught. MF, Beau Zane, is one text away. Or one phone call. He's right there. All at once she's so nervous, she could be carsick as they take the *S* curves down Mount Rainier, the steep drop-offs suddenly terrifying. "Can you keep your eyes on the road?" she snaps. She's the kind of mad you get when something's actually your fault. Her hands are sweaty. Her hands always get sweaty on roads like this, but it's intolerable.

More than angry, more than jealous, Ezra is kind, though. And he loves Harper. And so he drives in silence, his face somber, as he keeps his eyes on the road and as he takes each turn with care. There will be no dropping off a cliff and igniting into a ball of fire with Ezra behind the wheel.

They wind through the nerve-racking swirl of on-ramps and

off-ramps and speeding cars jetting in and out of traffic through Tacoma, and then race past the car dealerships of Fife and the water park, and the various outskirt-y stuff like the Last Living Denny's in the West, which was what she and Ez called that Denny's out by Renton back when he still liked her. And then, when they're just a few blocks from Harper's house, he pulls over. He parks in front of a semi-dilapidated Craftsman, with a string of prayer flags across the porch. *Their* dilapidated Craftsman, the one they park in front of when her mom's home and they want to kiss and hang out before saying goodbye.

"What are you doing?" She knows they're not going to kiss, that's for sure.

"Who was it?" he asks calmly.

This is the furthest thing from the perfect moment. But she can't have him thinking she's cheating on him or something. She's stuck, and there's only one way out.

"My half brother." It's so weird to say those words out loud.

"What?"

"My half brother."

"I never knew you—"

"I didn't know, either. I just found out. And I don't just have *one.*"

"What do you mean? Harper? Harper, are you okay? You don't look okay. You're shaking."

"I have, um . . ."

"Harper, what?"

"I have forty-one."

Ezra makes a scoffing sound and shakes his head. He leans against his door. "Harper, come on. God. Don't fuck with me."

"I'm not kidding."

"Just tell me what's going on."

"My, um, *father*? He was a sperm donor. So, suddenly I have all these . . . *people*." Her voice wobbles. It's all catching up, what she's been holding, and holding *away*. She starts to cry. Tears stream down, and her nose starts to run. "And this?" She shakes her phone. "Was a text from my half brother, saying they found out who he *is*. Who my father is."

Ezra looks shocked. Well, sure. Of course.

But he isn't shocked about siblings and sperm donors. He's shocked about something else.

"You didn't tell me." His voice has a quality she's never heard before. Firm and colorless as concrete.

"Ez . . ."

"How long has all this been going on?"

"A few weeks! I mean, I found out about Dario a couple of months ago." She sniffs loudly. She searches in his glove compartment for a Kleenex and settles for a Taco Time napkin.

"Dario? A couple of *months* ago?" Ezra's face flushes. It's as red as it was up on that trail.

"As you can imagine, this has been very—"

"Well, I can't imagine, actually, because you never told me any of this."

"Ez, come on . . ." Wait, wait. What about the part where he understands how hard this is? Or how embarrassing? Forty-one siblings, like she was one candy on a conveyor belt of candies, or one doughnut, or . . . Well, God, pick the processed food of your choice.

He starts the car.

"Ez, don't!"

Ez does. He pulls out, heads up the two blocks to Harper's house. Their front door is open, and some reusable shopping bags sit on the front step, her mom in the process of unpacking the car after a grocery stop. Ezra doesn't even turn the motor off. He leaves it running, his foot on the brake. Fine, fine! Harper opens the door and gets out. One of Mrs. Wong's chickens has gotten loose, and it's jabbing its beak into some marigolds, oblivious to the drama unfolding.

"You need to take your tripod, Harper," Ezra says. He's eerily calm. "I'm sure you can find someone else to take your picture."

"Ez, no. I'm sorry!"

"You might want to pay the next guy better, though. Or at least give him a lunch break."

She removes the tripod from the back seat and slams the door. Wait. Wait just a sec. He's not breaking up with her, is he? What? *Why?* And right after she just told him what's been going on? Because this is definitely more than a fight. "Are you breaking up with me? How can you do this right now, when this huge thing is happening to me?"

"I'm not your doctor. I'm not your photographer. I'm not here to support you when you decide you need it. We're here to support each other."

"You can't do this! You don't have to do this," she pleads.

"But I do," Ezra says, just before he drives away.

CHAPTER TWELVE

Mother's marriage manual warns that you should never delve too deeply into science or mathematics lest you sacrifice any portion of your feminine delicacy. And yet, I am compelled to follow the great inspiration of the sisters who came before me. To beguile the tedium of the long voyage, I have insisted on learning how to calculate the daily position of *Neptune's Car.* I took my first lesson in navigation last week and looked through the quadrant for the first time, studying to find the difference in latitude and longitude.

We calculate the ship's reckoning usually by the sun, or if the sun is not out during the day, using the stars after dark. I look through the sextant at the noon hour, and at night, using the two chronometers to determine the exact position of the ship to mark on the chart and in the logbook. Today, the last day of my eighteenth year, the captain paid me a great compliment by copying my reckonings into his book. He told me I have a rare talent for navigation, and in the ship's log, proudly noted: "Mrs. Patten is uncommon handy about the ship, even in weather, and would doubtless be of service if a man." It seems remarkable, to be so able.

Mary Ann Patten journal entry
April 5, 1855

SHE'S IN SHOCK. SO SHOCKED THAT SHE DOESN'T EVEN feel pain yet. He needs a little time to cool off, he needs some aloe for that sunburn, he needs some food (he was right about lunch), and then they'll talk, Harper tells herself as Ezra's car disappears. She can explain more fully. She'll apologize again, and swear to be better. She's exhausted, from the hike and the fight and the Beau Zane news, and she still hasn't texted Dario back. With her mom home, a call is out of the question.

"Harp, is that you? Can you bring in those bags?" her mother shouts.

Melinda shouldn't leave their door hanging wide open. This isn't some quaint little town where people leave stuff unlocked. Once her mom accidentally left her battered old flip phone in the cup holder of her car, and someone smashed her windshield in order to steal it. Little ice chips of glass were everywhere, threatening to cut them for months afterward. Harper hauls the groceries to the kitchen, where BPA-free, non-GMO, gluten-free, organic water and a box of Ancient Maize Flakes sit on the counter, along with several bulging mesh produce bags.

"When they say Whole Foods should be Whole Paycheck,

they're ri— Honey!" Her mom interrupts herself. "What's wrong? Oh no. Come here." She sets down a container of Guac-Kale-Mole and puts her arms around Harper, and that's when Harper starts to cry. You can't be mad at all your most important people at the same time, or you're alone, is how it feels. And in spite of her mom's failings (and who doesn't have those?), she's one-hundred-percent available when Harper is upset or sick or in need. More than one hundred, if that's possible. And she feels all those things, upset, sick, in need. Harper's chest heaves in a sob. "What happened?"

"Argument." Harper can barely speak. She wipes her eyes, and a big smear of mascara streaks her hand. God, she must look awful. No one's going to post a photo of *this*.

"What did he do?" Melinda's voice takes on a threatening tone.

"Me. *I* did. Or didn't. I don't even know!"

"Did you break up with him? Because good for you! You have a long life ahead to be so locked down now. You hardly see your friends anymore, you spend so much time together."

"He broke up with me! I think. I'm not sure. How can he do this? I mean, we're in love! If you could *see* us—"

"I *do* see you. He sure doesn't look miserable in all those photos, I'll tell you that mu—"

"Right? *Right?* Exactly! I don't even understand what's happening. Nothing's even wrong! He, like, *blindsided* me! I'm such an idiot."

"You're *not* an idiot. Far from it, and honestly, it's his loss. You have a rare combination, honey. Beauty *and* intelligence. Good luck to him ever finding that again. He doesn't deserve you."

Ugh! She breaks away from her mother's hug. She is not beautiful and not intelligent and not deserving, she's sure, as she stands there stricken and helpless, clutching a soggy Taco Time napkin, hating everyone and everything.

"Oh wait! Look what I got you." Melinda fishes around in one of the bags and then holds it up. A low-carb keto pizza, with a crust made from ground chicken and egg whites. "That pizza you like. We can have it tonight. Clean eating."

Clean eating!

She stops crying then. She gets it together. Her head pounds with confusion about Ez, but she's *lucky*, you know? To even be in a room where someone uses those words, where there are bags of food from an organic grocery store . . . She's so much luckier than so many people. She feels ashamed of herself, for this crying, her treatment of Ez, her half-hearted friendships, her self-involvement, and stupid posts, and emptiness, and fear. Just that morning she saw a bridge that had collapsed, and a landslide, and a dude who swindled a ton of old people out of their money. When you see the tragedy of the whole world, your pain is a stubbed toe. A stubbed toe hurts, but, God.

She splashes her face with cold water, forces herself to get it together, because poor Dario has been sitting in silence after his text. Is she ready? Who cares, it is what it is. If it's the prisoner, it's the prisoner.

Well? Which one is he? Harper types, then sends.

Can you talk? Dario immediately replies.

Not now. Prisoner?

The faceless dude. The wanderer.

The guy with all the addresses?!

Oh man, this is bad news. Who moves around like that? No one, unless you're trying to leave yourself behind on a regular basis. Why does it have to be *him*? Why not the casino manager? Harper has been hoping for the casino manager. He has a boat that he takes to Lake Tahoe on the weekends, and his wife and her two kids from a previous marriage, Jason and Kevin, go tubing. There's regular old beer, not fancy IPAs, maybe too much beer, but not TOO too much, and Jason and Kevin got ATVs for Christmas. Beau Zane takes them off-roading. Harper actually imagined herself going with them, even though in real life, she'd never do something that dangerous.

Just like that, Harper says goodbye to Casino Beau and his wife, Cathy, and Jason and Kevin, and Kevin's girlfriend, Misty, with her rose tattoo on her ankle. She says goodbye to all the other Beau Zanes, too—Nissan Beau, prisoner Beau, Christian Beau—boom, gone, after so many hours of tracking their life histories, and their extended families, their holiday decorations, enchilada platters, and Employee of the Month photos.

This is how it is with people online, the ones you snoop on, like Harper snoops on Ezra's ex-girlfriend Brie in California. First you spy out of need or jealousy or curiosity, and then you just kind of like watching that person's life. It gets as familiar as a TV series. Seeing Brie with her grandma, kicking ass in her track meets, and sharing funny stories with her friends, like the time she got tangled in her sports bra and had to call for help, haha . . . Harper thinks Brie is kind of great, actually. A few weeks ago, though, Harper forgot to check on Brie, and that turned into more forgetting, and lately Brie's the TV series she's finished and can barely remember. She's going to miss Casino Beau and the boat trips until she forgets him, too.

Yeah, the one with all the addresses and NO PHOTO ANY-WHERE. Wyatt figured it out. Can you meet?

When? Screaming-face emoji.

Tomorrow? Wyatt's parents go to church, but he can get out of it.

WYATT?! Another sibling now? No way, no way.

Me AND him. Don't chicken out. Buns again?

Oh God. She doesn't know what to do. The little bubbles start up on Dario's end. And then his text pops up. *I SAID, DON'T CHICKEN OUT, BAWK, BAWK.*

Okay, okay! How about Green Lake, on the steps by the rowing club? Outside is better. Outside is safer. Still safer, because who can ever forget *that?*

Sure. Eleven?

Fine.

Harper sticks her phone under her pillow so it'll shut up. She has a general feeling of *yuck,* a recipe of self-hatred, gross anxiety, guilt, and who knows what else. There are so many ingredients, it's hard to tell them apart: Ezra, her mom, Beau Zane, Wyatt. Harper stares out her window, spots Mrs. Wong and the chicken, heading through the back gate. She found the escapee, thank goodness. If anything had happened to it, Harper would have had a chicken death on her conscience along with everything else.

She takes the phone back out from under the pillow.

Can we talk? she texts Ezra.

She waits.

Nothing.

She starts to call Soraya but then changes her mind, because her mom's right—they've barely seen each other since she and Ez got together, even though Soraya keeps asking. Running to her now, the very second Ez might be gone, is just wrong. It's using her. She's been enough of a user already.

Are you there?

Nothing, and more nothing from Ezra. Harper scrolls through her phone. A video of a basketball being dropped four hundred fifty feet, a girl singing into a faucet nozzle. A healthy smoothie, cowboy boots with a dress, butt cheeks peeking from shorts, sprawled cat, sprawled cat, sprawled cat. Harper watches Ada pencil in her eyebrows.

She looks through the photos they just took. Harper, at the start of the hike, walking ahead on the woodsy trail; Harper, sitting on a crop of rocks, viewed from below; Harper, alone on the high, narrow path, with the mountain behind her. Harper and Ez, big faces in the camera, and big smiles, pre-fight. Ez sticking his tongue out, one shoelace untied, fight imminent.

Harper chooses the one of her with her hands on her hips, with a panoramic scene of jagged peaks dramatically in the background. Contrast up. Saturation up. Filter: Lark. Ethereal, and meaningful. Caption: *Soul-searching.* No. If Ez sees it, he'll think she's sending him a message, or looking for support, and he hates when people do that. Caption: *Staying grounded at high elevations.* Does that even make sense? Should she look up the exact elevation? Whatever. #mtrainier #takeahike #takeahikeday #adventures #hikingtrails #pnw #pnwwonderland #getoutdoors #goexplore #ilovenature. She posts.

Her chest aches. She pictures her ribs like the curved walls of a cave. The likes start pouring in, the compliments. *Beauty! Fire! You are my inspiration!* Talk about being a user! These people are real and alive somewhere, but they sure don't seem like it. They have a favorite food, their own toothbrush, and secret wishes, and bad days, but it's easy to forget that. Behind that screen they can just seem like pseudohumans, ones she has a fake connection with and can easily dismiss, even if she looks at their stuff, too. Another pet dies, and then another one, and on and on until any real empathy she might have is diluted to near zero. She scrolls right past, like a boring TV channel, because how many pet deaths can a person take in? How many hurricanes, how many shootings, how much cancer, until your heart shuts down? She can almost hear all the hearts, once warm and caring, just shut, shut, shutting down, like closed doors. She could pass any of them on the street, those followers, and not have any idea who they are. They, the internet They.

What's your rating, They? Five stars for the hurricane, two stars for the pet death, one star for the maybe-breakup. Restless energy fills her. Her head is filled with so much *noise!* She needs air. She can barely breathe, even though she's right here at the surface. She opens her window, and when she does, she sees the neighbor boy, Rainey, out on the street alone on his bike, God! He's setting up a small wooden ramp. Holy shit, is he going to drive off it? He could break his neck!

"Rainey! Don't do that! You could get hurt!" Harper yells.

"My dad helped me build it!" Rainey yells back. He pedals a figure eight, picks up speed now that he has an audience, his butt off the seat. Ugh! Everything seems potentially tragic; everything seems impossible and doomed. Everything seems so, so danger-ous.

Rainey's thin little legs pump. This day is getting worse and worse. She'll have to call 911. He aims for the ramp. Harper squinches her eyes shut.

And then she hears him whoop and holler. "YEEHAW!" he shouts. "COWABUNGA!" Harper peeks. Rainey is shaking one fist in the air in victory.

But she missed the part where he was airborne. She missed him flying.

CHAPTER THIRTEEN

After arriving just one day behind Captain
Hussey and *Westward Ho* in San Francisco, the
captain now cannot break his obsession to best
Westward Ho on our race to Hong Kong. Progress
is slow and the tropical heat unbearable, broken
only by the occasional violent downpours. I am
at work at my navigational skills, with noontime
and evening star sightings. The marriage manual warns that sometimes in a female breast,
there is a passion of a dangerous nature. In man
this passion is ambition, but in women it is a
selfish desire to stand apart from the many, to
be something of, and by, herself. And yet, in my
secret self, Hussey's one-thousand-dollar wager
is also on my mind. As I calculate our positions,
my heart thrills at the race.

Mary Ann Patten journal entry
June 16, 1855

BIKES ZIP PAST, BABIES IN RUNNING STROLLERS FLY BY, AND
pairs of women jog or speed-walk, arms pumping, checking their

heart rate on their Fitbits and smart watches. How unnerving, to see your heart beating every second. What is Harper's heart rate now, she wonders, as she stands there in front of two half brothers? A jillion, it feels like. As fast as a hummingbird's, at least. She looks at Wyatt, who's wearing clothes a guy would wear on a yacht—white shirt, blue shorts, those boat shoes—and she sees herself in him, all right. There she is, in male form times two, but this time with broader shoulders, edgier cheekbones. The three of them just stand under a cherry tree on the Green Lake grass. That cherry tree has seen a lot, Harper guesses, but never this.

"Hey," Wyatt says.

"Hey," Harper says. They take inventory. Who knows what Wyatt is noticing about her. She feels super awkward, realizing that noticing goes both ways. There isn't the immediate ease there was with Dario. They don't hug like two long-lost friends. It's more like that wedding they went to in California, her mom's cousin's, where you understood you were family but could only see the ways you'd never be alike: a chocolate fondue fountain, an ice sculpture in the shape of a leaping fish, a DJ in a sequin vest, lots of chiffon. Harper and her mom ate carob, and champagne gave Melinda a headache, and cutting loose to disco seemed outrageously brave, and chiffon was poofy.

Wyatt is wearing expensive-looking everything, an air most of all. Confidence. People that confident make Harper nervous. He looks popular, too. He looks like what he is, a football player at a high school in Mercer Island, the richest area around. Does everyone do this? The speedy mental calculations of hierarchy? You don't always even realize it's happening. It can be innate, like a chimpanzee who feels alpha-safe among the Darios, but who's definitely not alpha among the Wyatts.

"Girl version," Wyatt says, whatever that means. She sort of judges him for saying it, even though she kind of thought the same thing.

"So great, huh? So great!" Dario says, all jazzed up. He's holding Walter, and he kisses Walter's cheek in anxiety.

"Family reunion." Wyatt smirks. Apparently, the guy only speaks two-word sentences.

But she's making him an asshole before she even knows for sure. It's her own insecurity, really. The same thing that kept Harper and her mom in their chairs at the wedding while everyone else joyfully danced to the Commodores. Or the way she judges the perfect people online, using petty, snarky superiority to chip away at anyone who has more—more success, beauty, happiness. Harper hunts madly around for something to say, a way to connect. "Hey, I'm sorry," she says. "Dario told me, about how you found out about all this. I didn't know, either. I mean, I knew, but I didn't know I could know."

Ugh!

"It's strange," Wyatt says.

"For sure."

The conversation stalls. What can you really say about any of this? Large things just have to sit in the silence of truth sometimes. Harper stares out toward the lake and watches a group of swimmers. She hopes they checked the website for toxic algae blooms before they got in.

Dario's phone rings. "It's Simone!" he says cheerfully. "FaceTime!" Simone?! That fucking Dario! "Hey, Simone. I'm here with Wyatt and Harper."

He spins the phone in an arc. "Hey, Wyatt," she says.

"Cool shirt," Wyatt says. They all know each other already.

And her shirt *is* cool. A black-and-white hedgehog, with the words WHY DON'T THEY JUST SHARE THE HEDGE? Her hair is in two braids that are pinned up on her head, and she sits on the stairs of a building on her college campus. That wedding was nothing compared to this.

"Nice to meet you," Harper says. It sounds prim. Her built-in insecurity safety features activate, and the walls go up as she shuts down.

"We now convene the first meeting of the Beau Zane fan club." Dario cackles.

"Little sister, let me see you!" Simone says. Dario shoves the phone right up to Harper's face, God. And there she is, the incredible Simone, blue eyes sparkling, definitely looking that rare combination of beautiful and intelligent. In the background students keep calling her name and saying hi as they go in and out of the building, and she waves, a campus celebrity who's used to the attention.

Harper catches Wyatt's eye. *So* strange, she tells him with hers, and he nods.

"You're beautiful," Simone says, and heat fills Harper's cheeks.

"*You* are," Harper says. They're kind of complimenting themselves, and yet, Simone *doesn't* look like Harper in the way that matters, the light of individuality in their eyes. If Beau Zane meets them, he'll prefer Simone, for sure.

"Well, ducklings," Simone says, apparently finished with her appraisal. "Let's tell her what we know."

"Me?" Harper asks.

"We know where he is. His address. Makena Beach. Maui. South end, where there's no more road," Dario says.

"Here's the weird thing," Wyatt tells her. "*One* of the weird things. We've got a house there. Like, ten minutes from there. Palauea. Well, a condo."

"It's fate," Dario says. "How can it be anything else?"

"Wait, what's happening?" Harper asks.

"We need to catch her up," Dario says. "Wyatt—"

"I put all the addresses of the guy into one search and realized they all have something in common." He pauses for dramatic effect. "They're di—"

"Dive spots," Dario interrupts.

Wyatt scowls at Dario. Little brothers, right? "Dive spots. Key West, Florida. Bonne Terre, Missouri. Freeport, Texas. Carmel, California—huge dive location, Point Lobos, right nearby. Point Huron, Michigan, has *Lake* Huron. Huge diving area. Sitka, Alaska? Baranof Island, boom."

"Missouri?" Harper asks. "It's landlocked."

"They've got a freshwater mine," Wyatt says.

"Freshwater mime." Dario puffs out his cheeks and puts one flat hand up, like he's stuck in a box underwater.

Wyatt ignores him. "Creepy as fuck. It's the world's largest freshwater dive resort. Like, twenty-six miles of 'coastline.'" He makes air quotes. "In this deep cavern where they used to mine for lead, with all these old structures still down there . . ."

"Lead?" Harper says. "I wouldn't get in that water." Carcinogen city.

"Anyway," Simone says. "As Wyatt was figuring out they were dive sites like a goddamn *genius,* I was hunting down all the 'father's side' relatives I had on MyHeritage.com, seeing who else they were associated with online. I kept plugging in all the names, just hoping to hit on something."

"And then she hit on something!" Dario makes Walter's

paws applaud. "After she did a *deep dive*." Harper can understand Dario's excitement, but he needs to take it down a notch.

"A woman. Related to my father's relatives on MyHeritage. Greer Brody McClure. Makena Beach, Maui. Unlisted number. Right age to be Beau's mother, sixty-six, and Scottish—check. I just knew it when I saw her name."

"Yeah, like you just knew it about the sculptor," Dario says.

"Shut up about the sculptor," Simone says. "Anyway, I tried to find out more, but these people are super nonexistent on the internet. *No one* is entirely nonexistent, though. I found her name associated with a business license. Captain Neptune. I hadn't heard about Wyatt's dive find yet, but when I did, boom. We had him. Our Beau Zane, the faceless guy."

"The Texas address, the last one—he wasn't there," Wyatt says. "I called the owner of the house. It was a rental. Beau Zane hadn't lived there for two years or so. He couldn't tell me anything about him. He only talked to the guy, like, twice, over the phone."

"But then once they told me about the dive thing," Simone says, "I started zeroing in on Captain Neptune. It's a Makena Beach dive shack. Co-owned by Antonis Zane, now dead."

"AZ now D," Dario chirps.

"But more importantly . . ." Simone pauses, then raises her eyebrows for dramatic effect. "I fou—"

"She found a Yelp review that mentioned an instructor, Beau. A very *recent* review," Dario says.

"Dario!" Simone huffs.

"Sorry." He shrugs. You can tell he's used to being forgiven.

A dive instructor? A guy who moves around every few years?

If Harper's mom judges Ez for not having a CEO résumé, what's she going to think about the dude she chose to be Harper's father? "How recent?" she asks.

"Weeks," Simone says. "He's there."

"Did they like him? As an instructor, I mean." If they slammed him . . . it'll be a bad sign.

"*Loved.*" Simone beams. "And, wow, they really loved his dad, Tony."

"Don't get her hopes all up. Tell her the bad news," Wyatt says.

"We can't get an answer at the Captain Neptune dive shack, or at the home number for Greer Brody McClure," Simone says. "Believe me, I tried. Like, a hundred times. It just rings and rings and rings at the shop. No email, either. You just can't get ahold of this guy. Which makes me hate him way less, because I tried to contact him and thought he just didn't answer."

"Wait," Harper says. "I thought we weren't supposed to just go calling people."

"But it's him! And we know he's *right there* somewhere," Dario says.

"So, that's why we're all here today." Simone leans back, satisfied.

"What do you mean?" Harper asks. "Why?"

Simone stares right into Harper's eyes. At least, right into the tiny circle of her camera. "Well, we're go—"

"We're going to go see him," Dario interrupts. "We thought you might like to come. Didn't we, Walter?"

"We sure did," Dario-Walter says in a high, dog-human voice.

CHAPTER FOURTEEN

The first teas of the season have finally arrived in Hong Kong and have been loaded onto the ship, one million five hundred thousand pounds of it, 9,583 full chests, 2,609 half chests, 7,393 packages of the finest teas in the holds and in the staterooms and in every possible crevice. We now say goodbye to the *Westward Ho,* one thousand dollars richer after beating her by eleven days. Next we will race south through the pirate-filled Gaspar Strait, the thought of which has shattered my nerves, though Joshua says he is confident in my abilities to navigate toward the strong coastal winds of Borneo, and across the Indian Ocean. After that comes the South Atlantic, and, finally, London. What a sight it will be, the beam of the Lizard Lighthouse at Lizard Point, the welcoming beacon as we head at last through the English Channel.

Mary Ann Patten journal entry

September 28, 1855

THERE ARE MANY, MANY REASONS HARPER CAN'T POSSI-
bly go. Her mom will have to know. Her boyfriend will retreat
entirely into the past if she leaves now. She'll meet Beau Zane and
find out for sure if he actually likes her, approves of her, or could
even love her . . . or not. The expense, although Wyatt claims
to have plenty of air miles, and a place for them to stay. The
aforementioned "them." The aforementioned "them" all sharing a bathroom. Airplanes, germ capsules that they are, airports,
same, with so many moving handrails and fingers, fingers, fingers. Let alone the reasons people used to fear flying, actual plane
crashes and other "aviation accidents," defined (she looks this up
on Wikipedia) as "incidents that take place aboard an aircraft in
which (a) a person is fatally or seriously injured, (b) the aircraft
sustains significant damage or structural failure, or (c) the aircraft
goes missing or becomes completely inaccessible." And let's not
forget Hawaii itself. Hazardous swimming conditions from rip-
tides, winds, and swells. Shark attacks. Portuguese man-of-war,
which can grow to be a hundred feet long, with a bladder that
looks like a pink chewing-gum bubble, and with stinging tentacles. Box jellyfish, with one of the most venomous stings in the
world. Ocean water quality, tropical bacteria disease, sun poison-
ing. Also, Harper has nothing to wear.

And yet, and yet.

How do you explain the pull to know who you are?

Dario starts texting her the minute they all part ways at Green
Lake.

You can't pass this up.

I can.

Come on! Crying emoji, scream emoji, palm tree emoji.

You have thirty-eight other people you could ask.

I like YOU.

This chokes Harper right up. She almost bursts into tears as she stands there in front of Rosita's, with the smell of handmade tortillas wafting out. She likes him, too. A lot. She even likes kind-of-an-asshole Wyatt and too-amazing Simone, and Walter-never-Walt, of course. She could maybe, um . . . God, this could make her *sob,* but . . . she could maybe *love* them, you know? Someday? Love, in the mostly forgiving way of family. Still, Harper is a person who often says no before she says yes, a Melinda Proulx trait, for sure. No is easy—it spits from her lips like an olive pit—but a yes takes time. You have to ponder the ramifications. A no can become a yes, but a yes cannot easily become a no.

I'll think about it. I have to ponder the ramifications.

Did you really just say ponder the ramifications? Laughing emojis, all in a row. *You're kind of a dweeb,* he texts, followed by a row of hearts.

Wow. Harper's gotten herself into such a mess. And she hasn't even met Beau Zane yet.

Harper barely reaches her street when something awful happens. Rainey, the neighbor kid, has his dad's dartboard propped up on the seat of his bike, which is propped against a tree, a small pile of real darts, the kind with the metal tips, at his feet. Zoom, one hits the tree trunk. Zoom, another flies into a rhododendron bush. He has his arm in the air, flicking his wrist a few times in practice, when Mrs. Wong's cat crosses his path.

"Raineeey!" Harper shouts.

No, nothing bad happens to the cat! Or to Rainey, okay? She thought for sure it would, but it didn't. The dart misses the board and sticks in the soft padding of the bike seat. The awful thing that happens is that her phone rings.

Ezra.

"I was just going to call you," Harper says. "You want me to tell you everything, right? I tried to reach you last night, but you didn't answer. Ez, I met two other ones today. A half brother. A half sister."

She was sure, or else just hoping very hard, that he might forgive her. At least give her more time to do better.

"Ez?"

It's not the good kind of silence. Harper knows exactly what this silence is saying.

"Ez, no." She starts to cry.

"I think . . ." His voice is strangled. High-pitched. He's crying now. "I think we need some time apart," he manages to say.

"What? *Why?*" He's been telling her why for months, but she's been too preoccupied to hear him, she realizes. Too self-focused to really see him, either.

"Maybe you just need time to do your—"

She doesn't want to hear it. "No. No." Tears are running down her face, and stupid Rainey is staring at her, and Harper waves her hand to get him to stop.

"Harper, you just keep people *away*. From the real you. Me, even. I can't have a relationship with someone who shuts me out. I can't have a relationship with someone who isn't *here*."

"I don't shut you out!" She shuts him out. "I don't keep

people away from the real me, I just . . ." She has no idea what to say, because there is no *just*. She's wrong in a million ways. "You're doing this on the *phone*? You're *that* guy? What are you going to do, *ghost* me next?"

"I called because my heart would fucking break if I saw you," he says.

Grief—it's a tsunami. Harper sees it out there, the real wave, the biggest one, the thing you've really been fearing all along: loss. That wave is rising. "I've got to go," she says, and hangs up, just like that, because she can't take another second of this. She's devastated. So devastated that *mad* has to come to her rescue, and quick. Come on! Breaking up right before summer? What a jerk move. They only have three and a half days left before school's out, so he won't even have to really see her until September. Maybe he planned it that way. A whole summer, unattached, perfect. She starts to build the list of his wrongdoings, the list that will let her blame him. It's a short list.

She presses her palms to her eyes to stop crying. Her stomach is so sick, she might throw up. Rainey has returned to his darts, and one goes airborne and then lands in a prickly juniper bush. Harper hates the promise of summer and the warm, magical cut-grass smell in the air.

Thank God her mother isn't home. She slams her door as hard as she wants. The mirror falls, and she just leaves it there on the floor. She flops onto her bed, sobs into her pillow until it's all gross and wet. She turns around, and Freddie Mercury stares from the ceiling, defiant and brave, reminding her that people have gone through worse, way worse.

She scrolls on her phone in desperation. A row of bananas

made to look like farm animals. A tiny hamster getting a stomach rub. A guy catching grapes in his mouth. A toddler meeting an alpaca. A surprise proposal in a public park. A glittery manicure, a restaurant aquarium with mermaid, a side-view mirror reflecting a road, a rock stack by a river, a slice of cake, a yoga pose, a yoga pose, a yoga pose.

Harper hears the garage door go up. Her mother's purse clunks on the counter. The fridge door opens and then smacks closed, too fast for anything to be taken out, for sure. And then there's a covert silence. A too-long silence, when her mom would usually be heading to her bedroom to take off her bra, like any sensible person. It's the kind of quiet that makes you rightly suspicious, same as when Binx is playing in the other room, chatting to himself, and then goes quiet. A silence that means stuff is being stealthily destroyed. Harper's heart jabs at the thought of Binx. Will she even get to say goodbye to him, or to Nudo or Yanet? Will she get to say thank you? Or is this just *it*? She chokes in that tidal wave as she realizes the scope of her loss. It's not just Ezra, but Ezra's life, and her life with him.

What *is* her mother doing down there?

She tiptoes down the hall, avoiding the creaky parts she knows so well. And then Harper sees her.

Her mother screams. You'd scream like that, too, if you'd just been caught. "I didn't know you were home."

"What are you doing?"

Well, here's what she's doing: That papier-mâché mask of

Viola in Shakespeare's *Twelfth Night* Harper has been making for AP Lit? Melinda's fixing it. One side of the mask is female and the other side male, to show how Viola—after finding herself shipwrecked on the beach of Illyria, her twin brother dead—disguises herself as a man to take charge of her own fate, rather than falling apart in helplessness, like her upbringing has taught her. For weeks Harper has been sliding newspaper strips through glop, smoothing them, letting the mask dry, painting both sides of the face. Adding hair that looks like waves, and a dolphin along the bottom, since Viola's brother rides on the back of one. Now Melinda Proulx is holding a paintbrush, the tip dipped in black.

"The smile was a little off. . . ." Her mother's voice sounds guilty. She knows this is wrong and still can't help herself. Things just have to be perfect.

"I wanted it like that," Harper lies. Was it off? Whatever, whatever!

"I was just trying to help." Melinda doesn't even have her jacket off yet.

"I can't believe it. I just can't believe it." Rage is rising in Harper's body. She starts stomping around, pacing. Her mother may as well have fixed Harper's smile.

"For God's sake, Harp, calm down. I'm sorry!"

"I'm not just some . . ." Her mind swirls. "Lump of clay. That you *form*, to look like *you*. You don't get to just *design* me." Except in a way, Melinda did. She chose traits, Harper assumes, but isn't really sure. Which traits? How can Harper know anything when Melinda refuses to talk about it? Imagine you live in a house, but half of it is blocked off. Imagine a book where every other page is blank.

"I don't want you to look like *me*. You're *you*, beautiful, smart, wonderf—"

"Stop! *Stop it.*" Harper's had enough. She's done. With all of it. Her mother, herself, lies. Sure, this is the despair of Ezra leaving her, but not entirely. All the walls are coming down with his leaving. The structure is crumbling. "You lied to me."

"I don't know what you're talking about," Melinda says. But she does. She just stands there in her jacket, and Harper sees it right on her face.

"The sperm thing." She can't think of the words, "fertilization," "donor," words that imply a moment, not a lifetime. "It's open. It's always been open. I could have known more about him."

Melinda's face falls. It's a cliché, but that's what happens. Her cheeks actually sag. Her mouth gapes.

"I could have known more about *them*."

"What are you talking about? What do you mean, *them*?"

"My half sisters and brothers." Harper says it like that to shock her, and it does. Melinda's face turns red. "Didn't you know? You could look. You could find out."

"Harper, I didn't want to. This, you, us, it had nothing to do with anyone else. Science is not family."

"Oh yeah?" Harper thinks of Dario, his goofy self, kissing Walter's cheek at Green Lake. His-her-Wyatt's-Simone's eyes. Eyes feel like family. Dario's crooked tooth does. "They look exactly like me."

"Oh my God, Harper, what have you done?"

"What have *you* done?"

"I was trying to protect you. Us. Against all this needless

143

emotional . . ." Melinda waves her arms around, at a loss for words. "As you can imagine, these were very difficult decisions. . . ."

"Well, I can't imagine, actually, because you never told me any of this." Ezra's words pop out of her mouth. "*Forty-two children. So far.*"

Melinda puts her hand to her head. "I'm going to be sick. Oh my God. You should have told me. You should have told me you were looking. . . . Forty-two? How do you know?"

"Some are right here. Some are only miles away."

Silence. Silence and then her mom's voice gets all wavery, and she reaches out a hand, but Harper doesn't want to think about *her* vulnerability right now. "Honey. Honey, we could have been doing this together."

"Exactly." Now Harper's face is hot. She's so mad, she could sob. Or so sad, she could rage. Or else go cold for the rest of her life.

"Let me help you. I can . . . look into it further. Put some protective boundaries around it for you. Make sure that—"

"It's too late for that. It's way too late. We're going to go see him."

"What? No. No, we're not. Absolutely not. Harper, that's just not going to happen."

"Not we-we. *We, we.*" Oh, Binx would have loved that.

"Forget it. And who is *we* exactly? What in God's name have you been doing?"

"We. Me and a couple of the sibs. We're taking a trip." She makes it sound casual. Like they have way more of a relationship than they do. Somewhere in there, she's decided to go. It's one of those large, brave/reckless decisions you make when you just want to show someone, a *so there, fuck you!* Her mind has decided, without her full permission. Still, she doesn't know how she's even going to get to the airport, let alone onto a ninety-thousand-pound petri dish that doesn't belong in the sky, and over the threshold of a condo where other people will see, hear, and smell the evidence that she's an actual human being with a body.

"You're not taking a trip. First of all, I can't even afford a trip anywhere. For one of us, let alone both. Second, I'm *working*. I can't just take a vacation during summer quarter. And what about *travel*? It's not *safe*."

Airport handrails, public bathrooms, those trams where all the people hold on to the pole. Panic builds in her body, and she tries to beat it down.

"People are traveling! You're not coming, and I've saved a ton of money from babysitting and summer jobs. Plus, Wyatt has air miles, and his parents have a condo in Hawaii."

"Wyatt? Hawaii?"

"That's where he lives."

"He?"

"Beau Zane."

When she says his name, she sees it: Melinda recoils. She blinks, like a missile is heading straight at her.

CHAPTER FIFTEEN

Dear Mother—I expect to be boarding a steam-ship to Boston in the next few days. You and Father and Isabella and the boys will be a glori-ous sight, and so will our dear city, in spite of the dreaded smallpox. Since we departed Lon-don on February 23, our thirty-one days at sea have been ill-fated, with calamity after calam-ity. Frightful squalls awaited us when we hit the open ocean, and one sailor, our dear John P. Kearn, lost his grip and fell to his death from the topmast. You may be sure it was a solemn scene, kneeling by him and praying. We did everything that could be done, for we were both very attached to him. His body was decently dressed and wrapped up in a canvas with iron weights, and the captain read the funeral ser-vice, and his body was committed to the great deep. The squalls continued, bringing sleet and hail and lightning, and on the twenty-third of March, the topmast of *Neptune's Car* was struck by lightning and splintered, burning several of the crew. The men were confined to their bunks for the remainder of the voyage as I tended their wounds with liniments and oils. So close to home, with already heavy spirits, we were fog-bound for three days, until a tug, the *Huntress,* brought us in. On the way the jibboom of the *Adriatic* became trapped in our moorings, damaging the bowsprit. We limped into port, all wearing a melancholy appearance. I don't know how I shall ever rid my mind of these days. To see our figurehead, the great King Neptune, injured seems a terrible omen for our next voyage.

Mary Ann Patten to her mother,

Elizabeth Brown

New York, March 28, 1856

YOU CAN MAKE THE SOUND OF A UKULELE PLAYING HAWAIian music by pinching your nose rhythmically and humming, which is something Harper was not aware of until Dario demonstrates it when she FaceTimes him on Monday morning. They have plenty of time to talk, since she's walking to school. No rides from Ez anymore.

"So, Wyatt will fly in a few days early. They're already on summer break. You and I will go together, and Simone is coming later that day. Wyatt will—hey, are you listening?"

"Yeah. 'Simone is coming later that day.' I got it."

"You're looking all around. It's distracting. Like when people check themselves out in the little square the whole time, fixing their hair and trying to get the best lighting."

"I'm sorry. You're right." She *was* looking around, searching for Ezra's car on the street and in the school lot, but not seeing it. Ezra seems so suddenly gone. A huge part of her daily life, and then, poof, not. Oh God, her heart is actually aching.

"Are you okay?" Dario asks. His face is right up close to the screen, as if he's trying to get a better view. "Oh man. You were looking around for *him*. This has got to suck. All this find-your-sperm-donor right during a breakup . . ."

Harper has barely told Ada and Soraya the breakup details. She called them, sure, finally she did, last night, before they heard it from anyone else first. She cried, and they listened. But when she talked to Dario after that, she confessed how she made Ezra go on that hike, and how she stupidly thought she and Ezra were going to *last*. Dario—well, his own relationship experience is pretty limited, a crush on Nathan Benowitz in the fifth grade, and a few dates with Elizabeth Gary last year, including a home-coming dance, but he said all the right things. *It* will *last,* he told her. *No matter what. Plus, you never know what the future holds.* Somehow this concept is more comforting than terrifying coming from Dario.

"Hey, we'll talk more later? I'm here at school," Harper says.

"Watch for the ticket," Dario says. "No one checks their email, so check your email."

Harper doesn't see Ezra in the halls, either, when she lingers outside his Algebra II class. She doesn't see him by his locker, even though she passes it, like, fifty times. It sits as still and as closed as Ezra's heart apparently is. As cold and gray, too, locked with a secret combination.

"Jax said Ezra wasn't there during the algebra final," Soraya says at lunch.

148

He wasn't there during the final? The one they studied so hard for? This is terrible news, but maybe proof of his own heartache. "Oh no."

"'Oh no' is right. And Mr. Deon is such a butt about makeup tests. We should ask Trace if he's okay."

Soraya is already texting Trace. Ez and Trace and the rest of their group have second lunch. It's just Harper and Soraya and Zoe Marshall, this quiet girl from band, at first lunch. Zoe is heading over with her sack lunch.

"I hope he's all right," Harper says. Her eyes fill with tears, and Soraya hugs her right there in the cafeteria, as everyone eats pizza and dunks carrots in hummus and tries to lob half-eaten apples in the trash can before getting yelled at by Mr. Vern, the cafeteria guy. Harper crying, Soraya hugging—everyone will know that Harper and Ez broke up.

"Oh my God!" Zoe Marshall says as she sits down. "Did you and Ezra break up?"

Soraya's like a grandma, the way she always has Kleenex in her pockets. She hands Harper one. "Yeah," Harper says.

"Honestly? Wow. I don't get it. You two . . . You seemed so good together." Zoe opens the crinkled top of her lunch bag, removes an orange, and starts to peel.

"Really?"

"Yeah. You seem so happy. You guys are always cracking each other up, and your eyes just light up when you're with him. And the two of you on Instagram, so *romantic*."

"They do? They did? My eyes?"

Soraya shoots Zoe a *shut up, for God's sake* look and squeezes Harper's arm, because her voice is getting wavery again.

"Did *his* light up?"

"*So* up," Soraya says kindly.

"I mean, I'm in shock right now," Zoe says. "He was devoted to you. I don't get it."

"*I* get it. I was awful."

"Everyone is awful sometimes. And not awful. Both," Soraya says.

It seems so forgiving, to think of yourself like this.

"It's going to be okay." Soraya rubs Harper's back in a circle. *It's going to be okay* is a statement Harper has never understood. Not when there's so much evidence to the contrary.

By the end of second lunch, Trace has texted Soraya, and Soraya has texted Harper. Ezra is just *taking a personal day,* definitely Trace's phrasing. He's the president of Future Business Leaders of America and is always using terms like "metric" and "leadership" and "measurable results." He's an unlikely friend for Ezra, but Trace is kind, and he's the first guy Ezra met when he moved here.

When Harper gets home, her resolve crumbles, and she calls Ezra, but his phone is still off. She thinks about going over there, but it's Stalker 101. He can't just disappear, can he? Like Mr. Wong, here one day, gone the next? Harper still has his sweatshirt, and his copy of *The Alchemist,* and that Valentine bracelet he gave her with their initials, and his favorite T-shirt with the Earth on it, and one of his water bottles, and a pair of his headphones because hers broke, and those warm socks of his that were, like, two inches thick, and his dad's old hand weights, and that big, cozy gray sweater with the cables. . . . Harper tries to remember what he has of hers, but all she can come up with is Just-Okay Bruce's backpack. She has all those photos, too. Photos and videos and more photos and videos. She starts to look at them but stops. It hurts, too, to see his sweet face. They *do* look so romantic. It hurts to realize that she remembers all the hours of posing, and choosing the images that looked best, and editing, and even some of the filters, but not much about what they did before or after. She can remember him jogging away from her, heading to various spots to get a good shot, but she can't remember him jogging back.

By the end of the day, it's there in her email, just as Dario said it would be. A ticket to Hawaii, booked by Wyatt using his air miles. Leaving in eight days, no changing her mind now. Harper prints it out and lays it faceup on the kitchen counter, a proclamation.

An act of war.

A declaration of independence. *I want to break free,* Freddie-God sang.

Harper tries to summon Freddie Mercury's fire and determination, but she only feels terror. It reminds her of that Saturday she had the great idea to paint her room when her mom had to work. She got an old paint can from the garage, a blue from who knows what century, and she got as far as the doorframe before the *Oh my God, I don't want to do this anymore* regret and fatigue hit. Her mom was furious when she got back home, and they had to spend the next two weekends taping and painting to put it back the way it was.

It's *exactly* like that. Harper's mom gets home late. She's always late at the end of a semester, working more hours as she grades finals and papers. She's tired, and her eyes are red. But she's not too tired to fling open Harper's door, her eyes wide with shock.

"What is *this*?" Melinda waves the ticket around.

"I told you, I'm going." Huh. Maybe it *isn't* like the time she painted her room. Harper's voice surprises even her. She seems to mean it.

"You can't just *go*. How did you get this ticket anyway? How can a minor just book a ticket without a parent's approval? What, a child can just walk onto a plane? There are no rules against unaccompanied minors? There are no federal regulations? The airlines don't have *policies*?"

"Apparently not."

"This is unbelievable. This is nuts! Why not just open the door and say, 'Runaways welcome'?!"

"Just as bad as the library, those airlines."

Melinda scowls, but her eyes squinch in confusion, too. Clearly, she doesn't remember getting furious with the librarian at the Green Lake branch after Harper checked out *The Stud and the Sword* when she was thirteen. Harper thought it was a fantasy novel, even though the guy on the cover had his shirt off, and had muscles that looked like the lake on a windy day, and was stroking that sword like it wasn't a sword.

"I don't understand the plan, Harper."

"I told you the plan." She did, the night before, right after dinner. She answered all Melinda's questions about finding Beau Zane's address, and about meeting Dario, and Wyatt, and Simone, all of it. Melinda cried and apologized and told Harper she'd been trying to do what she thought was best. Openness would only lead to confusion and complications, unsolvable equations.

She couldn't bear to lose her, her mom said, and so she spilled the details, too, details Harper always longed for. How Melinda had been ready for a baby, how she'd made an appointment with the clinic, how she'd gotten pregnant right away. It all felt vague, though. Maybe that's always the case when one human being is reduced to their bodily fluids, a vagueness you just have to deal with.

"You can't just go spring yourselves on him."

"Not spring, just politely approach."

"You could write a *letter*."

"I told you a million times! Simone tried. Dario tried. The emails and letters bounced back. Even the agency tried. There's no phone number that works, either."

"You don't even know this man."

"That's exactly the point."

"This . . . *Beau Zane*."

Harper looks in her mother's eyes then, straight in. Because the way Melinda said his name—it's like she knew that name. Harper wonders what she'd find if she tore the house apart. Some big file, probably, with all the same investigation the half sibs had done. Or more. *Of course* Melinda would have looked him up, too. She probably knew his name for years. When Harper looks in those eyes, she sees a wall, with who knows what behind it. She feels betrayed, frustrated, shut out. *Shut out.* Ezra's words. Was this how *he* felt when he looked into *her* eyes?

"You're willing to use all your saved money for this?"

"I'll be frugal," Harper says. Her mother loves the word

"frugal." Then Harper thinks about that time in the second grade . . . No, that time in the second, and fourth, and seventh, and eighth grade, and year after year where the longing to know her father, the sheer ache for not only the man but the answers, caused her to burst into tears of frustration and loss. "Yes. I'm willing."

Her mother sighs.

"I'm going," Harper says.

"And where's the return ticket?"

"Wyatt said everyone might have their own idea about how long they want to stay. You know, *depending*. Maybe the whole summer. We'll book it when we're each ready to leave."

"The whole summer? Harper, you don't even know these people!"

"I'm related to these people."

"Some of the most dangerous people are the ones you're related to."

She may have a point there.

"Are you *sure* they're all vaccinated? And what about traveling alone? What about *flying*?" Melinda is also scared of flying. She was terrified even before everyone temporarily stopped getting on planes, at least everyone who wanted to stay healthy. The one time Harper and her mom went to California for her cousin's wedding, Melinda took a little white pill as soon as they were in their seats, and Harper had to shake her awake when they were about to land. "Airports, Harper. All those *people*! And what about finding your way around? In *Hawaii*, where we've never been before! You've shown zero interest in the ocean! Remember when I got you that Semester at Sea application, and you changed the *e* to an *i* in 'All Hands on Deck'?"

"This is different. This is important," Harper says. "And I won't be alone, and yes, I'm sure. About all of it."

At that her mom shakes her head as if this is entirely too much, which it is. "*We* could have done this together. From here. With boundaries. You didn't have to spring this on me, too. And right during my busiest time at school." She rubs her forehead. She looks beyond stressed, and Harper starts to feel bad. She's almost ready to rip up the nonrefundable declaration.

"I'll be okay," Harper says, but it doesn't feel true. Harper believes Melinda, that terrible things are about to happen. Things she can't handle.

"I raised you. I took care of you when you were sick and hungry and awake in the night for hours on end. . . . I *sacrificed*. I carried you in my womb for nine months," Melinda says.

"I hate the word 'womb.' Plus, isn't that a lyric from one of your Alanis Morissette songs?"

Melinda folds her eyebrows down. Harper's flip comments make her so mad, but her mom doesn't see that they're armor, not ammunition. It's taking so much courage not to back down that Harper is fighting the urge to cry. "You're mine, is the point," Melinda says.

"I'm mine." It sounds brave, but Harper isn't. Being Melinda's is easier, for sure.

Her mom is silent. She fusses with stuff on Harper's dresser, moves her earrings around to form the shape of a pyramid. Finally she whispers: "I don't want him to know anything about me."

Harper feels stricken. And stupid. And thoughtless. Because this isn't just about *her*. It never even crossed her mind, but that vial of sperm Melinda purchased in order to have Harper—it went into her mom's body, and that's intimate, no matter how it happens. That sperm came (ugh) from a man Melinda thought she'd never have to deal with again.

But wait. Those words also mean that Melinda is giving in. Harper's getting her way. It seems too easy. Much easier than she ever imagined. Her mom is letting her go away on a trip alone with mostly underage people she doesn't know to stay for an undetermined length of time to meet a strange man. How is this even possible? Guilt is how it's possible, Harper thinks. Lots of guilt.

"I get it," Harper says.

"You do?"

"Yeah. I won't tell him about you."

"Not even my name."

"Yeah, I understand."

"Promise?"

"Promise."

"And I want the phone numbers of everyone. Your, uh, relations, and their parents. I want to talk to the parents first, too. We all need to . . . maybe be in touch while you're there. If any of them, *this,* feels off or weird or wrong, I have veto power."

"Fine, fine! I already told you, Dario's mom Reba is great. His other mom, Dana, sounds great, too."

She's silent. "And don't like him better than me." Melinda tries to make it sound like a joke, but Harper knows it isn't.

Harper can see her worry. So much worry. She sees all that her mom has given, too, and then she understands it's not just guilt that allows her to take this trip. It's the biggest wave again, the biggest fear: loss. And her mom sees the possibility of that loss, off on the horizon. A person will do anything to avoid that, even let three teenagers, one semi-adult, and one dog go to Hawaii without proper supervision, for months, maybe, to a dangerous land of unknown siblings, and maybe-wild parties, and rough tides, and men who might break your heart.

Harper takes a photo of her mom's suitcase, open now, Harper's bathing suit casually draped over one corner. *Casually* takes her about a half hour. Redoing it all in better lighting takes another half hour. Editing it takes another half hour. #summervacation #beachvibes #Hawaiibound #maui #arewethereyet #gooutdoors #liveyourbestlife. Palm tree emoji. Wave emoji. Sun emoji. Beach umbrella emoji. There is no absent father emoji. Or little family emoji with forty-two siblings, or emoji where half of you is a question mark.

She's about to post, but there's something she has to do first. She calls Soraya, finally.

"I was just going to call to see how you were doing," Soraya says. "Do you need me to come over? We could eat ice cream straight out of the carton like they always do in the movies."

"We only have vegan almond milk, and I know how much you love it."

"I'd bring you whatever you want. I still can't believe you guys broke up."

"Me neither." The words "broke up" make Harper's heart jab with a fresh bolt of sorrow.

"I saw him when I was walking home."

"Ezra?" Oh God. She wants to know everything. Or maybe

nothing. It's hard to tell. She feels that dull ache in her chest again, the one that spreads outward and feels permanent, and she has that anxious feeling of something bad about to happen, even though something already did.

"He was mowing their lawn with one of those push mowers."

She knows the one. Adam bought it for fifteen bucks at a yard sale. "He was? Did you talk to him? How is he?"

"He looked awful. He could barely speak. I mean, he was carrying Binx on his back, and Binx's arms were locked around his neck, so that may have been part of it."

"What'd he say?"

"Not much. I just told him I knew about you guys, and he shrugged, and then Binx kicked Ezra's sides with his heels and said, 'Fasta, donkey.' And then he said he had to go."

Awful—that was good news. A *shrug*—bad. "Ya Ya?" This is Harper's love name for her friend. "I'm actually calling to tell you something else."

"God, Harp. What?"

"It's something that I should have told you a long time ago, but didn't, and I need you to understand even if you might be mad."

"Okay."

"And it means that I am going to take a sudden trip for I don't know how long, so I'll probably miss our girls' camping weekend, and—"

"Tell me!"

Harper can barely say it. No wonder she waited so long, really. It sounds made up, and the first time she tried to tell Soraya, Soraya cracked up. It's ludicrous, and horrifying, and semi sci-fi. The number forty-two. Seeing her own face again and again.

Dario and Wyatt and Simone and the others on that poster, names Harper has studied since Dario sent a copy. Roland and Sean and Max and Griffin. Chloe, and Savannah, and a girl, Amalie, who's only in kindergarten. Not knowing anything about Beau Zane sounds so wrong. Hawaii sounds like an irrational plan. Being gone for maybe the whole summer—ridiculous, let alone disappointing. A ticket to meet a stranger who helped make her—downright dangerous. "Are you there?" Harper says when she's done.

"Wow, Harp. Wow. I'm so sorry I laughed that time you mentioned it. I thought you were joking."

"Don't be sorry. Of course you thought it was a joke. It's weird."

"It's . . . fascinating."

"Normal isn't fascinating."

"Who's normal?" Soraya says. "My cousin has a photographic memory. My uncle collects trains and wears a conductor's hat. And hey, my mother didn't know her father, either. He left before she was born, and bam, no idea."

"Really?"

"He's always been a mystery. Heck, mine is, and we live with him. I don't even really know what his job is. His business card says 'Certified Registered Central Service Technician.'"

"I stopped listening after the second word."

"Something medical. And honestly, Harp, I don't know what he does in the garage all those hours. Why didn't you tell me any of this, though? God, you sounded so scared just now, I thought you were pregnant or something."

Harper laughs. Wow, what a relief to laugh. "It's . . ." What? "Embarrassing. I feel . . . like an oddity. Wrong."

"Secrets make a lot of things feel wrong."

"How'd you get so wise? You're like an old Buddhist monk in a girl body."

"It's just common sense."

Which, of course, is never really all that common. "I love you."

"I love *you.*"

"Still?"

"Oh my God!" Soraya shrieks. "*Now* is when you're weird."

Harper presses *post* on the suitcase photo. She hopes Ezra sees it. It might be the point, for him to see it and call her. She indulges in a great fantasy: Her phone rings. *This is really brave,* Fantasy Ezra says. *I totally understand why you never said anything! Secrets make a lot of things feel wrong. Do you want me to come?* Fantasy Ezra offers. He drives her to the airport instead of her mom or some strange Uber guy. They ride in the plane together, and he whispers reassuringly, and holds her hand when the brakes make the alarming screeching sound upon landing. He tells her that over forty-five thousand flights land safely every day. He does the rental car stuff Harper has no idea about. It all gets a little hazy after that, except for her and Ez in matching Hawaiian shirts, and doing that thing you see romantic couples do on TV, where she has her legs wrapped around his waist in the ocean.

None of these things happen. But after she posts that photo, the likes pour in. The comments, too: *So lucky. Maui is the best. Love your suit. I'm going in Sept.! Cooool. Jealous!*

Ezra is silent. Harper looks up his social media accounts. Nothing. Only the same four photos from last year. She takes her gratitude journal out from under her mattress. She crosses out *MF* and writes Beau Zane's name above it. She looks up *reunions with sperm donors.* She reads about people like her, of all ages. She reads about awful, egomaniacal doctors in the 1960s, doing bad stuff with turkey basters. She sees some guy who goes on vacation with his offspring every year. She sees the same eyes and the same noses and foreheads in their group shot. None of it is giving her the answers she's truly seeking, the ability to read the future, the reassurance that all will be okay, which is probably, 90 percent of the time, why we Google stuff. Harper looks up *professional divers.* She looks up *men who are sperm donors.* She looks up *personalities of professional divers.* She types, *Who works in dive shacks?* And *qualities of people who live in Hawaii.* Also, *Hawaiian Island Life.* She asks the oracle of Google, *Do absent fathers want to know their children?* And then, *Do absent fathers ever think about their children?*

Almost immediately after, she gets ads for Invicta dive watches. Ads for borrowing money at low rates, too, and ads for Hilton Hotels on Maui, and designer water shoes. She uses the emergency-only credit card her mom gave her and buys a T-shirt that says ALOHA STATE OF MIND. She regrets using the emergency-only credit card to buy a T-shirt that says ALOHA STATE OF MIND.

The next day Harper carries that papier-mâché mask to school. The two painted faces of Viola stare up at her: Viola as the helpless female, and Viola disguised as a male, capable and brave, after being shipwrecked on the shore. The half smile her mother managed to paint before she was caught makes Viola the helpless female look uncertain. When Harper remembers how in *Twelfth Night,* Viola loses her twin, Sebastian, when their ship splits in half during a terrible storm and then sinks, she remembers, too, how the sea is a wild and perilous place, a place where bonds can be destroyed, and her stomach twists with doubt and uneasiness.

She's glad not to look at it anymore. The face Viola is, versus the face her dire circumstances required her to be. The helplessness, versus the resilience. Those two sides of one girl are right next to each other on that mask. But inside Harper's body, in the Viola that is her, an unknowable voyage separates them.

CHAPTER SIXTEEN

Dear Mother—It was such a brief visit, after so long at sea! And now *Neptune's Car* is ready again, with a new set of masts, rigging, and a jibboom. Joshua has shown great generosity with the installation of a special innovation, a gimballed bed, installed for my comfort in replacement of the fixed berth. King Neptune has been repaired as well, even though I continue to see in my memory the damage that was done to him and to our crew.

Joshua is eager to further enhance his reputation and, confident of the *Car*'s sailing qualities, has declared his intentions to beat *Romance of the Sea* and *Intrepid* round the Cape to our common port of San Francisco. However, I am feeling an unease that cannot only be attributed to the oppressive heat, or to our trusted first mate, still in the hospital with a broken leg. Perhaps it is only memory of our so-recent calamities, and the news of the plague in China, as well as the 2,300 men taken by the plague over the last months in the shipyard of Portsmouth, where our ship was built. Or perhaps it is due to Joshua, who has suddenly been feeling poorly. He has an unrelenting headache, pallor, and weak appetite, which he assures me is certainly from the exhaustion of readying the ship.

Mary Ann Patten to Elizabeth Brown
New York, June 27, 1856

AFTER SEVERAL PROLONGED GOODBYES WITH REBA AND Dana and Harper's mom on their front lawn, where Harper's mother whispers, "Be careful, honey, and use the credit card if you need to," into her ear and hugs her hard, and then after more goodbyes at the airport with Dana and Reba, it's just Harper and Dario on the flight over. Harper and Dario and Walter, who's in a crate in the cargo hold. Harper is worried about him down there. What if he's hot? Or has to pee? Or is thirsty, or scared? She tries to keep her mouth shut because Dario's worried, too.

"I wish he could be here with me as my support animal, but we're really each other's support animal," he says. Because they have their masks on, she can only see his concerned blue eyes. "Pretty much like most dogs. I wonder what he's doing in there. I wonder what he's thinking."

"He's thinking he can't wait to get to Hawaii," Harper tells him. She's pretty sure this is what an older sister would say, but she also wonders if Beau Zane has some anxiety in his family tree. Then again, who isn't anxious these days, after endless months of worrying you might die, plus Lyme disease, global warming, white supremacists, and so much more? Well, maybe white supremacists and those people who never wore masks but still escaped the consequences aren't anxious, but she and Dario sure are. Every time there's a moment of silence, Dario tries to fill it, like nervous people do, or else he's just excited.

"What are *you* thinking?" he asks when Harper is gazing at clouds. He let her sit by the window, since he's been on airplanes more times than she has. The aviation gods have smiled down upon them and a seat is empty, so they have the row to themselves.

What is she thinking? He doesn't want to know. A swirl of Beau Zane and rejection and the way that wing is wiggling and the cartoon people going down the waterslide on the plastic card.

"How crops look like beautiful quilts from above," she says.

"I'd give anything to meet certain famous people in history," Dario says.

"So you mentioned."

"Did you know that Teddy Roosevelt was blind in his left eye due to a boxing injury?"

"I do now."

When she remembers "This Toxic Fat Will Make You Gain Weight" and "These Seemingly Innocent Signs Could Signal Serious Disease" that she read while waiting to board, she reaches for her phone to make sure there are no other unknown threats on the horizon. She feels the rectangle of it in her bag, but, that's right, she can't use it anyway, unless she pays for internet access. It's weird, how it's just a lump of metal and useless parts when it's turned off. Instead she cleans off their seats and their seat belts and tray tables again with her antibacterial wipes, glad for the jillion packages of them her mom gave her. Now their row is sterile enough for anyone's emergency appendectomy. She feels that tidy, superior sense of calm you get when you've put things in order.

After a while Dario teaches her how to play Snap, the card game. When she wins the Snap pool, it hits her that she's playing cards with a sibling for the first time in her life, and her heart blooms like a flower in one of those sped-up nature movies. She also learns that Barack Obama once worked at a Baskin-Robbins, and that John Tyler had fifteen children.

And when the brakes make the alarming screeching sound upon landing, she lets Dario squeeze her arm. She tells him that over forty-five thousand flights land safely every day.

Harper is grateful to be alive and to find herself in a tropical island paradise. She's only been to California before, but everyone on social media seems to go so many places, and here she is, doing the same. The air is different—it has the most calm, warm balminess, and palm trees are everywhere, and they tick-tick-tick in the breeze. *Breeze,* because even the airport is open to the outside, which seems wild and carefree when you come from rainy Seattle.

Her phone is already buzzing with texts from her mother and Soraya, and Ada, too, a flurry of *ARE YOU THERE,* and *HAVE YOU LANDED,* and *Tell us everything,* and *Hope you have a great time.* Wyatt's also texting now, since he's picking them up, and Harper wishes she could take a hundred photos to post even in the airport, but it's all a little frantic, trying to find their way as Dario bumps into her, rolling his suitcase and holding Walter's crate at the same time. Walter seems totally great after the trip, peering out the door grate with his sweet black marble eyes. Harper navigates to TAXIS, where Wyatt said he'd be, leading them like she knows what she's doing. Since Dario is following, she has no choice but to lead, even if she herself is lost. All at once she wonders if Ezra felt that way with her.

"There he is!" Dario says.

"You might want to lower your voice an octave," Harper says, but she's excited, too. People really *are* wearing Hawaiian shirts, which seems so confidently flamboyant and untroubled, and some even wear leis, too. Flowers around your neck—how cheerful is that? There's a serene warmth all around, and the tiny hint of a floral scent, and yeah, there's Wyatt, nodding his chin toward them in acknowledgment, standing in front of his mom and dad's SUV.

"Hey, you guys," he says. He arrived a few days ago, as planned, and he has a freckle tan starting. Once again he's wearing expensive-looking clothes, khaki shorts and a white shirt, rolled to the elbow, and dark sunglasses he doesn't take off. Harper feels the stranger-ness of him, the way he has his hands in his pockets all casual and self-assured, but then she notices the tiniest quarter-moon of sweat under his arms.

"Let me see your eyes," Dario says, getting to the point. Wyatt removes his glasses and then smirks, as if Dario's already being a pain in the ass, which he kind of is. Dario goes in for the hug, thwapping Wyatt on the back. Harper gives Wyatt an *oh my God* look, even though she loves Dario so much right then.

They get in the SUV, Harper and Wyatt in the front like a

mom and dad, Dario in the back. When they're underway, Dario lets Walter out, and Walter starts jumping all around the car, and Wyatt says he can't see, and Harper says, "Wow, wow," at everything. She's taking photos out the window, sending them to her friends and her mom, even posting a quick one, as Wyatt says, "This is just the freeway. We're not even there yet."

And then they *are* there, and Wyatt is right. Oh man, this trip is already worth risking her life for, because Wyatt's condo is like a house out of a magazine, and the condo complex has two pools and a swim-up bar, and maybe God is a woman because they each have their own bathroom, connected to their bedroom by a little hall. Wyatt's staying in his parents' master bedroom, which opens onto the beach through a set of sliding doors, and Dario is in Wyatt's usual room with a bed and a couch and his own TV, and Harper and Simone, who hasn't arrived yet, are in guest bedrooms, with large windows with views of the ocean. Just like Wyatt's parents promised Melinda, there's a security system, smoke alarms, an on-site manager, and neighbors who Wyatt knows, too, should anything go wrong.

"OH MY GOD, THIS IS AMAZING," Dario shrieks as Walter sniffs around, examining end tables and potted plants, his toenails clicking on the cool tiles.

"Make yourself at home." Wyatt tosses his keys onto the counter like a pretend grown man, which he isn't entirely, since he just graduated. And then Wyatt gets a beer out of the fridge, opens it, and takes a swig. Sure, Harper understands, they're all nervous, but she hopes he isn't going to make a habit of underage drinking, or underage drinking and driving, or underage anything else, since rebellion like that is nerve-racking. They're right smack on the beach, and are pretty much screwed if there's a tsunami or a volcanic eruption, too, but the place is beautiful.

Harper unzips her bag and takes off her Seattle early-summer clothes (leggings and a T-shirt) and puts on real summer clothes (shorts and a tank top). She pads around in her bare feet, taking more photos of everything, and posts three others right away, bird-of-paradise, palm tree with pool, ocean with palm tree. #paradise #maui #islandparadise #summervacay #relax. The likes and hearts are pouring in for the green mountains she snapped while still in the car—her followers are going to love this temporary island-y change-up. Her mom has already commented, *Beautiful, honey!* The world in her hand has followed her here, too.

Harper takes out her gratitude journal, the one that now sports Beau Zane's name, and she sticks it under her Hawaii bed. She texts a photo of her room to her mom, with a tossed-off *We're here!* The bubbles of reply start up immediately, but Harper ignores them. She types out a text to Ezra, attaching the bird-of-paradise, because this is all stuff he needs to know. *Here in Maui, and it's INCREDIBLE, and I wish you were*—she deletes it. Being away from home makes him feel even more distant. So much new stuff has happened already that the space between them is growing alarmingly.

Out in the beautiful living room now, with its bamboo furniture, Dario emerges in his bathing suit. Oh geez, blue with yellow sharks, and you'd never know his moms had a bakery, he's so thin, and it's possible the sun has never made the acquaintance of his chest before. "Let's hit the pool!" he says.

Wyatt busts out laughing. He just cracks up in a way Harper would never expect, so much light in his eyes.

"What?" Dario says.

"Nothing, bro," Wyatt says, grinning.

At the word "bro," Dario flushes, so pleased. Harper always thought blushing stopped at the face, but now she knows that you can blush right down to your bony collarbone.

CHAPTER SEVENTEEN

> We will set sail tomorrow, in the early hours of the first day of July, for our fifteen-thousand-mile voyage. Joshua has made every exertion within the bounds of prudence to ensure a quick passage, even while feeling terribly unwell. Abel Nickerson has insisted we not delay our departure for either illness or lack of crew. He has suddenly assigned William Keeler from Philadelphia as our first mate, in spite of Joshua's protests. He knows nothing about Keeler or his abilities, making this a very uneasy proposition.
>
> Mary Ann Patten journal entry
>
> June 30, 1856

"TOMORROW?" THERE'S HORROR IN HARPER'S VOICE, AND even she hears it.

"Well, I didn't come to just sit around the pool," Simone says, cutting a piece of grilled fish with the edge of her fork. Only someone who gets to do that a lot would have used the word "just." And besides that, none of them have sat around this particular pool with these particular people before. Harper could do it for weeks.

Wyatt grilled the fish, and the corn, too, and he made a salad, because he can cook, who would guess. They're eating late, almost nine o'clock, because after Simone arrived, after Harper and Wyatt got to meet her in person for the first time, they all walked the beach, swam in the ocean, and then played Marco Polo in the pool. Sometimes they split off, Harper talking to Wyatt, hearing his story, how he found out, how he sensed he was different from his brother, and then Harper talking to Simone, about the mural project she's doing with homeless teens in Berkeley, or books they both like, or about Simone's annoying roommate. And then they'd be a group again, swimming, splashing, and messing around. It's so fun that Harper forgets about the dangers of drowning and jellyfish stings and broken glass in the sand and the rising temperatures in our oceans. She even forgets Ezra, and Beau Zane, too, the supposed reason they're there.

"I thought we'd try bodysurfing." Dario presses a finger to his pink skin and watches it turn white.

"Dude, I told you that you were getting sunburned," Wyatt says. "You need, like, a two hundred SPF."

"*We* need a two hundred SPF," Dario says.

"You definitely don't need more beach time tomorrow," Simone says.

"Well, maybe we could just, uh, get to know the area at first." Harper drops a bit of potato to Walter, who decides he loves potatoes, communicating that fact by sitting up even straighter. "See where he lives, check out the dive shack from a distance, before we go launch ourselves on him."

"Like, spy!" Dario's eyes light up.

"You guys are chickening out." Simone plucks a papaya chunk from her plate with her fingers and then pops it in her mouth.

"We're bonding beforehand. Bonding is a good idea, so we'll have mutual support," Dario says. This sounds like it came straight from his moms.

"*They're* chickening out. I'm not," Wyatt says, walking over to the grill to make sure it's turned off, which he's done twice already. He doesn't look anxious when he does it, just confident and easy, though maybe it's the espadrilles.

"How cute, the way they have that in common, the chickening," Simone says.

"Yeah, like we have the bottom tooth that sticks out," Dario says.

"I have a bottom tooth that sticks out." Wyatt pulls down his lip to demonstrate. Sure enough, one steps forward like the bravest soldier on the front line.

"Braces," Simone says. "No idea."

"Can you guys do that tongue thing?" Dario pops his out and then folds it together.

"I can." Simone does it now. With her hair all pulled up semimessy, and her blue eyes more sparkly in person, Simone is beautiful, even with her tongue out. So beautiful that Harper still feels shy with her.

"Yup." Wyatt demonstrates.

"Same." Harper too.

"That'll get us far in life," Wyatt says.

"I can also wiggle my toes." Dario takes off a flip-flop for better viewing. Sure enough, even his baby toe waves.

"Nah," Simone says.

"Maybe that's a learned thing," Wyatt says.

"No one exactly sat around and taught me." Dario can be a dweeb, but assertive on his own behalf, in a good way. "Wait. Do you guys have Darwin's tubercle?"

"God, I hope not," Simone says, and they all laugh.

"Sounds deadly," Harper says.

"Or just painfully chronic," Simone says.

Dario lifts up his hair, shows them an ear, and points at a little bump on top.

"That gets a name?" Wyatt makes a face.

"Darwin thought it was because people's ears used to be pointy. Like, early man, or woman. Did you know that Darwin and Abraham Lincoln were born on the same day?"

"Negative," Wyatt says.

"Cool, and yes," Simone says, feeling her ear. "I think I have it. Do I have it?"

Harper leans to look. "Yeah." She aims her ear Simone's direction.

"Yup," she affirms. "You too, Wy. I can see it from here."

"You can see it from ear," Dario says, and cracks himself up.

Wy—it seems like an awesome nickname to have, Harper thinks, because *why* just about everything. Also, how amazing to get a nickname. From a half sister. It seems like you'd be on your way to sharing clothes next, and talking about how messed up your parents made you.

"They say if you have it, you're better at identifying noises, or hearing high-frequency sounds." Dario's hair is back down. The big day of travel has caught up with Walter, and he's curled up next to Dario's talented feet.

"Like bats," Wyatt says.

"Whales." Simone lifts one eyebrow.

"Now that's something I can't do," Dario says.

"What?"

"Your eyebrow."

"I didn't even realize I was doing it," Simone says.

"I can't do it, either." Harper tries, but both go up, per usual.

"My dad does it," Simone says. "But, my God, are we done talking about body parts yet? I say we go cruise by his house."

Harper swears her heart stops when Simone says it. They all knew who she means. His, He—it only refers to one godlike entity. Godlike, because God was supposedly an unseen being who created stuff, a complete enigma. "It's eleven o'clock," Harper says.

"Will you turn into a pumpkin at midnight?" Simone says. Harper's embarrassed. She feels like a child. She feels like . . . the little sister. "Just to check it out! You didn't go see it already, did you, Wy?"

"I promised I'd wait until we could do it together, so I waited."

"What Harper means is, it's late," Dario says. "We've had a big day. A big day of travel, and meeting in person, and swimming, and I have to call home still."

"I'll get the keys," Wyatt says.

The road out there is dark, so dark. The only lights are from the car dashboard, Dario's phone, and the green, alien glow from Walter's night eyes.

"What'd she say?" Harper whispers.

Dario just texted Dana to say he'd call tomorrow, and Dana just texted back. In seconds, same as you do when you're waiting by the phone. "She said, 'Have fun.'"

"'Have fun'? That's all? My mother would have asked a jillion questions. My mother *will* ask a jillion questions." Harper had lied and sent a *going to bed, all is well* text.

"They want me to check in, but they also want to give me the freedom and space to have a positive experience," Dario whispers back. "They trust me."

"You two okay back there?" Simone pops her head around. You know, to the back seat. This was one of the first things that happened on this little escapade: Harper's demotion to the back, with the oldest up front.

"We're fi— YIKES!" Harper screeches as the SUV smacks another unexpected pothole and her head nearly hits the top of the car.

"Sorry!" Wyatt sings. "Dirt roads, what're you gonna do."

Where is his anxiety when they need it? The pavement stopped a long ways back, and that sign, PRIVATE ROAD, was a long ways back, too. For miles there's only been the crunch of gravel under the tires, the sudden lurching from holes and dips, and the dark, dark midnight of the sea out there.

Dario rolls down his window.

"Hey, dude, the air conditioner," Wyatt says from the back-in-the-old-days father seat.

"No, it's nice," Simone corrects from the back-in-the-old-days mother seat. She rolls her window down, too, and Wyatt fusses with the knobs. The cool whooshing stops, and warm, tropical air blows in. The moon illuminates the ocean, turning the water a spooky silver blue.

"No wonder you can't reach the guy," Dario says.

"This is about as far south as you go on this island." Wyatt squinches in the darkness as the headlights bob and weave.

"Your destination is on the right," the GPS lady says.

"You don't know what you're talking about," Simone says.

"Hey, we come here every year," Wyatt replies, all touchy.

"I meant her, not you!" Simone points to the GPS. "Where's the house?"

Wyatt pulls over to the side of the dirt road. The only things Harper can see are scrubs of palm trees and the silver-blue ocean, and the big, white moon, and the brightest blanket of stars you can imagine.

"We've probably passed some driveways, but it's too dark to even—"

"Shh!" Dario says. They shh. "Hear?"

"Boats?" Harper guesses. Because, yeah, you *can* hear something, some deep beat rumbling, some high-pitched sigh coming from the direction of the sea.

"Whales?" Simone asks hopefully.

"Creedence," Dario says.

"Creedence?" Wyatt asks.

"Creedence. Like, Creedence Clearwater Revival. Reba loves them. Her own mom used to play them when she was a kid. I think it's 'Bad Moon Rising.'"

"Oh my God, how did you hear that?" Simone asks.

"It's my Darwin's tubercle," Dario says, and they all bust out laughing.

"We can't see anything from here. I'm getting out." Simone already has her door open.

"Oh my God, you can't!" Harper says. There's checking

something out, okay, fine, but then there's creeping around someone's house in the dark. He, Beau Zane, half maker of them, is probably in there. If he hears them . . . It isn't Harper's idea of an awesome first meeting.

"We didn't come down that fucking road at midnight to just sit here listening to Creedence Clearwater Revisal." Simone unbuckles her seat belt.

"Revival," Dario corrects. But then he shouts, "SPY!" and opens his door.

"I thought you were on my side." Harper wants to pinch him. She's got years of pinching to make up for, along with cries of *He did it first!* and *Stop annoying me!* Walter hops out, too, and now they're all heading down the pitch-black path, the four of them and one dog, looking like the cover of the Boxcar Children's *Island Mystery*. That is, they look like that until Dario starts playing air guitar.

" 'There's a place up ahead, la la la . . . Just as fast as my feet can fly!' " He leans back on his heels and does some mean riffs. Or something.

"You play?" Wyatt asks.

"Nah, but I taught myself harmonica," Dario says.

Right there on that path, with gravel in her sandal and a warm wind playing palm-tree keys, Harper learns something new about ultraconfident, semianxious Wyatt: he's kind. One look at Dario playing air guitar, and you know Wyatt's being generous, because no way, not in a million years, does Dario look like he plays guitar.

Simone is skipping down the path. "OH MY GOD, YOU GUYS!" she says way too loudly, gesturing madly with one arm.

Dario and Walter trip along toward her, and then Dario waves his arm, too.

"We're going to get arrested," Harper says as she and Wyatt catch up.

"SMELL," Dario whispers, dangerously loud now, because there it is, the house. A one-level, mid-century modern, only without the modern. The house is set on a long stretch of grass, and there's a pool, underwater lights on, the water all spooky and still. A ledge of rocky lava leads straight to the sand. The house, okay, it's a little rough around the edges. But that setting, wow. The house is mostly dark, but music thumps inside.

Harper sniffs.

"WEED!" Dario cackles.

And then, oh no, Simone starts laughing, and so does Harper, and Wyatt, too, and because it's late enough that anything is hilarious, let alone this whole situation, them, the ridiculousness of them, standing there in the dark with their matching hair and eyes and foreheads, right outside the house of their—wait for it—pothead sperm donor, they lose it. All of them. Snickering and trying to keep quiet, and bending in half, busting up, socking each other, and Dario even accidentally snorts, God. God, Harper laughs so hard, her stomach starts to hurt, and then she tries to say, "Shh! Shh!" but it has no authority. It just sounds like a snake laughing.

A new song begins. Same people, Creedence, high-pitched and pounding. *I hear hurricanes a-blowing.* "No worries, they're not gonna hear anything over *that!*" Simone says.

And then, right then, a light pops on. A floodlight, a huge, blinding white.

"OH MY GOD," Simone whisper-shrieks. They clutch each other, and as one entity they lurch behind some—well, who knows what it even is, because their eyes have been zapped with a laser glare—rock, maybe, a big clump of foliage. They hunker down, crowded together like a nucleus of cells. Dario is on Harper's foot. Simone's elbow is jammed in her side. The hot breath of Walter's *huh huh huh* is right by her neck. She can feel Wyatt's shoulders going up and down in a strangled laugh, and Dario's stomach going in and out, doing the same. It's like a slumber party, when you play that game, Sardines, where everyone smashes in to hide in the same spot.

They stay there, shoulders, stomachs, elbows, parts of a whole, until the light turns back off.

"RUN," Simone says.

And they do. They race back to the car, giggling like mad, and then they tumble in, sweaty, nerve-racked, kind of high them-selves, giddy from hilarity and almost getting caught.

"Oh my God, I peed a little," Simone says.

They crack up anew.

Wyatt throws the car into reverse, and the tires spit gravel. The windows are still open. Harper's breath, her complete in-the-moment joy, is just catching up to the rest of her when she looks out toward the ocean. She spots something. It's hard to see entirely in the dark, but the moonlight catches a raised arc out there, giving the crescent of rock a silver gleam. The light from space makes it look like an alien ship, submerged.

"What's that?" she asks.

"The island?" Wyatt says. "Molokini. It's the top of a vol-cano."

She almost feels magic entering her body at the word "Molokini." Or maybe it's the sight of that crescent that does it, the top edge of that sunken structure. She gets a similar flicker as love at first sight, with that potent sense of familiarity plus thrill. Harper knows she's going to have a relationship with that place. She knows it right at that instant. She can feel her heart trip.

She doesn't hear what's under there, though. Under the water. *Ticktock, ticktock.* If this is love at first sight, it's the kind where the new person is menacing, and the relationship dangerous, only you don't know it yet. You're taken in by the beautiful smile but don't see the troubled history hidden beyond it.

And then she searches around in her pockets. First one, then the other, then a mad scramble in her handbag. She shoves her hands down into the fold of the seat and hunts on the floor in a panic. Pure panic, like she's lost a limb. She reaches toward Dario's side now.

"What'd you lose?" Dario asks.

It seems like the right answer is *everything.* Or else, *my whole life.*

But then her fingers connect with the cool, rounded edge of her phone, and relief floods in. Huge relief, the kind of relief a mother might feel spotting her lost child in the cereal aisle. But then again, what does Harper know about what a mother might feel? The point is, disaster has been averted.

"Nothing," she says. "Found it."

That night when they get back, Dario goes straight to bed. Simone and Wyatt stay up late to talk. In her room Harper pulls out that gratitude journal. In the back she writes, *pot, Creedence, beach house.* She writes *Molokini,* but the word alone doesn't capture how that place made her feel. She tries to draw it—a crescent of an island, under the crescent of the moon. This is what they did long ago, right? Ancient people? They didn't have the words or the answers, or the ability to type a phrase into the ever-flowing internet and be rewarded with a jillion facts. They didn't explain, explain, explain with descriptions and hashtags of the thing itself. #island #moon #crescentmoon #crescentisland. They had scratches and markings, a drawing on a stone or a cave wall, and those had to tell the entire story, those had to speak to the mystery, and the drama, and the unknowns of all the big questions and feelings. Eons later we see that hunter chasing after the antelopes and understand the wild and perilous quest of staying alive. Those drawings spoke, plainly. Those spoke with a powerful and timeless silence about the wholeness of it all.

CHAPTER EIGHTEEN

We were barely underway, a matter of hours, when the captain's reticence over William Keeler was proven correct. Keeler is sullen, and orders of simple tasks must be repeated to no avail. This is terribly worrisome, since Keeler will be tracking our daily position, course, and speed. The heat is so oppressive, too, that my garments confine me unnaturally. I must loosen them somehow. The voyage stretches with ominous length ahead, and there is nothing to be done but mark each day of its completion.

Mary Ann Patten journal entry

July 1, 1856

IT'S TRICKY, BUT IF HARPER GETS ON HER KNEES NEXT TO the patio table, she can get the rainbow triumvirate of papaya, pineapple, and melon on that white plate, with a palm tree in the distance. She has to clear off the scrambled egg bits, and a cement grid is forming on her knees, but it's worth it. Her posts of this trip, wow, the likes keep pouring in. Sunsets, beach, sand, swimming pools, palm trees, God, an *extravaganza* of likes. She doesn't even have to try that hard. It all looks beautiful and shiny and perfect just like it is, and people are hungry for it, she can tell—to be somewhere they aren't. To be *someone* they aren't, a pretend someone in an enhanced place. It all spells escape. It all shows life, if life were perfect, and who doesn't want that. Who doesn't want to *believe* in that.

Her camera roll now has four lines of nearly identical shots, and as she scrolls, she can see that the pineapple only gets progressively less shiny. The first and second shots are probably the best, which happens pretty often, to be honest. Saturation up, vibrance up. #fruit #paradise #paradisefruit #Hawa—

"Harpo!" Wyatt calls.

"Just a sec!" she calls back. She doesn't even look up, because pineapple. She presses *post*, too hurriedly, and, ugh! She accidentally chose shot four and not shot two. The saturation is up too high, and the pineapple looks neon, no color of any true pineapple in nature. She wants to delete, but three people have already liked it. Harper's so focused that she almost misses what just happened.

He gave her a nickname.

Now when she *does* look up, there he is, Wyatt, standing in the doorway, freshly showered, in his stylish navy bathing suit and white T-shirt. His clothes look expensive, yeah, but he also just looks like Wyatt. The minutiae of pineapple vanish. The saturation angst does. Who cares about hashtags when you just got a nickname.

"Are you okay out here?"

She's not sure. She's smiling like a goof, but she feels choked up, too. "I was just . . ."

"You've been out here forever. We need you to break a tie."

"What's going on?"

"Simone and I want to go over to Captain Neptune today and see if Beau is there. Dario's gotten all nervous about meeting him since this shit got real, so he and Walter say not yet."

"Dogs can't vote," Harper says.

"Walter's a person."

This makes her like Wyatt even more. Man, you can really misjudge someone just by how they look.

"Good point."

When Harper follows Wyatt back in, Simone is already dressed to go, sundress on, sun hat, straw bag on shoulder. She sits in one of the wicker chairs, but you can tell she's impatient, the way her foot is rocking. Dario is in his shark bathing suit and tank top, smelling like coconut lotion, Walter in his lap.

"Okay, one more time," Simone says now that Harper is there. "Who votes Captain Neptune today?" Simone raises her hand, as Wyatt lifts his. "All right, who votes not?"

Dario lifts his arm and Walter's paw.

"Harpo, you have to vote," Wyatt says.

"I'm thinking."

"You can't please everyone all the time," Simone says, zeroing in on the problem.

"Okay, okay." Harper usually just goes along with the consensus, which makes tie-breaking extraordinarily precarious.

"What do *you* actually want?" Simone asks.

"Me?"

"Jesus!" Simone exhales in frustration.

Ugh! Harper wants what they want! She wants them to be happy, and happy with her, and searching for her own real answer is harder than you'd think. She imagines herself going, she imagines herself not going . . .

"Come on," Dario says. "I want to find a spot on the beach before it gets crowded."

"Right. This is all about the beach," Simone says.

"I can't help it! It's one thing to be brave when you're imagining it in your mind, and another when he's *right here.*"

"Harpo!" Simone barks. She can be kind of harsh, that's for sure.

"Captain Neptune," Harper says, and cringes, waiting for Dario's upset.

"Oh man . . ." He shakes his head at her, the betrayer.

"How many times do I have to say this? You don't have to come! Come when you're ready," Simone says.

Walter squirms out of Dario's arms. He trots over to Simone and gazes at her with love.

"Goddamn it," Dario says. "I can't believe this. Walter, geez."

"Relax, Dar. You've got his heart, I promise. I just gave him cheese this morning."

"Cheese love is not real love," Dario says.

"Profound," Wyatt says. "But if you had my mom's lasagna, you'd disagree."

"I have to change," Harper says.

"Whyyy?" Simone groans. "You look fine. You look great."

Harper makes a face. Her sundress doesn't feel adequate at all, not for actually meeting Beau Zane for the first time.

"Okay, fast," Simone says.

Back in her room, fast is impossible. Harper puts on the dress and heels she planned for their first meeting, but she feels like she's going to some job interview, and the stiff shift dress is all wrong for Hawaii. The heels hurt. Whenever she's worn heels in the past and her grandma or some guy would comment on how they look like they hurt, she's always told that girl-lie: *They're actually really comfortable.* But they're not. *What do* you *actually want?* Simone asked, and wow, here it is again, because does she even *like* heels? Or dresses? She never thought to really ask herself this. They're just what you do. *Girl, you can do hard things. . . .* Well, no, you can't, not wearing high, uncomfortable shoes and a tight dress. She yanks off the heels. She *doesn't* like them, especially not after wearing sandals and walking around in bare feet. She does like dresses, but loose and comfortable ones, light and airy ones, not that tight thing.

When she comes back out, she's wearing the same thing she was before. No one says a word. Maybe that's because Dario now has on a bright white T-shirt, along with his shark trunks, and Simone has ditched her sun hat and has pulled her hair into a ponytail. Wyatt has changed from a T-shirt into a polo with a collar. Harper's willing to bet that the other thirty-eight kids would have had a clothing crisis right then, too.

They let Dario sit in the front as a concession, like you do with a grumpy kid. Harper holds her phone as they drive because its weight and presence can be comforting, like a blankie for grown people. A phone can come to your rescue, too, especially in socially awkward moments. Once, at Ada's older sister's party, when Harper didn't have anyone to talk to, she pretended she got a call and had to take it outside. She stood around by their rhododendron hedge, moving her lips. More times than she can count, she's acted like she was reading exceedingly important and involving texts that needed her undivided attention, when they were threads going back years, or just a bunch of ferrets on National Ferret Day, or mustaches on National Mustache Day, or ice cream cones on . . . Well, you get the idea. Her phone is her escape and her excuse.

"It's just a couple of blocks from here," Wyatt says, looking at them in the rearview mirror with his hot-shit sunglasses on. "We can park in this mall, because parking is tough on the main drag."

"You said you didn't check it out before. You promised," Simone scolds.

"I didn't! I've been here a million times. You can't exactly miss this place."

"I'm going to throw up," Dario says.

"Seriously? Roll down your window, dude," Wyatt says.

Harper rolls hers down, too. Her stomach is swimming with nerves.

Wyatt parks in a strip mall in front of a shave ice place, next to a Safeway and a nail salon. They all pop out of the car.

"Hey, do you guys wanna—" Dario looks longingly at the rainbow heaps of shave ice.

"Forget it," Wyatt says.

"Maybe he won't even be there," Harper says.

"We'll know soon enough." Simone glides on a new swipe of lip gloss. Her mouth looks as slippery and shiny as a peach slice. But the shine seems scared, not bold. Simone keeps adjusting her sundress that doesn't need adjusting.

The main drag of town is busy enough that Dario has to hold Walter so he doesn't get stepped on. The long days where people stopped traveling (at least the nonspreaders did) are maybe behind them, now that vaccinations are common. The smell of frying burgers wafts out from restaurants, even though it's late morning. They walk past little shops stuffed with tourist trinkets—coconut cups, grass skirts, Hawaiian shirts swinging on outdoor stands; flowy, colorful sarongs hanging in doorways; and towels in all colors and styles. As they near the beach, the shops dwindle, and the rental places start up—helicopter tours, whale watching, catamarans, and parasailing. When their feet hit sand, other rental shacks appear. Kayak rentals, windsurfing, paddleboarding, with all the boards lined up along the sand.

"Oh my God, there it . . ." Simone doesn't even finish because, yeah, there it is, all right, and as Wyatt said, there's no way you can miss it. There's a small shop, with a shaggy grasslike hut next to it, an open-air counter for rentals, but even more, there's a giant Neptune-God merman statue on the beach out front. He's huge, with a pierced fork and bulging muscles, and with CAPTAIN NEPTUNE, SCUBA & DIVE painted on his pedestal.

"Wow," Dario says.

"You didn't mention *that*," Harper says.

"After a while, you kind of forget to see it," Wyatt says.

Dario's eyes swivel from the flowing hair and impressive six-pack of the statue to that outdoor counter. "He's there."

"Or someone is," Wyatt says.

"It's definitely him," Simone says.

Oh God! God, he is! Harper really feels sick with nerves now. They've only seen that long-ago photo of him from the file, but he's got that same grin and boyish handsomeness. And he's got a cocky confidence that allows for hair experimentation, too, because Beau Zane, human man, not a god, a regular dude, has longish auburn hair that's stuck up in a—gasp—man bun. He's helping a guy in a full-body wet suit and fins, handing him some scuba gear. Oh, Harper's mother would just die, seeing him there behind a counter, looking sort of worn and weather-beaten the way people who spend a lot of time near the sea do. His blue eyes—Harper can see them even from this distance—are vivid and flashing, and his tan face features some pretty strong smile wrinkles around them from all those days in the sun. He, *the* He, the giant Neptune-God merman of their own lives, former owner of the victorious swimming sperm that created the four of them—he looks like a surf bum. An old surf bum, who might still use the word "radical." Up one wrist are several hemp bracelets, and he's wearing a T-shirt with a turtle on it that says PUT ME BACK IN THE SEA.

"Why are we doing this again?" Wyatt's face has gone pale. All these years of mystery and longing, and here he is, a man.

The customer in the wet suit turns and heads toward the ocean, like a creature returning to its watery home. The four terrified people standing there like timid children in front of an ice cream counter move forward as a group. As they get closer, Harper spots a kombucha drink on the counter, along with a Styrofoam container holding a half-eaten breakfast burrito with a fly buzzing around it.

Dario notices, too. "Eyuw," he whispers.

Now there's nothing between them and Beau Zane, the real and actual person who gave them life.

"Welcome to Oz, dudes," Beau Zane says jovially. "Can I help you find something?" It's the first thing he ever says to them. For a moment Harper has no idea *why* he says that, until she realizes: the four of them, plus Toto-Walter, arriving at the gates of the Emerald City. This makes him the wizard, though, right? And can he help them find something? Courage, a heart, home? They all sure hope so.

Something is happening, though. The big smile is rapidly vanishing. Beau looks from Dario to Harper to Wyatt to Simone, and back again. His mouth drops open, enough that Harper can see the silver shine of a filling in the same spot she has one. It might be her imagination, but his tan does an instant fade.

Dario steps forward as their Dorothy. He even has a little quiver in his voice, but he's wearing shark trunks and flip-flops instead of a gingham dress and ruby slippers. He obviously knows, too, that Beau was referencing Oz, because he says, "The great and powerful Beau Zane?"

Beau Zane has gotten serious, fast. He knows. Somewhere inside him, he does. "Um, have we met?"

"Well . . ." Dario shrugs.

"If you're here for, uh, dive lessons, I can, uh, hook you up, but there's a waiting list."

"We're not here for dive lessons," Wyatt says. It sounds wrongly confrontational.

"We've tried to call and write," Simone says.

"I don't have a cell phone. I think the web has an old number for the shop, but we never . . . People pretty much know us, and just walk up, and—oh fuck." Beau rubs his forehead, then runs a hand over his man bun.

"We . . . We are all your . . ." Dario's face is red.

"Oh fuck," Beau Zane says again. "I always wondered if this might . . ."

"You were a donor at the Lakeview clinic?" Wyatt asks. He still has his police investigator tone.

"Oh fuck," Beau Zane says a third time. He moves things around on the counter, a cup of pens, some credit card thingy, that glass bottle of kombucha. "I mean, a good fuck! This is a good fuck, not a bad one!"

Oh God, he's trying to be nice, but it sounds all wrong. Harper's already worrying about telling this story to her mother. *And then he said, "This is a good fuck, not a bad one!"* Ugh!

"I mean, this is great, right? Wow. Just wow." He's shaken. The poor guy. It really is an ambush, but what were they supposed to do?

"Wow," Dario echoes.

"It is . . ." This is what comes out when Harper tries to speak. *It is,* but nothing else.

"Are there . . . ? Is it just . . . ?" Beau Zane shakes his head, as if it's a malfunctioning Magic 8 Ball. Swiftly the message in the triangle changes from *You've Got to Be Kidding* to *It Is Certain.*

Dario understands his question. "Forty-two," he says. "In total. So far." Dweeby Dario is merciless, dropping this information like a bomb.

"Oh fuck."

"Is it *still* a good fuck?" Wyatt asks.

"Absolutely," Beau says, nodding and nodding. "Absolutely, absolutely." He pauses. "Absolutely." It sounds like they broke him. "Wait. Let me come out. . . . Let me get out. . . ." He's rattling the knob of the hut's door, but he's having a hard time getting it open. "Shit," he says. "Shit. This thing . . ." He leaps over the counter instead, but it's awkward. He scrapes the back of one leg on the way down, and has to say, "Ouch!" and check for bleeding before he's with them on the beach. Any idea of him as the great and powerful Oz vanishes. He has his swim trunks on, too, and they're a faded blue, and his tan legs end up in a pair of beat-up sandals. The great and powerful Oz would next ask them to prove their courage, but this doesn't happen, at least, not yet.

"I wanna . . . Oh shit, I feel like I should . . ." He reaches toward them as if to hug, but no one steps forward, and so he just looks like one of those Jesus statues, with his arms out. "It's okay. Yeah, no. Hey. I don't know what to do here. This is fucking surreal."

"We just wanted to meet you," Simone says. She's licked off all her shiny lip gloss, and she looks so vulnerable standing there in her sundress that the bold young woman in her ethereal online photos could be another person entirely. She looks like a girl. One who could get very hurt. One who very badly needs him to say the right thing.

"Of course you did. Of course. Hey, I totally get it. I wanted to meet you, too. I've been dying to meet you."

In Harper's body it's as if an old wound opens up and relief pours in. She badly needed him to say the right thing as well. And he did. In some ways those words aren't much, but in some ways they're everything. In some ways, or at least by some crucial people, acceptance does matter. By those crucial people, acceptance, the idea of you, yourself as acceptable and worthy of love, is everything.

CHAPTER NINETEEN

Across the horse latitudes, the wind is light, and Joshua has given strict instructions to keep all sails up. His headaches continue, and so does his exhaustion. To add to our troubles, on this fourteenth day of our voyage, Second Mate William Hare has reported that he found Keeler asleep in the chart house at change of watch. Keeler is also an indifferent navigator, and his neglect of duties transfers extra care and watchfulness to the captain, when he is increasingly ill. It is exceedingly worrisome. I sit by, helpless, as my sex and youth require me to avoid everything masculine, and to be only the light of our home, now this ship. Yet, I can feel the peril on the horizon.

Mary Ann Patten journal entry
July 13, 1856

SOMEHOW THEY AGREE ON A PLAN. THEY'LL ALL TAKE A day to metabolize the news (Simone's word—you can tell she's been in therapy) and then meet the following night for dinner, at Beau Zane's house. His *mother's* house, he clarifies. Things get complicated in your mind and fast in this situation, because Beau's mother is technically Harper's grandmother, and the wider web of networks and questions just spins out of control from there. How many more pseudorelatives are there? By the look of Simone's MyHeritage account, *a lot.* Are they really relatives? What makes a relative? Wouldn't every single human in your genetic line, going back to the cavemen, be a relative? Why are the most basic things—identity, family—so hard to pin a definition on?

Harper's worried about going over there for a million reasons, but Dario handles a big one, with a swaggery, faux-casual *Hey, you guys vaxxed?* which is utterly humiliating yet relieving when Beau Zane says, *Yeah, man, of course.* Beau gives them the address for the house they already visited the night before, and when he does, Dario edges his foot toward Harper's and starts to snicker like a six-year-old who just heard a butt joke. And then Harper starts giggling like an eight-year-old sister. When Beau Zane tells them that the road can be hard to see because of all the *weeds,* Dario lets out an outright *Ha!* Beau's eyebrows go down at these mostly-strangers he might never understand.

When they get back to the SUV, that shave ice place and the nail salon and the Safeway all look different. It's all somber, even with clanging carts, and little kids with purple mouths, and tourists on vacation. No. *They* are somber. Harper carries a weight of emotion in her chest, but she can't define it. It isn't the thrilled excitement she was expecting. She feels embarrassed at Dario's "vaxxed," and a creeping shame that she's failed already. But even more, she feels *sad.* It's hard to tell if the sorrow she feels is because something is ending or is starting or is simply disappointing. Because, well, there he was. The guy. There were his/her blue eyes and his/her auburn hair; there was her origin story in beat-up sandals.

None of them are as changed as they hoped as they stand there by the car, Wyatt *beep-beep*ing the locks so they can get in. And, oh God, her mother really would die. After all her canceled relationships, after all the guys who never seemed good enough to be a father to her future child or a stepfather to her child, they now have Beau Zane, who doesn't have a cell phone and uses the word "dude" even though he's old. His fingernails were a little long. Bordering on icky long. That fly had landed on his breakfast like a small plane on a burrito island, and he didn't even notice, or care.

No one really speaks on the car ride back. Well, Dario says, "Walter, *move*," because Walter is standing on his legs in order to stick his nose out the window, and Simone says, "Should we just bring home chicken so we don't have to go out later?" and Wyatt says, "Nah, let's go out later," and Harper says, "That was weird, that was so weird," but no one replies.

When they arrive back at the condo, Simone carries her shoes inside, like a weary guest after a party, and Wyatt says he needs a nap, and Dario decides to go read by the pool. Everyone needs some space with the big thing they all shared. The bigness is larger than the shared.

Harper changes her clothes, as she sometimes does when she needs to shake off a hard feeling. She puts on her favorite old shorts and a soft tank top so they can offer their nonjudgmental compassion. She looks at that notebook but can't bear to write any details, the burrito, the good fuck, the giant Neptune statue with the muscled chest, the silver filling. Beau Zane, the answer to the mystery, clearly doesn't fill that empty space that she thought belonged to him, because here it is again, aching. Oh God, it's *still there*. She's as echoey and searching as ever.

She sticks the notebook under a bunch of clothes spilling from her suitcase. Maybe she doesn't need it anymore. Maybe not knowing *was* better than knowing, as her mother believed. At least then she could still tell herself that he could make every-thing better.

She takes her phone and a towel to the beach. When she passes the pool, she sees Dario on his phone, telling Reba and Dana about meeting Beau, she guesses. He gives a little wave, and Harper waves back. She spreads her towel out on the sand and applies a new layer of SPF 50. Her mom has sent a bunch of texts, which she ignores. Soraya has sent a few, too, and she ignores those as well. She normally hates Twitter, because a tweet about a parent's stroke can sit right next to one about ketchup, and because it can seem like a noisy party where it all becomes one loud sound, but she checks it. It's the best place to see ur-gent news, like if your government has been attacked again while you were meeting your sperm donor, but nope. There's only been another shooting at another mall and another earthquake in an-other foreign country, and someone hates a TV show, and some-one else hates that person for hating that TV show, and someone else is announcing they are taking a social media break, but no one cares.

Harper checks her Instagram account, pushing the little heart next to every single comment and giving out generous love and acceptance to prove to herself that she's not a cynic. The surf seems rough. Little kids are playing in it, too far from their parents. In the distance a riptide warning sign pokes casually from the sand. Harper takes a selfie with a grass hut in the back. #paradise #exhale #vacation #relax. She hopes that the people in that earthquake are okay. Where was it again? She's already forgotten. The sky gets hazy, and suddenly a warm, soft rain comes down, and then stops as quickly as it arrived. She sends a brief text to Soraya. *Dad meeting went great. More later!* And then watches Ada choose the perfect shade of foundation. She reads about an infestation of some gross caterpillar, the One Major Way You Could Be Eating Bananas Wrong, and the World's Volcanoes That Could Erupt at Any Moment, scrolling fast past Chile and Martinique to get to the Hawaii ones. When this gets too terrifying, Harper watches a cat swatting a TV cat, a guy falling off a skateboard, a pug wearing a bunny hat, a girl dancing in a bathroom mirror, a girl dancing in a bathroom mirror, a girl dancing in a bathroom mirror.

This sounds like one of those nauseating things on canvas art, but while she watches the endless swiveling in various bathrooms around the country, she might have missed a rainbow. When she looks up, she sees the last bit of it, fading.

Harper wants to cry but doesn't know why. Which now sounds like bad poetry, but so what. Whatever. She worries that *whatever* is a permanent state.

That night the four of them minus Walter go to a barbecue place. It isn't far from Captain Neptune. Restaurants are open again here, but they all head to one of the outdoor tables, where it's also cooler anyway. Out of their individual Styrofoam containers, they eat messy ribs, and an igloo of potato salad, and a spongy roll. Simone downs, like, three beers in a half hour and starts talking like her tongue has a knot in it. Wyatt picks a fight with Dario about leaving a tip or not in a place without full table service. Dario reminds him that his moms own a place like that, so Wyatt can shove it. It makes sense, him being especially protective of his moms right now. They all wanted Beau Zane to be part of them; they put themselves out there for it. Instead they got the fact of their strangeness to each other, and a reminder of where their true kinships lie. It's hard to put words to the big lump of feelings that they're passing around tonight, just like the stack of napkins. Maybe they all just needed too much from Beau Zane. They wanted the instant Oz magic and got the fumbling man with the levers.

"Why are we so morose? We haven't even given the guy a chance," Simone says. *Shansh,* it sounds like. "He didn't do anything wrong. He was perfectly friendly. What do we expect, jumping on him out of nowhere—a parade?" *A phrade,* it sounds like. Afraid.

"Maybe it was just all the f-words," Dario says prudishly. He's never been a prude before now. He let out a stream of profanity himself when he stepped into the too-hot shower that very morning. Harper heard him through the wall.

"It felt sad. The breakfast burrito," Harper admits.

"Don't be ridiculous," Wyatt says. "That fly thought it was delicious."

They crack up.

"Think of your regular day, and someone comes out of nowhere and judges you on that," Simone says. *Shushes you,* which is maybe what Harper wants to do to her. Simone's words don't even make sense all the way, but enough sense that Harper starts feeling bad.

"We're not judging him. We're just taking in information," Dario lies.

"There are flies here, too, you dicksss," Simone says, and waves one away. She's maybe going to be an angry drunk.

"A dick shouldn't be a slur," Dario says, his lips pursed.

Under the string lights, around this table, there's so much feeling, it seems like anything could happen. A bad fight, bad enough to destroy the new and fragile thing they have, is sitting right here as one possibility. Simone is pissing Harper off, too.

"You're right, so sorry. Give *all* genitals the respect they dessssserve!" Simone says loudly, and two guys eating ribs look over at them.

"Let's get out of here," Wyatt says.

They toss out their trash and, without speaking, amble their way to the beach. Not just the beach. To the Captain Neptune shack. They stand in front of the giant, bare-chested Neptune-God. Dario shakes the sand out of his shoes. The beach is quiet, except for a few couples strolling, holding hands, and the ever-present crashing of the surf, which roars in and shushes out, as the palm trees tick-tick-tick in a breeze, and the grass on the now-closed-up hut roof whispers. Moonbeams alight on the tips of the Neptune-God's spear and merman tail. Some beachgoer has balanced two shells on his nipples. It makes him look ridiculous. It deprives him of his majesty. Tacky majesty, but still.

Wyatt tries to hop up onto his tail but can't quite reach.

"You can hoist me," Dario says. He's the smallest, so it makes sense.

Simone and Harper spot from below as Wyatt balances on the

tail and raises Dario. He removes the shells and then flings them away as if they're something offensive.

They may have felt disappointment after their first meeting with Beau Zane. But right now it's clear that they all feel protective of him, too.

Simone runs off toward the water, like a tipsy sprite, holding up her sundress and kicking around in the waves. The rest of them follow and watch the moonlight sprinkles dance on the ocean. Out there Harper notices a dock she didn't see that morning, cordoned off with a thin, trusting chain, where dive boats are moored, bobbing uncertainly and banging into each other.

"Come back, it's rough out there," Wyatt calls to Simone.

She does. The hem of her sundress is wet. "It's beautiful here. Isn't it beautiful?" she says. The cold water has sobered her a bit, softened her as well, or maybe the night itself has.

"Did you know that whalers in the olden days could actually hear whale songs? Those ships were quiet. The enormous hulls were like amplifiers," Dario says. He doesn't only know about presidents and history.

"You're so smart, Dar," Simone says.

"No kidding," Wyatt says.

These people, these half siblings, they are all smart. But they are something else, too: kind. They are kind. God, Harper hopes that kindness is passed down in their DNA, too. It *is* beautiful there. There on that island, there with those exact people.

It's late, but Harper can't avoid it any longer. Telling her mother about Beau Zane is somehow proving her right. It's confirming what she seemed to believe—that Melinda is both all-knowing and all Harper needs.

Her mom picks up on the first ring. "Well?"

"You're up late."

"How was it?"

"It was a lot of things. Weird, mostly. You wouldn't have liked him."

She's silent.

"Kind of a beach bum surfer type, but old."

"Are you coming home, then?"

"No, Mom! We just got here! We maybe want to stay the whole summer, no matter what happens with him. We're supposed to have dinner at his house tomorrow."

"Oh. Wow."

"Are you okay?"

"I guess so. Are *you*?"

"Yeah. I'm fine. Everyone's so cool. It's great."

"I'm glad, honey. I am! Really. I've been so worried. This is a lot to handle. I just hope you have the support you need."

When she says stuff like that, Harper starts to doubt she has the support she needs. She can suddenly feel like she's falling without a net. But nope. There she is, just sitting firmly on the bed in Wyatt's condo. "Yeah, I do."

"Did you see your grades? Calculus?"

She totally forgot, honestly.

"Well, A minus. There's always next year. You did your best."

She *did* do her best. But why is *You did your best* so often an expression of failure? Of missing the mark? And it's weird, how little she cares. You can care so much about something, be downright obsessed with it, and then, boom, nothing. How *can* she keep caring, caring, caring about getting into an impressive college? How can she keep up that intensity constantly, huh? And *why*? Is her one single future so important that she has to destroy herself for it? And *calculus*? Come on, people are dying in whatever place that earthquake was.

"Oh hey! I wanted to tell you, too. I saw Yanet at QFC today."

Harper's stomach drops. It seriously feels like an elevator with a cut cable. Oh God. Yanet and all her lovely warmth appears in Harper's memory, bringing a hard pang of longing with it. Suddenly she misses Ezra so bad, it hurts. Sweet, wonderful Ezra, who used to love her before he found out who she really is. "What'd she say?"

"Oh, I didn't talk to her. I just saw her. She had her hands full. Her baby was eating a cookie and waving it around. I'm sure she hadn't even paid for it yet."

"QFC . . ." She's about to tell her mom that QFC gives those away to kids for free, so stop judging. Harper knows, because she made a few trips there with Ezra and Binx, but what does it matter. "So, you didn't talk?"

"She just looked at me with sad eyes, like we shared a mutual grief."

Harper feels awful. She can only imagine what her mother's eyes said back. Harper misses all of them so much—Ezra and Yanet and Adam and Binx. Nudo, too. She misses the crumbs all over Binx's chubby cheeks as he ate those cookies, and the way Ezra would wipe them away with his thumb. Heartbreak washes over her anew.

They say good night. It isn't until after they hang up that

Harper realizes it. Her mother didn't ask anything about Beau Zane. Not a single question. Harper's sure now that her mom has already investigated him. She probably knows stuff they haven't even found out yet.

Harper scrolls on her phone. Videos of a baby giving the finger, a cat in a lobster costume, a soccer coach falling through a net. There's an article about the dangers of tree nut allergies. A twenty-year-old died in a freak accident while hiking. Another new and especially deadly variant of the virus has been found.

When she goes out into the living room, they're all there. Dario sits on the couch, and so does Simone, and Wyatt's in a chair. Their heads are bent down as they look at their phones, even Dario's is, his thumbs typing fast. They don't even glance up. Everyone is in their own world, and she wants them to be in this one, with her, right now. *Stop that!* she wants to shout. *Stop that right now! Be here!* But she's one to talk.

CHAPTER TWENTY

While on the quarterdeck to check the *Car*'s speed and course, Joshua found Keeler asleep on his watch. The third mate, George Kingsley, was in poor command, with the ship under shortened sail, when the wind and weather were most conducive for making the run. Joshua was enflamed with fury, like never I have seen him, and the men shouted, in hearing of the crew. William Keeler will be relieved of his duties if he continues this disobedience. He has been warned. How we will manage if this happens, however, I have no idea.

Mary Ann Patten journal entry
July 20, 1856

"MARGARITA?" GREER BRODY MCCLURE OFFERS. MOMENTS before, she disappeared inside the house, followed by Walter, and now they've emerged again, Greer holding a tray of the green drinks, even though Dario looks young enough to be in junior high. They're sitting around that pool outside, waiting for Beau

Zane to appear, their butts hanging down in those old, worn lounge chairs. "He's changed his shirt three times," Greer says, holding the tray out to each of them. "He's trying to figure this all out. It's a shock, a lot to take in, you know, when you're just going along like normal?" She wears a large, forgiving muumuu, and she has the kind of body she seems to have made peace with, droopy boobs, generous arms, so different from Harper's stick-thin grandmother, who only eats dessert on her birthday, leaving the frosting behind.

There's that particular grassy tang in the air, pot again, and it's hard to tell if it's from Beau somewhere inside the house, or from Greer herself. Greer's hair is pulled back in a long gray braid, but her eyebrows are still the same auburn that Harper and her siblings share. Her eyes are a gray blue, while theirs are more similar to Beau's eyes, a vibrant hue. Greer's face is plain, no makeup, again so different from Harper's grandmother, with her circles of rouge and penciled brows, and Greer's face is wrinkle-etched, a map with winding country roads. She seems like she's lived a lot of life. Maybe a hard one. A wedding ring on a chain is looped around her neck, and her house has maybe lived a hard life, too, with outdated furniture, a tilting drainpipe, cracks in the cement by the pool. Greer's feet are bare, but they reveal a play-ful side, each toenail painted a different color so that her foot is a rainbow. "So, where're you from?" she asks.

For the second time. Harper's mom might be right about pot's effect on the brain.

"As we said, the three of us are—" Wyatt looks so corporate in this environment. Or maybe, with his white shorts and blue polo, he should have a clipboard, like an uptight cruise ship ac-tivities director.

"Oh! I already asked that." Greer sets the tray down on a small outdoor table, which is layered with a thin green-brown grime, and then tosses her hands up. "I'm nervous, too." She smiles, like she's okay with this. Harper, on the other hand—not so okay. She feels like a teacup trembling on a saucer. Fragile, delicate, about to spill. She sits on her hands so they'll stop shaking. That green-brown grime is such a reminder that she's sitting in a stranger's backyard, and that strangeness sits around them, tense and breakable. "So that took some balls, kids, just walking right up to the counter like that," Greer says.

Harper takes this as criticism, and a defensive wall begins to rise. Anxiety can be a set trap, just ready to snap at every threat. She feels primed and ready for rejection. "We tried to email and call first," Wyatt says. He sounds defensive, too.

But Greer clarifies. "I admire that, your persistence. Your courage. And you found us." She scratches Walter's head as the waves roar in and crickle out again just beyond.

"I've seen your place, your business, lots of times," Wyatt says. "The statue . . ."

"Quite a hunk, huh?" Greer winks. Harper's pretty sure that no one has ever winked at her before. "Made in the likeness of my late husband, the original Captain Neptune. Beau's father, Tony." She puts her hand to her heart. "God, he was a looker. That beard. No tail, of course." She laughs. "But boy, did he ever have those fine, hard abs from all that swimming and div—"

"Hey, all."

Their eyes turn to him, Beau Zane, standing in the doorway. He smiles. His smile is so big and infectious that you feel it, and you have to smile back. He's wearing one of those old Hawaiian shirts that look beautifully vintage, with muted greens and blues, featuring palm trees and a ship on the horizon, with two hanger bumps on the shoulders. He's got two bits of toilet paper stuck on his face, dotted with blood, from where he cut himself shaving. Now *he* puts his hand to his heart. He blinks, like he might cry. "This is . . . so fucking awesome."

"Dad's shirt," Greer says. Dad—Captain Neptune. It *does* look old.

"He should be here," Beau Zane says, and all at once Harper has a father and his father, hard abs and all, a line of fathers, going back and back, where she had none before. Fathers and all of their fathery things, old shirts, beards, shoe polish, shaving cream, leather wallets, who knows what else—she never had one before, let alone so many. It's a sudden abundance. She can almost see those fathers winding through the past, a parade of previously missing men.

Beau scrapes a chair across the patio to join them. They all gaze at him, and he at each of them. It feels different from the day before at the counter, when they ambushed him. His eyes look serious, and full of feeling. "I always thought, you know, maybe one day some eighteen-year-old would show up on my doorstep, and we'd maybe just get lunch or something. But here are *four* of you, the real *yous*. . . ." He shakes his head. "And so many more I haven't even seen . . ."

"Forty-two. Minus us. Thirty-eight," Dario says.

"Forty-two." Greer whistles.

"I want to ask about them, but—"

"It's up to them to decide all that," Dario interrupts.

"Right," Beau says.

"We're really glad to see you." Simone's voice breaks. "To know you."

And with that Beau Zane bursts into tears. Big, noisy tears. He just lets them come, looking at the four kids and one Walter with his full, open, crying face. It's kind of shocking. But it's happy crying. And it's just *honest*. So vulnerable that Harper feels a lift in her heart. If this were any other stranger, so much emotion might make her uncomfortable, and, oh God, he just turned his head to wipe his nose on his sleeve, but it's a fulfilled wish. He's *glad* they're there. It makes her feel wanted.

"This is so emotional for me," he says. He presses the tears from his eyes. The toilet paper flies off like little snowflakes. Greer is sniffing and blowing her nose into a Kleenex, too. "It's a miracle. You're all a miracle." Wyatt's eyes start to brim. Harper's throat cinches with emotion. Simone just stands there, blinking, as Dario runs his hand through his hair and lets out a long exhale.

It's funny, but it never occurred to Harper before. That the miracle might go both ways.

Greer slaps her thighs, as if something has been decided, and stands up from her chair. Walter snaps to attention. They head over to the barbecue at the far side of the patio, and before Harper knows it, there's the smell of burgers, and plastic wrap lifted off salads, which are laid on a long patio table with one wobbly leg. They eat with plastic forks on Chinet paper plates, and again Harper thinks of her grandmother's house, where they eat in the fancy dining room even if it's just the three of them, a full array of silverware on each side of the plate. Here Greer apologizes for forgetting the napkins, and they pass a roll of paper towels around. The bottom of the roll is all wavy, like someone acciden-tally dropped it in water.

One at a time, at Beau's insistence, they tell him about them-selves as he listens intently. They actually go around the circle, like they're in some strange group therapy session. Harper gets nervous, and her mind spins about what to say. Wyatt goes first. He tells Beau all about his life in Mercer Island, school, sports, skirting all around the important stuff, until he edges into the part about his "origins" and how angry he was at his parents, which leads Beau to tell a story about his own dad during the summer that he and the "old man" couldn't seem to get along.

Harper watches Beau as he talks, like he's a riveting show on Bio Dad TV. She tries not to look at his teeth, which are kind of yellow, but then she stops listening to Wyatt for a minute because she gets lost looking at Beau's wrists. She likes guy wrists gener-ally, and his are strong-looking, and his arms are kind of hairy but in a good way, and when he listens, he folds his hands and leans forward as if he's praying. She has a stupid fantasy of him carry-ing her around as a child, strong arms around her in a way that would make her feel safe and happy, her long kid-legs hanging down, her arms looped around his neck. It gives her a hard hit of loss. That would have been so, so nice.

Simone goes next, and it's kind of annoying because she's bragging like wild, and she takes a long, long time, and even shows him photos of her art, lots of photos, like those annoying students who are supposed to give a four-minute presentation, but it lasts for fifteen. The art stuff leads to the story of Greer's uncle Fredo, who was one of the creators of oil pastels. These eerie overlaps keep popping up, like they've been connected through time without knowing it, and yet, now there's an Uncle Fredo added to the picture, and it's getting crowded. Maybe it feels crowded because Simone is being a kiss-ass and laughing too loud, and wow, almost being kind of flirty, trying to keep Beau's attention.

Dario talks about his moms and his big family in a way that's shy and proud and protective. Simone keeps interrupting to say stuff about Dario like she's an expert, until he glares at her to knock it off. Dario tells Beau and Greer how he wants to study history, and then Greer and Beau both gasp and look at each other, because it's another connected thing. Beau's dad apparently loved history, like, *loved,* to the point that he was practically an expert in clipper ships of the nineteenth century. Dario beams and then does a really Dario thing and starts spouting off stuff about the nineteenth century, until Beau's and Greer's eyes start to glaze over, and so Harper interrupts to take her turn. She's careful to keep her promise to her mom, guarding her privacy, but she tells him about getting the message from Dario's friend, and how this led her here. She tells him about being a junior in high school, and living in Seattle, but what else is there to say, really? She's been practicing in her head the whole time they've been sitting there, but now she just kind of goes flat. At one point Beau's eyes drift to something he sees out in the ocean, and then back again, and she feels awful that she can't keep his attention.

Her life in Seattle leads to a few reminiscences of Beau's two years at UW, how he dropped out to do what he'd grown up with, diving. And that leads to the other places he lived, the ones they discovered—Carmel, California. Key West, Florida. Port Huron, Michigan.

"Bonne Terre, Missouri," Harper says. "I really liked that name when I heard it. Bonne Terre . . . I'd want to live there." Now *she's* being a kiss-ass.

"'Good earth.' Most scary-ass diving of anywhere I've ever been," Beau says.

"Baranof Island, Alaska," Dario remembers.

"Freeport, Texas," Wyatt adds.

"Hey, you guys are good! Yeah, I wanted to dive every one of the best places that exist. I wanted to make a name for myself as a diver, like my dad did." Beau leans back in his chair, as if he's about to tell a tale around a campfire, because it's *his* turn. You can hear it, though, a hit of the same ego Wyatt has. When he leans back like that, Beau has Wyatt's confidence, or Wyatt has his, for sure. It's even in the way they move. Certain gestures. And he has this same look that Simone does, a way of tilting his head when he's being sarcastic. "You guys saw that dive shack, his business, but that's not everything he was. Tony Zane started out cleaning the bottoms of boats and spearing fish for money when he was just a kid, and then he began one of the first free-diving clubs when he was only twenty. He went on to make over *five thousand* dives. He was just a young guy when he discovered his first wreck, the SS *Josephine,* right out there. Dude won two NOGIs. Not one, *two.*"

"Noogies?" Dario says. He pretends to give one to Walter, but you can tell this isn't something to joke about.

"The highest honor you can get as a diver," Greer explains. "Think of the Oscars without the dresses. Not bad for little Antonis Zanetakos, whose great-great-grandfather, Nikolaos Zanetakos, came over from Corinth in the hold of a ship when he was twelve."

"Corinth, cool. I was wondering," Dario says. "My mom Dana was curious. *Damaskenos*. We have the food, mostly, and everyone goes to this festival they have at St. Demetrios every year, but that's about all we do to celebrate."

"Tony's father and his father—it's not like today," Greer says. "They were ashamed to be immigrants. They didn't want anyone to know. They became Zanes, no more Zanetakos. His father, grandparents, they wanted Tony to blend in. They weren't *celebrating* who they were. But his Greek would show. The swagger, the tough guy with a heart of gold, the food, the dolmades, the leg of lamb, the baklava, and then, when the music came on . . ."

"Doo da da da, doo da da da . . . ," Beau sings. He holds his hands up, snapping his fingers. "Opa! Man, I remember some of those weddings as a kid."

"Hey, I know opa!" Dario says. "I've been to those weddings!"

"Tony's mom—she had a little Irish in her, too. She died long before I met him, so I can't tell you much," Greer says. "And on my side . . . we say Scottish, but we actually lost track of who had sex with who *long* ago." She laughs. "Marriages, divorces, lots of them. If I had one of those MyHeritage things, it'd show a pie with too many slices to count."

"Hey," Simone says. "Mine too."

"Tony . . . They were poor. They all started working when they were, like, *nine*. When he got that NOGI, when he had his own business, he kept saying, 'If old Papou Zanetakos could see me now.'" She smiles.

"Big shoes to fill, wow," Simone says. Okay, she's been annoying, but she also looks like a different person from the girl with the shiny lip gloss. She looks relaxed and happy. And it *is* a relief. Here they are, sitting around all together and having a great night. It could have gone very badly, but it hasn't, not yet anyway.

"Or big scuba fins to fill." Greer chuckles. You can tell they're both so proud.

"It was *all* I wanted," Beau says. "To be as big as him. Until I came back home last year. Then something else mattered more. Much more."

They should ask what he means, for sure. But they don't. They have other things on their minds, urgent things, the large question, or maybe the second largest. No one has dared to tromp right into the heart of what they want to know. Someone this important, someone this new, maybe you don't want to scare him off. He could flee or something, who knows. It's funny how precious he is, this guy who had TP on his face. And funny how delicate he's being, in spite of his wide, sturdy wrists. The sun has set, and the ocean has turned dark, and Greer gets up to light the old tiki torches. There's one of those awkward group silences, where every single person seems stuck for something to say. And that's when Simone asks it.

"So why'd you do it?"

They all know what "it" means. Beau fiddles with his hemp bracelet. "I figured I'd never have a family myself. My career was the most important thing to me. I'm not the marrying kind. I thought I could help women who wanted to have kids but couldn't. I hoped, I always imagined . . . maybe one day someone might show up."

"But then *four* did," Wyatt says.

Beau looks down at his fingernails. Harper almost can't believe what he says next. "I hope they *all* do. All forty-two."

"Wouldn't that be something?" Greer says.

Beau Zane and his life, any life, it probably could never fit into one little gratitude journal, never.

It's getting late, and suddenly Greer's face starts looking tired. Walter has curled into a sleep doughnut, and there are longer and longer spaces between their words. In some ways Harper just wants to get out of there, to be in her own room, to be home, even, away from all these people—there's been *so much*. But she also doesn't want to leave. Here he is, this huge life person, and they've only had him for hours. And what if he's . . . *gone* after this? What if this is it? She doesn't even know what's fair to expect. If you father a bunch of kids, do they get to see you for a few hours, or forever, or what?

"We should get back," Wyatt says, though he doesn't get up. Beau Zane could have been anyone, but it turns out, he's this emotional, open, and cool guy who does interesting stuff, even if he's a little scruffy and disorganized and has flashes of ego. His family is interesting, too, and it's all so much better than Harper's dream of casino manager Beau.

"Beau," Greer says, and her eyes flicker with the lights of the torches. "You know what you should do?" She waits a dramatic beat, and they all look at her expectantly. "If you all want to get to know who he is . . ." She thumbs her finger toward Beau. "That guy, who *we* are . . ."

Beau gets it right away. "You guys wanna learn to dive?"

"Oh my God, *yes,*" Simone says.

215

Oh my God, no. No! Absolutely not! "Dive? Like, dive-dive?" Now Harper's the one who sounds broken.

Beau grins. "Yeah, like, dive-dive."

Ugh! Why is she the boring one who says stupid stuff? But *diving*? There's nothing Harper wants less. The ocean is pretty, sure, especially from a distance, but that doesn't mean a person needs to be in it or under it. Just that afternoon she stood up to her thighs in the surf, and a hard wave dropped her smack on her butt, bubbles whooshing around her head and up her nose. This is not a *feel your fear and do it anyway* situation, okay? She gets claustrophobic even watching people diving on TV. Wearing some weighted-down gear and trying to breathe underwater is against all sense. Harper *needs* the surface.

"How deep would we go?" Dario looks nervous, too. He likes his boogie board, but this is next level.

"Sure, I'm game," Wyatt says, as if this will likely be as easy as everything else is for him.

"I really don't know," Harper says.

"This isn't just who we are. It's what we *do,* every day. We certify tourists," Greer says. "You'll be in the best hands. We've been doing it for thirty-plus years. Ever since Tony decided that this place right here had a hold on him."

"Do you dive?" Harper asks. It's hard to imagine it.

"Hell yes," Greer says. "Can you swim?" She looks directly at Harper, as if maybe it's in doubt.

"Yeah," she admits.

"Eight laps? Tread water for ten?"

"Probably," she says. "I mean, in *a pool.*"

"I never swam in an ocean myself, until me and a girlfriend

216

came here on a trip. That's when I laid eyes on Tony on the beach in that little red Speedo, and now look," Greer says. "It's my life."

"How long does it take?" Wyatt asks.

"Open Water Diver certificate, three, four days," Beau says.

"That's all?" Harper is shocked. It doesn't sound nearly long enough.

"First day, coursework. Second day, pass the test, learn the gear in the pool. Third day, two open water dives. Fourth, two more, and a test, and boom. You're certified to dive anywhere in the world."

"We're in," Simone says. *We're?* You can't group–kiss ass, Harper thinks.

"All of you? No pressure, though," Beau says. You can tell he's excited.

"Yup," Wyatt says.

"I guess." Dario doesn't look too sure.

They're all looking at Harper, waiting. Those two large questions for Beau Zane . . . There's why he did it, and then there's the largest question of all: Will he like them? *Her.* Will he maybe even love her, or be proud, or just be glad that he helped create her? She wants that. It feels really important. Crucial. And, God! He stared off at the ocean while she was talking! She has to make up for her usual self already. There's a lot to prove to *all* of them. Sometimes you do stuff for the wrong reasons, until you do it for your own reasons.

"Okay." Okay? What the heck! Panic thrums. She's supposed to say no before she says yes, not the other way around! Well, she'll just have to get out of it somehow, if it gets to be too much. If worse comes to worst, she can call her mom and use the code word she gave her in case Harper ever got abducted and was able to get to a phone: "gymnasium."

"Damn!" Beau says. "This is so great. This is incredible. This is a dream come true."

They are his dream come true.

If Harper weren't sick with fear, she'd be so happy.

"When?" Wyatt asks.

"Wanna start tomorrow? Come by the shop. Around ten?" Beau addresses his mom next. "I'll have Dean take over my classes, and Amber can work the counter."

"They'll figure it out," Greer says.

Simone rubs her hands together. "Can't wait."

They help collect plates and platters and bring them inside. The house is stuck in a different era with teak tables and wicker furniture, a stereo, a stack of records Beau is flipping through with Wyatt, and a bookcase holding odd items collected from wrecks, which Greer shows Dario as they wait for Simone to pee. The house has the smell of a stranger's house, that musty something that the people who live there don't smell anymore. Harper realizes she left her handbag on the patio, and she steps out to get it. After she does, she keeps walking toward the edge of that grass, where the lava rocks dip toward the sand. She can see it, Molokini, that odd island, a crescent moon curve. It draws her. What she sees, it's the top of a volcano, and all the rest of it, its great mass, is underwater, hidden from view.

She gets that fate-feeling again, the sense that they—she and the island—have a future together, same as she got when she first saw Ezra in that Zoom box. She was sure that they'd share *more* sometime, a more of hope and possibilities, though maybe she was wrong about that, since she's now standing here alone, with no Ez in her life. Or else, they already got all the more they'd have.

"Cool, huh?" Beau Zane says, and Harper jumps. He's walking quietly across the lawn in his bare feet, and until he gets closer, she can mostly only see the orange glow of his joint.

"Yeah."

"And the most beautiful parts, you can't even see." He exhales, and the air fills with the burning-grass smell of pot.

"Is that right?"

"Can you hear them?" he says.

"Whale calls?"

He looks at her quizzically. "Whale calls?"

Why did she say that? It's so stupid! It just popped out. She's nervous all of a sudden out there, just the two of them alone. She always feels anxious when people do drugs, especially adults, even though marijuana is legal where she lives, but it's more than that. It feels too intimate out here, father and daughter, without the protective layer of the whole group. Being alone with him is nerve-racking. She shakes her head to say *never mind.* "I was thinking of something Dario said. How sailors used to be able to hear them."

"Bombs," Beau Zane says. "I can hear them in my sleep. *Tick-tock."* His eyes look slightly wild. He offers her the joint, and she shakes her head. The alcohol fumes from the tequila rise off him, too. Once again she's reminded that they don't know this guy. For the first time, Harper wonders if they should be wary of him. Or maybe even scared.

"Bombs?"

"This could all be gone. *Kaboom*," he says, exploding his fingers out like fireworks.

And then out they come, Dario, and Simone, and Wyatt, and Walter and Greer, too. Holding dishes of leftovers, hugging goodbye. Beau is jovial again.

"Tomorrow, dudes!" he says, his eyes all alight. "Tomorrow!"

CHAPTER TWENTY-ONE

A repetition of misdemeanors by First Mate Keeler have occurred. He is freely defiant of orders, and mutinous in view of the crew. He has attempted to incite disaffection among the seamen. Additionally he has set our course over reef beds! The captain has arrested him at gunpoint, and he has been placed in irons in his own cabin and will remain there until reaching our port. Joshua's headache continually worsens, and I have bathed his head in vinegar and applied mustard to his feet to no avail.

Mary Ann Patten journal entry
July 27, 1856

"IT'S TEN-FORTY-FIVE," WYATT SAYS. HE KEEPS CHECKING his phone like the disgruntled supervisor.

"It's *only* ten-forty-five," Simone says.

Dario's being annoying, rattling something in his pocket to make an irritating *click, click, click.* Harper glares at him to stop. More minutes go by.

They sit in metal folding chairs behind several long tables in the back room of the Captain Neptune shop. The whole place is much bigger than it looks from the outside. When they first stepped through the doorway next to the beachside rental counter, they found themselves in a store full of shirts and sarongs and gear, like fins and goggles. Kitschy stuff, too—snow globes with seashells in them, and key chains that say HAWAII but are made in China. The walls are a bright aqua blue and feature murals of swimming turtles. A friendly girl named Amber, who has long blond hair and is wearing what is clearly the uniform of the place—blue shorts and a blue short-sleeve shirt decorated with a tiny Neptune with his spear—waved them in and then guided them toward this small classroom. It's the employee lunchroom as well, Harper can tell, with its tiny fridge and stained coffeepot, some forgotten Tupperware and a collection of chipped mugs by a sink, and a small bathroom with toilet paper stacked in one corner.

"Raise your hand if you've ever been forty-five minutes late to anything, because I sure haven't," Dario says.

Before anyone responds, Amber pops her head in. "Everyone good? Awesome! Bo Bo should be here any sec!" She hands around notepads and pens. She gathers up all the forms they filled out, basically promising not to sue if anyone dies. Amber yanks down a white screen in the front of the room, where Harper assumes they'll be watching videos on how to succeed at the never-intended act of breathing underwater. "Just hang tight!" Amber bops out again.

"Bo Bo?" Wyatt says. "Like Bobo the clown?"

"Bobo the gorilla?" Harper says.

"Like Bo Bo Bohemian." Dario snaps his fingers to a song made up on the spot, but his eyes look stressed.

222

"Amber got a double shot of espresso." Simone makes swirls on her pad.

"This is not good," Dario says.

Dario's right. Things are definitely heading in a very bad direction. It's getting later and later, and there's no sign of Beau, and the feeling is creeping in, that he's had a whole lot of second thoughts since they left that house. Let alone those wild eyes and the bomb talk the night before. The whole evening had been going so great, *so* great, and then, wow, he was standing out there with his joint and his booze breath, sounding like those guys who live in the mountains and hoard weapons. For the hundredth time, they *don't know these people*! At all. They barely know *each other*. A panicky paranoia fills her.

"I'm just going to say what we're all thinking," Wyatt says. "What if he doesn't show?"

"Um, he's clearly not showing," Harper says.

They've been trusting. They've been hopeful out of need. And they should have known better, too. They've had tons of conversations, tons, about the various horror stories they've heard, about men who denied being donors at all, or who were angry at contact, or friendly at first and then, bam, gone. Guys who started getting freaked out that they were after money or something. Their families getting all insecure, like they were going to be the new favorite, or demand a piece of the inheritance. Beau Zane moves around every few years and now lives with his mom. He slips up on basic hygiene and doesn't even own a phone, and all that stuff he was saying last night . . . Harper couldn't even tell everyone else about it, at least not right when they got home, when everyone was so happy and talkative and excited.

Beau said that he'd *hoped* they'd show up one day, but what

223

does *that* say? He didn't want to be there for the hard parts of raising an actual child but was happy to be there for the prize at the end. Harper plays around on her phone while she waits. She posts a photo of her breakfast omelet. She posts another of ripples in the pool. She posts two others from last night: a tiki torch, the moon over Molokini. #dreamlife #Hawaii #liveyourbestlife #paradise. It's like trying to plug the holes of a sinking ship. What'll be worse, him not showing up, or him showing up, and then having to strap on some tank of air and go underwater? Or him showing up and raving about bombs again? She kind of wants the whole thing to go away. Harper watches Ada dab highlighter onto her cheeks with a sponge and leaves an enthusiastic *Looooove this!* comment. She misses Ada and Soraya, the simplicity of being together, because, so what if her life is boring? Boring is better than some dude-father hurting you. She watches a guy dive from a high ledge, a guy falling from a trampoline, a broken-nail repair, a puppy hugging a goose, a waterfall, a waterfall, a waterfall.

"Want to play hangman?" Dario asks. He's already drawn the scaffolding. Too close to home, thanks.

"Nope," Harper says.

A loaf of bread, a girl folding her legs over her neck, girl dancing, boy dancing, girl and boy dancing, grandma dancing, baby dancing, vintage VW bus, vintage VW bus, vintage VW bus.

"You're *always* on your phone," Dario whines.

"He's not coming, you guys," Wyatt says.

"Would you just *stop*," Simone snaps. She's gone back to testy, pre-Beau Simone. "Have you *ever* had something come up when you were expected somewhere? Maybe he's stuck in traffic."

"He lives five minutes away," Wyatt and Dario both say at the same time, and then look at each other in surprise. Their faces—they look exactly the same. Harper has gotten used to it, but there it is anew: four mirror versions of each other in that room. She has an awful flash image of all forty-two of them in there, same, same, same, just tapping their pencils, waiting for him. Crushing disappointment, multiplied again and again.

"If you really want to be somewhere, you'll make it a priority," Harper says. She sounds just like her mom. Well, good, because her mom has *always* shown up when she said she would. Harper's whole life long, she has.

Amber reappears. "So!" She beams, as if delivering great news. "Mr. Beau had to do something extremely important today, and I mean *extremely*. But Big Dean will be filling in! Dean Martini!" It's hard to tell if this is another nickname, or if Amber just likes the sound of it.

Dean Martin? Dario mouths. He snaps his fingers and pretends to swagger, but Harper has no clue what he means.

"Friends, introducing Big Dean! Dean has more experience than anyone here, and you'll be in excellent hands!" Amber gestures toward the door, but nothing happens. Finally he appears. It's easy to see why Dean has more experience than anyone there. He's a jillion years old. Nearly bald, with the wisps of gray in the back pulled into a ponytail, face as lined as a cracked vase. But he looks strong, his muscles ropy and hard in his navy shorts and navy shirt.

"Special friends of Beau's, huh?" he says to them. "Special class not on the schedule? You family or something? You look just like the kid."

"Yeah, family," Simone says. "Distant family."

"Very distant at this point," Dario says. He's pissed.

"He's our biological father," Wyatt says. He's pissed, too. He's been jiggling the car keys in his pocket and looking at Simone with a *See?* expression, since Beau has skipped out on them.

Big Dean snorts at the joke but then notices their somber faces. "No shitting? I thought I knew all the stories. Linda, Maggie, Mary? Melanie? Melinda? Margaret? Natalie? Nadine? Who?"

"Wait. Are those all his *girlfriends*?" Dario sounds disgusted. Harper feels gross, too. No wonder he's not *the marrying kind.*

"I don't know their names. I don't keep track. He's a good-lookin' kid." Dean shrugs. "Hey, I'm not one to judge. I've known him since he was this high." Dean sets his hand knee-level. "His dad and me were like brothers. My ex-wife, she made that statue out there."

Dario glances at Harper and lifts his eyebrows, and Harper lifts hers back. That statue is, um, anatomically generous and done in great detail. Clearly the ex was an admirer. That family has stories, all right.

"Hey, it isn't my business. *This* is my business." He reaches into a box under the table and plops large blue ziplock bags in front of each of them. Harper unzips hers and finds a book, pamphlets, and a notepad of quizzes. "Think of me as your ocean ambassador." You can tell he's said this hundreds of times. "This here's Knowledge Development, your first step to your Open Water license. Okay. Go to page one in your manuals. If I go too fast, you tell me. If you have a question, you ask me. No point keeping your mouth shut. We start with talking about staying warm in the cold."

"Ninety-two," Wyatt brags.

"Ninety-one, fine," Simone says. "You win."

They stand outside with their test results, on the sand right near the Captain Neptune statue. The afternoon light shines on his ripply abs.

"Eighty-nine," Dario says, disappointed.

"Dar, that's great!" Simone says. "What are you down about? We only need to pass."

They're all looking at Harper now. "Ninety-nine," she admits.

"Oh man!" Wyatt says. "You weren't even watching those videos."

"Yeah, I was." Mostly. First she was distracted, trying to figure out what they should do now, and remembering the way Beau's phone just rang and rang. But those videos were also just hard to watch, especially when they demonstrated a diving crisis, someone getting low on air, cold body temperatures, equipment malfunctions. Of course she got a ninety-nine. When you're always on guard, you don't let anything slip.

"What'd you get wrong?" Simone asks. They all have another thing in common, Harper has noticed. They're very competitive.

" 'True or false. An object is neutrally buoyant when it displaces an amount of water less than its own weight.' "

"Oh my God!" Dario screeches. "That was, like, the first question on our first quiz."

"Thank you, Mr. Eighty-Nine," Harper says to him, and he shoves her.

"Let's get out of here," Wyatt says. "I'm starved."

"Amber's tuna sandwich and the bag of chips didn't fill you up?" Simone rolls her eyes.

"That was actually a really good tuna sandwich," Dario says.

"I always picture those tiny bags of potato chips with tiny cartons of milk and tiny breads in an elf grocery store," Simone says. They might all look alike, but no one else's mind works like Simone's.

"Well, say goodbye to Captain Neptune," Harper says.

"Goodbye?" Wisps of Simone's hair have escaped her braids, and it makes her look like a little girl again.

"What, we're not coming back, are we? I mean, he had the whole day to show, and he never did."

The whole day, and every time someone walked through that door, they all looked up expectantly. It was sad. No, it was *heartbreaking*. When she says the words "he never did," her voice even wobbles because she wants to cry. Ugh! Harper isn't going to keep hoping like that. No way. She's mad, too. How could he? How *dare* he? After all they'd done to find him, after all his big lovey, lovey words and fake tears. It's horrible. Do you know what the biggest danger out there is? People, that's what. Your fellow unfeeling, selfish, and cruel human beings.

"Big Dean said he had an important meeting. A meeting he'd been trying to get for weeks," Simone says. "He said he'd be there tomorrow."

"*Simone,*" Harper pleads. "Really? I mean, how important could 'a meeting' have been? He skipped out on seeing us after we just met him for *the first time!*"

"Why do you always believe the worst is about to happen, Harpo?" Simone asks. They've all begun calling her that.

"Why?" Where to begin. Doesn't Simone see the dangers

everywhere? Is she totally unaware? How can you be unaware? Every day the news is alarming, from the universe and the Earth, down to your very cells. Just that morning Harper read that the shark population has diminished, and that they (the mysterious *they*) discovered a dangerous ingredient that has been in our shampoo for years, and that ridged fingernails are a sign of disease. Let alone all the ways, large and small, that people fail each other. Human beings, with their flawed and disappointing selves, up against the dangers of the world—it seems pretty hopeless, to be honest. It can feel kind of pointless to be anything but afraid. "There's a lot of worst" is all Harper manages to say.

"I believe in him," Simone says. "I saw goodness in Beau's eyes."

Dread whooshes into Harper when Simone says that. Oh God, right there, there's no way she's going to break Simone's heart by telling her what *else* was in those eyes. They were wild, wild in a way that doesn't make sense. Well, maybe it does if you add in alcohol, weed, and a transient life. In some ways she's crushed he didn't come, but in other ways it's a relief. The sibs can have fun together this summer, and life can go back to what it was. What it was: anxiety-ridden and apparently empty and pointless, sure, but not full of false hope about some disappointing old dude who mutters scary stuff about *bombs*.

"I don't necessarily believe in him," Wyatt says. "But we might as well come back. These courses are, like, five hundred bucks. And they're just giving them to us."

"Absolutely. We already got fitted for the equipment," Simone says.

"The equipment is cool, but I don't know about actually using it," says Dario, who walked around the store in his fins, making *slap-slap* sounds, his eyes big and googly behind his mask.

"Yeah, no way. That whole section about oxygen regulation . . ." Harper shivers.

"You were good at this stuff," Wyatt says. "You got a ninety-nine. You're practically a natural. Like, it's in your DNA."

He's just trying to get her to go along, but it still makes Harper feel oddly good. In spite of Beau being such a letdown, the funny thing is, diving *is* something that, in a way, has been in her family, their family, for generations. Beau can ditch them all he wants, but it doesn't erase what's in her.

"*You guys!* Come on! Ten-year-olds can take this course. All we're doing tomorrow is driving to some pool to play with our new toys. Totally harmless. What else are we going to do? Do you two just want to go home?" Simone asks.

"I don't want to go *home,*" Harper says. "I thought we could all just still . . . be together." When she imagines actually having to say goodbye to these people, people who she now likes enough to feel free to *dislike* on occasion . . . her heart aches. Walter, even—he sometimes trots into her room and sleeps in her bed. Sure, she could rejoin Soraya and Ada on their camping trip, or she could stay in her room and pine for Ezra, or try to spot him when she goes with her friends to Green Lake, but they're not finished here. She's not finished with her siblings, and she's not finished with that island, Molokini, and whatever it might mean to her.

"Then let's just go to the pool tomorrow. If he shows, he shows; if he doesn't, fuck him," Wyatt says. It is so sad, because this is Wyatt, Harper understands, just wanting to give Beau another chance. They all need so much from him. No wonder he fled.

"Everyone is such a cynic lately," Simone says cynically. "I'm going."

"Okay," Harper says. "I'll go." But she's doing it for them, not Beau Zane.

Dario hasn't answered. He's just making that annoying clicking again with whatever's in his pocket.

"What *is* that noise?" Simone says.

Dario holds out his palm and shows them. "A cool piece of coral I picked up that day we first met Bo Bo." He puts that one back in his pocket. "And this." Now he holds up a long, flat yellowish strip, which looks purposefully rounded at one end and broken at the other. You can almost see through it. "Greer gave it to me. It's whalebone."

"Whoa," Wyatt says. He runs a finger along it, and so does Harper.

"What are these notches?" she asks. She feels them, and she sees them, too. She doesn't count them, not now, not yet. She just sees a handful of small lines, etched in.

"No idea. Greer said Tony found it on a dive. Right out in front of their place. This round end, because it looks so finished, he thought it wasn't just regular, natural whalebone, but maybe, like, part of a corset? A corset stay."

"Part of a *corset*?" Harper asks. It makes no sense.

"That's what she said. I don't know. They could never really tell what it was, because part of it is missing." He rubs his finger along the ragged, unfinished end.

"Très meaningful, très metaphor. Missing part, et cetera," Simone says.

"It *is* meaningful," Dario says. "I like it."

231

"What's a corset stay?" Wyatt asks. Harper doesn't know, either.

"I looked it up," Dario says. "Stays are the hard ribs of the corset. You know, those tight, laced-up girdles in Victorian times? They often used whalebone for the ribs. Know what else I read? Women weren't expected to wear them because of fashion, or to make themselves look thinner, like people think. The real reason was that, in the nineteenth century, they thought that a woman's body was so weak, she needed support around it at all times."

"No wonder we're still so fucked," Simone says. "A Brief History of Spanx and Misogyny."

"What's it doing in the ocean?" Wyatt asks. "I mean, no one's out there swimming in a corset."

"From some old ship, maybe?" Harper guesses.

"She didn't give *me* anything," Simone says.

"Pool or no pool, Dar?" Wyatt asks. "You never said."

"Fine, pool. He gets one more chance, and that's it. I'd rather boogie board with you guys than sit around and wait for some hurtful loser."

"That thing was in a whale's actual body," Harper says, and makes a face.

"Exactly," Dario says, and tucks the whalebone back into his pocket like a treasure.

That night, even though they're well aware that Beau Zane doesn't have a phone, Harper hears Simone awake in her room. She hears Wyatt get up and rummage around in the fridge. And she hears

Dario get up, too, and brush his teeth twice. They're all waiting for Beau to call, *somehow,* to explain himself, and apologize. Harper is sure of this, because that's what she's doing. Sitting there in the dark, just hoping her parent will be who she needs him to be. Then again, you don't need to be one of forty-two kids of a sperm donor dad to know how *that* feels.

CHAPTER TWENTY-TWO

It is day thirty of our voyage. Joshua's exhaustion and headaches are without pause. Now I join him in my own delicate condition. I have ceased to be unwell in the monthly way. I also have a depraved appetite, a depressing foreboding of impeding evil, and dry skin, multiple signs of impending motherhood.

Mary Ann Patten journal entry

July 29, 1856

"IF YOU STAND IN THE ROAD FOR A SEC, YOU'LL GET SOME of the ocean in the background," Harper says to Dario the next day.

"Are you trying to get me killed?"

"Real quick!" Harper says. She's wearing her BCD over her swimsuit and her goggles on her head. BCD—buoyancy control device, a vest that inflates to let you stay buoyant at any level, and that holds your tank and gear and stuff. That's about all she knows, but it looks cool. They're standing at the side of the road nearest to Captain Neptune, waiting for "the bus that'll take you to the pool." Amber shoved the gear at them and pointed the way, because it's Saturday and the shop is busy. Dario raises

Harper's phone and snaps a few photos, runs back to safety, and hands it to her.

"Good enough, okay? I don't want to get hit by a car out here."

"Thanks, I'm sure they're great," she says.

She wanted to wear her whole wet suit, but after she got one foot in, her leg started to feel claustrophobic. If a leg feels claustrophobic, what will happen when her whole body is in that thing? Besides, Simone says she'll die of heat in the bus if she wears it now.

The photos aren't great, but she doesn't dare ask him to take more. They're all a little irritable after staying up late in a quiet condo. Also, because they're all waiting for the last, killing jab when Beau doesn't show up again, the moment when they really have to face the truth that he never will. That morning Wyatt slammed stuff around when he made coffee, and Simone and Dario got in an argument about maple syrup versus honey. No one, not even Dario, called their parents to let them know about the no-show yesterday. *Scuba adventure!* Harper types. #beyondthehike #challengeyourself #thenextadventure #divedeep #maui #bestlife #pacificocean #buoyant #joy. The hearts pour in, and for a moment she believes it, that she can do this. That vest, though, it's heavy and complicated, and Harper mostly posts that photo so Ezra will see. Harper is someone who hides her eyes every time she watches an underwater nature show, hyperventilating on her couch when the cameramen seem to be submerged for too long. Ez definitely knows this. He's lifted up the couch pillow and peeked at her under there more than once.

But it isn't Ezra who immediately responds. Harper doesn't even want to answer the phone right now, but she'd better, or she'll make things worse. She still can't believe she's even allowed on this trip.

"WHAT DO YOU THINK YOU'RE DOING, HARPER PROULX?!"

"Mom. Ten-year-olds do this program."

"I DID NOT GIVE MY PERMISSION FOR ANYTHING OF THE KIND. Don't they require parental permission? A signature? A waiver? Anything? You mean, kids can just get on airplanes, and go scuba diving, and buy stuff on the internet, and have sex, and the parents can't even do a single thing ab—"

It's wrong. It's very wrong and mean for so many reasons, but she says it. "I have my dad's permission."

For a moment Harper's mom is silent. And then she quietly says, "Oh my God, Harper. I cannot believe you used that word. That is a word that has to be earned. Deserved. That is—"

"It's just in a *pool*. I'll be fine. I'll call you later. I've got to go."

And she does have to go. Because a bus is coming, and it's hilarious, because it's an internet celebrity: a vintage VW bus. God, people love those things. Stonehenge, manicures, Neuschwanstein Castle, rocks in a stack next to a river, vintage VW buses . . . rock stars, icons, beloved images of the web, guaranteed heart-heart-heart payoffs.

Quick! Harper opens her camera. It's a yellow bus, too, an audience fave, coming down the road, oh so perfectly under the blue sky. Snap, snap, snap! It's all she's thinking about. Like catching a big fish, she has to reel it in. She doesn't even think to look at who's driving.

But then the vintage VW bus pulls over. It's apparently the bus they've been waiting for. He pops his head out the open window.

"Hop in, kids," Beau Zane says.

"VW rules, you gotta have music," Beau says after they'd flung all their gear in the back. "See this? Cassette tape." He waves it at them.

"The good old days, huh?" Wyatt says, doing something Harper's mom does all the time—saying one thing with his words, and delivering a whole different message with his cool, withholding tone. He's still pissed. There's not going to be some easy forgiving and forgetting of Beau Zane's absence yesterday, and he wants Beau to know it. After Harper's rush of *thank God* when she saw him, a brief, outright giddiness, all the daunting stuff comes whooshing back. She got herself all geared up to let it go, the whole voilà-here's-a-father thing, but now she has to crank up the excitement machine again. Hey, maybe *he'll* want a relationship, and *she* won't. A few days might be plenty. Hope and need are a roller coaster, and who wants to be on one of those for very long.

"Abso-fucking-lutely," Beau says, ignoring Wyatt's tone altogether, snapping the tape into place and pushing *play*. A grainy, faraway *Buh bub buh buh!* works its way through two tinny speakers, and he turns the dial until the music's blasting. Harper's glad that Walter and his sensitive dog ears are back at the condo.

"Retro, baby!" Simone shouts from the front seat next to Beau. She looks at Harper and lifts her brows to say, *See?* It's annoying, like she's saying she knew him better than they did.

"Creedence!" Dario shouts, too, from the back seat next to Harper. His cheeks flush. Oh, he's so happy. He's just so darn happy that Beau is back. He's like a human being made of relief.

Beau plays air guitar and steers with his knees before putting his hands back on the wheel. Jesus, he's going to kill them before he kills them. "'Welllllll, take me back down where cool water flows, yeh,'" he sings loudly. "Roll down your windows for the full effect." They already are down, but he doesn't seem to notice.

"My moms love them," Dario says. "Especially Reba."

"Hey, mine, too. This is her bus, her tunes. I'm more of a Growlers, Peach Pit, Hunter Eden dude myself."

"Hunter Eden's my favorite." Simone smiles at him.

"How'd you guys do yesterday? Big Dean said *awesome.*"

"We did awesome, all right," Simone says. "Harpo even got a ninety-nine."

"Is that right?" He catches her eyes with his in the rearview mirror, and his have those really great smile wrinkles around them. He also has that forever-bare ring finger, the kind of charm that lures you in and then breaks your heart, and he's wearing a wrinkled T-shirt that smells kind of musty, like he plucked it from a pile on the floor. He's got some shit stuck in his man bun, too, and when Harper squints, she's pretty sure it's French fry–related. After yesterday's no-show, she's definitely still mad, same as Wyatt, but, ugh, un-mad is trying hard to slide in. She can't help herself. "Hey, didn't I tell ya? Easy! Wait. You gotta crank this guitar part." It already is cranked, if you ask Harper, but now he turns the dial to the point of distortion and bams the steering wheel in rhythm. Simone sways her shoulders and shimmies in her seat. Dario bobbles his head like a goose pecking a bread crumb and taps one sandal, giving Harper clear visions of awkward high school dances.

It's a love fest, but Wyatt's face is aloof, and Harper wants answers, too.

They pull into the parking lot of the Kihei Aquatic Center, where Harper can see a giant outdoor swimming pool. Beau turns off the engine, and suddenly it's quiet. She's afraid to ask the necessary thing, but more afraid not to. And no one else is, so who's being chicken now, huh?

"So. Yesterday . . . ," Harper says as they pop open the doors and pile out. "Where were you? We were sort of surprised, um, that you—"

"Oh hey, yeah! Couldn't be avoided. Those bombs I told you about, they're gonna go off, okay? Ten weeks. BOOM! All I can think about is bombs. I sleep bombs. I eat bombs. I had a meeting with the Man."

His eyes are shiny and wild again, and this time they're all there to witness it. Dario freezes with one hand on his bag, and even Simone stops what she's doing, too, her BCD slung halfway over her arm, her face dropping. Wyatt's brows knit together in a concerned V. Harper can feel one giant *oh no* held between them. She's sorry that they have to witness it, but better sooner than later.

"The Man?" she asks.

"Head of the entire navy. The big guy. The admiral."

"Really?" Wyatt asks.

"Yup." Beau purses his lips and nods in serious belief. "I sat by the kitchen phone, worried it was maybe broken, since we never use it, until the dude finally called. The junior guy kept postponing, until there he was, four hours late, what an asshole."

Dario sneaks Harper a look. She rubs her forehead in response. *Bombs?* he mouths, and makes his eyes wide. Harper shrugs. It is what it is. This settles it. They can finish whatever they're doing at the pool today and slowly back away. Oh God, imagine how smug her mother is going to be, after she's said all along that it's sometimes better not to know.

"Shit," Dario whispers under his breath as they walk from the parking lot to the pool.

"I know," she says.

"He's totally . . ."

"I know."

After all they've done to get here, neither of them can bear to say it.

Delusional.

Captain Neptune holds all their classes at the Kihei pool, and Harper spots Big Dean down at the far end with five other people in wet suits. He waves when he sees them. They drop their gear at the shallow end near the bleachers. Beau's eyes are calm again, and so is his voice, as if he's been transformed back into the other Beau, the one not obsessed and possessed. He eases into teacher mode, showing them how to put on their wet suits, starting with them inside out and then rolling them up "like a granny puts on pantyhose." This makes Dario ask, "What are pantyhose?" and Simone answer, "A corset for legs." Next he teaches them how to put their masks on and take them off, and how to clear them when they get fogged up. He's one of those encouraging kinds of teachers who's always saying stuff like "Great job, man" or "That's the way to do it."

They get in the water. Yeah, even Harper. Those smiling eyes in the rearview mirror, those you-can-do-it words are louder than anything else, even Beau's bomb obsession, even her own fear, because wow, that idea is so great—that she can do it. It's like a little mini pill of power, like those cellulose ones that melt and there's an enormous foam dinosaur inside. Okay, she also doesn't want her half siblings to think she's pathetic, because there they are, her mirror images, getting right in. Squeezed into that latex suit like ground pork in a casing, with a tank on her back and twelve pounds of lead on her waist, against all logic and good sense, she eases below the surface.

Her heart is unnervingly loud in her ears, and so is the chlorine-scented, bubbly whoosh, the sense of separation between above and below. She reminds herself again and again that she's just in a stupid swimming pool, same as she has been lots of times before, even if strapped-on lead weights and doing everything you can to stay under is the opposite of any instinct for survival. Here's the thing, though: being exactly where you want to be underwater, going under, navigating that world, as Beau is teaching them—it requires slow, deliberate breathing. If you get nervous, if you panic, you'll hold your breath and stay at the surface. But when you control your breathing and exhale, you can submerge and experience what's beneath. When you stop trying to climb out of the water, stop the mind and body thrashing, when you *relax*, keeping yourself trim so your legs and arms are calmly, neutrally horizontal, you can go forward. You can rise or fall at will, too, you can go the direction you want, just by controlling your fear. It seems like a magic trick. Or a piece of secret life knowledge shared by only a few.

It's . . . *Wow.*

And if you get into trouble, you have a buddy. You can share air. You can help each other out, if you communicate. Beau demonstrates, and then Harper and Dario, her buddy, the sea creature across from her in the pool, practice. She gives him the *hey, I'm out of air* signal, waving both hands, making an unnerving slice across her throat, and then he shares his Octo (short for Octopus, heh) line with her as they connect up to each other. Then it's Dario's turn. He signals. He points at Harper, makes an okay sign, and then a thumbs-up: *Are you. Okay. To go up?* And she signals back, with a nod and her own okay sign. Air for him, air for her, and now they can rise together. But you have to think more about the *together* than the *trouble*.

You want to maintain that connection, Beau Zane said. *To each other, to your environment.*

What is most memorable about this day at the pool, though, besides the fact that she does it, that she actually *does it,* goes underwater with lead weights on her waist, breathing beneath the surface, is what happens when that class is almost over. Big Dean walks to their end of the pool, and Beau leaps out.

"Your *kids?*" Dean says. They all hear him. Their heads are popped up out of the water, like a seal family. "That's what they said yesterday."

"I know, dude. Surprise. Sperm donor, years ago," Beau says without any embarrassment. He gestures toward his wet suit crotch, adding unnecessary detail.

"Tadpoles now," Dean says, looking at them in there, and they both crack up.

"Yeah," Beau says. "My tadpoles."

And right now it doesn't matter how delusional he is. It doesn't matter if he talks about bombs or having meetings with navy admirals. What matters is the pride in his voice.

On the way to the van, they were all a little high and excited from succeeding at something new and challenging, but heading home now, Dario and Harper are both distant, the way you are when a day is great but has to end, and Simone gets quiet after she settles into her seat. They've got to face the whole wild-eyed bomb thing. It's all pretty awful, because how do you back off when you came on so strong? How do you shut the door on the guy when he's maybe lonely and not well? Strangely, though, Wyatt isn't aloof at all anymore, and he isn't even reserved. He's talking to Beau with a new respect in his voice. What the heck? He's in the front seat now on the way back, and when you look at them up there, his and Beau's profiles are identical.

"Football, huh? I never played, too scary for me, all those big guys," Beau says.

"I don't really like it, to be honest. My dad played."

"But *you* don't like it?"

"I've never even said that aloud before."

Wait. Wyatt doesn't just have a new respect in his voice. Wyatt is *confiding*. And, also—Wyatt, who looks like a football player and acts like a football player, doesn't even like being a football player.

When they get back to Captain Neptune, they drop off their gear. In the store, standing next to that mural of sea turtles, Beau moves his hemp bracelets up and down his arm, nervous, like he's asking them out on a date. "So, do you guys wanna . . . ?"

He doesn't finish, but it's getting toward dinnertime. "I've got to get back to Walter. He's been at the doggy day care all day," Dario says. "I don't want him to think I disappeared."

"I'm exhausted," Simone says. "But this was so great, thanks."

"We sure appreciate it," Harper says.

Beau looks sad. It seems surprising, but rejection can go both ways. Harper feels sorry for him, but ready to get the heck out of there, too. "Yeah, yeah, I get it. We've got a full day tomorrow anyway. We *are* going tomorrow, right? I mean, two dives, and then two dives on Monday, and you're certified. You can open water dive anywhere in the world."

"Of course! Of course we are," Wyatt says. "And hey, I'll meet up later, after I drop these guys off."

Beau brightens. "Great, great! Love it! The Y Knot has killer onion rings." He whirls his arm like a cowboy with a lasso, catching a red plastic basket of onion rings, maybe, instead of a calf.

"Seven?"

"Nice! Awesome. See you dudes tomorrow!" he says to Harper and Dario and Simone. He hugs them, and they hug back. Harper's hands are on that wrinkled T-shirt of his, and it kind of makes her uneasy, but she tells herself to remember this. She's not sure if she'll ever see him again. They all need to have a serious talk about what happened that morning. How they should go forward, what the plan is. There were no delusional bomb guys on the donor-conceived forums.

Beau waves as they head out. "Great job, you knocked it out of the water today, hahaha!" he calls. The bells on the door of Captain Neptune jingle a goodbye.

They're barely outside again when Wyatt spins around and snaps at them. "What is *wrong* with you guys? Why are you acting so weird?"

"Why are *we* acting so weird? Why are *you* acting so not-weird?" Dario says.

"We had a great day. That was incredible!" Wyatt says. "I've never done anything so cool in my life. I actually *loved* it."

"It *was* very cool, and *I* loved it, but, uh, 'bombs, bombs, bombs'?" Simone makes an alarmed face.

"The other night he said the same thing," Harper admits. "'Kaboom.'" She explodes her fingers out and makes her eyes *yikes* big.

"What are you guys talking about?" Wyatt says. "You don't know? There *are* bombs. They *are* going to go off. Right out there! Right out in front of Molokini Island."

"What?" Harper looks at that mysterious curve of volcano ridge, just above the surface, and now it doesn't just look mysterious. It calls, with a silent urgency.

"They are?" Dario says.

"From World War Two. The military used Molokini for bombing practice. Bombs are sitting there, under the water. The US Navy wants to detonate them for 'safety' reasons." Wyatt makes the quote marks with his fingers. "A teenager was killed way back in 1971 after he tried to take one apart, and then, like, twelve years later two soldiers were injured during a military exercise. So they think these bombs, which have been just sitting there undisturbed for eighty years, pose a serious risk to the public. This has been going on for *months* now. My parents signed a petition last summer when we were here. All kinds of environmental groups, leaders of the community—they're trying to stop it from happening. Beau's obviously one of them. What did you think, that he was just making shit up?"

"He sounded . . . um, unhinged," Dario says. "Uh, very worked up."

"Well, *yeah.* He *should* be unhinged. So should *you.* So should every human being on the planet! After that teenager was killed, after those military guys were injured, they *did* detonate some of those bombs. The first time, in the 1970s, the detonation left a *crater,* damage in a hundred-foot radius, hundreds and hundreds of fish dead. The coral turned to ash. And the second time, in 1984, it was worse. Thousands of fish, dead or floating at the surface. You should see the pictures. All these years later the pulverized coral just looks like gray talcum powder, for miles. And there are options, you know? Other ways to remove them. Do you know what will happen when they detonate those things in a few weeks? The reef, marine life, every living creature around that island . . . Gone."

"Wait, did you say *weeks*?" Harper's anxiety ratchets up right there. It feels larger than just her and her own body. It *is* larger than her and her own body. Shit, that bomb is going to go off *right here.*

"They're going to do it at the end of August."

"This is horrible," Simone says.

"Shit. No wonder he looks obsessed," Dario says. "Down there since World War Two? I need to read about this."

By then they're standing under that huge Captain Neptune statue. This time someone's climbed up and stuck a beat-up pair of goggles on his head. Apparently this is a regular thing, dressing up the guy, and now he looks like a joke again.

"No one can get any definite answers from the navy," Wyatt says. "No matter what the environmental groups say, no matter what *anyone* says, they won't commit to listening. And they're powerful enough to do what they want, you know? So if Beau Zane got a meeting with some admiral . . . he's a fucking hero."

Shivers run up Harper's arms. And she's contrite, fast. She wants to run back into that shop and apologize. It's so easy to make assumptions with little information, and it's so easy to believe that we should all be only one thing. Perfect people in perfect squares, brief encounters, first impressions, they can never tell the whole story. Looking up at Captain Neptune in his silly goggles, Harper thinks it, how each and every one of us is a messy world, fearful and brave, cocky and insecure, a hero under a crumpled T-shirt. So much stuff lies below every surface. So much.

Dario is looking up at those beat-up goggles on Neptune's head, too. He starts to climb the statue again. But Simone tugs on his swimsuit.

"Leave it," she says. "We don't have to guard his majesty. That's what's great. He's a goof *and* a king. He is who he is."

"You're right," Dario says. He hops down. "And, wow, you know? Those other thirty-eight kids . . . They don't even know yet that the dude who sperm-doned us is taking on the Man."

"Pretty sure that's not a verb," Simone says.

"*You're* a goof and a king," Dario says, and shoves her.

"You are." She shoves him back.

"You two are," Dario says to Wyatt and Harper, and they leap back so they won't get shoved, too. They're like a bunch of kids getting to babysit themselves for the first time. Giddy. Giddy because they get to maybe love him again, and he gets to maybe love them back.

Still, when Harper catches Wyatt's eyes, she sees the horror of what he is remembering, that ash of pulverized coral, stretching for miles. The lifeless gray, caused by an unyielding allegiance to safety.

CHAPTER TWENTY-THREE

> With Keeler under arrest, Joshua has been at-
> tempting to discharge the mate's duties as well
> as his own, in snow and sleet and lightning, as
> we head south to Cape Horn. Without a sec-
> ond watchkeeper, he has refused sleep for eight
> days. Tonight our troubles deepen, as he has
> developed a brain fever, with trouble staying
> awake or thinking clearly. Second Mate Hare is
> incapable of navigating, and there is no quali-
> fied man to take command of the ship.
>
> Mary Ann Patten journal entry
> August 6, 1856

THE ARC OF MOLOKINI IS RIGHT IN FRONT OF HARPER, MUCH larger and even more magnificent this close, as they bob and slosh aboard the *Greer Brody*. It's an island in an adventure story, green with succulents in its rocky surface, mystical, old, where there's treasure buried somewhere. It's ancient enough to be comforting—at least that's what she's trying to tell herself.

The whole way over to the dock near Captain Neptune, where

the *Greer Brody* waited, Harper's half siblings talked her down from the ledge, or rather, her visions of herself on the side of that boat. *You don't have to if you don't want to,* Dario said, which is what his moms told him. *You did better than any of us on the test and in the pool,* Wyatt reminded her. *What're you worried about?* But Simone put it most plainly: *Get your shit together,* she said.

Which seems like an impossible task after the phone call she had last night with her mom, who has forbidden her to do this. Melinda also madly called around to the other parents, trying to find someone who'd back her on it, without luck. *What is wrong with these people? A pool is one thing, the ocean another. Do you want me to fly down there?* Answer: absolutely not. Getting her shit together is also impossible because Soraya called her, too. She wanted to know if Harper was okay. Harper's actions seem "out of character." Soraya's mom thought something was up, too, because the real Harper (whoever *she* is) wouldn't do dangerous stuff like that. *Beautiful girl, you can do hard things,* if those hard things are calculus, or camping, or wearing something slightly out of your comfort zone.

After those calls Harper stayed up all night reading about diving accidents, air bubbles in regulators, the bends. She wanted to know everything that could go wrong, so she'd be ready. She also read about those bombs, and the planned devastation of the protected species that live around Molokini, the monk seals, the green and hawksbill turtles, whale sharks, manta rays, bottlenose dolphins, great frigate birds, wedge-tailed shearwaters, and Bulwer's petrels, creatures with names like poetry. She looked up the whale shark, because *shark*. If she went in, they'd be sharing the same pool. But he's not what she expected—there are no sharp teeth to yank off her leg, and he survives on plankton and supposedly poses no danger to humans. But he averages forty thousand pounds, and he's up to sixty feet long, the largest known fish species. He's elaborately decorated, too, with a gaily polka-dotted head and a grid-and-dots body, but he wears a somber expression in his photos, like someone unhappily dragged to a costume party.

If she saw him in person, that whale shark, she'd have a heart attack, she's sure. She looked up *heart attack in water* and *coast guard rescue,* which somehow led to an article about a fatal disease that is killing apes and that might transfer to humans, which somehow led to dangerous levels of toxic metals in baby food, which somehow led to an emergency alert about a lettuce recall. Let us recall all the things that might kill us. Let us recall all the things that might fill our hearts with overwhelming grief.

Now, though, they're on the boat, and she's trying very hard to hold on to Dario's advice, because she doesn't have to do this if she doesn't want to. They came here to meet MF, mystery sperm donor, and they can get to know him without doing *this.* Waves are so much bigger when you're right up close to them, more hotheaded and reckless and full of secret plans. Being in them is definitely unwise. On that boat, too, you can barely stand up straight without holding on. Harper feels like a marble on a tippy table, about to drop off, and she remembers that time in Ada's dad's boat, when she posted that first shot of herself in her bikini. Then Ada's brother drove so fast, Harper's teeth knocked together, and the next day her whole body was sore from the effort of staying on the seat.

The *Greer Brody* rocks and sloshes because this is the spot. The one where they're supposed to dive. Wyatt is bragging about his waterskiing skills, and Simone looks like she belongs in a sun lotion commercial, and Dario is spouting facts about World War II out of nerves. (Harper knows this about him now, the way he jabbers when anxious.) Harper watches the waves with dread. Her mother has forbidden this, so right there she has a get-out-of-jail-free card if she needs it. The wet suit, though—she kind of likes it. She kind of *really* likes it, even if she'd prefer not to use it in the way it was intended. It makes her feel slick and streamlined, as powerful as Catwoman, though maybe squeakier. It makes her smell like a tire, but in a nice way. It's definitely not baby powder or lavender—it's the scent of action. Dario must feel the same, because he keeps pretending to karate-chop things until Simone tells him to cool it.

Beau is up in the front of the boat, telling who knows what to their driver, Jake, who works at Captain Neptune while on summer vacation from Kihei Charter High School. From the minute they got on the boat and Wyatt met him, Wyatt's been all tongue-tied and keeps looking Jake's way. Amber's up there, too, in her own wet suit. Everyone at Captain Neptune plays all the parts, from retail rentals to dive master. Harper has all the gear on, all of it, and even if she never gets in the water, she wants to post this. Ezra will just die if he ever sees it, although maybe he won't even care. She hasn't heard anything from him, not a single word, since they broke up. Maybe he can forget about her just like that, but obviously she can't.

"It's cute," Simone says, and hands Harper her phone.

She looks at the shot. It *is* cute. She doesn't even want to adjust anything, or add a filter. In spite of the anxiety jittering around in her whole body, she looks surprisingly happy. She *is* surprisingly happy, even if this is her last day on Earth. Everyone is—Beau's bopping around on the boat, in his element, not losing his balance no matter what the boat suddenly does, so at ease and capable that she totally forgets any of his stumbling on land. Simone is being sweet and mellow, and dotted Harper's nose with sun lotion in a spot she forgot. Dario might be scared, but he looks proud, too, in his wet suit. It's the first normal day they've had, if you can call any of this normal. At least they're just here doing something together, them and Beau, without all the awkwardness and fear and superhigh stakes of their first meetings. This is just regular fear and the superhigh stakes of some terrifying adventure-y thing. Harper posts the photo. She refreshes, wanting to see the likes flow in, hoping her reassuring friends are out here with her, too.

The boat jostles. And right then Beau *does* lose his footing. He bumps smack into Harper. Her phone—it leaps from her hand.

It's airborne. Oh shit! Shit! It's airborne, and then it isn't. It plops and makes an actual *glub* sound as it dives straight into that ocean, like it has the courage she lacks.

"No!" Harper cries. She leans over the side of the boat and reaches, but already, just like that, it's gone. "My phone! Oh my God, I just lost my phone!"

"Oh hey," Beau Zane says. "I'm so sorry." He doesn't look all that sorry. He's grinning the Beau grin, but there's nothing funny about this.

"Oh nooooo! I can't believe it! Shit, shit, shit! Goddamn it!" Ugh! Her mom is going to kill her. Do you know how expensive those things are? It cost practically as much as their living room furniture! But even more, her *whole life* is on that phone.

"It's okay, Harpo," Dario says, but he looks stricken on her behalf. The ocean has now swallowed her phone as if it never existed. That little rectangle now vanished . . . It was everything. It's like one of her arms just dropped off and sank, or worse, a vital organ.

"My whole life is on it," she says. That phrase again—it's what she keeps thinking. Her voice wobbles. She wants to cry. "Shit."

"You can get another one, Harpo. Major hassle, though, yeah," Simone says.

Like it's that easy? Like they can just afford that, no problem? "All my photos," Harper says. It's just . . . despair. "All my contacts, texts, everything."

"Hey, it's okay," Wyatt says. "It's in the cloud, right?"

The Cloud. It's like saying a person is in heaven, their soul is, even if their body is gone. A part of them is fine and whole somewhere else, wherever and whatever The Cloud is. A fluffy and safe place, with golden gates. Maybe Mr. Wong is in The Cloud, too.

"Yeah," Harper says. The Cloud is comforting like heaven, sure, but you have to believe they both really exist. "I hope so. I mean, I save my stuff, I back it up."

"It's there, it's there," Dario says.

"Try not to think about it right now," Wyatt says.

"It was a really old phone, Harpo," Simone says.

There are other death/heaven similarities, only Harper doesn't know it yet. *It's in a better place. Everything happens for a reason.*

"Hey, I'm so sorry for your loss," Beau says.

"Ugh, this is so unfair," Harper says. She's devastated. She just wants it back so bad.

The day already feels ruined. Harper has this intense anxiety being away from her phone. It's even worse than those times that she worried she lost it, because it's actually gone-gone, forever gone. What if someone's trying to call her right this second? No one but her mom and Soraya has called her for days, but still. There could be some kind of emergency, and she's way out here, *disconnected.* What if she needs to . . . What? She thinks about what she does on her phone, and all she can come up with is, what if she needs to look something up, or what if people are commenting and she doesn't know it? What if she *misses* something? Let alone all her superimportant things that are now down in the sea.

There's a lot of the day left, though. It's only morning, and they're supposed to have this first dive, and then lunch, and then a second one. Simone and Wyatt have already gone over. They're under there somewhere with Amber, beneath those choppy waves that have turned blue now, same as the sky. Dario's head bobs out there, too, waiting.

"Come on, Harpooooo!" Dario yells. She's counted to three with Beau a bunch of times, but she's still stuck on the edge of the boat with him. She's frozen there in that suit. Only not frozen, because it's getting hot. She wonders if heat will make her wet suit stick to her forever, like a wrapper on a candy that sits in the sun.

"I'll go with Dario if you want," Beau says. "You can stay with Jake."

Harper shakes her head. She doesn't want to be the only one left behind. "Just give me a minute." She's kind of pissed at him for bumping her, because it's pretty much his fault she lost her phone. Plus, it's hard to trust a guy who fathered forty-two children. Why are they out here doing the thing *he* loves anyway? Why aren't they doing . . . She tries to think of her favorite thing to do but draws a blank. He let his man bun free, and now his hair is loose. Loose and long to the point of stringy, but wow, is he patient.

"It'll be worth it, I promise you," Beau says.

"One, two, threeeeee," Dario shouts again as he treads water out there.

"Do it for him," Beau Zane says as they both look out at Sea Monster Dario. "Sometimes it's really great to do things for other people that you can never imagine doing for yourself. Like, really great."

He means the forty-two women who got to have the babies they desperately wanted, and look, here are the kids now. But she thinks again about how those women and their partners did the hard parts. It's not the time to have this talk, with poor Dario treading water, but she asks it. "Why didn't you just have your own kids?"

"I told you about the summer my old man and I weren't getting along? He said I was a selfish asshole, and I believed him. Hell, I *was* one. The way he grew up—you worked hard. You weren't a taker. You did things for other people whenever you could. I went to the clinic a few weeks after that. I figured, do something unselfish, right? I would have messed it up bad, raising kids, and your parents did such an awesome job."

She stares into his eyes, and he, Beau Zane, MF, stares back into hers. He smiles, and she smiles back. When she looks into those blue eyes, it's like she's been looking into them her whole life, which she has. It's a comfort, the way eyes go back and back through generations, through all the hard times, even. It almost makes Harper believe in something bigger than herself, a grand plan, but a plan from a nature-science-DNA-universe-ocean God, not a religion God. That kind of God seems so much more worthy of faith, so much more generous and kind.

"What if . . . ?" There are so many, but she means those waves.

"What if you can totally do this?" Beau says. "You can. I saw it yesterday."

Oh, oh, her heart fills. *You can totally do this* is pretty much what anyone just needs to hear, and for a second she believes him, and a second is enough. The part of her that wants to see what's under there is bigger than the part of her that's afraid. One second, that's all it takes, and she goes over. She feels the cold, even through her wet suit, and she sees bubbles, bubbles, all around, and her panicked mind shrieks *Go up!* The part of her that can totally do this, though, the part that wants to show Beau Zane that he is right, tells her to go down, to keep her body trim, to not think about the weights around her waist but about breathing.

She sees a murky Dario across from her, hair like seaweed. She sees Beau down there now, too, even more in his element than before, maybe in *their* element, the same element as Captain Neptune and Greer Brody. He's gesturing, and they follow. They *can* follow, wow. The smallest fin flap sends her forward in a marine mammal glide. She forces herself to breathe calmly and then forgets about panicking, because of what she sees. There, where Beau leads them, is a rocky reef, and flat yellow fish, and chubby orange striped ones, and ugly brown fish with scowling faces, popping in and out from little caves. She's in a film, she's *living* a film, and it's too captivating to think of anything else but being in it, all the way, without fear or other thoughts barging in to distract. She sees the shadows of Simone and Wyatt and Amber, and then they're gone. She feels the presence of someone behind her, and then he passes her, calm and old, in his slow daily paddle—a turtle. A turtle! Huge enough to seem unreal, and then there's a second one, unconcerned with her, just being a turtle on his way to who knows where. They're just doing their thing, with their own turtle plans. Beau gestures, and they follow. They follow those turtles like they're part of them.

After they surface, Harper spits out her mouthpiece and flings off her mask. She treads water, bobbing with waves that sometimes smack her face, but she doesn't care.

"Wow!" she shouts. "Wow, wow!" For one brief second she remembers something Ezra said: *We lost wonder.* But he was wrong. Wonder might have gotten misplaced, but it's definitely still here.

Dario flings off his mask, too. He has the outline of it on his face, and his eyes are giddy. "AWESOME!" he shouts.

Simone and Wyatt climb the ladder to the boat. On deck, Amber peels off her mask. They climb in after them.

"It's just like *Finding Nemo*!" Dario says.

"Or *Finding Nemo* is just like that," Beau says, shaking the water from his hair, removing his flippers. He's right. You can forget which came first, the real or the image of the real.

"That was fantastic!" Simone says. She has that mask outline on her face, too.

"You guys have a good time?" Jake asks.

"SO good," Wyatt says to him.

"I've never experienced anything so incredible in all my life,"

Harper says. She's exhilarated, that's the only word. A jazzy party is taking place in her chest, pure fizzy gloriousness.

"Did you guys see the turtles?" Wyatt asks.

"They were so calm. They were just doing their thing." It seems like a miracle to Harper, that they have *always* been doing their thing, through wars and lettuce recalls and riots and pandemics. It's so reassuring, that nature keeps being nature throughout all of it, that turtles keep on paddling as they have always paddled.

Everyone has their flippers off now. They stand in a circle on the sloshy boat. Feet and feet and feet. Harper looks down. "You guys," she says.

Dario looks down, too, and starts to laugh. Beau's second toe is significantly longer than the rest, and so are Harper's and Dario's and Simone's and Wyatt's. They never noticed it before. Wow, all those toes together with their creator toe, and they crack up.

"What's so funny, gang?" Amber asks as Jake starts the motor. She pops her head into their circle and gazes down. "Oh geez! It's like your toes are giving all other feet the finger," she says.

"Rebel toes, furious feet!" Simone says.

"That's right, man!" Beau says. He makes that lasso motion again. Their circle disbands. Wyatt heads to the front to talk to Jake, and Simone undoes her tangled braids and shakes out her hair. The boat picks up speed, and Dario sits on the boat bench and watches the horizon of their fabulous day.

"I am so proud of you," Beau says to Harper.

"Hey, I didn't die," she says.

"Hey, you lived," he says.

CHAPTER TWENTY-FOUR

Within hours of arriving at the Strait of Le Maire, Joshua collapsed on deck, and he was brought below to his bunk in delirium. He is tossing violently. He may have been disabled by a malarial disease contracted in the east, or a virus, or a debilitating tuberculosis. He is suffering greatly. As an illiterate, Second Mate Hare is ill equipped to handle the duties of captain. It is now in this moment of quiet that I am having clarity, the increasing dawning that I will have to do something no woman has ever done: assume control and command of this vessel myself.

Mary Ann Patten journal entry

August 7, 1856

FOR A WHILE THERE HARPER TOTALLY FORGOT ABOUT HER phone. But as soon as they're motoring back, she remembers. Ugh! Why, why, why did she use it while the boat was so sloshy? If only she'd left it zipped up in her bag . . . When they order takeout at the PP Shack (Pork and Poke), Harper keeps reaching for it. This happens again and again, especially at those life-pause moments when nothing is *actually* happening, like when they're waiting for their food or just riding in the boat. She just wishes so bad that she could feel the cool weight of it in her hand. This is weird, but it's like her hand misses it. It's a *craving*, like the time she and her mom tried to quit sugar, and Harper gave in because she couldn't stand it. Its absence gnaws at her in a way that's restless and distraught, as if everything would be okay again if only it were here.

They get back on the boat to do their second dive. There are *so many* awesome photos just *missed*. The light is different, and now Molokini looks prehistoric but in an inviting way, and it's wildly frustrating because no one will ever see it.

Everyone goes over the side, one by one, until here she is again, sitting on the edge in panic, as Dario paddles in the waves, waiting.

"Harpo, we're missing stuff!" he calls.

Oh man—sitting here thinking about missed photos is making Dario miss actual stuff he wants to see right now. "I'm sorry! I'm trying!" she shouts back.

"Man, it's beautiful out here," Beau says, as if he's seeing it for the first time. He has two speeds: hyped up and super mellow. Now it's like he has all the time in the world. She did not inherit *that* quality. She's more like her mom, always frantic, her mind spinning a million miles an hour.

"Doesn't diving ever scare you?"

He curls his three middle fingers, extends his thumb and pinkie, making the Hawaiian *hang loose* sign, reminding her that it's not how it's done here, the rush and the worry. She realizes all the other parts that make a person who they are, because maybe she'd be calmer if she lived on this island. She thinks of his phone, ringing and ringing, a demand ignored.

"You look like my mom when you do that," he says. "That nose-crinkling thing. It's freaking me out, you look just like her."

"This?" She crinkles. "You do it, too."

"I do?"

"Harpoooooo," Dario yells.

That second of bravery strikes. That's all it takes to be there again, in that vibrant, flashy real-life aquarium. And it's easier, regulating her buoyancy, staying trim, even adjusting her eyes so she can see this new place. When they rise again and are back on the boat, there's that same exhilaration, the same elated discovery of wonder, as the wide sky turns the enchanted gold of early evening. God, how frustrating to not get a shot of that.

"This is so fucking awesome, having you guys here," Beau Zane says, pulling his hair up into the man bun Harper is growing surprisingly fond of. She feels a greater closeness with *all* of them, as if today has been years of togetherness. They traveled to a different land together. They had an adventure that no one else could understand.

"Let's do it again tomorrow!" Dario says. It's the plan anyway, but you can tell he wants to show Beau that he's truly excited and happy to be here.

"I can't wait!" Harper says, for the same reason. Also, she *can't* wait. She really wants to go under there again and see every bit of that world. Yeah, they're doing Beau's thing, but wow, she likes it, too.

Wyatt looks out at the ocean. "Can you even imagine?" He shakes his head.

"It's fucking criminal," Beau says. "It's *evil*."

Those bombs. It makes Harper sick to think about it. She imagines her old turtles on the day it happens. She imagines those fish, and that coral that looks like the Earth's brain, alive and essential and full of marvel. That kind of devastation . . . It's unbearable. Unbearable, and too much. What can she even do, really? She's one girl, and this is so much larger than she is. She's not in charge. All she can think to do is be anxious about it. Being anxious takes so much time and space and energy that you can forget that being anxious isn't really doing anything. It seems like action, but it isn't. It's just thoughts in your head, equal to all the other thoughts, like debating what to have for lunch.

That anxiety—it makes her reach for her phone. It's what she normally does in times of stress, picks it up, starts scrolling. All that commotion of kittens and catastrophes—the noise causes fear, but it shuts out the fear, too.

No phone, no phone!

Ugh, now it's just her and the world, with no screen between them.

They're all so tired after the second dive that Beau goes home and so do they, and Wyatt just orders them a pizza. Walter spent the day at the doggy day care of the condo complex, and he clearly had a blast, too. He's all revved up, and he has a tiny plastic lei woven around his collar, and he keeps jumping on the couch and on Dario's lap, staring him in the eyes, tongue hanging out, like he wants to tell him everything. Dogs smile, you'd better believe it.

"She's going to freak when she sees your number," Harper tells Dario. She's borrowing his phone to do her nightly check-in with her mom, since her phone is at the bottom of the ocean. Melinda is going to be so pissed that she lost it. Before that, though, she'll see Dario's number come up instead of Harper's and assume the worst.

"Give it to me. I'll pretend I kidnapped you and ask for ransom," Simone says.

"Abducted by the Hawaiian drug cartel," Wyatt says.

"Pineapple ransom," Dario says, which doesn't make sense, but they're all tired enough to cackle. He has that piece of whalebone in his hand again, catching his thumb along each notch. By now they've discovered more ways that they are different, not the same. They all know about Harper's mom and her *tight leash* (that's what Simone calls it), the same way they all also know about Dario's moms' cozy but sometimes smothering love (*If they try to tie your shoes, smack their hand,* Simone said), and Wyatt's arrogant dad (*What an asshole,* Simone said), and Simone's own hands-off, ultraprogressive parents (No *leash would be scarier to me than a tight one,* Dario said). They know that Simone always forgets something when she leaves the house and has to go back, every time, and that she always acts tough but frequently has bad dreams, and they know that Wyatt hates cashews and can find a parking spot in even the busiest places, and that Dario often hums annoyingly and eats any pointy food—tonight's pizza, pie, quiche—backward.

They know things about Harper, too.

"Deep breaths," Simone advises.

"And don't use my phone to stalk your ex-boyfriend afterward," Dario says.

"Okay, okay. Wish me luck." Harper heads to her room. She feels bad about it, though, her mom as their joke. They had such a great time with Beau that it seems doubly disloyal. When Harper was seven and Jolene Harris made fun of her, Melinda called Jolene's mom to make her apologize. And during the pandemic . . . Well, sure, Harper had her classes online, and yeah, she saw Ez and Soraya, but she and her mother and Grandma Patricia—they were her true pod.

It's such a relief to have a phone again, even if it's Dario's. So weird, though, how using someone else's phone can feel like you're holding their secrets. She signs into her Instagram before she does anything else, and aside from the regular old likes and comments, it's pretty much the same as she left it. All day she had the panicky worry that something huge was happening without her, but nope. She hasn't missed anything. She goes down the line to like the comments and then DMs Soraya and Ada to tell them that any phone calls or texts will go straight into the Pacific Ocean. Soraya answers almost immediately. *I'll tell everyone you're out of touch!* Crying emojis. *I'll be gone, too. Going on vacation with the fam. Mom finally agreed to stay in a hotel again.*

Harper sends Soraya a line of scream emojis. Finally she dials home.

"IS EVERYTHING ALL RIGHT?" Her mom doesn't shriek, but her voice has that panicked intensity.

"It's me, Mom. I'm fine. I just lost my phone."

"Oh, Harper. Oh my God. Don't scare me like that! I saw Dario's number come up, and . . . Jesus. What happened? And, no, *really*? How could you lose it? I finally just made the last payment! We don't have insurance, either, since you *promised* you'd be careful."

"I'm really sorry. We were on Beau's boat, and he bumped my elbow when I was holding it."

Melinda goes quiet at his name. Harper can hear her breathing. It's a complicated silence. Harper doesn't know what to say.

"His boat, huh?"

"I should also tell you that I went di—"

"Oh my God, Harper. Don't say it. You didn't."

"I did. I did, and it was incredible."

"Ughhh! Tell me you won't make a habit of it, please! Are you trying to kill me over here? I'm worried sick."

"I was fine. I totally could do it."

"All it takes is one little mistake, you know that?"

Now Harper is silent.

"Well, I'm going to have to contact the phone company, and I'll see what I can do about getting it replaced, but it might take me a while," Melinda says. "I don't have any free time until the end of the week, and we'll have to get on some payment plan, and a new chip thingy, and . . ."

"I'll pay you back."

"Really? How? You don't have a *job*."

"You don't *want* me to have a job. You keep saying I have my whole life for that."

"Babysitting is a job. Camp counselor is a job."

"A *real* job." She can't help but think of Tony Zane, cleaning those boat bottoms when he was a kid.

"Harper, I don't want to argue."

"It's fine," Harper says. "I'll just do without." Without, like *none*. Like *not having*. The thought sends her into the depression part of the grieving process. But geez, she feels so guilty about the money part.

"It's not fine if I can't contact you."

"I'll email. Wyatt said there's a computer here."

"I want regular communication, not like when you're supposed to send a thank-you note to Grandma and you forget. How've you been sleeping?"

"Sleeping? Fine."

"I haven't slept at all since you've been away, and especially since you started those classes. I can't even *breathe*."

"Was this, like, the first computer ever made?" Harper says. The thing is huge. It's set up in a small office where the decor is nothing like the rest of the condo, with a serious, weighty desk and a stuffed marlin, yikes, covering one whole wall.

"The first computer ever made took up a whole room," Wyatt says.

"I know that. It was just a joke." She punches Wyatt's arm. He seems distracted. When he turns on that beast, the computer hums loud enough that Walter starts to bark, as if he heard an intruder.

"You have to wait a minute for it to connect."

"Is there a password?"

"They didn't have passwords in those days."

"I hope I don't subject you to identity theft," Harper says.

"That's already happened. At least to my identity," Wyatt says, and then leaves Harper in front of the large screen. Wyatt has never gone into the details of it, but for the first time Harper thinks, really thinks, about what it would be like to be told your biological father was one guy when he was really another. Damn, that hurts. And a father who you played football for when you didn't even want to, too. A man you wanted to please, a lie. Wyatt's world must be *rocked*. His confidence and certainty definitely aren't what they seem. She feels a new respect for him, handling all this, and still being so *kind* to them.

Harper can open her old email account, which she hasn't used in a hundred years, except for that hurried grab of her plane ticket to Hawaii. There are all these emails for lowering her mortgage rate and stylish dining pieces for everyday prices and hot girls twenty-four hours and rekindling her romance with their February specials. She doesn't know who they're talking to. They sure don't, either. She sees an email from her grandmother from January, asking if Harper got her gift, because she hasn't received a thank-you note.

Harper sends an email to her mom with the subject line *Testing, testing.* Twelve years later it actually gets sent. She opens a browser to catch up. A whole frantic day has passed, so she's expecting a monumentally altered world, but Ada's just lining her lips. Ezra's feed is as unchanged as ever. Harper watches two babies hug and then fall, a wedding dance, a complicated hair braid, a complicated hair braid, a complicated hair braid. There was a bear attack in Alaska, though, and a bridge nearly collapsed in the Midwest, and pollen season is lasting longer and starting earlier than thirty years ago.

Harper can't post any photos onto her feed from a desktop, but she can look at her profile again. There's the image of Harper just before her phone leapt over the side of the boat, and just before she did, too. She looks at that girl and knows her future, the way she used to look at photos of her and her friends right before the pandemic and know theirs. The whole planet's future, shocking and unbelievable. But this girl is about to get joy, not despair. A new magical universe, not a lockdown in a small house, and those awful photos of people on respirators and covered head to toe in protective gear. The funny thing is, no one will ever see what happened down there, under the surface. No one will ever see her moment of courage and what it led to, but when she looks at the before-girl, she can feel the way that dive has changed her.

"Technological time warp," Harper says to Simone and Dario when she emerges. "Prehistoric fossil. Early man used that computer." They're watching the History Channel. Walter's on Simone's lap, zonked after a big day, and she's rubbing one of his triangle ears. Wyatt must have gone to bed. It's wild, Simone's and Dario's two noses, sitting on their faces like twin statues. Harper has gotten used to the way they all look and mostly forgets to notice. But sometimes it strikes her, like it does right now, both of their sets of blue eyes, watching that screen through matching beams. It makes her think about the other thirty-eight half siblings, maybe watching TV too right now, or sleeping, or partying, or doing who knows what. Real people, not numbers, people she might one day get to know like she has these guys.

"You really miss your phone, huh?" Dario says.

"It's got my whole life on it." Why does she keep saying this? It seems wrong, after this day. The actual ocean is part of her whole life, and so are they, a big part of it now. Seeing them there, she realizes that she pretty much loves them, and love is filling in some places that only echoed before.

"You check it *a lot*," Dario says.

"No more than anyone else!" It sounds way too defensive.

"Yeah, okay. You probably have a lot more friends than I do."

"You gotta keep watching, because what if," Simone says. Her eyes are still on the screen, and for a moment Harper thinks she means the show. But then she understands what Simone is saying, and it's so true, the way she keeps scrolling for imminent disaster. "During the worst of the pandemic shit, I was checking mine forty-five thousand times a day. Well. Before, too, to be honest."

"When can we stop checking? How do you know when it's finally going to be okay?" Harper asks her.

"You're asking the wrong person. I still check it forty-five thousand times a day."

"It's never going to be okay, Harper," Dario says. "You just have to stop thinking about how it's not okay all the time, so you don't miss out on all the great times when it is."

Simone looks at Harper and shrugs, and then Harper shrugs back, and they both crack up, even if he's right.

"Shut up, you guys. Sometimes it's better to watch all the stuff people got through in the past anyway," Dario says. "I mean, they had to be strong through things we can't even imagine." He's maybe telling us to be quiet so he can watch his show, but he's probably right again. "Or turtles. Them, too. Think of what they've survived through *eons*."

Harper was going to go to bed, but she changes her mind. She races to the couch and flings herself on Dario and Simone and Walter.

"Harpo, shit! What the hell, ow!" Simone says.

"God, you got me right in the balls!" Dario says. "You're crushing me."

Walter leaps up in alarm but quickly rearranges himself.

Simone scooches to make room for her. One of Harper's legs hangs over Simone's. Dario scoots, too, and Harper's arm is smushed next to his bony side.

She's not even paying attention to the show, so she's really got no idea what it's even about. People just getting through stuff in the past, probably. It's the sort of life-pause moment where she'd normally pick up her phone, because it seems like nothing is really happening. But *a lot* is happening, she notices: She's jammed on a couch with two half siblings, and she's happy-tired from a whole day of swimming. There's an old war on TV, but there are turtles doing their thing right at that moment, too. She can't see them, they aren't posing for any photos, yet they are still just doing turtle life. They swim through her memory. Simone's hair tickles Harper's nose. Walter settles into Harper's lap this time. Dario falls asleep, and his mouth hangs open, and Harper can see a filling in the exact same spot where she and Beau have one.

CHAPTER TWENTY-FIVE

> Today I called the crew together and briefly explained the state of things. I avowed my resolve to command the ship, to lay the vessel's course and perform the duties of captain. With no man aboard capable of the delicate mathematical calculations, they have all agreed to obey my orders.
>
> Mary Ann Patten journal entry
> August 8, 1856

ON THE SECOND DAY THEY DIVE, AND THE SECOND DAY without her phone, Harper still keeps reaching for it. She still keeps forgetting that she doesn't have it, but the forgetting has gone down by half, and the craving has subsided, transformed into a dull ache. She wishes she had it, absolutely, but she's not pacing some cage with need. Anyway, they've been busy, the whole day so full that there's barely time to think about texts, photos, and "The One Food to Give Up for Better Skin."

Twice more, in a protected cove of Molokini, Beau sits with Harper on the edge of that sloshing boat as if he has all the time in the world while Dario bobs in the water, Wyatt and Simone already below. Those few moments are great, if she's being honest, because Beau seems like such a *dad* next to her. It's how she always dreamed she'd feel with a dad—safe in his strength and experience. Okay, his breath smells a bit like coffee and smoke, but what matters is the solid feeling he gives her, sitting there. She gets it all to herself, too, at the expense of Dario, though. Maybe she's a selfish asshole, same as Beau, same as Simone and Wyatt occasionally, but never Dario, who's never either of those things.

As the waves smack the side of the boat, she sneaks in a question. *Do you have a girlfriend or anything?*

Not since Barbara.

What happened to Barbara?

Pandemic, different political views, and she wanted me to move to Montana.

No ocean.

No ocean, Beau agrees.

And on the second dive: *What's the best thing you ever did?*

Before this week I would have said conquering Bonne Terre, but now I'd say walking into Lakeview.

Dario shouts, "Hurry up, for God's sake, Harpo!" and finally, helped along by steadiness and safety, a growing trust, wow, she does it. Splash, and then the cold, the bubbles, the brilliant Technicolor hues, Mother Nature's wild creativity, all the crayons, all the glitter and imagination, eyes that aren't eyes, rocks that aren't rocks, a hundred yellow fish that look like one mosaic swirl. So mesmerizing, so fantastical that Harper forgets fear. She forgets everything—calculus, her mother, Ezra, even the imminent destruction of that very beauty. She's just in it, marveling, because all of it *has* existed for eons, and every minute that Harper has been sleepless or worried, every minute that she's spent taking and editing photos, or reading "Ten Signs of Kidney Disease" or "I Drank a Gallon of Water Every Day for Two Weeks and This Is What Happened," or fretting about stupid Rainey cracking his head open while he does wheelies, the sea has been here, being the sea. *Wonderful:* full of wonder. Saturation, perfect; shadows, yes; contrast, as it was always meant to be.

"Look at this. Isn't she a beauty?" Greer says, plopping the tuna on the grill with a smile and a happy swing of arm flab. "Our neighbor old Mr. Mamoa brought it over. To help us celebrate the new grandchildren, he said."

"Nice!" Wyatt says. "Man, that smells great."

Greer and Beau have a ton of friends. So far they've met Big Dean and Amber and Jake and, when they first got to Greer's house, Teva, the pool boy (a pool man—he's Beau's age), with his beautiful Polynesian tattoos covering both shoulders. And they've heard about old Mr. Mamoa and lots of other neighbors and shop owners: Bob Alualu and his wife, Maureen, who own the Surfside Restaurant; Loyale Grant, former chanteuse (Greer's word) and neighbor, known for the hit song of the 1960s "Sand in My Pocket," who always wears all pink. Beau briefly spotted Dirk Cooke from the Oceanography Institute, too, with his deep tan and his white beard, and waved from a distance. Mr. and Mrs. Nuu from the PP Shack, who look like twins with their matching shirts and black curly hair, who rang up today's lunch order and slid it across the counter, making inside jokes to Beau. When you find your MF, you get a whole crew of new people.

Beau and Greer aren't embarrassed to let everyone know about Harper and her siblings, either. It makes her own embarrassment dim. Their openness just airs out the secrets and lets the light in, and wow, the truth just seems like a normal part of being human. Their neighbor Heiani even came over with her own little granddaughter, Beatrice, and brought forty-two pieces of what looked like green glass, good-luck charms to be given to each of Beau's new children. *It's actually olivine,* Greer told them, *which in its highest form is peridot. It's a volcanic gem known as the tears of Pele, the great goddess of the volcano.* Harper has hers in her pocket right now.

"So much to celebrate!" Beau says. "Let's have another cheers! To the newly PADI-licensed open water divers!" He raises his glass, and so do they, clinking in another round of happiness. Harper's mom would have rolled her eyes—it's a pet peeve, when people use the word "cheers" like that when they give a toast. Beau is beaming, and maybe drinking a little too much. Simone, too. Harper hopes *that* isn't something that came down the genetic line. Still, they have reason to celebrate—they've officially completed their course, receiving their temporary PADI cards, the official ones coming soon.

"Photo!" Simone shouts. Harper doesn't reach for her phone this time. She knows it's gone. For a second she feels jealous that Simone will have this great shot, because people love family reunions. But weirdly there's a new awareness—it's kind of freeing not to take the photo. It's a job she doesn't have to do. She doesn't have to take the photo and edit the photo and post the photo and follow up with the comments about the photo.

They all clump together and squeeze in, one giant selfie, with all their similar faces. "Say 'PADI,'" Simone says. It's not just being a kiss-ass, either, Harper can tell. Simone owns it. They *all* own it as they shout "PADI!" and smile. The achievement . . . It feels awesome.

Greer runs out to take the fish off the barbecue, and Harper has to go inside to use the bathroom.

"I always like to imagine it, before," Greer says when Harper comes back out, and takes her chair inside their circle.

"Imagine what before?" she asks. The torches are on, and it's a warm but windy evening. The waves boom and then crash, and overhead the palm trees hula.

"The volcano. Molokini. Before it blew up some, what, two hundred fifty thousand years ago," Greer says.

"Two hundred thirty thousand." Dario's been reading about it.

"It was one of seven out there . . . ," Greer says.

"They were just telling us that the seven volcanoes made, *formed,* a whole big island, Maui Nui," Wyatt says.

"Maui Oldie." Dario feeds Walter a noodle from the pasta salad.

"So old, so, so old," Beau says. He pops a bit of fish right into his mouth with his fingers, and then licks one. Patricia Proulx would be appalled at his manners. It's hard not to think about the ways her family would disapprove of Beau and Greer, and even Captain Neptune, with his beach nipples draped in seaweed like they were today, especially as Harper feels the judgmental Proulx parts of herself loosening like a once-tight knot. "Pleistocene old. Two million–plus years ago. And then, boom, *blast.* All that was left, all that was visible—you're looking at it."

They all gaze out at the bluish dark curve. "The sea monster," Harper says.

"The battleship. That's what the navy thought it looked like," Dario says. "That's why they used it for bombing practice. That's why all those old bombs are out there."

"Fuuuuck," Beau says. Imagine Patricia Proulx's eyes going cold here. *It's just a word, Grandma,* Harper imagines saying back. *Righteousness is way worse.* She's not out to disown every part of her mom's side of the family, but she wouldn't mind disowning the prissy-superior-virtuous thing, her own included.

"Did you hear anything from the admiral yet?" Wyatt asks.

"Yeah, no," Beau says. "He wasn't too pleased about how I got through. We told his secretary I was the president of the Model Trains Association and wanted to do a Q and A with him for *Model Railroad News.* He loves that shit."

They snicker.

"Our friend Loyale did the intel."

"Chanteuse who wears all pink?" Simone asks.

"Her tech skills are killer for an eighty-year-old," he says.

"That's because she's hot and heavy with Aaron Wilkes from Island Realty, fifteen years her junior," Greer says.

Now they really snicker.

In spite of the serious subject, Harper feels a warm coziness there with them. A belonging, like being part of the popular group, with their inside jokes. The small differences don't matter that much when you all laugh at the same time.

"I FedExed twelve pounds of environmental reports to him, and four separate petitions with some ten thousand signatures that we got in days."

"It's at fifty thousand now," Dario says. "I looked. I signed it."

"I want to sign," Simone says. "I'm going to sign right now." She gets out her phone.

"Me too," Harper says.

"Seriously, though, what's going on? I mean, what are their plans?" Wyatt asks.

"They're going to detonate those bombs," Beau says.

"I just cannot believe this," Simone says. "What about endangered species? They can't just *do* this. Here, Harpo." Simone hands her the phone, and Harper signs the petition, too, and hands the phone back.

"Yeah, they can. August twenty-seventh. That's the plan. And we wouldn't have even known about it until after the fact if some whistleblower hadn't told Pauline, a dive guide over at Severns Diving. They've been planning it since last year. Our state rep is outraged. Even NOAA can't get answers. They told the navy that they're supposed to be consulted about the effects on protected species before anything happens, but NOAA also put out a statement that they're 'not clear' if the navy intends to do it anyway."

"There's *no way* they can just—" Simone ties her braids under her chin anxiously.

"Yeah? They already have. *Twice.*"

"Wyatt told us," Harper says.

"It took *decades* for that area to grow back to what it is now," Beau says.

"We dived it after those detonations," Greer says. "Tony and me. All over, all along the bottom . . . gray ash, wherever you looked, hundreds and hundreds of yards of it, spreading outward. It looked like the end of the world after a nuclear bomb. And the sharks! You could see them from here, from the yard. So many sharks, because of all the dead fish."

"Oh my God. We can't let it happen. We can't," Harper says. But those words ring false. They feel like the helpless statements of a girl sitting in a lawn chair on a summer night. What can *she* possibly do? It's all so large, so awful, that it seems separate from her, like those earthquakes happening somewhere else, distant enough to forget about. What is *wrong* with her? Her heart has blown a fuse, because every horrific thing is another internet pet death. It feels cold out suddenly. The wind has picked up, and goose bumps rise along her arms. Even the sturdy birds-of-paradise and the huge, wide leaves of the elephant ear plants sway.

"All those beautiful species," Greer says. "Not to mention the wreck. We were just plain lucky the last times. She was covered in ash for a while, but that ship was built to last. But it's gonna go this time, I just know it. Who knows how much of it will be left. Dad would have been heartbroken," she says to Beau.

"The wreck?" Simone says.

Greer looks at Beau. "You didn't tell them?"

CHAPTER TWENTY-SIX

> The *Car* is caught in a horrendous gale that threatens to swallow us.
>
> Mary Ann Patten journal entry
> August 12, 1856

NO, BEAU HASN'T TOLD THEM, AND SO GREER *SHOWS* THEM. They leave the dark arc of Molokini and go inside, into the living room of the house, with its sagging couch cushions, and the teak tables, and the framed maps. She brings them over to those shelves again, the ones she showed Dario the last time they were there. The largest item is a murky photo in a frame, propped at the center. It's hard to tell what it is, actually. Harper can only see smeary brown-green until she looks closely. Then she can see faint outlines, and when her eyes adjust, the partly buried skeleton of a ship.

"There she is," Greer says, and taps the photo's glass with her nail. "Our Tony—he did *thousands* of dives. He was one of the men who discovered the SS *Josephine*, like we told you. But this is the one he couldn't let go of, the one that gnawed at him. No one knew her identity, and, goddamn it, he was going to find out. The first time he saw her, with that figurehead of King Neptune, he was a goner. Do you see it?" She runs her fingertip along the bow.

"I think so," Harper says. She sees a hazy male figure, and maybe a spear.

"I totally can," Simone says.

"Definitely big hair," Dario says.

"I kind of see the tail." Wyatt points.

"He dived this wreck so often, Dean started calling him Captain Neptune, and then everyone else did, too. He even changed the name of the shop."

"Well, the original name pretty much sucked," Beau says. *"The Dive."*

Simone winces. "Yikes."

"Missy, Big Dean's ex, even made him that statue," Greer says. "The likeness is incredible, I'll tell ya. That bod of his! He . . ." She blinks. She has to stop to clear her throat, as if she might cry. "Ah! He wanted to know the identity of that ship so bad."

"It was his, um . . ." Beau's voice has gotten high-pitched with emotion. "Dream. Desire. *Need.* To find out. But he never did. It never happened."

"It was right out there, right in his own backyard. Or front yard. Right near the deep center of Molokini. Imagine being so close and never knowing who she is. He just kept going out, trying to find some proof that would tell us for sure."

"Are all these things from that wreck?" Wyatt asks.

"Not all. Most of this stuff is from other dives. Just these things here." She indicates a single shelf.

"This?" Dario takes the whalebone from his pocket.

"That." Greer nods.

"There's actually *a lot*," Harper says.

"There's all kinds of shit down there," Beau says. "I found this just last month." He holds up a small round object.

"A button!" Simone says.

"Did he have any *guesses* even? About the ship?" Dario asks.

"Oh, he had guesses," Greer says. "One big guess."

"You could call it a *hope*," Beau says.

"*Neptune's Car.*" Greer pauses, lifts her eyebrows, and waits for their reaction, as if this name is an important and known name. But Harper's never heard of it, and everyone else seems clueless, too, but no one wants to admit it. They each do a version of the pretend *hmm*, the all-purpose social face-saver for any lacks in your common knowledge. Wyatt actually makes a *wow, you've got to be kidding* face, but he's totally faking it. *Neptune's Car,* whatever it is, seems to mean so much to Beau and Greer that no one's willing to risk the failure of not knowing. "The evidence was building. First of all, that figurehead."

"Well, that's logical," Dario says. "With King Neptune right there, it should be Neptune-Something."

"Nah," Beau says. "He was a pretty popular figurehead for ships. Him and mermaids."

"Tony knew it was a clipper ship—" Greer says.

"So that narrowed it down to the nineteenth century," Beau interrupts.

"He knew it was an *extreme* clipper ship, from the shape of the hull. Sharp." Greer forms her fingers in a triangle. "Which means it was built for transport, but also for speed. *Neptune's Car* won herself some races, for sure."

"He also got the idea in his head," Beau says, "because of

this." He picks up another disk, a large metal one, and he holds it in his palm and shows them. It features a design, a strange design—a star and a moon, and on one side a creature with a beard and a sailor hat, and on the other a creature with a horse head, both with the tails of a whale.

"A coat of arms," Dario says.

"A horse with a whale's tail?" Harper asks.

"It's supposed to be a sea lion and a sea unicorn," Greer says.

"A sea unicorn? Awesome," Simone says.

"It's the Portsmouth coat of arms. Portsmouth, Virginia. And Tony recognized it. It's a marker from the shipyard where it was built. And the only clipper ship builder in Virginia, or in the whole south, was Page and Allen," Greer says.

"This is the hope part," Beau says. "Because his own great-great-grandfather Nikolaos had been a welder in Portsmouth. At *that* shipyard, back in its heyday, in the 1850s. Remember the kid who came over on the boat? Some cousin gave him a job there when he was twelve, and he stayed, learning the ropes. So he could have worked on that very ship. He was sort of our original link to boats, to the sea, all of it. Going way back. After Dad found this, he *really* couldn't let it go."

Beau's own great-great-great-grandfather? *Her* own great-great-great-great-grandfather. A father and a father and another father. She imagines this welder, her ancestor. Well, she imagines stuff she's seen in movies—a hardworking kid, one who becomes a man with big hands, a helmet, a torch. That man lives on because of her, and this is such an unbelievable fact that she shivers.

Dario's thoughts are there, too. "*Our* great-great-great-great-grandfather," he says. "If this meant so much to Tony, we've *got* to be able to figure this out. It's narrowed down to clippers built by that shipyard, then, right?"

"It's not a short list. And who knows what happened to most of them," Beau says. "This just might be something we'll never know, Dar, because he tried to find out for *years*. I understand it. I do. Wanting that connection to the shipyard, let alone to such a famous ship."

"Okay, I really don't want to seem like the stupid one here, but I have never heard of it," Simone says.

"Same," Harper admits.

"Well, 'famous' is probably stretching it," Beau says. "I mean, like, ten people even know or care about this."

"Famous," Greer insists. "And he didn't just *want* it. He *felt* it. That wreck—she's *Neptune's Car,* he was *certain.*"

"So, why was it famous?" Dario asks. "I don't know, either." He shrugs. Oh man. Harper is grateful for them, her siblings.

"In 1856 a nineteen-year-old girl navigated it around Cape Horn, the most treacherous seas *in the world,* while she was *pregnant,*" Beau says. "She was the first woman to captain a ship. Ever."

"Wow," Simone says.

"That's incredible," Harper says.

"Yeah, maybe *too* incredible?" Beau says. "That it's right here, this ship my great-great-great-grandfather likely worked on? The measurements add up, though—two hundred sixteen feet, by forty by twenty-three or so . . ."

"And there was evidence that a woman was on board at one time." Greer picks up another object. It's a clump of rusty something with rings attached.

"No idea," Wyatt says.

"It's a gimbal," Greer says. "For a gimballed bed. These two pivot points here, and the rings—they keep a bed flat in rocking sea. In the time of these ships, beds like that were built for the comfort of a captain's wife. Pretty strong indication that one was once on that ship. *Which* wife, on the other hand . . . And he also found this down there." A brass syringe, with a longish bent handle, some sort of medical device maybe. "Definitely belonging to a woman."

"It looks like a big metal tampon," Simone says.

"At first we thought it was maybe a needle case or a device to grind spices. But our friend Sylvie S. O'Sullivan—she's a marine archaeologist—told us it's a douche, from the mid-1850s," Greer says. "Common back then, to maintain 'cleanliness' and prevent venereal diseases. Women even gave these contraptions to each other for wedding presents. Can you believe it? Give me a Cuisinart, thanks. This *definitely* meant there was a woman on board, at least once."

"Still, that doesn't tell us which woman, either," Beau says. "It's not enough proof. I wish it was."

"We need something else," Greer says. "It wasn't all that uncommon for a wife to accompany her captain husband out to sea in Victorian times. She was still a delicate lady, though, keeping the home in order and her husband happy, but *home* was a boat."

"Well, that girl was sure more than a delicate lady," Harper says.

"Mary Patten," Greer says. "Her name was Mary Patten. And her story . . . Let's just say she was one delicate Victorian badass. Right around *your* age, too." She points her finger at Harper and Simone.

Mary Patten. It's hard to imagine it, a real girl just two years older than Harper herself, navigating a ship in the most treacherous waters, as Greer said. *Beautiful girl, you can do hard things.* Yeah, now *that's* hard.

"There's *got* to be a way to find out," Dario says.

"Not if those bombs go off," Greer says. "It'll be in pieces."

"So there's this historical thing out there, let alone the marine life, and they're just going to blow it all to shreds? It's sickening." Simone folds her arms, shakes her head.

"Well, in terms of the historical thing—there are millions of shipwrecks," Beau says.

Wyatt's eyes pop. "Actually *millions*?"

"Millions! The seafloor is covered with them. From every era. Canoes, ten thousand years old. Right out here, even?" He hooks his thumb toward the ocean. "A *ton* of shipwrecks! The marine life, though . . ."

"Wait. Did he think, uh . . . ?" Dario grimaces. "That *she's* down there? Mary Patten? Like, her bones or something? Some of those shipwrecks are graveyards. Like that one in Pearl Harbor."

"No, no. We know what happened to her. She made it back home to Boston, where she was from. We just don't know what happened to the ship, *Neptune's Car.* At least, at the end," Greer says. "The *Car* went on to have many more voyages. God, what it went through—pirates, yellow fever, cyclones, even a murder in her history after that. But in 1869, the last record of her, she was 'sold to local interests' in Hong Kong. It's said that she sank into the mudflats of Kowloon Bay, but Tony said the purchase price was high, too high, if they just planned to break her up. There were rumors that she was on her way back to either New York or San Francisco. He and Dirk Cooke, after examining the wreck down there, both think the mast snapped. And she was already damaged, after the last trip on record."

"Why would the girl's personal stuff still be on the ship? If it went on many more trips?" Wyatt asks.

"You can say the word 'douche.'" Simone pokes him, and he scowls at her.

"Oh, we found stuff from other trips, too. You ever been on a ship at sea? Anything not nailed down slides around. Lots of cracks and crevices in a ship. You break it apart, it's like hitting a piñata." Greer picks up what is clearly a coin and hands it to Harper.

"From where?" Harper asks. "I can't read it."

"Peru. 1860. Which jibes with a trip *Neptune's Car* took there for a shipment of guano."

"Bird shit?" Simone asks.

"They used to use it for gunpowder," Greer says.

Dario snickers.

"There's another coin from Madagascar. Also jibes with her record," Greer says. "This stuff . . . We could be here all night."

"It's so sad, that Tony never got to *finish* this," Dario says.

It *is* sad. Harper understands wanting to know something so bad that it consumes you, a mystery that's part of your own lineage. Sad, too, really sad, that they'll never meet him, Captain Neptune with his spear and his muscly chest. She wishes she could see a photo of the real guy. The *real guy*? Her *grandfather*. She never met her other grandfather, either, Raymond Proulx. And weirdly, right now, she feels closer to Tony. Hearing about someone's deepest desire can do that. All she hears about Raymond Proulx is how successful he was, and how much he loved chocolate-covered cherries.

Greer must be reading her mind. She takes an album off another shelf and opens it to a particular page. "My favorite photo of him." She still sounds so in love. This is also really different from her grandmother and grandfather. When her mom and grandma talk about Raymond Proulx, he sounds less like a real man than an idea to admire. Now here he is, Antonis "Tony" Zane. Brown hair, solid build, beaming smile. He's muscly, all right, standing in his wet suit, holding an old-fashioned globe diving helmet. It's a photo from the 1970s or so, with that particular retro yellowing, but you can still see them, their blue eyes. He really is hers. What would it have been like to grow up with him? He seems like he'd have a big, loud laugh.

"How'd he die?" Simone says. "If it's okay to ask."

Beau looks stricken. "The . . ."

They wait.

Beau puts his head down, rubs his temple.

"Virus." Greer's voice is hoarse. "The fucking virus."

Oh no. *No.*

"And, um. Uh, we couldn't be there. You know, with him." Beau says it so softly, Harper almost can't hear.

Their grief hits her in the center of her chest. She thinks of Mr. Wong on that stretcher. And she remembers the anguish in Mrs. Wong's stooped shoulders, the way she disappeared into her house afterward. It's heartbreaking, so unbearably heartbreaking. She wishes she could push this singular tragedy away from her, too, along with the larger ones like earthquakes and hurricanes, but it drills into the center of her chest. And she understands now why Beau Zane came home. Why just seeing beautiful diving spots wasn't the biggest thing anymore.

"God, I'm sorry," Simone says.

Simone sets her hand on Beau's shoulder, and Wyatt stares at the floor and doesn't speak. Dario loops his arm around Greer's waist, and then Harper does the same. She feels awful, but kind of embarrassed, too, because this woman, the one she has her arm around, isn't the grandma she's known all her life, and Harper doesn't truly know their tragedy. *Her* tragedy during the worst of it was sitting in front of a screen for months on end, stuck at home with her mom. *Her* grandma was just fine, staying inside and ordering box after box from Amazon.

Other things *did* happen, though. She lost so many experiences, ones she'll never get back—school dances, hallway banter, the chance to care about small things, like gossip and crushes. She was going to join band, but it didn't matter to her anymore afterward. The set of the school play she helped paint got abandoned halfway through, a half-finished city backdrop. Harper's mom worried about losing her job, her coffee cup deserted on her desk the day they were told to go home. For months they wiped down groceries and were afraid to breathe anytime they passed another human being, if they went outside at all. The images stay and stay with her, a wound that refuses to heal even after you stop picking at it: Feeling so trapped that she wanted to climb out a window, even if there wasn't anywhere to go. The eeriness of empty streets and boarded-up stores. The lull of sameness and depression. So much is still here, too: the half faces, eyes only, the stuff that makes us human—smiling, touching each other—gone. Fear of the next thing happening. News of the next thing happening. Mostly Harper wants to forget all about the pandemic, just move on, but it's still hovering and threatening. It's the kind of change that doesn't change back, even if you can go to restaurants again. Knowing that regular life can end so swiftly is something you can't shake, and maybe never will.

Harper's eyes are drawn to that photo of the wreck. The murky waters. Greer and Beau and Mrs. Wong and people who got sick or lost loved ones—they were actually *on* that boat, Harper thinks, the one that sank. But the wreck belongs to everyone. Everyone has been through something large. Everyone has been battered.

Greer and Beau walk them out to the SUV, and they all hug good night. The palm trees sway hard in the wind, and Harper can smell that particular heavy dampness of rain coming. Beau is congratulating them again, bouncing around, happy.

"PADI open water divers!" he says. "You can now dive anywhere in the world!" He's said this enough times that it could sound like a tired advertising phrase from Captain Neptune, but it doesn't. It sounds like something she's earned, that's hers now, and that no one can take away.

"There's got to be a way to find out about that ship," Dario says. "Maybe you just need to find the right object. Maybe you already have it!" Oh man—history, facts, an open question about identity, a *hunt* he can get all obsessive about—it's Dario's favorite stuff. Harper can see the hook set. Wait, wait . . . *Tony's* favorite stuff, maybe. God, it's so weird how these pieces of them, tiny and large, just keep surfacing in Beau and his family, like some weird DNA treasure hunt.

"Tony had been trying for *years,* Dar," Simone says.

"I wish I could look all this up," Harper says. "Like, right now, but my stupid phone . . ."

"I'll take you guys if you want," Beau says. "To the wreck."

"Hell yeah," Wyatt says.

"Didn't you say it was at the center of Molokini?" Harper asks Greer. "Where the waters are rough and super deep?"

"They need more practice for that, Beau," Greer says.

Beau ignores her. "Hang on a sec," he says. He jogs back inside. When he comes back out, he hands Harper a book. The cover is old, red leather, with the title embossed in gold: *The Voyage of Mary Brown Patten.* "You don't need your phone. It's all right here."

Wyatt beeps the horn as he pulls out the drive, and Greer and Beau wave goodbye. Everyone is quiet on the way home. Walter's eyes glow that demon-dog iridescent green with every passing streetlight. Harper runs her fingers along those embossed letters. *Mary Brown Patten.* It's the same way Dario runs his fingers along the notches in that piece of whalebone.

"I know there's tons of stuff we could be doing here this summer," Dario says just before they're back. "But, man, I wish we could at least *try* to help Tony. He seems like such a great guy. People *love* him. Did you see that T-shirt someone put on him today? 'Don't hassle me, I'm local,' with a pineapple?"

"That's a statue, Dar, not the real guy," Simone says. "And we gotta remember that he had his shit, too, you know."

"No one deserves to die like that," Dario says.

"I'm into it," Wyatt says as he pulls into a parking spot.

"I just like being around them," Harper says. "I don't know about diving in a *shipwreck,* though."

"I hate this about myself, but if he wanted me to jump out of a plane, I might," Simone admits.

Harper's been jealous of Simone, and sometimes she gets on Harper's nerves, but after tonight she admires her, too. Simone's the most honest one of them. *That* is something that takes courage.

CHAPTER TWENTY-SEVEN

Writing is mostly impossible. I take up the sextant daily, at meridian and at night, and make the necessary observations, tracing out the position of the ship from the charts in the cabin. I then give orders to the men as to the course to be steered. They have never gotten orders from a woman before but are resigned to it. Joshua is still delirious with fever, and I have shaved his head and keep him bathed to bring down his temperature. The men have no idea of my condition, and all eye me curiously through the little windows of my cabin, making the calculations on which their lives depend. In quiet I mark the passage of each day, and in this manner I gain clarity.

Mary Ann Patten journal entry
August 19, 1856

"WY!" HARPER SHOUTS FROM THE OFFICE. IT'S LATE, AND IF she doesn't get an email out as promised, her mom will freak. That old computer isn't connecting.

"What?" Wyatt pops his head in. He sounds annoyed, like an older brother might. And she's mildly happy at bugging him, to be honest, the way a little sister would be, too.

"Nothing's happening."

"Harpo, come on. You know what to do."

"No, I don't."

He reaches back behind the desk, unplugs it, and plugs it back in again.

"Oh," she says.

They wait as the beast hums and whirls. Wyatt's phone rings. He takes it from his hoodie pocket and looks, and Harper sees it, another reason why Wyatt might say *hell yeah* to more diving. A name, already a contact in his address book: Jake. She raises her eyebrows. He blushes. Confident Wyatt actually blushes.

"He's hot," Harper says.

Wyatt shrugs.

"He seems really nice, too."

Wyatt exhales.

"What are you waiting for? God! Go talk to him."

The corner of Wyatt's mouth goes up in a small smile. "Okay, okay."

"Hot," she says.

He hurries out of there, but Harper can hear him in the hall, answering the phone. "Hey," he says. It's a shy *hey.* It makes her so happy. Love is so great, and she's sorry she messed it up so bad.

Harper types a hurried email to her mom. She reads Melinda's. It's full of questions, and updates about her new phone, how they have to do something-something with her account, et cetera, et cetera. Basically they aren't going to be getting a replacement for a while.

Now she catches up with the world. First her own profile, where everyone has gone silent. She has, so they have, too. No one new has liked her last post. She's stopped interacting for, like, two days, and so, boom, nothing. She's struck with a sudden awareness: if she stops for good, she'll basically be forgotten, and fast, at least by all those strangers. The she in those squares will disappear, the perfect girl who doesn't really exist. What does it say about the perfect girl? She didn't mean much, that's what it says. Harper opens a browser. "Subtle Symptoms of Disease Your Feet Can Reveal." An ab-roller workout. "Healthy Foods That Are Actually Ruining Your Diet." "Five Signs That There's a Snake in Your House." A kitten licking another kitten. A plate of macarons. Hey, Neuschwanstein Castle again.

She scrolls past Neuschwanstein Castle and the kittens and the ab-roller workout. Weirdly, after this second day of diving, none of this seems like the world at all. Those fish did, that coral did, Wyatt out in the hall saying a shy *hey* does. Captain Neptune with his six-pack abs did. Harper going over the side of that boat—that definitely did. But this all seems like . . . *noise*.

She realizes something shocking: She doesn't care about Neuschwanstein Castle. Or the rest of it, actually. Not a single bit. How long has she just been staring at this shit, not caring? No idea, but she just kept looking and looking like she couldn't help it, and now some wire has been snipped, and this noise . . . It seems really annoying. That perfect girl in the squares is pretty annoying, too. She's afraid to make one wrong move.

Right now, right at this very second, while she's still logged in to her email account, the number of unread emails changes by one. Her mom has probably been sitting there waiting and has already answered. This bugs her beyond words, the waiting. The focus on her is so irritating! Harper's ready to get all worked up and pissed, and so she clicks to her email account to read her mom's response.

But then her heart stops.

She swears it's a thud, like heart brakes on a heart road, or maybe heart breaks, because there's the subject line, all in black: *I hope you're okay.* And there's his name: *Ezra.*

She's scared to open it. So scared that she paces the room a few times, gathering up her courage. Same as when she sat on the side of the boat, though, she has a second of bravery, and that's all it takes, because there are his words. His very own voice, she can hear it.

Hey, Harper. I've been trying not to reach out, and, oh man, it's been tough. But I'm caving because you didn't post in a few days, and the last one was of you about to GO DIVING. Well, I hope you're okay. We don't have to talk, but I sure as hell would feel better knowing you're all right.

She starts to cry. Tears of relief, love, who knows what else, roll off her nose and drop down onto Wyatt's dad's desk. Those make more tears because sun lotion and salt and Ezra, Ezra, Ezra. Because missing and grief. Because he's not *gone.* She wipes them away. She blows her nose.

And then she emails him back. She's cautious. She reads it over, like, a hundred times. She tells him that she's more than okay. She tells him about the word that's been whirling in her brain lately, something she's been wishing she could tell him. *Remember when you said that wonder was gone?* she writes. *It isn't, Ez. Not at all.* She tells him about the yellow fish and the turtles and the Technicolor hues, and what it feels like to let go of the edge. She tells him about Beau Zane and Greer and Antonis Zane and Dario and Simone and Wyatt. She wants to tell him everything. Maybe because there actually *is* an everything, real stuff from just *being* and *doing,* instead of the secrets and pose-y nothingness that she held on to so tightly before. God, she realizes it, like, it smacks her right in the head, the way she tried to jam all that stuff into an empty place. The way, too, that she thought that hole belonged to Beau, and would be fixed by Beau, when it was hers all along. It's not there anymore, not like it was, that hollow spot.

It's way too long, and she says too much, but there's one more thing—she tells Ezra that she's sorry.

Blink.

In a few moments, a response. The mailbox number goes up, by a single, perfect one. Oh, beautiful life, there he is again. And he tells her about Binx getting a new stuffed star that glows, and how they're spending a lot of time in the bathroom with the door shut, just sitting quietly in the dark watching the star be light. He tells her that his mom got him some charcoal pencils and a drawing pad, to shake him from his sadness. He drew a bird, and when Binx saw it, he said, *Hey, good-lookin',* like a sleazy guy at a bar.

She doesn't care about Neuschwanstein Castle, but she cares about those fish, and her sibs, and both her families, and her real, actual friends, and she cares about Ezra.

Writing to each other, *reading* each other, feels so different from their old being together. In the stillness of Wyatt's dad's office, she can really *hear* him, even though reading is a silent act. She is concentrating on him, *being* with him and him alone. It makes her miss him so bad. Not because he looks artistic or takes photos of her like a devoted boyfriend, but because he's a good person. She says, *I never knew you went to Cuba.* And he says, *I never knew you were so brave.*

It's hard to get to sleep now. Harper is energized, but self-doubt is creeping in, too, because what if this is over? What if it's just these emails, and that's it? What if she messed it up in there somewhere? That familiar worry about messing up is usually handled by reaching for her phone and scrolling. In some ways, it's *too* quiet without makeup tips and singing and kittens and hidden signs of illness and catastrophes. She's just about to get out of bed to pace around when her door cracks open. Walter pops his head in and then makes a running leap to jump on her bed. It's her and him, and she focuses on Walter and Walter alone, same as she did with Ezra. She studies his eyelashes, and his funny chin. She pulls up one of his lips so he looks fierce.

"Grrrr," she says on his behalf.

Quiet—it gives you unexpected space to play in, too. Quiet is a once-crowded dance floor, now cleared, where you can cut loose with no one watching. It's roomy.

"You've had a big day, Walter," Harper says as he curls up like a doughnut. He's a good friend, and his little warm body is a comfort. Now Harper decides to fold herself into the quiet like it's a feather duvet.

Under this island sky, they sleep.

That night, she dreams she's Viola, from *Twelfth Night.* With two faces, same as the mask she made. The girl, the helpless female. The girl, disguised as a male, shipwrecked on the shore, capable and brave. The dream is about Mary Patten, too, she realizes. The girl, the helpless female, pregnant, Victorian delicate. The girl, standing at the helm of a clipper ship, as capable and strong as every human woman throughout time, no disguise needed at all.

CHAPTER TWENTY-EIGHT

I have received a letter from Keeler, still impris-
oned in his room. He has reminded me of the
great dangers of the coast, and of the perilous
responsibilities I have assumed. He has offered
to resume command of the ship if I will free him.
I replied that he is unfit to be mate, and that I
will not consider it. When my husband was well,
he did not trust him, and now that he is ill, I
certainly won't trust him, either. I will keep the
man locked up, even if this will incite his fury.

Mary Ann Patten journal entry
August 26, 1856

HARPER SETS THE BOOK DOWN. IT'S THICK WITH INFORMA-
tion about clipper ships, and life at sea, and captains' wives,
sprinkled with bits of the journal Mary kept at sea. It's not thick
enough, though, so she has to portion it out and read slowly, like
you do with the best and most important books. If she doesn't
get greedy and gobble it all up, she can make it last the rest of
the summer. She's had the book for two weeks now, and Mary is

on day fifty-seven of her voyage. That asshole first mate, Keeler, is trying to get her to let him out. *Don't do it!* Harper urges from the future. She's worried about Mary. Every bit of the world Mary lives in is telling her that she can't manage this, and Harper is hoping she doesn't cave and let Keeler take charge. Mary's only nineteen, too, and going on six months pregnant or so, and trying to handle mutinous creeps and a sixteen-ton ship.

Harper hasn't had time to read in years, but she has time now. Since that day she realized she didn't care about Neuschwanstein Castle or ab rollers or the rest of it, her scrolling has gone down to practically zero. She's gone from six kittens and four elaborate doughnuts, down to two kittens and one elaborate doughnut, down to one elaborate doughnut. The noise, so recently annoying, now seems . . . pointless. It's an intrusion, like someone interrupting an important conversation for pointless chatter. Now when she picks up that big old book, it feels so good in her hands, and she remembers how fun reading was, how much she loved it when she was in middle school and before. She was the sixth-grade reading champ, and her mom used to take her to the library, and she gets to have it again, that great way you can disappear into a fantastic book, let alone this one, a *true* story. She even sniffed it, yum, pages, and she hasn't stopped to smell book perfume in a very long time.

Harper wishes she could read just a little bit more, but Wyatt is jingling his keys. "We're all waiting! Come ooooon, Harpo!" he says. "Dario and Walter and Simone are already in the car."

They've been doing other stuff, too, during those two weeks, of course. They've been getting ready for today. The day they dive the wreck.

Getting ready . . . Harper doesn't feel ready, even if they've practiced pretty much every day. They went to the Tako Flats on the inside of the crater, with its channel of sand and heads of rough red coral and, oh God, lots of octopuses squeezing in and out of narrow places, changing shape like the goo in a lava lamp. And then to Enenue, where there's little current and medium visibility, but where they saw a flat, wide manta ray, and an enormous maroon-and-pink antler coral with red dotted crabs hiding in its crevices. They dived Middle Reef a few times, too, deeper still, though the visibility is good as far down as you can go, a hundred feet or more. Harper had to force herself not to think about *a hundred feet.* But before she knew it, instead of forcing herself, she was *losing* herself in those blue trevallies, with their silver bodies and electric, neon-blue outlines, and the yellow-and-white pyramid butterfly fish, and the wide, vibrant, pointy-nosed yellow tang. When Harper spotted a thin white fish with a yellow head and a shockingly red tail featuring a fin like a hook, Jake said, *A fire goby. Did you know they're monogamous?* and Wyatt turned shy. Jake is supersweet, and if you see any cool creature under the surface, he can tell you all about it.

Once, when classes were full and the store busy, Greer took them out, along with Dirk Cooke, who drove his boat, the *Reefer.* Greer scooched into her wet suit, and then she patted her sides and tummy and said, *A nice chocolate babka,* but lovingly. She waited with Harper on the side of the boat as Dario paddled patiently in the water.

You guys have heard a lot about Tony and his family, but I haven't told you much about mine. My sister was one of the first women to do the Iditarod, back in the early seventies. You know, the sled dog race, Anchorage, Alaska, all the way to Nome, nine hundred–plus miles.

Wow.

Uh-huh. My mother raised three of us alone while working in mountain rescue. You know, where you take a sled up to some injured skier? Her mother gave birth to her alone in the rooming house where she lived. She almost died. Walked half a mile to the hospital after, in a blizzard, and that isn't some made-up tale.

Geez, Greer.

But you know what? Being strong isn't about doing some big, brave thing, not mountain rescue, not this. Being strong is A LOT of different things. Speaking the truth, or being up against it and getting through some shitty, terrifying situation. And sometimes being strong is saying no. Saying, "I don't want to do this. I'm not gonna do this." Right?

Right.

So, do you want to do this?

I do. I really do. It's just scary.

Okay. Then, in that case, being strong is letting go of the damn boat.

Greer grinned, and Harper grinned back. Then, splash. Over the side Harper went.

After a day of diving, Dario would ask, Are we ready now? and Greer would say, Nope. Beau would just shrug, because they know who the boss is. It's a little unnerving, honestly, that Beau didn't insist on this practice himself. It shows a reckless enthusiasm, something Harper doesn't have. She doesn't have his sloppiness, either, and she doesn't ignore the tip jar at the PP Shack like he does, and she'd never swear in front of Heiani's granddaughter, Beatrice, especially since Heiani winces whenever Beau does it.

At this point they've each taken their turn at having a prickly, awkward silence with Beau because of something he's said, like when he joked *Hey, loosen up* to Harper, or *Take it down a notch, bud* to Dario. When he said that, Harper wanted to cry. She felt devastated. After Beau hurt Dario's feelings, Dario got stony and cold. Simone stomped off when Beau said she was being dramatic. *Is that something your dad taught you?* Beau said to Wyatt when Wyatt kept trying to pay for lunch. The thing is, those observations are all true. And they've also pretty much said the same things to each other a bunch of times, no huge problem. But when Beau said it, he became He again, the one capable of creating them, and destroying them. No one got destroyed, though. He apologized each time, and a slow forgiveness would creep in, laughter would return, and the rest of them would exhale. The whole relationship was on the line every time, but after that, after you could have been destroyed but weren't, the need to be perfect was gone. You could say the wrong thing, he could, and everyone was still there.

It was easier having the romantic image of the guy, the MF. Reality is harder than mystery. It got tiring, smushing seventeen years of feelings into a few weeks. The day he said that she should loosen up, Harper just wanted to go home. She was done having an actual relationship with Beau. Her mom, *she* was the one who deserved her time, her love and devotion. But then Beau took her arm. *I'm so sorry, dude,* he said to Harper. *Ma keeps telling me, a joke from me isn't the same as a joke from you guys to each other. You're awesome, you know, exactly like you are.* They got back in the boat. When he smiled at her after that, it's hard to explain, but it meant more. She *felt* his smile. He didn't have to, and she didn't have to, either, but they did.

MF—he's the dude with ketchup on his shirt, who's patient, and easygoing, and whose reckless enthusiasm gave life to forty-two children.

During those two weeks, after a day of diving and being together, Harper would also write to Ezra.

We saw, like, five octopuses, she typed. *They were red-blue and moved like the slime we made when we were kids, oozing and flowing forward, flattening themselves to glide into narrow openings of coral. Jake told us that they're day octopuses, and that they have three hearts.*

One is more than enough for me, Ezra said.

Same, Harper said, though hers is feeling lighter. Hope is soul-helium.

I used to know a girl who got nervous at the aquarium, Ez wrote. *I took her photo beside the shark tank, but she said she worried there'd be an earthquake right then, and the glass would break, and they'd come whooshing out.*

Who was she? *I can totally handle the aquarium,* Harper said.

For you, he said, and attached a charcoal drawing of an octopus with a globe diving helmet on, its tentacles wildly enchanted, the words *Sink or Swim* written in scrolled letters underneath. It turns out that Ezra doesn't just look artistic. Ezra *is* artistic.

This, all of it, has become her life this summer. It's so far from calculus and posing for photos and cauliflower pizza. Far, too, from all the things she might drastically fuck up, from eating the wrong and deadly food, to failing to see the warning signs, to simply choosing the wrong place at the wrong time. Here, she's a different person in a different existence.

But she worries, because vacation is never permanent. They've been here for five weeks, but time is just flying, and the summer is over in only three and a half more. After that, she'll have to go home, and whenever that reality slips in, it hits Harper that she loves it here, and that she loves these people, her sister and brothers. A lot. And she's maybe starting to love Beau and Greer, too. No one has said those words to Beau and Greer yet, and they haven't said them, either, though they all constantly show affection to each other, hugging, joking, giving big smiles and meaningful looks. Maybe "love" is too big a word for such a short time, or maybe no one wants to risk being the person who says it first. Or maybe because they're saving that word for their own families, their "real" ones.

The sibs, though—they sneak the word in all the time. A joking punch, *Hey, love you, you doof.* A *Love you, buttheads* shouted through a bedroom door at night. And *If I didn't love you, I wouldn't*... How can she possibly leave them? It seems so wrong, that the bigger the love, the bigger the loss. It seems so unfair. Already she has the kind of missing you feel when you haven't even left yet.

Now they're almost at Greer's house. Harper recognizes the particular banyan tree that comes just before the long driveway. "You nervous?" Dario asks Harper.

"My stomach feels like *that.*" She points to the tree's twisty, complicated trunk and branches. "I don't know if I'm ready. God, what are we doing, diving a shipwreck?"

"I'm nervous. Nervous *and* ready," he says. "It's going to be so cool."

"Don't die," she says.

They pile out of the SUV, and Wyatt *beep-beeps* the lock. "If Greer's pissed, it's your fault, Harpo. You know how she hates it if we're late, especially if she made breakfast."

"Who's going to steal your car out here?" Simone says, and gives Wyatt a shove, and he shoves back. It's true. It's lush and jungly, with the hard leaf and white flowers of the hibiscus, and the thick, fleshy succulents, and the sudden red of a dragon flower, with Greer's house set in there next to the crashing surf. Anyway, a pissed-off Greer is her waving a sausage and complaining that it got cold, and breakfast means stacks of pancakes and bacon and waffles, with perfect, deep squares to fill with syrup, like seawater fills a tide pool. They've made a habit of stopping by the house first to drop off Walter, who prefers Greer to doggy day care. At her house he gets pets from Beatrice next door, and boxes of gourmet dog cookies from Loyale Grant, and dried jerky from old Mr. Mamoa. Walter has his own fan club.

"Yum, bacon," Simone says.

Harper can smell it, too, shoving out the warm floral breeze of the island. It makes her think of home, when that glorious smell drifts from Rainey's house and he appears an hour or so later, sticky-faced and wild, doing something dangerous with a pointy twig.

But this time *pissed* doesn't mean Greer waving a sausage. She's pacing by the pool, her arms gesturing in a rant, loose old skin flapping, the hem of her muumuu whipping back and forth around her ankles, as Beau sits in a lounge chair looking glum.

Their lateness isn't the problem.

"Are you okay?" Simone asks, dropping her backpack on the patio. "What's going on?" Walter races straight to Greer, but she's stomping into the house, and the screen door shuts with Walter on the other side. He looks devastated. Oh man, Harper thinks. There are so many little ways that we're hurtful when we're wrapped up in the swirl of our own thoughts and feelings.

"They finally made a public declaration," Beau says. When he looks up at them, his eyes are teary and pained. "The detonation is absolutely happening. Two and a half weeks from today. 'Public safety concerns must be our priority.'"

"No." Dario runs a hand through his hair.

"Fuck," Simone says, and Wyatt just shakes his head.

"Oh my God," Harper says. But honestly, there's that distance again. That's one thing that hasn't changed. Like it's just too horrific and unbearable, you know? Like maybe it's not about feeling too little, but too much. So much that it loops back to a flat nothingness. It's a storm you have to protect yourself from.

"'Public safety.' And what about all the damage, huh? How many consequences, how many unforeseen reverberations lasting for *decades*?" Beau says.

"I just don't get this," Wyatt says. "Creating a whole new catastrophe to prevent a catastrophe? It doesn't make sense."

"Two and a half weeks, do you know what this means?" Beau drops his head to his hands.

Harper nods, but she doesn't really. Not yet.

Greer's back. Harper can see her bathing suit straps under

her muumuu, and she has her wet suit over one arm. She scoops up Walter with her other one, much to his and Harper's relief. "You are going to have a glorious day, little man," she tells him. "With Beatrice and her grandma. I've got to go to the wreck with this motley crew. I don't know how many times I'll ever see it again."

"Mom . . . ," Beau says. It's a whole conversation in one word.

But maybe Greer is feeling too much, too. She ignores him and just bustles around, stuffing towels into her bag. "Hurry up, friends. This bacon isn't gonna eat itself," she says.

In the boat Jake accelerates with urgency as the *Greer Brody* plows forward through azure waves. The unknowable arc of Molokini is ahead, that old volcanic ridge, and there's the gasoline smell from the boat merging with the salty, cold, deepwater smell of the sea. A sailboat's in the distance; a bird dives toward breakfast. Harper's hair whips in her face, and her eyes water from speed and from the glare of the sun. If she squinches, she can see Greer and Beau's house, a tiny dot on the shoreline, a reverse view of what they normally have as they sit by the pool and look out toward this place. Jake slows. The boat motor sputters. He knows right where to stop, just beyond Middle Reef, where the waters are deepest. It's eerie and frightening and fantastic that the wreck is right there below them.

The boat sloshes and rocks, and for the first time out there, Harper might be seasick, or maybe it's nerves. "Let's go," Beau says. "Guys, stay right along the hull."

Hull—the word shoots terror through Harper. It sounds like something that's capable of swallowing.

"No wandering in," Greer warns. "I don't care how cool it looks. That means *you*." She jabs a finger at Dario. Today Harper's diving buddy might be nervous, but he's gotten more and more brave and wants to get out to the wreck badly, with the sort of impatience that makes Harper worry about the way Viola's brother fell into the sea and vanished.

"Remember the map," Beau says. He's shown them the one his father drew. It'll be hard to make out its form down there, where the visibility isn't what they're used to. "We're about to view an endangered species." He looks at Harper, and she nods. She gets it. If any part of her wants to see this, now is the time.

Splash, and in Simone goes. "Enjoy, dude," Jake says to Wyatt, who flashes him a thumbs-up. Splash.

The waves look huge and choppy and maybe even cruel. Splash, Dario, her brother. For a moment she worries if this is going to be one of those stories where there's a diving accident. Where there's an emergency, and someone doesn't come back. Where a brother disappears, like Viola's. As Harper sits on the edge, she looks into Greer's old, kind eyes.

"You know what to do," Greer says.

Harper breathes and imagines that old banyan tree inside her untwisting. She reminds herself that she's nervous and ready, too. One second of bravery. *Splash*.

There's a flurry of bubbles. A rush of cold. And then a smack of fear because, shit, she jumped. But after that her own capability slots into place, wow, as she extends her arms and descends. She sees Dario beside her, and the murky shapes of Simone and

Wyatt up ahead. A cyclone of bubbles blurs everything, but it's just Greer. There she is, her chocolate babka form, *her* capability. *That's my grandma right there,* Harper thinks.

It's quiet beneath the surface, but not silent. There's the blurble of water in motion, and the whoosh of her own breath. In, out, she reminds herself. It definitely *is* murkier here, and there's not the instant clarity of vibrant fish, but a smeary haze she has to decipher. Beau arrives in another flurry of bubbles, and he and Greer swim ahead so they can follow.

It doesn't take long before she sees it—a shape. A purposeful shape, like that of a whale. How could you miss it? It's *enormous,* even if it's partially hidden in the ocean floor, and covered in a fuzz of brown-green. It's huge, and, wow, wow! Harper can even see the three broken shafts of masts in varying heights, dripping with seaweed and plant life, and the passageways like caves that they're forbidden to enter but that fish travel freely through, darting in, zipping out.

The story of it, this ship and everyone ever on it—it rises and fills her with an immense awe. It's so eerie and unbelievable. And it's undeniable, too, that this ship was a once-living beast, designed and crafted, set on voyages with once-living human beings standing right on those murky planks, sleeping in those murky caves. People built this ship, maybe even Nikolaos Zanetakos did. They lived and worked on it, they steered it through still, moonlit nights, and ones where the waves were thirty feet high. Was she here, Mary Patten? Was this the clipper that went around Cape Horn with a pregnant girl at its helm? Harper understands why it's so hard to know who she is, this ship. She's obscured. She's unseen, here below the surface, and history and nature have taken over and covered who she truly is. She's in pieces and half buried.

Harper's eyes adjust. Simone kicks her flippers neatly until she's nearly at the bottom. She reaches out an arm, and silt spins up. They follow Beau to the halfway point of the ship, where a giant hole carves the hull and stern into two. Harper can see the once-alive layers of the clipper, the storeroom bottom, the officers' quarters; the deck, split in half, like a model in a museum, draped in seaweed and muck. Broken, as if the truths might spill out. Harper swims right up to it. She sets her hand on its big side, and it's such a large creature that she almost expects it to breathe. It's slippery and slimy, but it's *real*. And it's magical, the way it's real and wrecked, but still here. Transformed now, with an unexpected purpose, home to all these species.

Harper adjusts her buoyancy so that she remains in place, floating in midsea. She gazes into that dark space, imagining what it was before, taking in what it is now. She sees the spooky, majestic outline of the figurehead, King Neptune, at the bow.

And then her attention is snatched away. A flash of unearthly purple catches her eye. Something glowing. Something swaying. And there it is, there *she* is, an alien being, elegant, astonishingly beautiful, her center a translucent dome encasing an intricate purple design, part flower, part stunning extraterrestrial technology, her tentacles a hundred threads of purple-pink iridescence. She hovers in front of Harper, and Harper hovers in front of her, and she pulses like a heartbeat, and Harper's heart pulses back.

Harper is aware that this creature, this jellyfish, might sting her, but it's not her primary thought. Instead her mind is focused in a moment of pristine awareness. The same way that Ezra and Binx sit in the dark watching the stuffed star be light, Harper watches this creature be light. But it is watching her be light, too. This vivid, miraculous underwater astronaut who has no heart but who is all heartbeat, who has no brain but who is all thought, pure feeling, is clearly witnessing the vivid, miraculous under-water astronaut who is Harper.

Many people think a creature like that, with no heart, brain, or even eyes, a creature made almost entirely of water, can't feel or can't communicate, but right now Harper is sure they're wrong.

You here, the creature says.

You here, Harper says back.

Harper's heart—it's so full. She is. Her whole body, her whole self, is alive on this planet with this singular being, also alive on this planet. She feels a vast, deep, nameless connection to her. Maybe that name is *compassion,* maybe its name is *humanity,* a shared humanity, even if that creature isn't human. She feels that creature's story, too. The whole epic story of every living thing.

The jellyfish rises from that wreck. No, she *emerges* from that wreck; the wreck is all around her, and the murky mess of it only makes her look more beautiful, a true and real and unseen beauty. And right then Harper is so there, so present in this profound moment, that if you reminded her again that she once felt empty, she'd hardly believe it.

The creature pulses, and then she's gone. Harper is so full of wonder that she feels the shock of a near miss. She might have never seen this. Oh God, the girl in the squares might have been at home, instead of here, trying to determine whether she looked better in Clarendon or Ludwig.

Now Harper rises from the wreck, too. She gasps when she surfaces. Oh God, oh God! What if she'd missed it? Not just the stunning jellyfish, witnessed during a wildly adventurous act, but *this*—the *Greer Brody,* bobbing in the ocean. Wyatt boarding, and then kissing Jake, who playfully swats his wet-suited butt. Simone, on the boat already, whipping off her mask and wringing the water from her hair. Jake's hand reaching out to help Harper up. Dario just behind her, and then Greer and Beau. Beau shaking her shoulders and saying, "You did it, girl. You dived the wreck!" Exhilaration, pure exhilaration, and no way to record it or photograph it or ever forget it. She could have missed all of it.

"Did you see her?" Harper shouts.

"Wasn't she incredible?" Beau says. "You understand the old man's obsession now, right?"

"Two hundred and sixteen feet long," Dario says. "You can't imagine how enormous that is until you are swimming right next to it!"

"She was magnificent!" Simone says. "And I found this! I saw something shiny, and I grabbed it. Look." She holds up a tiny object. She sets it on her pinkie, like a hat.

"Oh wow. Fucking wow. It's *fantastic,*" Beau says. He reaches out his hand, and Simone drops it in, and they, this strange family, bend over it.

"A thimble," Greer says. Her wet braid is a long rope of ribbon kelp.

"Yeah. For a *very* small hand," Simone says. She takes it back. It doesn't fit on her forefinger, that's for sure. "It *had* to belong to a woman. Mary?"

"No way to know," Beau says.

"But it belonged to a real person, you know? God, that's so incredible. Did you see the second layer? You could almost make out rooms," Simone says.

"I want to go in them." Wyatt's eyes are bright.

"It was great, it was so great! Did you guys see her, though? That *jellyfish*?" Harper asks.

"Jellyfish?" Dario says.

"She was . . . incredible. Like, unearthly. Purple, and pink, glowing! She had this curved globe over this purple center. . . ."

"A firework?" Jake looks at Beau. He seems doubtful.

"They're usually much deeper. Much, much deeper."

"Then again, think of all the weird shit we've seen recently. Early migrations, species where you don't expect them. It's what she's describing. Under the globe, was it purple, like . . . ?" Jake spreads out his fingers.

"Yeah! Like a flower. A precise and otherworldly flower."

"A firework jellyfish," Jake says. "Did you know that jellyfish are some of the oldest creatures that exist? Five hundred million years, they've been here."

"Those spineless survival dudes are practically eternal," Beau says.

"Super resilient," Jake says. "Sometimes so resilient, huge numbers of them appear in a bloom. In the earliest stage of life, they can clone themselves, so you can get an army of them. Seen from space, it looks like one mass, but it's a just a ton of identical jellies."

"More than forty-two?" Dario grins.

"Dude, don't freak me out," Beau says, laughing.

"Definitely more," Jake says.

"You were out of your depth, and she was out of hers, but you both were there," Greer says.

"We *cannot* let anything happen to that ship," Dario says.

"We cannot let anything happen to all of it," Harper says.

And, God, she means every word. If she thought her empathy was gone, she was so, so wrong, what a relief. She feels that empathy like a pure and permanent thing, a cherished gift, a birthright. Harper cares, deeply cares, about her, the firework, and all of them—the flat yellow guys and the ones with the bright red tails and the huge antler coral and the turtles and that polka-dotted whale shark, wherever he is, and her poor, struggling, radiant fellow human beings, and she cares about the seaweed and the silt, even. And that ship, too, that old beauty.

"There's got to be something more we can do," Simone says.

"All we can do is all we can do," Greer says, which sounds both nonsensical and profound.

Beau puts it more succinctly. "Dudes, we gotta stop them."

CHAPTER TWENTY-NINE

> Keeler is in a raging fury and, made feeble
> against female command, has tried to stir up
> a mutiny against me. I will not weaken to his
> power. This morning I called the other mates
> and sailors aft and appealed to them to support
> me in my hour of trial. To a man they resolved
> to stand by me and the ship, come what might.
>
> Mary Ann Patten journal entry
> September 2, 1856

THEY SET UP SHOP IN GREER'S HOUSE. SIMONE STARTS work on a new website, featuring links to the Molokini petition and the photos that Dirk Cooke took after the detonations in 1975 and 1984, showing the grim, end-of-the-world devastation. Wyatt usually phones his parents every few days, but today they talk a bunch of times as he asks them to share the news of the upcoming bomb blast with their circle of friends in Mercer Island, which includes some of the big names in business and tech companies in Seattle. For the first time in weeks, Harper posts to her page, using Simone's phone. It's not an image of her looking cute by the pool—this time it's a different kind of posting entirely, one for a crucial purpose. She chooses that photo from 1975, depicting the dead underwater landscape in the center of Molokini. She links to Simone's new site. She urges people to share. And then she posts.

Dario, he has other connections. A web of them. A dozen of the thirty-eight half sibs he's spoken with so far. J. C. Mandelli, a college sophomore in San Diego, a surfer and guitar player, texts back: *Dude, this is so fucking awesome, what you're trying to do. Sharing with everyone I can think of.* Eamon Auberge, a high school senior in Vancouver, Canada: *All respect, man.* He shares it with his lacrosse team, and with his mom, who works at a CBC station. Lara Brooks, another college sophomore in eastern Washington, says, *I wish I came with you when you mentioned it,* and Max Perez, history major at the University of Texas at San Antonio, with two braids just like Simone's, says he'll fly over if they need him. Sullivan Cleary, on the UCLA swim team, reaches out to Beau directly after hearing from Dario, and now he's coming to meet Beau next winter break. Iris Jahan, mom of kindergartner Amalie, shares the petition with her mom friends at Challenger Elementary in Issaquah, Washington.

"Dudes, dudes," Beau says every time he hears about another one of them. "Fuck, man." His eyes water. He runs his hand over his scruffy, unshaven chin. "Riches raining down. *Riches.*" And it does feel like riches. Them, him, the whole giant mess of it.

Tick, tick, tick—a bomb, those signatures. Fifty thousand, then seventy-five, then a hundred and seventy-five. Two hundred and fifty thousand. Harper does not watch the likes pour in on her post. Instead she watches the number of signatures go up and up.

Noise isn't all bad, only when the useless kind consumes you.

They're back in the lounge chairs the next afternoon, having an end-of-day meeting before they hit Greer's pool. Beau is home again after working the counter at Captain Neptune, and they fill him in before dinner. They pretty much live in their bathing suits, but Dario already has a towel draped around his neck.

"Five hundred and sixteen thousand!" Beau whoops, and makes his lasso gesture.

"I didn't want to get your hopes up yesterday, but my dad told me that he went to school with the Commander of Regional Commands in the navy," Simone says. "He was always an asshole, according to Dad, but he emailed the guy."

"Commander of Regional Commands?" Dario makes a face. He's getting so tan. They all are. Everyone except Walter, who's still white with brown spots, as usual.

"Kinda redundant," Harper says.

"I don't know! It's what Dad told me. No word back yet, though."

"My mom's having lunch with the head of the Centre for Science and Environment for the Gates Foundation next week," Wyatt says.

"But if we find the truth about the ship, it'll change every-thing," Dario says. "If it's really *Neptune's Car,* the whole area will also be a historical landmark."

"As if the sea life, the environment, and the ocean aren't rea-son enough," Harper says.

"It's so disgusting." Simone swigs a can of beer. "I can't even believe we're having this conversation." She's sitting there in her bathing suit, one flip-flop dangling. Harper hasn't even combed out her hair since they were in the water, and her skin has a salt-water crust. The day when they changed their clothes a bunch of times to meet Beau seems so far away.

"Greer put me in touch with Dirk Cooke," Dario says. "The thimble didn't necessarily belong to a woman. They usually had sewing stuff on board to repair sails."

"It's so small, though," Harper says.

"Even if it did belong to a woman, there's the ongoing issue of *which* woman. Something will practically have to have Mary's name on it," Beau says, chomping on a carrot. The day where he changed *his* clothes a bunch of times seems far in the past, too. He's wearing a holey red tank top with his sailboat bathing suit. He's got three that go in rotation—sailboats, blue stripes, palm trees. He also has the habit of just grabbing something from the fridge and chowing down—a carrot, a tomato, a chicken leg, a tub of yogurt with a spoon.

"The exact same dimensions. The Neptune figurehead." Dario checks off the evidence. He's been studying Tony's notes and research. "A gimballed bed. Portsmouth. Tony thinks that the shipyard used a certain kind of ore in their solder, the same ore they found on pieces of frame and bulwarks from the iron hull. The coin, the high purchase price at the end, the gossip that she hadn't sunk in the mud after all. Pieces of copper fixtures, and signs of floral carvings, same as the *Car* when she was built. What more do they want?"

"Something specific. Something definite," Beau says.

"Two weeks," Harper moans. It feels hopeless. "I mean, Greer told us the Maui legislators already voiced *outrage*, and so did all those environmental groups. The Hawaii Wildlife Fund, NOAA . . ."

Greer herself now pops out of the house. A waft of pot smoke follows her. Oh, Harper's mom would just die. Harper barely notices it anymore, and no one snickers, either. It just blends in after a while, with the musty smell of the house, and the sweet, citrusy smell of the island.

"Well, we still have one option," Greer says.

"Ma . . . ," Beau groans.

"What?" Simone asks. "Whatever it is, we'll do it."

"Damn right," Greer says.

"Ma, we gotta send these kids back home in one piece."

"One piece?" Harper says. She gets a hit of anxiety. "Tell us."

"We'll Greenpeace 'em," Greer says.

"Greenpeace 'em?" Dario asks.

"What we did in 1977. Me and Tony and Dirk, and Big Dean, and old Mr. Mamoa, when they were killing whales. Even Loyale was there."

"*You* almost got killed," Beau says.

"But the whales didn't," she says.

"What did you do?" Harper's really nervous now. That look in Greer's eyes—Harper's afraid to even ask. She remembers the women in Greer's family, the Iditarod racer, the mountain rescue worker. And she feels this in Greer, too, an iron core of stubbornness and will, something that didn't come straight through the DNA, at least not to Harper. Harper will do anything for that firework jellyfish and the rest of them—at least she thinks so—but she's scared to know what *anything* might turn out to be.

"These giant, stinking death ships in the Pacific were massacring whales by the thousands," Greer says. "What those whales have been through . . . God. We went up to Vancouver. We waited until we heard the radio transmission from this Soviet whaling ship, and then we got in these high-speed inflatable rafts."

"Oh shit!" Wyatt says.

"You better believe it! We zoomed out there. Got right between the harpoons and the whales . . . One of those harpoons, *zzzzzooooo*!" She makes the sound of a spear flying in midair. "Went right over our heads, could've killed us! But we stayed. Finally they retreated. They heard us. We put our lives on the line for those whales, and they understood we'd do it again. And again. It was what they called a 'major incident.'" She chuckles. "And we *did* do it again and again, in other places, too, until there was a moratorium on commercial whaling."

"Badass," Simone says.

"This is not done," she says. "Race you to the pool." It's more of a slow jog than a race, but her cannonball splash is fierce.

"My grandmother hates to even get her hair wet," Harper says to Wyatt.

He cracks up. "Same, Harpo. Same."

We may have to Greenpeace it, Harper writes to Ezra. She's been telling him all of it, the embarrassing parts, the imperfect parts, the faults, the whole. She types late into the night, and he types back, sometimes long paragraphs, sometimes only a line or two, as if they're texting. Yesterday, he got his whole family, cousins and second cousins, like, fifty of them, all throughout the country, to sign the petition. And they got *their* friends to sign. Harper had no idea he has such a big family. She's learning so much about him.

Greenpeace it? he writes back.

She explains. As she types, the anxiety zings around. The idea of putting her body between a navy ship and a jellyfish seems too far-fetched to imagine. It seems unreal enough that she can sound fearless, writing that email. But then again, she never could have imagined seeing that firework to begin with. Harper, so out of her element there beneath the surface.

Be careful, Harp, Ezra writes.

It's not like him. He's always encouraging her to feel safe. Maybe she's gone too far toward the other edge, pushed there by Greer and Beau, these people in her life she's only known for weeks. She starts to feel uneasy. Deeply uneasy. Their strangeness to her can just barge right in sometimes, erasing all the connections they seem to have built.

What's happening at home? I miss home. Well, she misses Ezra.

Binx threw his Barbie down the heater vent, and Mom had to use the garden hoe to get her out. Me and Jax and Ada and Maya and Trace are supposed to go to El Corazon. El Corazon is an all-ages music venue in Seattle. For a moment she wishes she were going, too, instead of doing dangerous stuff against the navy. *Hey, it's our favorite band, Slow Change. Still weird, though, thinking of going somewhere with so many people in one room. It'll be my first time since the pandemic. It's creepy. And there's, like, all this Covid-variant talk, and numbers creeping up again. I don't even know if we should go. Fuck! We thought this was going to be over.*

I didn't even know you felt like this! Anxious. You always seemed like you were taking it in stride. I can't believe we never talked about it. I mean, you feeling fear. Well, they never talked about a lot of things.

Yeah, OF COURSE I do. Who doesn't?

Lots of people. Lots of people weren't even all that scared during the worst of it. Ada's family! Harper answers.

I kind of flinch now every time I see a crowd scene in a movie, or an old TV show where people are all jammed in some bar.

You do? I never knew that! SAME! I see it, and it's like, STOP HUGGING STRANGERS. Or DON'T TOUCH THAT HANDRAIL! Remember when we thought masks were weird? Now my mom has different ones to match various outfits.

Sometimes it's like it'll never end, Ez answers. *And other times it seems like . . . did this really happen? When life feels pretty much normal, I think, "What was THAT?" Did we just really do all that strange shit? It was surreal. Totally unbelievable. I mean, even in the moment, it'd hit me, like, I ACTUALLY JUST USED THE WORD "PANDEMIC." But, now, God, is this just going to be our life forever? Is what we knew GONE? And what does it all even MEAN?*

Before, the whole idea was a bad sci-fi movie, Harper writes. *Nothing that could ever actually be REAL. Something "they"—your government or whoever—would protect you from if it ever showed up somewhere. You could totally ignore the possibility of "pandemic," but not anymore. Now we know what can happen. And so fast, too.*

Yeah. We had to be different so suddenly. I mean, fear—weird, shocking fear like that. . . . It goes in deep. Maybe it never comes back out.

It changes you, Harper writes.

It changes you, he agrees.

For a moment neither of them replies. But then he's back.

You're still changing, he says. He's right about that. So right.

WE are, she tells him.

My mom always says, "Most of the time, change is a verb," Ezra writes.

She's been trying to ignore the messages until she and Ezra are done. It's hard, though, and maybe wrong, because the first email reads, *Call me,* and the second one, *CALL ME,* and the third the same, but in bold, with four exclamation points. Maybe something has happened to Grandma Patricia.

"Can I borrow someone's phone?" Dario and Simone and Walter are on the couch watching a movie. It's one of those kinds where some guy has only days to save the world from destruction.

"Not *Wyatt's,*" Dario says, and tosses her his. Wyatt and Jake have been meeting or talking on the phone nearly every night.

Dario and Simone giggle and elbow each other like two elementary school kids on Valentine's Day.

"Hey, thanks," Harper says.

"You can borrow mine anytime to talk to Ezra," Simone says. "So much love in the house is making me feel all warm and fuzzy."

They giggle again.

"We *like* emailing," Harper says. "I don't know why."

"It's new-fashioned old-fashioned," Dario says.

"Now unpause the movie, would you, Dar?" Simone says. "I wanna find out if mankind survives."

Melinda answers on the first ring.

"Is everything okay?" Harper asks. This is her mom's line, but after today, with the harpoon noises and the talk of Greer nearly being killed, she's reminded again that she and her mom are alike, too, and that her mom and grandma were the ones who raised her. *Their* iron core is prissy anxiety, and so is Harper's. *Was?* She has no idea. What her core is made of seems up for grabs.

"I'm not going to beat around the bush, Harper. But you need to come home."

"Is it Grandma?"

"Yeah, it's Grandma! I made the mistake of telling her about what you guys are doing, the whole navy thing, and—"

"She's not sick?"

"No, she's fine! But she actually looked at that post of yours. We both did. She used the word 'radical.' She said I was irresponsible, letting a minor stay in a house with other minors *at all,* let alone for a summer, and she's right. God, she is! I've been so stupid. She said I let this whole thing—you, him, those kids—get out of control, and it's true, Harper. You've been there almost *two months,* and this is ridiculous. I mean, I wanted to support you and all, but it's been *weeks,* and you keep doing one dangerous thing after another, and now going up against the government, I mean, your grandfather was in the navy for two years, how could I forget, and—"

"*Radical?* I'll take it as a compliment if that means caring about our environment, Mom, God."

"I booked you a ticket. For Saturday morning."

"You can't have booked a ticket. You didn't even ask me. Saturday morning? That's in three days. I can't leave now!"

"Don't you understand? You could get arrested. Your whole future could be at stake. Do you want *that* on your résumé your whole life long?"

"I'm not going to get arrested!" She might get arrested.

"I never should have allowed this. She's right, it *was* irresponsible, four kids in a condo for the summer, what was I thinking? Jesus."

"I'm not coming home, Mom. I'm supposed to be coming home in three weeks anyway! What's it going to hurt now? No."

"You've been gone *two months,* Harper. That's plenty of time to have gotten to know him. Them. I mean, God knows what you guys have been doing there, teens in a condo on your own. And now this variant stuff is cropping up again. What if you get stuck there or something, away from home? I just, ugh! I'm furious with myself. It was stupid. You used the word 'detonation' in your post, for God's sake! My *father* was in the *navy,* for *two years,* did you hear me? And you kids are diving right out there where there are *bombs*—it's insane. How *he* would allow this . . . Well, *of course* he would."

"You don't even know him. Don't talk about him when you don't even know—"

"I know what I'm seeing right now, don't I?"

"No. I'm not coming home."

"Do I have to call him? Do I have to talk to him directly?"

Harper feels sick. Beau has been so amazing and so generous, and everything he's done—it's been with the assumption that their parents are okay with it. With *him.* What will he think if her raging mother is suddenly on the phone? Maybe he'll feel betrayed, like she's been sneaking around and lying about the permission she has. He'll feel responsible. She can just see him, running his hand all stressed through his hair. She can *hear* him. *Fuck, man! Hey, you gotta go home if your mom wants.*

"Go ahead," Harper says. But she doesn't mean it. He'll be in the middle, and she's under eighteen, and if her mom objects, she knows what he'll do. One way or another she'll have to get on that plane.

"I'm only looking after—"

"This is wrong," Harper interrupts. Her voice wobbles. She can't leave *now*. The detonation is going to happen in *two weeks*. And she can't leave *them*—her sibs, and Beau and Greer and their friends, and, yeah, the turtles, the firework, *all* of them.

"Parenting is always about trying to figure out what's right! Do you understand that, Harper? Always, and I do the best I can, don't you see that? I make the best choice I can at a given moment. That's all I can do!"

She sounds desperate. She sounds like Harper often feels, sure she'll get it wrong, destined to fail. Sure, too, that failure will lead to a permanent disaster.

"This has been good for me! Can't you see that? Great, actually."

"No, I can't see that. Because I'm here, and you're there! I have no idea what you're doing half the time, until after it happens. You just keep getting further and further out on some *edge*—"

"Edges can be good, Mom. You can stand on them and be okay, and the view is awesome." It sounds brave, but she doesn't know how much she even believes that. They *do* keep getting farther and farther out. She can still hear Greer, making the *zzzzoooo* sound of that harpoon. And it's probably true that no "reasonable" parent would allow their kid to do any of this. She pictures Soraya's mom, also a no-sugar nutrient tyrant who, since Soraya got her driver's license, always makes her call whenever she arrives anywhere, even if she just goes to Harper's house a mile away. Or Olivia's mom, who stomped in to intervene with every unfair teacher and even called Jasmine Tibbett's parents that time when Jasmine was mean, even though Jasmine was six. Or Jax's dad, who called a friend and got him a job, who went to every soccer practice and game, to make sure—what? That no harm would come to him, or that he wouldn't make some fatal mistake like not scoring a goal, or not do his best, or what? And by the way, do you always, always, always have to do your best? How about a break, huh? How about doing a pretty good job, or a just-okay job, and saving the best for what matters most?

No way Melinda will risk all those years of applying SPF 50, and avoiding toxic plastics, and arranging disappointment-free birthdays, and doing FBI-level checking of friends, and clutching Harper's coat when they're in a crowd, and soothing, and comforting, and cheerleading, just to have her screw it all up now. Letting her fly by herself was a miracle, let alone the rest of it.

"You're coming home. I was such an idiot. And I've overnighted you a phone, because you are not traveling home by yourself without one."

"Mom!" she wails.

"That's it, Harper."

It *is* it. Harper might be learning a lot about Beau, but she already deeply knows her mother. She knows what every flinch

328

and intonation and half smile means, and she knows when she can push further and when she can't.

It's done.

It's so done that she doesn't even bother to rage against the wrongness. Harper, Dario, Wyatt, Simone—they started this together and need to end it together. Leaving them now . . . They're not finished. *She's* not finished, with Molokini, with Beau. Going home will mean that *she's* the one left behind, too, as the rest of them keep getting closer to each other, doing this huge thing together, maybe even getting to the point of love, while she's back at home staring up at Freddie Mercury, with his own iron core of stubbornness and will and his "I Want to Break Free" eyes.

Defeat just grabs her ankles and pulls her straight down to sorrow. She'll have to say goodbye to these people, and the time she's had here, on this beach, with the mystical curve of Molokini Island in front of her, and there below the surface of that sea, in and around the crater of a prehistoric volcano, where unimaginable creatures go about their daily lives, and have gone about their daily lives, for centuries. In a matter of hours, a new phone will be here, too, traveling everywhere she does, practically connected to her. It will all be back, it will all be hers again—hair-braiding tips, a dog with a watermelon-rind smile, signs of high blood pressure and reasons to always avoid soda. Six Ab Secrets, hospitals at capacity, Twenty-Seven Things to Never Buy at a Walmart. Two species cuddling, a beignet, a cupcake, a croissant, a bagel, a driver's seat selfie, landslides, and hurricanes. A taco plate, a taco plate, a taco plate.

CHAPTER THIRTY

> Joshua's condition worsens. His hallucinations
> cause great distress, and I must sedate him
> with whiskey and laudanum. He has gone blind
> and thrashes in darkness, and sometimes does
> not appear to hear us. There is little else to do to
> relieve his suffering, and I fear we may lose him.
>
> Mary Ann Patten journal entry
> September 9, 1856

"THERE'S GOT TO BE AN ANSWER HERE SOMEWHERE,"
Dario says. He has all of Tony's files spread out over the table in
Wyatt's condo. "There's just *got* to be!"

"I'm totally with you, Dar, but you're starting to worry me,"
Simone says. "Have you been up all night? You're like an obsessed
detective in a movie trying to stop the killer."

"This is not dissimilar," he says.

"His forehead is damp," Wyatt points out.

It's true. Dario's eyes have the same wildness as Beau's when
he talks about the bombs. Maybe Tony's had that same wildness, too.

"But *look* at this." Dario jabs the sheets of paper. "Look at all the evidence that the wreck is indeed *Neptune's Car.*"

"He just used the word 'indeed,'" Wyatt says.

"It's the right width, right length, right year. Built in Portsmouth, et cetera, et cetera, et cetera! And the Portsmouth thing is critical here, especially that year! A pandemic . . ."

"What?" Harper pops her head up from her phone. Her new phone, which arrived in a padded envelope that morning. She's trying to get all her dearly departed files to return from The Cloud.

"A pandemic. In 1855, the year the ship was built. Fewer ships were built there that year because of it, especially in Portsmouth, where it was raging. So, you know, there's not that many ships that it could even actually be."

"You're kidding," Harper says.

"Yellow fever," Dario says. "No cure."

"Wow. If I read that in the book, it didn't sink in. Our great-great-great-great grandfather was maybe building that ship in a pandemic? And Mary got on it during a pandemic?"

"Yup," Dario says. He's been kind of cool toward her, ever since she made the announcement at breakfast that she has to go home. Simone, too.

"A *pandemic.* On top of nursing Joshua, and dealing with those misogynistic creeps, and captaining the ship. . . . Did you guys know she came in second after all that?" Harper says. When she looks up, she catches Simone making an annoyed face to Dario. "What?"

"It just seems like you're pretending to care when you're leaving anyway," Dario says.

"I can actually care and still leave," Harper snaps.

"It doesn't seem like you care that much if you're leaving right *now*," Simone snaps back.

"Geez, gang, lay off," Wyatt says. "Not everyone gets to talk back to their parents and get what they want."

"Exactly. Thanks, Wy," Harper says. He's an unexpected ally. But this is how it works with the four of them, shifting to each other's sides, two against two, three against one, she and Simone agreeing, and then the three of them piling on Simone. It hurts, though. It hurts a lot. Is she going to lose them when she goes? This scares her, bad. "I can't help it!"

"It just seems like you could *try*. Try *harder*. The navy is coming in two weeks. We need you. I told you, my moms can talk to her."

"It's not going to help, Dar. You have no idea what she's like. You guys are being so mean." Harper wants to cry. "Not you, Walter. It's okay, boy." The dog has worried eyes and is leaning anxiously against Dario's legs. Walter hates tension.

"We just don't want you to leave," Simone says, softening her tone. "And you're going to miss out on meeting Max, too." Max Perez, their half sibling from Texas, decided to fly in after all and is arriving in two weeks.

"*I* don't want to leave," she says.

"It seems . . . wrong." Dario looks sad. "Really wrong. For you to just pack your bags and go. We're supposed to fly home together. This isn't *done*. What are you going to tell Beau?" he asks.

"I don't know!" Harper's stomach feels gross. What *is* she going to tell him? The truth, that her family disapproves of what's been happening—it's the furthest thing from *loosening up*. The small hill of similarities they've been building is sure to collapse in his mind. She can feel the circle being drawn, with all of them in it, and her outside of it.

"You guys, come on. Apologize," Wyatt says.

"Sorry, Harpo," Simone says.

"Mean it." Wyatt glares.

"I actually do mean it," Simone says. "I'm just kind of . . . hurt."

"Same," Dario says.

"Do you think I'm not hurt?" Harper says.

"Let's get out of here," Wyatt says. "We're a group, no matter what. And hey, maybe we'll find something else today at the wreck. Some hard proof. You never know."

In the car Harper reads all the messages that piled in when her phone came back to life, none of which really need an answer, at least not anymore. She's about to text her friends to tell them her phone is working again when she stops. She kind of likes the away-on-a-deserted-island feeling of no texts. Honestly, texts are pretty demanding, like a rude person constantly butting in. She's been guilty of this herself, but there are also those times when you're talking to someone and a text comes for them, and they stop the conversation with you to look or answer. But why, you know? Why is the interrupter more important than the person who is *right there*?

This phone—it feels like some of her post-lockdown friendships. After being away from some people, you just don't have that much in common anymore. She's not sure what their relationship should be, her and this phone, or if she even wants one at all. It's heavy in her hand. Was it always heavy? No idea, but it is. And it's also been incredible, to spend time living life instead of portraying life.

It calls to her, though, the all and everything that is the noise. She opens and scrolls. Stonehenge, skydivers, concealers, ads. Feet on the beach, feet on the beach, feet on the beach. "Six Things You're Doing to Wreck Your Health." All the mistakes she might be making, all the potential disasters and calamities. All the shaky and bold ways people say *here I am* but aren't *here*, and *I* is a carefully constructed image. All the ways we are objects with our objects.

She makes a vow not to get sucked in, not to do the aimless scrolling anymore. She doesn't want to be an object with an object. She wants to be a real person in the real world.

She plunges. Down, down, the hit of cold, the blurble of bubbles. Knowing what to do. This is magic, that she's learned and now she can. There's the sound of her own breathing, in, out. It's probably the last time she'll do this. She can't really imagine buying or renting the gear somewhere at home, finding some diving club to keep this up afterward. Maybe it's just one of those things that are of a time and place. Maybe Beau is. It's hard to envision how—if—any of this will be a regular part of her life.

She can see the bottom of the boat above her until it disappears. The water gets murkier, almost thicker, with poor visibility, but she knows what's coming. That sea-serpent shadow over there, that hulk—the wreck.

There it is. That old clipper ship, grand, so, so grand and alive in its day, with its three masts and twenty-five sails that spread as wide as forty feet. Maybe built in a pandemic in 1855 with the help of a young kid from Corinth, Greece, in Portsmouth, where people were filled with uncertainty and fear, and dying of yellow fever in huge numbers, same as everyone has been filled with uncertainty and fear so recently, with people dying in huge numbers, too. Maybe taking off from New York on its first trip with a girl on board, a girl around Harper's age, who did brave and fearless things when they were required of her. She probably wasn't brave in advance, already brave, sure that she could stop a mutiny and nurse a sick husband and sail a two-hundred-and-sixteen-foot ship around Cape Horn. You don't know what will be required of you. She didn't have a choice. She just did it, and could do it. Bravery isn't a feeling, a feeling you begin with, Harper understands, a quality you have or don't have. Bravery is just the fact that you do what events ask of you when they ask it.

What Harper wants to see, *who* she wants to see, is her. Not just Mary Patten, but the jellyfish, the firework, one of the oldest creatures on Earth, one living being in the long line of them who have survived and keep on surviving. She wants to see her vivid purple, the ongoing soul of her, the magic. It would seem like a sign to stay, maybe, no matter what. To stay, even though it'll anger her mother, and put Beau in an awful middle. Even though them in a boat against a navy ship is dangerous and likely impossible besides.

But Harper doesn't see her. And Dario doesn't find anything. No one does. Maybe this is just over.

When they get back into the boat, Dario looks near tears. Simone pats his shoulder. Wyatt sits on the bench, his head in his hands, as Jake starts the engine. Harper still hasn't told Beau she's going home.

"We're in the fight," Beau says. "And no matter what, we have *this*." He opens his palms to mean them, this day. It's corny but true. It's too bad, Harper thinks, that so many sweet and kind things are labeled corny. Water drips from Beau's long hair. With him in his wet suit, and them in theirs, they all look more alike than ever, dad seal and his seal offspring. It breaks Harper's heart. "We have this, right now," he says.

They return to the condo to shower and dress, and then go back to Greer's. Every now and then, they've gone to a restaurant, some outdoor spot, dotted with people drinking tropical drinks, and a few times Beau came to the condo and Wyatt cooked, but mostly they head back to the house. *Every now and then* and *mostly* means they have a pattern; they have stuff they now do with each other that they can count on.

Dario is splashing around in the pool as Walter stands on the step like a toddler scared of the water. In a moment he'll jump, and his little body will be in midair for a split second before he splashes, paws going a million miles an hour until his head pops up to the surface, his Civil War soldier beard wet and pointy as if he's just bathed in ye olde pond. Walter always has his own moment of courage.

From her spot by Greer's pool, Harper watches Wyatt dive in now, like the athlete he is, his body forming a cool, adept arc before his fingertips hit water. "Thanks a lot, Wy!" Simone shouts, because he got her a little wet, as she lounges on a chaise, poking at her phone. Greer and Beau are inside the house somewhere. She's rehearsed what she'll say to them a hundred times, but it keeps changing, and then she erases and starts again. He's such an easy, go-with-the-flow guy that she's sure he'll understand, but still, the idea of telling him she's leaving forms a worried lump in her chest. Probably it's her who doesn't understand, and does not want to go with this particular flow. It's hard to tell someone something that you yourself don't want to hear. When she thinks of Beau just being himself, sitting beside her on the boat edge, making his lasso move, his wide smile, her heart clenches. A longing returns, the sharp claw of unfinished business. She gazes out at the other unfinished business that is Molokini.

When Dario and Wyatt and Walter get out and towel off, Harper opens her camera.

"Hey, you guys!" She motions for them to gather in, and no one complains, because they know this is an ending. She snaps a photo of them, all with their similar eyes and noses and hair, each with their funny and sweet and beloved uniqueness. Wyatt is caught with his head tilted and a doofy expression on his face, and Dario has one eye closed, and Simone's and Walter's tongues are both half sticking out. Over the weeks Wyatt's hair has grown long, and Dario's arms have grown strong from swimming, and Simone has grown more real and open. She has a Greer-like brashness, but a few nights ago, she and Harper sat on the bed and talked about Simone's depression, the way she wished there was a reason for it but couldn't find one. Simone felt bad about it, like it was a failure, since other people had real reasons to be depressed but weren't.

Now Harper lifts her phone high, reverses the lens, snaps a photo of all of them with her big face in it, too. When she looks at it, she's beaming. Even though her heart is breaking, her eyes are bright in the company of those people. They shine with purpose. It's the kind of beam she used to think she had to manufacture. But it's just there, all light.

"She's ba-ack," Wyatt says after she puts down her phone.

"No," she says. She's changed, as Ezra said, changed again, and she has grown, too, more brave, more present. She doesn't want to constantly see everything through her camera lens, or see herself in squares when the world is so wide and deep, as she is, too.

Simone heads into the kitchen, and when she emerges again, she stands at the barbecue with a pair of tongs, placing pieces of chicken onto the sizzling grill. The wind blows smoke their way, making Harper's eyes water, but then it shifts. Greer comes outside, freshly showered herself, her hair still wet, holding a giant bowl of potato salad, and Wyatt brings out his signature Greek salad with cherry tomatoes.

Now Beau appears. He's wearing the blue stripe bathing suit and the dressy vintage Hawaiian shirt of Tony's that he wore that first night. He's giving this grin-smirk, all cocky and self-assured, a totally Wyatt vibe. He's shaking a padded envelope in the air.

"Look what I got, my friends. Hey, this is a celebration, and we didn't even know it." He uses that expression a lot.

"Ooh! How exciting," Greer says.

"What is it?" Dario shouts from back in the pool again.

"Save it for after dinner," Greer says.

"Ceremony," Beau agrees.

All through their meal, they eye that packet on the table. By the time everyone is finished and the dishes are cleared, they've each spotted *PADI* on the return address. They know what's in there.

"Okay, dudes," Beau says, and rises from his chair. He is smiling so wide as he rips open that envelope.

"Dario Damaskenos," Beau proclaims. He really is the Wizard of Oz now, the way he's showing them the heart and courage they've had all along. "You are officially a PADI open water diver. You can now—"

"DIVE ANYWHERE IN THE WORLD!" they shout in unison, and then they all laugh.

"Congratulations." He gives the card to Dario and shakes his hand, like the principal at graduation.

"Thanks, Captain," Dario says.

"That's Sperm Daddy to you, son," Beau says, and everyone cracks up again.

"SD!" Dario hoots, like a drunk guy in a bar.

"Simone Van Den Berg," Beau announces.

"I can now dive anywhere in the world!" she says, as if the idea has just occurred to her. She takes the card and shakes his hand.

"Wyatt Groveland. Proud to know you."

They shake hands and Wyatt beams.

Now Beau pretends to rattle the envelope as if it's empty. "Whaaa—oh! Sorry, Harpo. There's nothing else."

"So cruel, so cruel!" she says.

"Okay, wait. Here it is. Harper Proulx, I now proclaim that you can dive anyw—"

He stops. He drops his arm, still holding the card. His face gets a puzzled expression.

Something is wrong. Very wrong, and all she can hear is the roar of the surf and the palm fronds swishing, and Dario clacking that whalebone in his pocket. Her stomach goes sick with alarm. Something is wrong, and he's just staring at her, looking stunned.

"Beau?" Greer says. "You all right?"

"Proulx?" Beau says. "As in . . . uh . . ."

"What's going on?" Dario asks.

"As in, Melinda Proulx? Your, uh, mom? I can't believe I didn't know your last name before. We never even . . . I didn't even realize . . . Melinda Proulx, right? She was a calculus TA at UW?"

"I don't know," Harper says. "I mean, yeah, that's her name, but she teaches economics, so maybe, back then . . ."

"Sang in a punk band for, like, three weeks? The Bloody Nails?"

"What?" Harper can't imagine it. "I don't think so. Um, she said she'd been in *choir*, but . . ."

"A really demanding mother with impossible expectations?"

"Mine?"

"Hers."

Oh God.

Oh God, oh God.

"You *knew* each other?" The shock presses outward in her skull. Her head starts to ache. "Like, knew-knew each other?"

Even in the glowing light of the tiki torches, she can see him blush.

"Ho-ly shit." Simone exhales.

"I had no idea. I swear to God, Harper, I had absolutely no clue," Beau says.

CHAPTER THIRTY-ONE

In the frigid waters of Drake Passage, there is
only the roar of the tempest and the huge bil-
lows that seem ready to swallow us, and the
dark nights of watch and fear during these
awful thunderstorms with the lightning's flash
and the loud crashes of the great waves. We
passed the *Rapid,* her ensign flying upside down
in a signal of distress, but there was nothing
we could do, as we ourselves are in a fight for
survival.

Mary Ann Patten journal entry
September 11, 1856

THEY GET OUT OF THERE. OR RATHER, HARPER DOES, AND
the rest of the sibs just go with her after awkward goodbyes and
lots of meaningful eye contact between them. No one says anything on the drive back. Her vow about her phone, gone. If she's
an addict, she needs a drink immediately, and bad. Harper fury-
scrolls. You can scroll because you're bored, or honestly curious,
or just do it mindlessly, but you can also scroll when you're mad,

a finger flick, flick, flicking, *I don't care, I don't care, I don't care,* angry rejection of all of it. "Ten Major Mistakes You Should Never Make While Walking," fuck you. *Really?* Harper glares at her phone. *We've been walking since we stood upright, it's our thing, it defines us as a species, and you think we don't know how? You think there's some fucking hidden danger?* She scrolls through the images of the accounts she follows. A sushi plate, a night-vision camera with a dangerous animal, a gerbil eating a berry, a grandfather in a uniform, a—goddamn it! Some wound! Some bloody gash! God, she hates when people do that. Hate, hate, HATES! Innocent scrolling, maybe eating your scrambled eggs, when, bam, some horrible thing you'd never want to see, never ever, gushy blood, raw-meat skin, or the gruesomely black crisscross of stitches, or a pale leg poking from a hospital sheet, all so that people will show they care. Or those posts hinting at some secret behind-the-scenes tragedy or emotional breakdown, *I'm about to scream, I'm about to lose it, I can barely take any more,* and the next day a photo of a squirrel, or an *I'm sorry I worried you* post. Really? How sorry? Look! Look at the comments right here, all the *Oh, I hope you're okay!* shit pouring in for the wounded.

If she's an addict, the drink disgusts her now. This noise . . . She just wants it to *shut the fuck up.*

"God, I hate that!" she snarls. No one in that SUV asks what she means. Dario just takes her hand. A tear drops off her nose, she's so mad.

She scrolls some more until she hits one of those obnoxious, despised selfies, the kind where someone thinks they look so awesome that they pretend it's just a casual post. *A good day at work!* #nofilter, #Augusteveninglight. GOD! Or, no, worse! Accounts where *every single square* is a self, self, self, false, false, false in some vintage clothes, skirt the exact color of the accompanying park bench, pop of color lipstick, fuck. Why not just say it, huh? Why not be honest? *I think I look really good here. It took me a few hours, but, man, am I ever fabulous.*

"UGHHHH! Look at this!" She shows Dario. "How much time did all these take, huh? It's sickening."

Dario shrugs. He does not say it, that she used to do this herself. Okay, okay, fine, but it looks different than it did before. She wants to throw this new phone into the ocean.

When they get home, she flings off her shoes and stomps inside, even though big emotions make Walter anxious, make all of them anxious, really. She slams the innocent door of Wyatt's parents' innocent condo.

In her phone she jabs at her mom's name. All this time she's been focused on the absent, unknown MF. But hey, you can also not know someone you know. She's lived her whole life with the missing Melinda Proulx.

"The Bloody Nails, huh?" she says when her mom answers.

"Harper, what?" She sounds honestly confused.

"Calculus TA? Beau Zane was no sperm donor, not to you."

The silence is so . . . silent that Harper can feel the shock in it. How can her mom possibly be shocked? Did she think this wouldn't come out? That Harper's promise not to give him identifying details was protection enough? Did she *want* to get caught? Or was she rushing Harper home now since she'd gotten away with it so far?

"You didn't even *tell* him you were pregnant?"

"I knew him for a few *weeks*, Harper. Weeks. It was just a—"

"Were you going to say meaningless? Because none of this is meaningless."

"Misguided. I was going to say misguided. He was not some-one who . . ."

She trails off. Oh, Harper can fill it in, though. She thinks of Ezra and how he never measured up. "Not someone who was good enough?" Harper says. "Because let me tell you, he's good enough. He's more than good enough."

"He wasn't someone I saw a future with! I'd already dated so many people by then. I badly wanted a child. The clock is tick-ing, everyone said. My family. My mom! She even suggested in-semination! He donated sperm anyway. He *told* me. He was open about it. Proud, even. He wanted to help people have the families they longed for. So, I just . . . I figured, what's the difference, really? This was his plan anyway! And, I mean, my mother would have *died*. Beau Zane? And me? We were so entirely . . . *different*. It didn't even last more than those few weeks. I was just in some phase, even the band, it was only maybe for a month. It was just some silly acting out. . . . My friends were like, *Melinda . . .*"

"How do you know?"

"What?"

"How do you know it was a phase?" Harper's crying now. She hasn't gotten to all the important parts, the fact that her mother lied, the fact that she never told Beau. *Has* lied—a million lies, not just one: outright lies, changing-the-subject lies, lies by omission. Well, those things will probably take years to sort out, if they ever will be. But right now Harper feels something besides anger. She feels sad for her mom.

"I was on my way to a full professorship. My father opened the door for me at the college. The plan was in place. It was a good plan! And, really, look at us, was it not a good plan? Look at you, you're so perfect, and—"

"Stop. Please stop."

"My God, if my mother even saw that stupid band. . . . I was *thirty-two*! I had no business being in that at my age! It was just reckless acting out."

"You stepped out of the box for five minutes, Mom. You tried to be yourself for all of five minutes." Harper is crying hard, and it's cruel, but she can't help it. She is also a daughter squeezed into a box, and she doesn't want to be a daughter squeezed into a box, too afraid of disapproval to ever step out. "That girl in the band—you never gave her a chance."

When they finally hang up, Harper is exhausted. She's nauseous. There are so many questions and feelings and betrayals, and Harper just wants to be alone.

There's a gentle knock at her door. "Harpo?" Simone says.

"I can't."

"Okay. We're here if you need us."

A moment later, another knock. "Harpo?" Wyatt asks. "If you need me to drive you back to Beau's so you can talk or whatever, I'm happy to—"

"That's all right," she says. "Thanks."

A few minutes pass. A knock again. She knows who it is. She hears the *click-click* of approaching toenails and the jingle of tags, and now she sees the shadow of a small black nose under the crack of the door.

"Harpo?" Dario says. "You never got this. And you earned it. You really earned it."

Here it comes, the small white PADI card, under the door.

"Now you can dive anywhere in the world," he says, and Harper smiles in spite of herself.

"Thanks."

She stares at it on the floor and then rises to pick it up. Her name is there. Her name, this representation of her, whoever that is.

I'm not going to be like you, she tells her mother in her head. But that's a lie, too. She will be, and she won't be. She already is. Her hands and her mother's look exactly alike, and so do their eyebrows, and their funny knees. Her voice sounds just like her mother's sometimes (oh man, does that ever freak her out), and they both say no before they say yes.

Are they alike? Are they different? Is she more like Beau? Who is she, compared to them? Who is she in general? Isn't that *always* the question?

One thing's for sure—she isn't that girl in the box. She isn't that girl with a filter covering her, edited to perfection, overwhelmed to the point of flatness, bombarded with enough *you are not capable* arrows to paralyze her. She is someone with a caring heart, deserving of a purpose.

She thinks of Mary at the helm, who never knew she'd be at the helm, and she thinks of that submerged ship. A wreck that holds so much old and unseen beauty, but so much beautiful new life, too. She thinks of carelessness—not the kind from eating the wrong food, or choosing the wrong shampoo, or missing the twelve hidden signs of danger, but the thoughtless acts to others and the Earth, acts with ramifications that echo through the generations. Where's the daily mass of articles about *those*?

Is Harper her DNA, her experiences, her successes, her failures? Is she the things she loves?

Who is she in dark times? Who is she after them? Is your real self revealed in the moments that ask something of you, that call for you to be something more? Everyone has been in a storm, everyone has been at a helm, and now, *tick, tick,* they are in another one.

Sometimes being strong is saying no. Saying, "I don't want to do this. I'm not gonna *do this."*

Harper sends her mother a brief text. At least now she has *leverage.*

I'm not coming home. Not yet.

She waits for the bubbles of reply, but her mother is silent. She hates those bubbles. She likes the real ones, and only the real ones, the ones that rise from her very own breath as she explores what's beneath the surface.

She types one final message. *I'm only using this phone for emergencies. You can reach me by email.*

She zips the phone into her bag. She will keep that noise away from her, at least as long as she's here.

And then she writes to Ezra. She tells him everything about who she is and how she came to be. Knowing your full true story, telling your full true story, living your full true story—it seems like the most basic right of every human being.

CHAPTER THIRTY-TWO

I count eighteen days ago, when Third Mate Kingsley called, "Ice ahead!" We bore a torture for four indescribable days and nights, as I and Hale and the men changed watch on the half hour, to warm ourselves from the frigid conditions. With lowered sails, and over the next weeks, we navigated through a mournful land of ice peaks and troubled glacial waters. There was no lull, only the fearful boom of the tempestuous sea, like a thousand cannons. I have not changed my clothing in fifty days all total. But at last we are around Cape Horn, with its particularly hazardous waters, strong winds, and strong currents. We have done it, I have, and when the sun shines on the icebergs, it looks like frosting. I have come to understand that our resilience is not composed of stunning acts of courage, but the way we mark the passage of each day, still here, still here.

Mary Ann Patten journal entry
September 29, 1856

THEY'RE BEING SO NICE TO HER, THAT NEXT MORNING AS they head over to Greer's. Harper doesn't think she'd be that nice if, say, Simone were suddenly Beau's "real" kid. She'd feel pissed and jealous. Simone wouldn't actually be part of their group then, would she? She wouldn't be donor-conceived.

Harper would feel resentful, but Simone and Dar and Wyatt and Walter know she's hurting, and Simone offers her sun lotion, and Wyatt asks if she wants music or not, and Dario pats her knee, like a kindly grandfather. No one says a word about the weird thing sitting between them, Harper transformed into his "real" kid, like some twisted version of *The Velveteen Rabbit*.

But what the heck does *real* mean? Harper stares out the car window at the misty gray clouds that often cover the morning sky, and that sometimes ease in without warning and depart again after a soft rain. Oh God—is *real* about the involvement of an actual penis, another patriarchal, penis-trumps-all BS concept? Is *real* about her mother and Beau actually having sex (and, God, get *that* image out of her mind)? Is it about them *choosing* each other? But those other forty-one women chose Beau, too, or at least a description of him, and he chose all of them by walking into the Lakeview clinic. He *knew* he was making *that* choice. Harper is less real, honestly, by that measurement.

"It's no different," Dario finally says as they bump down the road to Greer's house. Wyatt turns on the wipers as gentle drops dot the windshield.

"Nothing has really changed," Simone says as they get out of the car.

They wouldn't have to say these things, though, if they were purely and simply true.

It *is* different, and things *have* changed, at least this morning. Instead of having breakfast and dropping off Walter, and then piling into the VW bus to head to the dock, everyone is tiptoeing around the house, and Harper and Beau are sitting at the edge of Greer's bed with the door of her room shut for privacy. Harper has hardly ever been back here, to their rooms, but she knows that Beau's is tiny and strewn with clothes. Greer's is spacious, but cluttered, too. A bong sits next to a photo of Greer and Tony on her nightstand. Harper stares up at a painting of an ocean sunset, a palm tree in one corner.

"The work of yours truly," he says. "When I was fifteen. I don't know why she loves that thing. It's pretty awful."

"Beautiful in a mother's eyes," Harper says, and feels a jab. It's what her own mom says about that hideous clay pot with the glitter that Harper made for her in the second grade. "Hey, you were an artist like Simone."

Like Simone. Of all of them, Harper's sure that she herself is the least likely to be *real*.

"Harper. Is there *anything* I can do?" he asks. She looks into his blue eyes. They seem worried. His eyebrows have a few spiky gray hairs she never noticed before. They probably popped up after four kids came into his life.

"You met in her *calculus* class?"

"Shit, I know. I was awful at it. Actually, not awful. I was good at it. I just hated it."

"Same," Harper says.

Same.

"Who broke it off?"

"I hope this doesn't sound bad, but there wasn't a lot of *it* to break."

The giant swirl of questions telescopes back down. *Real* does. It *isn't* that different, and this is slightly disappointing, but also a relief. A moment doesn't make a father, and sometimes years don't, either, probably. "We are what we've been so far, I guess."

"Hey, it gets to be what we make it," he says.

And then they go on. Beau takes time off work, leaving the shop and rental and classes to Amber, Big Dean, and Ray, a part-time employee, and they all go out to the wreck every day. They want as much time there as they can get before it's gone. Harper goes over the side. She descends. She travels deep into the damaged pieces of a narrative they don't fully know yet. She watches the yellow-and-black-and-white reef triggerfish (also magically and impossibly known as the humuhumunukunukuapuaa, according to Jake), and the grumpy white-spotted puffer, and the abstract Picasso triggerfish, with its neon eyeliner running down its face, and the yellow trumpet, more writing instrument than fish. It seems impossible that it all even exists, let alone that it might be destroyed. And Harper wonders for the millionth time: How can humans do so much harm to each other and our one ancient and amazing planet? Can they not see the danger of looking for danger? Of seeing it in all the wrong places?

Nothing, Dario would say when he was back up on the boat again. He's still sure they can solve the mystery of the ship, that its identity as *Neptune's Car* might be ammunition against the ammunition threatening to destroy the best of what's under there. But so far they find no more clues.

Their relationship *is* the one they've built so far. She freaks out when she sees a really large octopus (*an ornate octopus,* Jake tells them, *each arm has a small brain, and it has DNA like no other creature on Earth*), and Beau teases her that she looked like an octopus herself down there, the way her limbs were swirling when she saw it. He and Simone go off on tangents about places they might want to travel to. Dario points out fresh facts from Tony's notes, and Greer turns on Creedence, Walter following her to her old turntable.

"Two more days," Wyatt says one morning, drinking the last of his coffee before they go.

"I'm glad you're here for this, but I'm sorry you're here for this, Harpo," Dario says, sticking his cup in the dishwasher.

"Same," Simone says.

"I couldn't be anywhere else," Harper tells them.

On the boat that afternoon, their mood is somber. The detonation is still scheduled for this coming Friday. As they head out to Molokini, Dario looks like he might cry. Jake, who sometimes whistles when he drives, is silent, and even the boat doesn't sound as enthusiastic as usual—the engine is a monotone drone. Simone watches the beach, all the people with their towels and coolers, swimming in the surf and getting smaller and smaller. Beau looks defeated as he applies sun lotion to his wrinkled neck. The sun is still bright, making Harper squinch.

She isn't even the last one over the side this time. Wyatt and Simone are still on the boat, talking to Jake, Jake's and Wyatt's fingertips trailing together. Beau and Big Dean, who has come along this time, are still on the boat, too, Big Dean hunting through the cooler to see what Amber packed for lunch.

"Ready?" Dario asks.

"Ready."

Dario's on a mission, and he can get too far ahead of her. He goes places he shouldn't. He swims into the wide passage where the ship has split, where there are dark spots and narrow crevices, where it's too deep and you can get in over your head. Harper sees him hovering around where he said the captain's quarters would be, the topmost layer above the deck, which is hard to define and, in some spots, not defined at all, just an absence, one large cavern. They've seen the drawings, and Dario has shown them Tony's photos of the *Cutty Sark* in Greenwich, London, so they understand what it would have looked like, the cold, hollow bottom, where the hammocks of the crew would be slung and the food stored; the deck above, with the infirmary and the crew dining area; and on the top deck, the captain's quarters, as well as the first and second mates' snug little bedrooms. Each had a desk and one small porthole, tiny but much roomier and more private than the rough canvas slings below.

Harper gestures to Dario to get out of there, but he isn't watching her. He's too intent on finding something. This is how you get into trouble. Harper forces herself to stay calm, since panic is your quickest route to a bad end. She breathes. She keeps her eye on Dario, watching out for him, her eyes fixed on the murkiest depths.

At the far edge of her peripheral vision, something catches her attention—movement, a startling flash of color. With one stroke and one kick, she spins around, and this is when she sees them, this is her view from that wreck: a hundred glows, a hundred purple otherworldly beings, pure and pulsing, with translucent globes over marigold centers. A hundred shimmery, ethereal grass skirts of radiant pink. Fireworks, in the crater of an ancient volcano, and her own firework most certainly there, too.

Oh wow, wow. It's such an astonishing sight that it's almost dreamlike. They are *wondrous,* this mass of pink-purple light, so wondrous that Harper is filled with that rare all-of-life feeling, where you're a witness to the whole of it, the grand tapestry. Those jellyfish have been here since the beginning of time, going through stuff, surviving stuff, and somewhere in there, that triggerfish entered the scene, and then that spotted puffer did, and the whale shark, and all the rest of them, one by one, same as their wreck joined the millions of other wrecks down here, going as far back as those ancient canoes.

And right then, with all those breathtaking creatures in front of her, Harper is sure of it, absolutely sure, that every living being has its own heroic story, and together they are telling a single, whole story, a long story, about oceans, earth, and sky, about volcanoes and plagues and tidal waves and wreckage and storms and tragedies. A story of endurance and courage and connection and resilience and love. And she is sure, as well, that she has a place in that story, and she should never forget that. She should never *miss* that. She feels so . . . *consoled* by this, the going onward–ness of life, and her own going onward–ness. She feels so hopeful as she watches the exquisite pink-purple hula, right where Mary's story also sits, and where she herself now paddles quietly.

So many purple-pink luminescent tentacles sway, and in a burst of color so marvelous and shocking that it makes her blink, they are down, down and then gone. Harper stares, looking at the place they were, the space they just traveled. At first it looks like they were never there at all. But then Harper realizes that the mass of creatures has shifted the area around them, and her eyes catch on something, a flash of brightness that doesn't belong.

She dives. She reaches. When she lifts the object, it's much larger than it seemed. It's actually a long piece of metal, buried deeply in the sand, a thin white object attached to it with two bent nails. Harper's heart starts beating hard, but not out of fear.

She holds it tight and kicks to where Dario is. And no, Dario has not gotten stuck somewhere. He has not run out of air or come to some terrible end.

Dario sees her this time. She shows him what she found, and he nods in excitement. *Ready to go up?* he gestures.

Ready, she gestures back.

They surface. Dario flings off his mask right there as they tread water a short distance from the boat. The waves smack Harper's cheek.

"Harpo!" he cries. "Oh my God! What is it?"

"Come on!" She clutches it, that band of metal with a familiar strip of white attached, and she swims. They lift themselves back into the boat. No one else has even left yet.

"Everything okay?" Beau asks. They're back so soon.

He drops his gear, and so does she. "Harpo found . . . Show them, Harpo."

Under those bent nails is a piece of whalebone. It's just like Dario's. And it has notches in it, and those notches are purposeful. They were made, each one, with intent, with meaning, and each is a victory. Harper can feel it as she runs her thumb across them—the triumph over an impossible day, similar to her own *X* over each square of her pandemic calendar. *I survived it,* the notch says. *Still here, still here.* And Harper can feel Mary Patten, too, the actual girl, a pregnant nineteen-year-old girl. Holding a knife in one hand, carving a mark into her old corset stay, affixed to the ship so it wouldn't be lost. Proof of her daily resilience, her strength. Proof of her being up against it, and getting through a terrible and terrifying situation.

"Please," Beau says, and that's all. *"Please."*

Dario is rummaging in his stuff, and then he's back. Beau and Big Dean and Simone and Jake and Wyatt gather in a circle to look.

Harper's hand is shaking.

She understands what's about to happen, and chills run up her arms, and tears spring to her eyes.

Dario holds out his half of the whalebone, and Harper holds out hers. They fit them together. Dario, her half brother, Sebastian to her Viola on this ship. The pieces join, connect as a whole, and tell the truth. They tell what happened. Dario runs his fingertip over each notch and counts. They're silent through this counting, because each number deserves respect. Dario's side has seventy-six notches. He counts down the length of Harper's until he reaches the end.

"One thirty-six, one thirty-seven . . . one hundred and thirty-eight."

He looks up. His eyes are wide. Harper is so full of emotion, she can't speak.

"Oh God," Simone says. By then they all know that number. One hundred and thirty-eight, the number of days between New

York and San Francisco on that perilous but victorious trip aboard *Neptune's Car*.

"It's her," Big Dean says. His voice is hoarse with feeling. "It's *Neptune's Car*. Oh, if your old man could have seen this."

Big Dean is slapping Beau on the back, and Beau pulls him in for a giant hug, practically lifting Big Dean right off his feet. "He knew it, man! He knew it!"

"It's too unbelievable," Harper says. "This can't be happening."

"How is this even possible?" Dario whispers.

"Dudes, my dudes!" Beau's eyes shine with joy. "A *pandemic* is unbelievable. A bomb is unbelievable! The sinking of a sixteen-ton ship is! If things that bad are possible, things this good are, too, right? Right, Pops?" He raises a fist of power to The Cloud.

Harper's throat tightens with emotion. Wyatt presses his palms to his eyes. Simone is beaming, and Dario's face is almost reverent. As she stands there holding her half of the whalebone next to Dario's, Harper gets it again—that wonderful sense of the whole. Something astonishing has occurred, but it's also just her bare feet on that boat, trying to stay balanced in the sloshy waves, and it's the arc ridge of a volcano in front of her, and Dario's face in front of her, too, and Simone's beam, and Wyatt's grin, and Beau, still smelling of sun lotion, just shaking his head in awe. All of them singular without even trying. Oh, she's full.

The world, the real one, the one outside those squares? The messy, scary, unpredictable and hard one; the natural world, with its frightening power and powerful beauty; the human world, with its horrific wrongs and its moments of shining rightness—it's worth it. The risk is worth it. The squares are nothing in comparison. Nothing.

CHAPTER THIRTY-THREE

Alas, our troubles are not over. With warming weather, Joshua's condition improved, although he is far too weak for any mental or physical exertion. Believing that I need to avoid all unnecessary fatigue and peculiar exertion, and given that I should be in confinement in my condition, he has restored Keeler under promise of doing better in the future. Now for a week I have not been allowed to take the navigational sights! I am alarmed at this turn of events and have Keeler in my sights instead. I am also supposed to preserve a serenity of temper for the health of the unborn child. I have failed at this, most certainly.

> Mary Ann Patten journal entry
> October 6, 1856

THAT NIGHT AT GREER'S, DIRK COOKE COMES OVER WITH their old friend Sylvie S. O'Sullivan, the marine archaeologist, who has short, efficient gray hair and wears fraying khaki shorts and a gray T-shirt that reads MAUI CANOE REGATTA, 2010. She's an expert on "archaeological diagnostics of women aboard ships of the nineteenth century," according to Greer. She studies what hasn't been given much attention—the presence of women aboard ships throughout time. Sylvie S. O'Sullivan examines documents, photos, and objects from shipwrecks, like sewing notions and baby toys, writing instruments and navigational tools. Like thimbles. Like douches. Like the mysterious whalebone.

"It's definitely a corset stay," she says. Her tone is take-no-shit brisk. "When we only had the smaller piece, I told Tony that's what I thought it was, but yup. For sure. Oh, he would have loved to see this."

"I read about those," Dario tells her. "How the Victorians thought a woman was so weak that she needed support all the time."

"Yeah," Sylvie says. "Look how weak Mary was." It seems so sad to Harper right now, the lies you're told about your own capabilities.

"I can't believe she would have worn one even on a ship," Harper says.

"No kidding. I take my bra off the minute I'm home," Greer says.

"Even on a ship." Sylvie S. nods. "Even during pregnancy. It makes sense, though, doesn't it? She found a way to loosen the corset without removing it and, at the same time, crafted a pretty ingenious permanent surface to mark. She probably affixed it to the desk in the captain's quarters."

Everyone is listening so hard that even Walter is still, aside from one ear twitching. Harper feels close to Mary. It's like she's right there in the room.

"When you guys say 'whalebone' . . . To be clear, this isn't actually a *bone*. It's baleen, the blades in a whale's mouth that allow them to sieve the plankton and small fish from the seawater. The stays, those rigid pieces inserted into the corset casing so that it keeps its firm structure, were made out of baleen because it didn't crack like other materials, and was flexible enough to get shoved inside the narrow seams."

"That's so awful," Simone says. "To think of the blades in the whale's *mouth*."

"Whaling was a *huge* industry then," Sylvie says. "The whale oil, especially. It was an illuminant and lubricant, the base for all artificial light. But these stays—they were part of a woman's regular life. A constant. Never forget your weakness, right? And keep that waist slim, even if you can't breathe!"

"Spanx goes way back," Simone says.

"True, true," Sylvie says. "Sometimes the baleen corset stays were given as gifts from one woman to another before marriage. More often, given by a sailor to a woman, a gift that could be kept as close to her as possible, an intimate gift. A *romantic* gift. And he would often decorate them, or engrave them. Some were beautifully, intricately carved, with images of ships and whales and scenes of life at sea. Symbolic images, like palm fronds that might represent a place the sailor had been. Even love poems, and extravagant hearts, sunrises, images of mothers with children."

"They had a lot of time on their hands out there, when they weren't about to die in a storm or from some horrible disease," Harper says. She knows all about it from the book Beau gave her.

"And to bide that time, the women on those ships, they also sometimes took up this same art, this scrimshaw, when they were at sea. So this corset stay—it's not an unusual choice for Mary to make. Ingenious, but not unusual. She carved a design, for a different purpose."

"A notch—it means you survived something," Harper says.

"A notch means you survived something, and that you intend to *keep on* surviving," Greer says. She puts an arm around Harper and gives her shoulder a squeeze.

"We know who she is now," Sylvie says. "At least, I have no doubt about it. That ship is *Neptune's Car,* and that area is a National Historic Landmark."

Greer gets the list, the one with all the numbers of every single official they've been calling again and again.

"It's late," Dirk Cooke says. "No one will be there."

"We'll leave messages," Dario says.

"It'll be the first thing any of these people hear in the morning," Wyatt says.

"I didn't even know shipwrecks could be historic landmarks," Simone says. Harper didn't, either.

"Yeah. Of all the, what, *thousands* of National Historic Landmarks, some five percent are shipwrecks," Dirk Cooke tells them. "They're archaeological sites."

"Seventy-seven acres down there near the crater have been a Marine Life Conservation District since 1977," Greer says. "That should've been enough. But nope. That little fact was completely ignored in '84. Well, they can't ignore this now, too."

"We only have one day," Harper says.

"Fuck, man," Beau says. "We gotta work fast."

"I've got to stop us for one second here," Greer says. "Just one second." She scurries to the kitchen, Walter all jazzed at her heels. Cupboard doors open and slam shut again. They look at Beau for clues, but he only shrugs.

"No idea," he says.

And then she's back. Greer holds a stack of small glasses and an old champagne bottle. A really old bottle. A retro label, for sure. She hands out the glasses, one for each of them. "This . . ." She clears her throat. "From our wedding. We were saving it . . . for a special occasion. Never got to use it. But *this* is a special occasion." She unwraps the brittle foil, picking it with a fingernail until she reaches the cork.

She presses her thumbs to it. "This is for you, stud," she says. The cork flies and bounces off a lampshade, and they all cheer as the white froth spills over the lip of the bottle.

When all their glasses have been filled, Beau lifts his. "To Antonis Zane," he says. "Great-great-grandson of Nikolaos Zanetakos."

"To Antonis Zane," they say.

"And . . . to all the mothers," Beau says. "Including mine, right here." He puts his arm around Greer and grips her tight.

"To all the mothers," they repeat as Harper's eyes fill.

The liquid is discolored and weird-tasting and kind of flat, but it doesn't matter. They drink, to all the history that is theirs.

I'm a mess!

I'm really worried.

Do you need me to fly out there?

This is too large for you to handle alone.

I'm losing my mind over here.

That night Harper answers a bunch of panicked emails from her mom with one of her own. *I'm fine. I can do this. I'm totally capable.* It's a bullshit story that she's not. It's a bullshit story that Mary's body was so weak that it needed support at all times. *We'll talk when I get home. Please. Give me some space.* Right now Harper needs to concentrate on the world and on the people around her, and not on how her mother feels about the world and the people around her.

And then she writes to Ezra. She can call him, but she doesn't. This writing—it's so intimate, the way the real him and the real her are truly getting to know each other. *That's* romantic. She tells him about the dive, and about the mass of fireworks appearing, and the baleen from inside the mouth of the whale. She tells him about Mary, marking the days, same as she did on that pandemic calendar. She tells him about the shipwrecks and the National Historic Landmark.

But his mind is mostly on her, and on those trumpet fish, and the antler coral and the turtles, and the firework jellyfish.

Hurry, he writes.

CHAPTER THIRTY-FOUR

In the past days I took sights in secret, charting our position, and determined that Keeler was steering the ship off her course. He was making for Valparaíso, where the cargo might be destroyed. I apprised my husband of this fact, and after watching the telltale compass, he again ordered Keeler in irons, this time belowdecks. Afterward Joshua slipped back into fever, hallucinations, and total blindness. I have taken back command of the ship. Today I mark our hundredth day.

Mary Ann Patten journal entry

October 10, 1856

BEAU FLINGS THE LIST OF NUMBERS DOWN, THE NUMBERS of their state rep, and the head of NOAA, and his contacts in the navy. He pushes away the pages of photos and notes and evidence that Tony collected. "I don't know what else to do." He's been using their old phone, stuck on a wall in the kitchen, and he's had a couple of beers already. A few minutes ago he pulled at the armpit of his T-shirt and sniffed, to see if it smelled. If Harper's mom had seen him like this—a guy with tired eyes, in a dirty T-shirt, a haze of alcohol fumes around him—she wouldn't have chosen his genetic material, Harper's sure. But it's easy to mix up what looks good with what actually *is* good.

Dario's head is in his hands. The light is golden, and the waves crash and roar as the sun sets on another day that isn't just another day. It's the last day.

Simone crinkles up an empty bag of chips. "Ugh, I just stress-ate most of those."

"We did everything we could," Wyatt says.

"They're avoiding us," Beau says.

"I don't think that they even *believe* us," Dario says.

"This just doesn't seem possible." Harper thinks of that stunning blast of color as the fireworks retreated, and she thinks of those photos of gray ash, coral turned to dust.

"It's possible, Harpo," Dario snaps. "It's not only possible; it's happening."

"I *know* it's happening, Dar." She doesn't snap back, because he looks near tears. They are all near tears. And she doesn't snap, because Walter looks worried, and they're responsible for him, and they shouldn't do anything to harm him.

"Did we get any more details on *when* tomorrow?" Simone asks.

"They won't broadcast when, but Dirk Cooke said he saw boats out there, getting ready to mark off the area so no one goes in."

"It'll be early," Greer says. She opens the old fridge, and now she pops the cap of a beer. "It's always early when they do bad shit. They think we'll be asleep. Well, we aren't fucking going to be asleep. Fuck those fuckers."

Harper can see where Beau got his swearing skills.

Harper can almost hear it. *Ticktock.* The clock, the bombs.

"It's last-resort time, kiddo," Greer says to Beau.

"Damn." He looks worried. Very worried. "*Harpoons,* Ma."

"It's all we got left. We gotta do it. We gotta Greenpeace 'em," Greer says. "Get me the old address book. It's in the junk drawer somewhere. Underneath the batteries and matchbooks and shit."

They all stay the night at Greer's. They let Dario have the couch since he's the youngest, and Greer pulls out some musty-smelling sleeping bags and air mattresses for everyone else to sleep on. They huff and puff until they're nice and full, but they're flat in minutes anyway.

It doesn't matter. No one sleeps. Harper lies awake, watching palm tree shadows dance on the wall, imagining every possible scenario for tomorrow. The navy ship barreling toward them as they shout defiantly. The navy ship forcing them out of the area. Them in a standoff with the navy ship. She's never been in a standoff, so this is hard to imagine. It mostly involves her saying brave and fierce things to guys in short haircuts. Maybe she'll get arrested, her hands locked behind her. She also imagines covering her ears and feeling the explosion throughout her body.

Dario is shifting around, and in the darkness Harper can see Wyatt propped on one elbow and Simone staring at the ceiling. "You guys awake?" she asks.

Dario sighs in response.

"Yep," Simone says.

"Uh-huh," Wyatt says.

Walter stirs.

Harper hears Greer tiptoe down the hall. Her floral-robed ghost moves toward the bathroom.

"We're awake," Harper says to her.

"Hey, you guys are awake?" Beau shouts from his room.

"I gotta pee," Greer says.

"Let's just get up," Beau shouts again.

"Really," Simone says. "This is torture just lying here."

Greer's back. "This always happens right before you Greenpeace it," she says. She turns on a light. Her hair is out of its braid, all wild and gray. Beau straggles from his room, zipping up a pair of raggedy shorts and wearing a T-shirt that says STYX WORLD TOUR.

"Anyone hungry?" Greer asks. "I'll make some pancakes. It's gonna be a big day."

"Ughhh," Simone groans. "One bag of potato chips has inflated to six bags of potato chips."

"What time is it even anyway?" Wyatt reaches for his phone. "Two-forty-five."

Everyone who's been called, all the boats, are meeting at the site at five a.m.

"Who can sleep?" Dario says. "Let's just get going."

Harper unzips her bag. He's right. He's so right. The fireworks are under that water right now, pulsing, flowing like magic, unaware of this particular peril, unaware of what's heading their way.

They decide to leave, even though it's so early. It's better to wait on the boat, in place, than at home.

"Jake's awake, too," Wyatt says. "He texted back in, like, two seconds." Jake's going to drive his parents' trawler, with Amber, Big Dean, and Ray on board, since the more boats the better. They have no idea how many people will show. "He's got to wait to pick everyone up at the agreed-on time, so he said he'll see us out there."

See us out there. Harper's stomach flips with nerves. That whizzing harpoon sound Greer made is in her head, but a bomb will make a different sound. It's terrifying, but she's ready. She wants to put herself in front of that firework, in front of that wreck. She's ready to Greenpeace it.

They throw their stuff into the SUV and head down to the dock. There's an electric energy between them, made larger by the fact that it's still night, with only a ridge of light on the horizon. On the way down the beach, they stop to look up at the Captain Neptune statue, now wearing someone's discarded bikini top, the life of the party with his grand spear. Beau salutes him, and then they move on. The ocean is still dark, with only glitters of moonlight on the waves, and when they step onto the boat, it feels like they're committing a crime, even though that boat has Greer's name on it.

The motor sounds so loud when Greer starts the engine and pulls away. She picks up speed as the dock retreats behind them.

"It's beautiful out here," Simone says to Harper, and takes her hand. It *is* beautiful, which makes what's about to happen even worse. Harper gazes at Simone's profile, similar to hers, but not her, her half sister.

"Who would have thought, huh?" Beau says, standing next to them. He means all of them here together, right now on this boat, the sky lightening, the deepwater smell of the sea around them, Dario sitting on the bench staring out, his nose the same as Beau's, and Wyatt, not seeming cocky at all but sharing the same contemplative look that Beau has. And there's Greer at the helm, her gray hair back in its braid, the short sleeves of her Hawaiian shirt flapping, her leather sandals planted firmly on the deck.

"See all those?" she shouts. Her cheeks are rosy with thrill. Harper can see the buoys in the moonlight, placed around the whole area and posted with warning signs. Greer accelerates through them.

They've almost reached the center of the site. It's just dark waves all around, the horizon line turning to a sliver of orange.

"We'll just anchor?" Greer shouts. "Wait for everyone else?"

"Yeah, sounds good," Beau shouts back.

The arc of Molokini is around them. It's three-forty-five. They have a little over an hour before the other boats show up.

But then Beau grabs Harper's arm. "Wait."

"What?" Simone asks.

"Do you hear that? I don't know if I told you guys, but I have really good hearing. Like, exceptional."

"Darwin's tubercle," Dario says.

"Darwin's what?"

"Tubercle," Dario says. "Do you have a little pointy bump on your ear?"

Beau lifts his shaggy hair.

"Affirmative," Simone says.

Harper folds her ear forward so he can see hers. "If you have it, you're better at hearing high-frequency sounds. Dario told us. We all have it."

"Huh," Beau says. "Wait. Did you hear that? There it is again."

"I think so," Harper says, but she doesn't, not entirely. She still wants to please him; that hasn't changed.

"I heard it," Dario says.

Then Harper does, too. It sounds like the creak and moan of a ship, a high-pitched cry, maybe the creak and moan of a ship before a wreck. She has no idea what it is, but she can recognize suffering.

"Cut the engine, Ma!" Beau shouts.

"Huh?" She can't hear up there. Maybe Darwin's tubercle came from Captain Neptune's side of the family. Maybe the guy who worked at the shipyard making *Neptune's Car* during the yellow fever had it.

"Cut the engine," Wyatt calls. He stands at the side of the boat, looking out. He hears it, too.

"It's a whale," Beau says. "Fuck, man. It's a whale."

CHAPTER THIRTY-FIVE

A monumental day. After one hundred and three days, we have crossed the equator. Trade winds are strong, and we are keeping sails up to make up for our time off course. I am clearly not meant for confinement. It is pleasant to witness the men's cheerful obedience to my orders, as each man vies with his fellows in the performance of his duty. Even the roughest sailors call me "the little woman" but with affection. Now, without a rival, I direct every movement on board. While we never know what each day will bring, the men manifest their compassion and respect by the great will and alacrity they show in following my orders. Together we have crossed the center of our great planet.

Mary Ann Patten journal entry

October 13, 1856

IT'S A WHALE.

Greer spins the wheel, heads in the direction they indicate. They go farther and farther out, away from the crater, away from the site, away from the protest about to happen. Wyatt searches through a pair of binoculars.

"There she is, there she is, there she is!" he cries.

There she is. The whale of every imagining, the largest, most awe-inspiring creature, ten times the size of their boat, at least, with a triangle tail, with huge oar fins. This whale, though—she's not leaping in the air and smacking the water like you see in videos. This whale is lying flat in the water, a gray island mottled with white. And there are buoys trailing behind her, and there's a thin rope line that looks as if it goes straight through her mouth.

"A humpback," Beau says. "What's she doing here this early?"

"Late September last year, but I remember late August at least once before. In 2012. But yeah, she's early," Greer says.

"Fuck!" Beau runs his hand through his hair.

"Some kind of crab pot. Who knows from where," Greer says.

She's so huge, she's scary. It seems like a bad and dangerous idea to be this close. One giant *bam* of her tail could upend them. She's more powerful than they are by an unimaginable degree. But then comes that sound again, a sound Harper will never ever forget—a plea, that's what it's like. A plea, grief, an outright cry for help. Despair.

She sinks just below the surface and rises again. She shoots a stream of water through her blowhole in an enormous whoosh.

"Oh my God," Simone says. "What are we going to do?"

"We've got to call NOAA." Beau rubs his forehead now. "Ah man."

"I mean, do they know what we're . . . ?" Dario says. "We can't *tell* them why we're out here!"

"It doesn't matter. We've got to call," Beau says. "We can't leave her. I'm not fucking going to leave her."

Greer's already on the radio, her head bent down. She hangs up. "He said, 'What are you guys doing out there? That whole area is supposed to be clear. Don't you know about the detonation? No vessels allowed.'"

"This is a disaster," Dario says.

"Then the guy says, 'No. Don't tell me. I don't want to know.' They want us to stay with her. If we leave . . . it's going to be impossible to locate her again." Greer looks at her watch.

"Four-forty-five," Wyatt says.

"We are Greenpeacing it, but not in the way I'd anticipated," Simone says.

"Kids, we are gonna babysit this whale," Greer says.

In their boat they sit with the huge beast, and wait and wait for the boats from NOAA to arrive. Every few minutes the whale lifts her enormous head and splashes it down again. She submerges and rises, shooting water through her blowhole. Harper sees one of her eyes. She looks into it. Harper can't tell if the whale looks back, or sees them at all, but she hopes so. She wants her to know that they're there, that *she* is there. This whale isn't a photo of a whale; this whale is so real that Harper can see the horrors and the majesty of *her* epic story, taking place right now. Harper can't believe she ever thought her compassion was gone. Her heart aches so bad for that whale that it's an actual physical pain in her body.

"What can we do?" Dario asks. It's almost five. Their own protest is about to go on without them.

"Be here for her," Beau says. His voice cracks. "Okay? It wasn't what we planned, but we can be here for her. Fuck. I couldn't do that for my old man."

The boat rocks and sloshes. " 'Welllll,' " Greer sings very slowly.

" 'Take me back down where—' " Beau chimes in.

" 'Cool water flows, yeh,' " they join in. By now they all know these lyrics. "Green River," by Creedence Clearwater Revival, Greer's favorite, Reba's, too. It's never had this tempo before, though. It's never been sung like a lullaby.

"Long ago whalers could actually *hear* whale songs," Beau says. "Because ships like those old clippers . . . Hulls like amplifiers."

Harper does a double take. Dario's eyes go wide. He said that same thing. "Yeah, I know," Dario says.

"Cool, huh?" Beau says.

Dario nods. "*So* cool."

Whoosh. Water sprays from her blowhole.

"You got me," Harper says to her, wiping water from her cheek. She is awe and wonder, that whale, with her gray-and-white island body.

"Those creatures have incredible old memories," Greer says. "Memories of migration routes from prehistoric times."

Impossible. *Unbelievable.* Possible. *True.*

No one will ever see this. They're just *here* with her. Harper won't need a photo to remember, and maybe this whale will also remember them. Time passes, and now it's six a.m., and the sky is a brilliant orange. The sun rises as it has forever, a fiery circle of hope slowly climbing to its place above them, as the orange turns to pink to yellow to blue. They sit quietly with that creature and show their love, as people have been doing forever, too. Harper imagined facing off with a navy ship. She imagined a detonation. She imagined being arrested, her hands cuffed behind her. But she never imagined this: the sound of waves slapping their boat, the sound of waves slapping the whale beast island next to them. Her oval eye, appearing above the surface, descending. Her presence. That *whoosh!* as the water shoots through her blowhole and rains. Her silence as they sing, as if she's listening. The sound of Dario as he asks, "Did you know about the Golden Record? Phonograph records that were put on the *Voyager* spacecraft to depict life on Earth? The third track is a whale song. It's still floating around up in space somewhere." The sound of Beau answering, "That's so cool, dude. *So* cool."

The NOAA boats finally arrive, carrying the team specially trained to do disentanglement, along with the tools that allow them to reach her and cut her free.

"Do you know what's going on out there?" one guy shouts, shaking his head.

They do, but they're here instead.

"It's wild. All these boats . . ."

It takes another three hours until she's free. It's almost ten-thirty. They've babysat that whale for nearly six hours. But they watch until she's free, until she slips under the surface and is gone.

They stand together. Beau loops his arms around Wyatt's and Dario's shoulders, and Dario loops his arm over Simone's, and Wyatt loops his arm over Harper's, and Harper loops her arm around Greer's.

"I'm proud of you kids, you know that?" Beau says. "*So* proud. I'm not sure if it's right to say this, because, you know, you got your own parents. But hey, man, it's what we got—showing up, showing our love . . . Why hold back, huh? You guys came here, and wow, was I happy. But now that I actually know you . . . I love you guys. I love the people you are."

Harper's chest fills with emotion, and then it brims to the point of overflowing. When she looks into his face, with its smile wrinkles and deep tan, it's clear that he *means* it. What he just gave, that word, "love," that longed-for word, well, she knows, okay? She knows it isn't some endpoint, some finished *worthiness* or whatever, but it pours into her. It pours in like something new and joyful, a foundation on a spot of land. Something both completed and only beginning. Wished for, but somehow unexpected. God, being seen and loved? It seems so simple, deserved, maybe even *owed,* yet how many people actually get it, huh? Every like in the world, every good grade, every success, every photo where she looked cute, every compliment, wasn't *this,* and never could be. "The person *you* are" is all she manages to say.

She sees it on their faces, too, her siblings'. She sees what this means. Simone's eyes are filling, and Wyatt actually has his hand to his heart. Beau sees them struggling. "Aw, man. Aw, you guys." He shakes their shoulders with affection. It's so funny, you know, how they needed *this* man to say these words, such a regular, flawed man, and yet no one else would do. Only the man-bun guy with the ketchup-stained shirt, him.

Dario squinches his eyes hard, the way he always does when he tries not to cry. It's weird, but he seems older than when the summer started, and he looks so much like Beau right now. So much that Harper can almost see Dario as a grown man. "Fuck, man," Dario says. "We love you back, dude."

They reverse course and putter home. It's creeping toward eleven o'clock. Clearly, there's been no detonation yet. Maybe they're still in a standoff, or maybe it's over, the navy chased away for now. Harper expects empty waters. She expects that they'll return the same way they arrived, alone.

She's wrong, though. She can see she's wrong the moment the crescent ridge of Molokini Island comes into view. There it is, its magical, prehistoric self in the distance. But even that far away she can see them. There are so many little dots, the water is an impressionist painting.

"You guys!" Wyatt sees them, too. They all do. Greer pumps her fist in the air.

"Oh my God!" Simone says. "I have never seen so many boats in my life."

Boats of every size and shape—small boats, big boats, speedboats, sailboats, catamarans.

"Not just boats," Dario says.

They motor closer. Not just boats, all right. People on Jet Skis. People in kayaks, and on paddleboards. So many surfboards, it's a surfboard sea. Someone spots them and shouts, "Hey, Greer! Beau!" and then everyone starts shouting and waving and cheering. They motor closer still, until they are with them, until they are one of them.

"Greer Brody!" a young woman yells from her surfboard.

"Captain Neptune!" a guy shouts from another surfboard.

"Those kids," Greer says. "So many that Tony taught! Look at them all! Remember Kai and his sister, Kalani? I see them on those surfboards over there!" She cups her hand around her mouth and shouts, "KAI! KALANI!" Greer waves, and they wave back. Those kids, and so many more, and there's Jake and Big Dean and Amber and Ray on the trawler, too. Harper sees old Mr. Mamoa, Greer's neighbor, in his green runabout. She sees Loyale Grant, former chanteuse, in a pink bikini and oversized sunglasses, with a much younger guy on a catamaran. She sees Teva, Greer's pool boy/man with his beautiful Polynesian tattoos covering both shoulders, on his surfboard. She sees Dirk Cooke, waving from a sailboat, and Mr. and Mrs. Nuu from the PP Shack in twin polo shirts and shorts, bobbing in a speedboat, riding with Bob Alualu and his wife, Maureen, who own the Surfside Restaurant. She sees Heiani with her granddaughter, Beatrice, out in a little dinghy. She sees Sylvia S. O'Sullivan in her canoe. She sees a guy with two older adults, probably his parents, on another small sailboat, and that guy looks familiar. Really familiar. He has two braids, like Simone's, and he has their nose, and their auburn hair. Max Perez, here now from Texas.

They pull up alongside Jake's parents' trawler. And Jake jumps right down onto their deck. He steps toward Wyatt, and he picks him right up, Wyatt's surprised legs dangling.

"We did it! You all did it! Look at that! Look at that!" Everyone looks in the direction he points. Harper spots the dot of the navy vessel heading out. "There were too many of us to arrest."

"You fuckers!" Greer shouts toward the back end of the vessel. She gives them the middle finger with both hands. She's making up for all the action she missed. She's Greenpeacing it. They are all Greenpeacing it. There's elation all around them, in them. Everyone is beaming, radiating with purpose. Dario hugs Harper. She hugs him back so hard. He tries to lift Harper like Jake lifted Wyatt, but they almost fall over. Beau has both fists in the air, his face jubilant.

And Harper sees it, with all of them around her, the great big mess of being human. Being flawed, and up against things bigger than they are. And she hears it, *Way to go, man! We chased those assholes! Captain Neptune, man!* People showing up, showing their love, for each other, for the things that matter to them. They are *all* showing their love—Loyale Grant; Bob Alualu and his wife, Maureen; Teva the pool boy/man. Love for Greer and Tony, and even more, love for their home and this ocean.

"Fuck those fuckers!" Greer is happier than Harper has ever seen her. This time she's high on life, for sure. "Let's party!"

"Ma," Beau says. "Mom."

"What? Hey, I see Fran! Remember Fran? She used to have that burger place, called the Joint!"

"We've got to do something before they get too far," Beau says. "We gotta go catch that vessel. We can't chase them off every time they come. And we need to tell them we know who she is, that ship, and what she's been through."

"Is there a speed limit for these things?" Dario shouts. His hair is flying so far behind him, Harper can almost imagine him bald. He clutches the side of the boat, and so does Harper, and her butt cheeks are gripping the seat so hard, they hurt. Wyatt and Jake and Simone have their arms linked.

"We're going to get arrested, one way or anoth—"

Bam! The boat hits a wave, and Harper's teeth clang together, and she swears she sees Dario levitate. She grabs his arm. He's the lightest of them, and there's still time for them to go full-on Sebastian and Viola after some accident.

"Almost there, almost there!" Beau shouts. He whirls his arm in that lasso motion again. "Hit it, Ma."

Wyatt widens his eyes at Harper and Dario, and they widen them back, because if this isn't "hit it" already, then what is?

"Oh shit!" Simone cries.

This is.

The boat surges, and the white froth wake behind them grows, and the boat's bow tips up. The old girl has a lot of power, for sure. The *Greer Brody,* the boat, but also Greer Brody, the woman.

There it is, right in front of them now. The navy vessel, gray and large, and no doubt it looks official, but it's certainly not the enormous warship of Harper's imagination. Greer starts honking the boat's horn, and Beau waves his arms.

None of this seems wise.

"Hey, hey, you! Stop!" Greer yells.

The boat slows, and an officer appears at the side. Harper doesn't even know if "officer" is the right word, honestly. He's wearing white, and he looks all crisp and angular-jawed, like a navy guy in a movie, but there are other people on board, too, in diving gear. "We've already told you," he calls down to them firmly, "we'll take your concerns back to be—"

Another officer joins him. This one is older, also in uniform. Higher in rank, likely, since he has two stars on his jacket, and the other guy only has one. He's carrying a megaphone. "Back away from the ship *now.*"

"We have new information," Beau yells. "About what you might be destroying down there, with your messed-up, reckless disregard for—"

Okay, it's probably not the best approach.

"BACK AWAY FROM THE VESSEL," the officer's voice blares through the megaphone. Overkill, honestly, since they're bobbing along right beside them, but the whole thing, the detonation, all of it, is overkill.

"Excuse me," Harper says. She can't even believe she spoke. And she has her hand raised, like the Goody Two-shoes she's always been, asking politely for the teacher's attention, and oh God, it works.

The officer puts down his megaphone. "Yes?"

"We really *do* have information about a shipwreck down there. A historic shipwreck."

Dario, the copycat, raises his hand, too.

"Yes?"

"Permission to board, sir?"

Haha! Harper almost laughs out loud. Simone snorts, and Wyatt elbows her. Dario has watched a bunch of war movies, clearly. He stands straight. "Dario Damaskenos." And then . . . he actually salutes! Hahaha! Oh geez. It's hilarious, but he's serious. Beside Harper, Simone gets the giggles and tries to stifle them. She's holding her stomach and has to turn away.

"Rear Admiral Michael Nimitz," the second guy says, and grins at the first officer like the seven of them are the idiots they actually are.

"Wait," Dario says. He looks honestly surprised. "You're not related to *the* Nimitz, Fleet Admiral Chester W. Nimitz, are you? Who brilliantly led American forces to victory in World War Two?"

The sun is bright, and Harper has to hold her arm above her eyes to see, and maybe it's just a sunburn, but she swears she sees Rear Admiral Nimitz blush.

"Let the kid up," he says.

They have gone to Oz and used their hearts and courage and brains that they had all along, that's for sure, because when Dario returns, after the navy vessel pulls away again, as they rock in the waves, he pulls a card from the pocket of his shorts. It bears the name of Rear Admiral Michael Nimitz, and Dario gazes down on it like it's a prize. But there's more. When he turns it over, a phone number is written on the back. It's time to remember the thing Harper always forgets when she thinks about *Twelfth Night:* Sebastian survived that shipwreck. It doesn't seem like it, but he did, and the two of them, he and Viola, are reunited at the end.

"Rear Admiral Michael Nimitz is the great-grandson of Fleet Admiral Chester W. Nimitz, one of the most important historical figures of World War Two," Dario says. "This is his private cell number. He said he's looking forward to speaking more at length."

They are all too tired to cook, so Greer orders food from both the PP Shack and the Surfside Restaurant. The restaurants suffered, Greer told them, when the island was basically shut down for tourism during the worst of the pandemic. They *all* suffered. Captain Neptune's rentals did, too. So Greer gets enough food to feed all of them plus ten more. There are lots of ways to show your love.

The food stays in its foil boxes, tucked under foil lids. They're waiting for Beau. He's meeting Max Perez and his parents for the first time, privately, away from everyone else, since it's less over-whelming that way. They understand. They remember.

"Maybe we should just go ahead," Greer says. "There's a life of questions."

It's true, so true. One notebook could never hold all of them. So they gather plates and forks, and Greer makes margaritas, even though it's irresponsible since they're all too young, and Walter pees on a coconut that fell from a tree, and they all laugh and maybe embarrass him.

"Oh, Walter." Simone picks him up and kisses his cheeks. "You know we love—"

"Hey, guys," Beau says.

Here he comes, around the corner of the house. And with him are Max Perez and his parents. He has sweet eyes up close, and he's taller than any of them, but there's that auburn hair in braids, and that nose, same as Wyatt's and Simone's and Dario's and Harper's and Beau's. Max grins shyly, and Harper can see that it's an ever-so-crooked grin, same as Wyatt's, same as Beau's.

"Hey," he says.

"Hey," they say.

And it begins again.

CHAPTER THIRTY-SIX

In the North Pacific, gales have submitted to the doldrums, and the ship pitches and rolls on swells, or lies nearly motionless. In the tropical heat and after these increasing months in my interesting condition, I have removed the confines of my corset and now wear a nice short wrapper. In the dead calm, with Joshua in total blindness, I see with utter clarity—our current position, where to go next, how I will get us to our final destination.

Mary Ann Patten journal entry

October 21, 1856

ON THE LAST DAY OF THEIR SUMMER, BEFORE THEY'RE ALL supposed to fly home, they step aboard the *Greer Brody*. Jake speeds them out to the crater, to the deepest center of the curved arc of Molokini Island. They want to dive the wreck again. On the boat they scooch over to make room for one more. Max does not have his PADI Open Water Diver license, which will allow him to dive anywhere in the world, but he has a snorkel and a set of fins.

He can begin to go below the surface, even if he can't go as deep as they have learned to.

Down, down they go. Dario's hair sways like seaweed. Beau dives with them for a while and then goes up to where Greer and Max are. Simone and Wyatt travel toward the antler coral. Dario ducks into the broken rooms of *Neptune's Car*, but no harm comes to him.

Harper takes in that wreck, its massive body, and the places it was battered and then became something else. That area there, that's where the crew would have slept, and that's where a jail cell would have been, and up on the deck, a mutiny occurred, and right there, that's where the wheel would have been. Mary, just a girl like Harper herself, would have stood *right there* and taken command over a situation she never could have anticipated. *Right there,* she discovered what she was capable of. *Thank you,* Harper thinks, because she will never forget her.

She takes in all the new life that's grown around the wreck, too. All of it just goes right on while people are up above, swearing at traffic lights, posting photos of a new haircut, fighting about who said what, breaking up and falling in love again—turtles being turtles, fish being fish, sharks being sharks. Harper watches the yellow-and-black-and-white reef triggerfish (humuhumunu-kunukuapuaa, *thank you,* Jake), and the grumpy white-spotted puffer, and the abstract Picasso triggerfish, with its neon eyeliner running down its face, and the yellow trumpet fish. *Thank you, thank you* to all of them, too. She swims in that ocean, where, somewhere, their whale also swims, along with the luminescent pink fireworks.

They *all* fill her. *Thank you, thank you, thank you.*

That night there are too many people for Greer's house, and so there's food from the PP Shack again, and the Surfside Restaurant, and the Conch, too, home of the best breakfast burrito and much more, and from Pork You, their favorite barbecue place. It's all laid out on some tables around the Captain Neptune statue, right on the beach. Flies buzz and land. Who cares? Mr. and Mrs. Nuu, in twin-patterned Hawaiian attire, stuck some tiki torches out there. And Teva the pool boy/man set up some speakers. Harper has no idea how it all got done, but it did. Max and his parents are here, and Big Dean, of course, and Amber, and Ray, and old Mr. Mamoa. Dirk Cooke, Sylvie S. O'Sullivan, and Loyale Grant in a pink, genie-like jumpsuit are also here, and so are Bob Alualu and his wife, Maureen. Kai and his sister, Kalani, and a few other people who were on the surfboards yesterday are here, too, and so is Fran from the Joint. Heiani and her granddaughter, Beatrice, are here, even when it gets late and past Beatrice's bedtime. Jake, of course, is getting in some making-out time with Wyatt before Wyatt leaves tomorrow.

Everyone eats and talks and laughs loud, and gets a little choked up, because this will be their goodbye for now, and it all happens beneath majestic old Captain Neptune, with his six-pack abs and sea-creature tail. Tonight he's wearing a sun visor and a seaweed cape and a lei, heavy on the accessories. No matter what anyone places on him, he's still himself, silly and grand.

"You've got to come back," Beau says when the five of them are standing together. "You've got to come back, because I'm going to miss you guys so much. You are all so fucking awesome."

He is.

"Group hug," Simone says, and makes Beau's lasso gesture to bring them in. Sure, it's a kiss-ass move, but who cares.

Wyatt grabs Beau's arms with affection and says, "Love ya, man," and then Beau hugs Wyatt tight. "Love you back, man."

"Love *you*, man," Dario says, like the smart-ass he can be, but his voice wavers.

"Love you, bud," Beau says, and hugs him next, and Dario's face squinches with tears.

"You," he says to Simone next, and points at her, shaking his head like he can't believe his eyes. "Love *you*."

"Hey, I love you, Beau. I sure do," she says into his shoulder as they hug now.

"Harpo . . ." He shakes his finger at her, and then raises a fist of power. "Bring it in, my girl." He's hugging Harper hard, and she's trying not to lose it. "I love you," he whispers.

"I love *you*," she whispers back, but she can barely get the words out. "Thank you."

He lets her go and just stares at all of them, and then he bursts into tears, same as he did that first time at his house. He is the same open and vulnerable guy he was when they arrived, but he's so much more to them after all this, too. And why not be open? Why not be vulnerable? Why not show your love, when it's the best thing you have? Beau presses his palms to his eyes. "Fuck, man. Fuck. You guys just have to come back," he says for the hundredth time. God, they're all a mess. Dario sniffs hard. Harper gets a tear-streaked mascara face. Wyatt's shirt is all askew, and Simone's cheeks are wet and her hair is out of her braids.

"Will someone turn up the goddamn music?" Greer shouts.

Someone does. They crank it high. *Buh buh buh buh,* the riffs begin. Dario air guitars, and they all point and laugh, which makes him do it more.

"Wellll," they sing. Dario's eyes are bright in the tiki torch light, and so are Simone's and Wyatt's, and Walter's are that dog-night neon. " 'Take me back down where cool water flows, yeh!' " They sing so loud, Harper's throat will be sore tomorrow, and who knows where her sandals went. Oh, it's all tempo, no lullaby. They party like it's 1969.

A summer of love, for sure.

"Will you guys stop crying?" Simone says. "Jesus, I can't take all this emotion." Now it's their goodbye, the half siblings, at the airport. Simone, she's one to talk, because her face is wet with tears again. Simone always tries to seem stronger and tougher than she is; that's one thing they've come to know about her. She's a great big softy inside. "We're going to see each other. Harpo, we *will.*"

"This was the best summer I ever had," Wyatt says. They step out of *their* group hug, in that open-air airport where warm breezes come right in. It seems impossible that this is the same place they arrived in a few months ago. It should be a different place, as they are different. Harper wipes her eyes. Dario honks his nose into a hankie like an old man.

"We will *see* each other," Simone calls over her shoulder as she and Wyatt walk toward their own gates, Wyatt heading to join his family for a week in Cabo. They each wave one last time before Simone's flowered sundress disappears around one corner, and Wyatt's palm tree shirt disappears around another. Harper's pretty sure she's seen that shirt on Jake. Luckily, she'll still get to see Wyatt when he's back in Seattle.

Dario, well, she'll get to see his beloved self, too, as often as they want. She'll see him right beside her on the whole plane ride home.

"I hope Walter's okay," he says when the plane lifts off and they are in the air.

"He's totally fine," Harper says, though of course she's also a little worried about him. When she glances at Dario, it hits her again, how he seems older than he did on the trip there.

After the thrill of a packet of pretzels and a Sprite, they both get bored. Dario pulls out a book about shipwrecks that Greer gave him. Harper takes out her phone, and she spends ten bucks to use the Wi-Fi. She wants to see how she feels about this whole phone thing, if it's different now that she's heading home. She sends a text to Soraya, and one to Ada. *On my way. Can't wait to catch up. Just wanted to say . . . you've always been there for me. Thank you.*

And then she scrolls. A girl applying fake eyelashes, the Taj Mahal, a tortoise with an inspirational slogan underneath. The variant, the numbers tick-ticking up, and another variant on the horizon. "Ten Ways Your Diet Is Sabotaging Your Health." "The Alarming Side Effects of Not Eating Enough Greens," no, no, no.

No. This noise is its own tsunami, its own disease, its own catastrophe. Living in fear is. Fear is a shutting out; love is a letting in. Fear is a shutting out; wonder is a letting in. Fear is a shutting out; living is a letting in.

She decides to look something else up instead. Something Beau told her about, if she's interested.

She's interested.

Ballard Maritime Academy.

The Ballard Maritime Academy is an alternative academic program at Ballard High School, which strives to educate its students in maritime skills, in addition to maritime history and marine science. . . .

She fills out the application right there. It's completely impractical; it's her senior year. Probably past all deadlines, too. But she also notices that phone number there, of the program director. She can make things happen for herself, things she wants, that's one thing she's learned. Oh, her mother is going to freak out, but she has a plan.

She's going to Greenpeace it.

CHAPTER THIRTY-SEVEN

> Yesterday my trusted first mate, William Hare, sent rockets skyward as a call for a tug to bring us in. Now after one hundred and thirty-seven days at sea, we are passing through the Golden Gate, at last, at last.
>
> Mary Ann Patten journal entry
> November 15, 1856

"I MADE YOU YOUR FAVORITE. A ZUCCHINI-AND-CHICKPEA lasagna with cashew nut cheese," Harper's mother says.

Sigh.

"How about I make dinner tomorrow?" Harper says. She remembers Wyatt's signature Greek salad recipe.

Her mom looks surprised and smiles. "That's so wonderful. I can't believe how tan you got. I didn't even think that was possible with SPF fifty. You did use SPF fifty, right?"

"I did. So, Beau Zane, huh?"

"Harper, I don't know what to say. I am so sorry. I made mistakes, I know, but they were always because I thought they were in your best interest."

This is going to take a while, Harper understands. They've got a lot to work out. But her mom is not her enemy, far from it. And she has her own epic story.

"I want to hear about the punk band. The Bloody Nails?"

"If you ever tell Grandma about that, I don't know what I'll do," Melinda says. Her eyes plead. She means it.

"Noted. Blackmail material."

She pretend-scowls. "God, I missed you. I worried the whole time you were away. Don't ever do that to me again."

Once more, it's going take a while.

"Harper, you're eating so fast! And save a little room. I made a lemon lavender yogurt cake."

"I've always got plenty of room," Harper says. "But I may have to have it when I come back. I'm going to head over to see Ezra."

"Ezra?"

"Ezra."

"You didn't tell me." Her lips press together.

Harper shrugs.

"You just got home. I've barely seen you for five minutes. Driving home from the airport doesn't count. All that nerve-racking traffic, I had to have eyes everywhere. And you're going to be back at school next week. We're barely going to have any time together."

"Um . . . about school . . ."

"What do you mean, 'Um, about school'? Don't tell me you're dropping out or something. Just like . . ." She doesn't say it. Just like Beau dropped out of college.

"I'm not dropping out. I just want to go somewhere else."

"Somewhere else? Now? In your senior year? How? And, like,

where, *Hawaii*? Do you think it works like that? You can just, boom, change everything at the last minute? Go be with him? A summer doesn't mean you know someone. You can't just go 'somewhere else.'"

"This isn't about Beau." And it isn't. Not just. When she found him, she found parts of herself, too. Her *own* self, her own story within the larger one. Beau showed her how to go beneath the surface, but what she discovered there . . . It's *hers*.

"Well, your school is expecting you on September eighth."

Harper will put her ship between her mother's ship and the thing she wants. She'll protect it, even if the harpoons whiz past her head.

"Can we talk about this later? I need to get to Ez's."

"Oh my God, Harper. Ughhh!"

It's okay. She can handle being a disappointment. She can handle a lot of things.

She grabs a hoodie in case it gets cold. From the front yard she can see Mrs. Wong outside, gardening, taking care of Mr. Wong's dahlias, the first time Harper has seen her do this since Mr. Wong died in the darkest days of the pandemic. Her curved back makes Harper smile, and her little yellow sweater does, and the way she holds the garden hose, water spilling down gently. Mrs. Wong, showing her love.

Harper starts to walk. Down the street Rainey's made some kind of go-kart with his wagon and a box and an orange traffic cone with a flag on it. He's carrying it to the top of the small hill at the end of their cul-de-sac.

Harper stops to watch. She doesn't squinch her eyes, even when the thing is airborne for a moment and lands with a clatter. She watches him fly.

"Whoooey!" he cries.

She cups her hand around her mouth. "WAY TO GO!" Harper shouts. She makes that lasso motion that's hallmark Beau, and Rainey lassos back.

Harper reaches Ezra's house. Her heart fills just seeing it. Man, she missed it, him, all of them, Yanet and Adam and Binx and Nudo, too. The smell of something buttery and cheesy escapes through their screen door. She rings the bell.

"Helloooo," she calls.

Nudo starts barking, and he's the first one to greet her. Nudo, who just full-on lives in the moment, all the time. And now here's Yanet, opening the door. Harper sticks her hand into Nudo's fur as his butt swivels in joy. "You are a sight, yes, you are, come here," Yanet says, hugging her.

Adam pops his head around the corner. "Harper!" he says. "I'll tell Ez you're here."

Binx rolls into the room in a little car. He crashes it into the wall and then gets out and races over, a living room hit-and-run.

"Wait," he commands Harper. Yanet rolls her eyes. Binx hurries back to the car, removes the goods from the pretend trunk. It's Ken, in a grass skirt and a ballet tutu stretched tight across his body. Binx shoves him at her. "Pway Hawi," he orders.

"Ezra's been showing him Hawaii on the globe," Yanet says by way of apology.

"*Please* play Hawi," Harper says.

"He swims," Binx tells her about Ken. You can tell. His hair is all matted, like doll hair gets after spending hours in a blow-up pool.

"Well, sure, who wouldn't?" Harper says.

And then there's Ezra. Standing in that doorway and, God, just taking her breath away. She feels almost shy. Her throat tightens with emotion. She can barely speak.

"Harper," he says as Yanet ducks out. "Harper. I just need to look at you for a minute."

"Wook at *you* for a minute," Binx repeats. He reads the room, makes a lovey kissy-face, and then shimmies in a somewhat provocative dance.

"Ez," Harper says. Ez, with his grin, and his kind eyes, and his goodness. Ez, his own beautiful self.

It's like she's seeing him, really seeing him, for the first time.

"Oh shit! Oh shit!" Harper cries.

"It's fine, you're fine." Honestly, Ezra looks kind of pale himself. "Accelerate," he says, even though his own foot in the passenger's seat is clearly on the brake.

Harper accelerates. She channels her diving lessons and breathes. She also channels Beau and swears. "Fuck!" She merges. Full-on freeway driving.

"I'm doing it."

"Yeah, you are," Ezra says. He takes a pinch of his shirt and waves it in and out for air. He's sweating pretty hard, that's for sure. "You're doing great."

You're doing great. Isn't that what she needs, what most people need, to hear? Just that? The words are so right and necessary that she almost cries, but they fill her with a confident joy, too. "Hey, maybe we need the radio," Harper says.

"Um, no. Just concentrate on keeping two car lengths behind that Subaru."

"It's changing lanes!"

"That Escort, then. I think a nice old lady is driving, perfect. I see a helmet of gray. Or better yet, that camper." It's a big, lumbering thing, with a license plate that reads CAPTAIN ED, and it's going about twelve miles an hour.

"No way. And next time, we work on some speed," Harper says.

She's just being cocky like Wyatt, like Beau. She's not ready for speed yet.

"Just stay in your lane, and watch for the signs. Rattlesnake Ridge." She's two weeks into the new term at school, a week behind at Ballard Maritime Academy, but she's in it. She's shy there, but she's in it. She's new, the curriculum is new, but she's in it. She's late to the whole thing, but she's in it.

"That car's on my butt," Harper says, glancing into her rear-view mirror.

"That's his problem. Let him pass. We don't give a fuck."

"Right."

"Five miles, steady on."

"Steady on," Harper says.

She can do this. It's a bullshit story, the one she's been told, that she should be afraid all the time, and that she isn't capable of handling hard stuff. The whole summer taught her that. Mary Patten has. If she ever doubts this, all she needs to do is look at the end of the book Beau gave her. That red leather volume, with Mary's journal entries in it, and more. It's after the part where Mary returns home and has her baby, a son, Joshua Patten Junior, on March 10, 1857. And after the sad information that Joshua never recovered from his illness and died in July at age thirty, leaving Mary to find a different strength once again. It's a page from a newspaper, an article in the *St. Louis Post-Dispatch*. The headline: "A Heroic Woman—How She Brought a Ship into Port with Mutineers on Board." And yeah, it's all there in the newspaper, everything that happened, but it's another article *right next to it* that also speaks to Harper. That one has the headline "The Duty of a Woman Is to Be a Lady." The article says, "Wildness is a thing which girls cannot afford. Delicacy is a thing which cannot be lost and found. . . . Self-possession, unshrinking and aggressive coarseness of demeanor, certainly merits that mild form of restraint called imprisonment for life." Mary had to face the bullshit story, too.

They reach Rattlesnake Ridge. Poor Ezra, he has big sweat rings under his pits from nerves, so he has to take his shirt off, what a shame. When they get out of the car, Harper gives his butt a squeeze because, damn, he's so freaking adorable, and his goodness just makes his hotness hotter. They hike in a little. They find a patch of beach next to Rattlesnake Lake. "You're not going to take photos?" Ezra's still getting used to the Harper who will leave her phone behind. Who only takes a photo every so often but keeps it for herself as something precious. Who only takes her phone out to make a call or text something important to a friend, because she wants to use her phone, not be used by it. The Harper who understands that when you're asked to feel everything all the time, your heart will batten down the hatches like a ship in a storm. The Harper who opened her Instagram account one final moment and imagined Beau's elbow knocking it into the ocean. Who said, *Hey, Siri. We're through.*

"Nope."

"I love that," he says.

"Anyway. You can't take a photo of how this feels," she says, and leans in to kiss him.

That ragged peak jutting over that lake, the September light on the trees, the pointy evergreen tree soldiers, the triangle glints of silver on the water—it's too beautiful for photos. And so is the rest of it. She just has to take it in: Ezra's profile; the smell of, yes, SPF 50; the feel of Ezra's lips on hers; her heart beating hard when she looks at that guy. The fullness.

CHAPTER THIRTY-EIGHT

Among the passengers from California who arrived by the steamer *George Law* on Saturday, there was an invalid who had to be borne from the vessel to his hotel upon a litter. By his side, superintending every movement, was a young lady of prepossessing person, but with a countenance careworn and anxious from long watching. The invalid was Captain Joshua P. Patton, late of the ship *Neptune's Car* of New York, and the lady was Mrs. Mary A. Patton, his wife, both of whom return home under circumstances of peculiar misfortune. . . .

Those who saw her enter the harbor say no vessel entered that port looking better in every respect. The *Romance of the Seas* had arrived only eight days before her.

The New-York Daily Times

(February 18, 1857)

The readers of the *Herald* will remember an account taken from one of the California papers, relative to the heroic conduct of Mrs. Martha Ann Patten, wife of Capt. Patten, of the ship *Neptune's Car,* who, during her husband's illness, took charge of the vessel and navigated it safely into San Francisco. The lady, together with her husband, who is now so sick that he is not expected to live, arrived in this city in the *George Law,* and are now stopping at the Battery Hotel. Her story is an interesting and painful one, and shows how much a weak, delicate woman can do when a great emergency calls out her powers. . . . Her labors are the more surprising in view of the fact that she was all this time in a delicate condition, and soon expects to give birth to her first child. . . . The *Neptune's Car* arrived safely at San Francisco on the 15th of November last, it having been for fifty-six days under the command of a delicate female not twenty years of age. What a splendid text for the women's rights people. . . . Mrs. Patten's case is one of the most remarkable on record, and adds one to the many instances that history records of female devotion and heroism. . . .

The New York Herald (date unknown)

Mary Ann Brown Patten managed to guide the ship through sixty-foot icy waves from Antarctica during an eighteen-day gale. Undaunted, she continued tending to the charts, logs, and her sick husband. . . .

The Boston Semiweekly Courier

(February 18, 1857)

Among the noble band of women, who, by their heroic bearing, under great trial and suffering, have won for themselves imperishable fame, Mary A. Patten may claim a prominent posi- tion. . . . By her good deeds, she has added an- other laurel to the honor of her sex.

The New-York Tribune

(February 18, 1857)

THEY GET TOGETHER AGAIN THE NEXT SUMMER, AND THE summer after that, and that, and there's no doubt they will keep on gathering, those kids with the rare combination of auburn hair and blue eyes; with the cocky grin, and the funny toes, and the excellent hearing; with the anxiety and the bravery. When mid- June arrives, Harper and Dario and Walter will catch a flight from Seattle, and Simone flies in from California, and Wyatt drives over from his parents' condo, where he lives full-time since he graduated from college. Max Perez from Texas will join them, and so will J. C. Mandelli from San Diego, and Nell Bauman from Port Townsend, and the next summer Mia Alani from Portland, along with Eamon Auberge, Vancouver. They will meet the man who was once only an absence, and he will be both less and more than they imagined. They will each be given a piece of what looks like green glass, an ancient, volcanic good-luck charm. Harper's stomach will fill with nerves meeting someone new. From across the patio Dario will see her, and he'll signal as they were taught. He'll point at Harper, and then make the gesture. *Are you. Okay?* And she'll signal back. *Okay.*

During those summers Harper shuts out the noise and stays present. Dario gets too sunburned. Walter stands in the shallow end of the pool for a while before he jumps. All of them—the children of Beau Zane—watch each other and him. *Are we alike? Are we different?* Yes, and yes. They are self-reflections, self-reflecting. They're stopping the noise for a while to ask the important questions: Who am I, and what matters? How do you survive the shocking and unforeseen things that happen?

Well, like this: Greer makes food. They swim in the pool, and in the ocean, and order takeout from the PP Shack. Beau says, "Fuck, man, this is so awesome," a million times. Big Dean comes by, and Jake, too, and sometimes he and Wyatt are back together again, and sometimes not. A new kid marvels at an ancient turtle. They party at the beach with the studly Captain Neptune. They show their love. One summer they stand at the grave of old Mr. Mamoa after he died that July, shoulder to shoulder. Another they celebrate the comeback of chanteuse Loyale Grant, with her new hit single, "Let Me Be Your Heat Wave." Creedence begins to play, and a drift of pot smoke comes from Greer's room. A new individual among the forty-two (so far) begins to really understand their story, the magic of what happens when a sperm meets an egg and creates its own big bang, the beginning of a mini universe, a story within a story: a human being with all their frailties and power and beauty and possibilities, now alive in a natural world with all its frailties and power and beauty and possibilities.

Each summer the original five of them—Beau, Simone, Wyatt, Dario, and Harper—and whoever is around to drive the boat, maybe Jake, maybe Greer, maybe Big Dean, will also take their own trip aboard the *Greer Brody.* They'll talk about their whale, and wonder where she is, and if she remembers them, too. They'll dive the historic landmark, the wreck of *Neptune's Car.* Over the side Harper will go, in a sudden moment of *yes,* down into the waves that have been waves forever, a whoosh of bubbles surrounding her in that old, old ocean. She'll take in what is buried and broken there, searching for the spot where Mary stood, taking command and charting her course, and searching for the firework as well—for her unbelievable self, made of light, resilient and self-protective, being all wondrous down there, even if no one sees her. And Harper will watch for whatever else might rise from the wreck, too, because you never know, it's always something. She will marvel, once again, at how there is so much more below the surface, more than you can ever imagine, when you finally have the courage to look.

ACKNOWLEDGMENTS

All love and thanks to Liesa Abrams, my treasured editor and friend. Over our four books together, her incomparable support has been life-changing, and her downright brilliant insights have made me a better writer, and I am so honored that this book is one of the first releases of her Labyrinth Road imprint. All love and thanks, too, to my one-of-a-kind, immensely talented and trusted guide, my dear agent and friend, Michael Bourret. I am so lucky to have these two people in my life.

Huge gratitude, as well, to the many people at Labyrinth Road and Penguin Random House who helped my words become a book. I appreciate every one of you.

And to my family, especially my beloveds—my husband, John; and, in order of their beautiful arrivals in my life, Sam, Nick, Erin, Pat, Myla, Charlie, Theo, and dogs Max and Luna. You each have your own epic story, and you are the light and the magic and the meaning in mine.

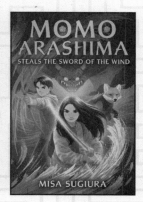
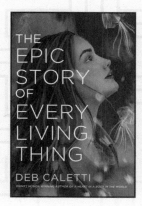

Underlined

A Community of Book Nerds & Aspiring Writers!

READ

Get book recommendations, reading lists, YA news

DISCOVER

Take quizzes, watch videos, shop merch, win prizes

CREATE

Write your own stories, enter contests, get inspired

SHARE

Connect with fellow Book Nerds and authors!

GetUnderlined.com • @GetUnderlined

Want a chance to be featured? Use #GetUnderlined on social!

Art used under license from Shutterstock.com